DEATH
SENTENCES

Otto Penzler is the proprietor of The Mysterious Bookshop in New York City and an Edgar-award winning anthologist.

Ian Rankin is the bestselling author of the *Rebus* series.

DEATH SENTENCES

Stories of
DEATHLY BOOKS,
MURDEROUS BOOKSELLERS
& LETHAL LITERATURE

from the
WORLD'S BEST CRIME WRITERS

Introduction by

IAN RANKIN

Edited by OTTO PENZLER

HEAD
of ZEUS

Each story was individually published in the USA between 2011 and 2013 by
The Mysterious Bookshop, and as an anthology by Assembly! Press, an imprint of Bookspan,
New York, USAby arrangement with The Mysterious Bookshop.

This anthology first published in the United Kingdom in 2014 by Head of Zeus Ltd
by arrangement with The Mysterious Bookshop

9 7 5 3 1 2 4 6 8

A catalogue record for this book is available from the British Library.

ISBN (E) 978-1-78185-955-1
ISBN (HB) 978-1-78185-674-1

Contents

Introduction

I AM OFTEN ASKED for advice by aspiring writers. Most of what I say is changeable, depending on my mood, but there is one constant: it's hard to be a good writer without also being a good reader. When I get together with other writers we always seem to spend the majority of the conversation passing on hot tips for new books we've enjoyed, or reminiscing about great books from the past. There will be anecdotes about bookshops and libraries, and we will vividly remember favourite books from childhood. It is through reading that we became writers, because we found it impossible to conceive of any finer vocation in the world than storytelling.

In the village where I grew up, there was no bookshop. The newsagent had a carousel displaying the works of Sven Hassel and Frederick Forsyth, but the small local library fulfilled additional needs. I would haunt that place, and I still recall the thrill of being told I had reached an age where I need no longer be confined to the Children's Section. Books immersed me in different lives and worlds, far from my immediate surroundings. As soon as I could, I began writing them for my own amusement, copying the styles of favourite authors (and, yes, sometimes stealing bits and pieces of their plots, too). When I went on to university, I studied English and American Literature, eventually specialising in Scottish Literature for a never-to-be-completed PhD. A group of like-minded students would meet after classes in a local hostelry, sometimes inviting a lecturer or two along, so that our discussions could continue. It was around then I gritted my teeth and started buying hardback fiction. The prices were steep for a student (and this was in the days when books had to be sold at the cover-price), but I was unwilling to wait six months or a year for a paperback fix of the latest William Golding or Angela Carter. I cherish those well-thumbed editions to this day – they sit on groaning shelves in my house. And when I visit other people's homes, I'll head directly to the bookshelves to get a sense of the inhabitants' inner lives.

When my first few Inspector Rebus novels were published, they failed to make ripples, but eventually my publisher in the USA decided I should tour there. This was in the late 1980s, and I discovered that many American towns featured at least one small independent bookshop specialising in crime fiction. Flash-forward quarter of a century and most of them have gone, alas, but some remain. One of these is The Mysterious Bookshop in New York, and its owner, Otto Penzler, was an early champion of my work. He was – and is – an expert in the field of crime fiction, a collector, and a fan. He pens bibliographies and scholarly essays, edits short story collections, and for many years has commissioned authors to write one-off Christmas tales which are then presented as gifts to the bookshop's loyal customers. It was Otto who came up with the idea of a series of 'bibliomysteries' – basically stories of a certain length in which books play a crucial role. As a fan of the genre, it seemed irresistible and fun to him, and when he started contacting authors, they agreed. Why wouldn't they? Books have often played an integral or peripheral role in tales of mystery and adventure – Otto's offer proved catnip to so many writers who share a passion for the written word in all its forms.

Hence this collection.

And what treats you have in store! What struck me when I first read these stories was their variety. Reed Farrel Coleman takes us deep into harrowing historical territory as a book rescued from a concentration camp comes to define one man's life. Anne Perry reworks 'The Maltese Falcon', but adds theology and the supernatural with gripping, twisty aplomb. Jeffery Deaver focuses on a pair of assassins in Mexico as they attempt the execution of a book-loving criminal. Andrew Taylor shifts the action to London in a tale of libraries, lost love, and jealousy both professional and personal. Thomas H. Cook meantime provides a delicious slice of alternative history, revolving around a famous book – to say more might spoil a thought-provoking twist. Then there's Mickey Spillane, with an unfinished story brought to a satisfying conclusion by contemporary author Max Allan Collins, a story where the search for a gangster's notebook brings Mike Hammer a series of clients including cops, politicians and the mob.

And those, dear reader, are for starters.

The bibliomystery then is by no means a narrow sub-genre but rather one that contains multitudes, and it is fascinating to see how different authors approach the task. There are books real and imagined, with stories set in past, present and future. Some will prickle the scalp, others raise a smile. You'll nod in appreciation of a piece of sleight-of-hand, or find your pulse quickening as a bomb is primed to explode. There are pleasing twists at the ends of some, while others resonate long in the mind, having left something at their conclusion for the reader to consider and chew on. All show their authors to be masters of their craft, their delight at the challenge set by Otto Penzler evident in the writing and plotting.

Now read on.

Ian Rankin, 2014

I

An Acceptable Sacrifice

Jeffery Deaver

WEDNESDAY

THEY'D MET LAST NIGHT for the first time and now, mid-morning, they were finally starting to let go a bit, to relax, to trust each other. *Almost* to trust each other.

Such is the way it works when you're partnered with a stranger on a mission to kill.

"Is it always this hot?" P.Z. Evans asked, squinting painfully against the fierce glare. The dense lenses of his Ray-Bans were useless.

"No."

"Thank God."

"Usually is *hotter*," Alejo Díaz replied, his English enriched by a luscious accent.

"You're shitting me."

The month was May and the temperature was around 97. They were in Zaragoza Plaza, the picturesque square dominated by a statue of two stern men Evans had learned were generals. A cathedral, too.

And then there was the sun . . . like burning gasoline.

Evans had flown to Hermosillo from outside D.C., where he lived when he wasn't on the road. In the nation's capital—the nation to the north, that is—the temperature had been a pleasant 75.

"Summer can be warm," Díaz admitted.

"Warm?" Evans echoed wryly.

"But then . . . You go to Arizona?"

"I played golf in Scottsdale once."

"Well, Scottsdale is hundreds of miles *north* of here. Think about that. We are in the middle of a desert. It has to be hot. What you expect?"

"I only played six rounds," Evans said.

"What?"

"In Arizona. For me to only play six rounds . . . I thought I'd die. And we started at seven in the morning. You golf?"

"Me? You crazy? Too hot here." Díaz smiled.

Evans was sipping a Coke from a bottle whose neck he'd religiously cleaned with a Handi-wipe before drinking. Supposedly Hermosillo, the capital of Sonora, was the only city in Mexico that treated its water, which meant that the ice the bottles nestled in was probably safe.

Probably.

He wiped the neck and mouth again. Wished he'd brought a miniature of Jack Daniels to use as purifier. Handi-wipe tasted like crap.

Díaz was drinking coffee, to which he'd added three or four sugars. Hot coffee, not iced. Evans couldn't get his head around that. A Starbucks addict at home and a coffee drinker in any number of the third-world places he traveled to (you didn't get dysentery from boiled water), he hadn't touched the stuff in Hermosillo. He didn't care if he never had a hot beverage again. Sweat tickled under his arms and down his temple and in his crotch. He believed his ears were sweating.

The men looked around them, at the students on the way to school, the businessmen meandering to offices or meetings. No shoppers; it was too early for that, but there were some mothers about, pushing carriages. The men not in suits were wearing blue jeans and boots and embroidered shirts. The cowboy culture, Evans had learned, was popular in Sonora. Pickup trucks were everywhere, as numerous as old American cars.

These two men vaguely resembled each other. Thirties, compact, athletic, with round faces—Díaz's pocked but not detracting from his craggy good looks, reflecting some Pima Indian in his ancestry. Dark hair both. Evans's face was smoother and paler, of course, and a little off kilter, eyes not quite plumb. Handsome too, though, in a way that might appeal to risk-taking women.

They were in jeans, running shoes and short-sleeved shirts, untucked, which would have concealed their weapons but they weren't carrying today.

So far there was no reason for anyone to wish them harm.

That would change.

Some tourists walked by. Hermosillo was a way station for people traveling from the U.S. to the west coast of Sonora. Lots of people driving, lots of buses.

Buses . . .

Evans lowered his voice, though there was no one near. "You talked to your contact this morning, Al?"

Evans had tried out shortening the Mexican agent's name when they first met—to see how he'd react, if he'd be pissed, defensive, hostile. But the man had laughed. "You can call me Al," he'd said, the line from a Paul Simon song. So the test became a joke and Evans had decided then that he could like this guy. The humor also added to the infrastructure of trust. A lot of people working undercover think that saying "fuck" and making jokes about women creates trust. No. It's humor.

"*Sí*. And from what he say . . . I think our job, it will not be easy." He took the lid off his coffee and blew to cool it, which Evans thought was hilarious. "His security, very tight. Always his security man, a good one, Jos, is with him. And word is they know something's planned."

"What?" Evans's face curled up tight. "A leak?"

And this, Díaz seemed to find funny, "Oh, is always a leak. Every egg in Mexico has a crack. They won't know about us exactly but he has heard somebody is in town to kill him. Oh, *sí*, he has heard."

The "he" they were speaking of was Alonso María Carillo, better known as Cuchillo—in Spanish: "Knife." There was some debate about where the nickname came from. It probably wasn't because he used that weapon to kill rivals—he'd never been arrested for a violent crime . . . or *any* crime, for that matter. More likely the name was bestowed because he was brilliant. *Cuchillo*, as in sharp as a. He was supposedly the man behind one of the cartels in Sonora, the Mexican state that, in addition to neighboring Sinaloa, was home to the major drug gangs. But, though it was small, the Hermosillo Cartel was one of the most deadly, responsible for a thousand or more deaths . . . and the production of many tons of drugs—not only cocaine but insidious meth, which was the hot new profit center in the narcotics trade.

And yet Cuchillo was wily enough to avoid prosecution. The cartel was run by other men—who were, the *Federales* were sure, figureheads. To the world, Cuchillo was an innovative businessman and philanthropist. Educated at UCLA, a degree in business and one in English literature. He'd made his fortune, it appeared, through legitimate companies that were known for being good to workers and were environmentally and financially responsible.

So due process wasn't an option to bring him to justice. Hence the joint operation of Alejo Díaz and P.Z. Evans—an operation that didn't exist, by the way, if you happened to bring up the topic to anyone in Washington, D.C., or Mexico City.

"So," Evans said, "he suspects someone is after him. That means we'll need a diversion, you know. Misdirection. Keep him focused on that, so he doesn't figure out what we're really up to."

"Yes, yes, that is right. At least one diversion. Maybe two. But we have another problem: We can't get him into the open."

"Why not?"

"My contact say he's staying in the compound for the next week. Maybe more. Until he think it's safe."

"Shit," Evans muttered.

Their mission was enwrapped with a tight deadline. Intelligence had been received that Cuchillo was planning an attack on a tourist bus. The vehicle would be stopped, the doors wired shut and then the bus set on fire. The attack would occur on Friday, two days from now, the anniversary of the day the Mexican president had announced his most recent war on the cartels. But there the report ended—as had, presumably, the life of the informant. It was therefore impossible to tell which bus would be targeted; there were hundreds of them daily driving many different routes and run by dozens of companies, most of whom didn't want to scare off passengers by suspending service or cooperating with law enforcement. (In his groundwork for the mission, Evans had researched the bus operators and noted one thing their ads all had in common: they began with variations on *Mexico Is Safe!!*)

Even without knowing the specific bus, however, Díaz and Evans had found a way to stop the attack. The biggest cartels in Sinaloa and Sonora were pulling back from violence. It was very bad publicity—not to mention dangerous to one's health—to kill tourists, even accidentally. An *intentional* attack on innocents, especially Americans, could make the drug barons' lives pure hell. No rivals or anyone within his organization would challenge Cuchillo directly but the agents had learned that if he, say, met with an accident his lieutenants would not follow through with the attack.

However, if Cuchillo would be hiding in his compound until after the bus burned down to a scorched shell, then Díaz's contact was right; their job would not be easy. Drone surveillance had revealed that the house was on five acres, surrounded by a tall wall crowned with electric wire, the yard filled with sensors and scanned by cameras. Sniping wouldn't work because all the buildings— the large house, the separate library and detached garage—had thick bulletproof windows. And the walkways between those structures were out of sight of any vantage points where a shooter could set up.

As they sat bathed in the searing sun, Evans wondered if your mind slowed down the hotter it got. Oatmeal came to mind, steaming sludge.

He wiped his forehead, sipped Coke and asked for more details about Cuchillo's professional and personal life. Díaz had quite a bit of information; the man had been under investigation for the past year. Nodding, Evans took it all in. He'd been a good tactician in the Special Forces; he was a good tactician in his present job. He drained the Coke. His third of the day.

Nine fucking forty-five in the morning.

"Tell me about his weaknesses."

"Cuchillo? He has no weaknesses."

"Whatta you mean? Everybody has weaknesses. Drugs, women, men? Liquor? Gambling?"

Weakness was a very effective tool of the trade in Evans's business, as useful as bullets and C4. Usually, in fact, more so.

Díaz added yet one more sugar to his cup, though there was only a small amount of coffee remaining. He stirred elaborately. Figure eight. He sipped and then looked up. "There is maybe one thing."

"What?"

"Books," the Mexican agent said. "Books might be his weakness."

❧

The weather in Washington, D.C. was pleasant this May evening so he picked a Starbucks with an outdoor patio . . . because, why not?

This was in a yuppie area of the district, if yuppies still existed. Peter Billings's father had been a yuppie. Shit, that was a long time ago.

Billings was drinking regular coffee, black, and no extra shots or foamed milk or fancy additives, which he secretly believed that people asked for sometimes simply because they liked the sound of ordering them.

He'd also bought a scone, which was loaded with calories, but he didn't care. Besides, he'd only eat half of it. At home in Bethesda, his wife would feed him a Lean Cuisine tonight.

Billings liked Starbucks because you could count on being invisible. Business people typing resumes they didn't want their bosses to see, husbands and wives typing emails to their lovers.

And government operatives meeting about issues that were, shall we say, sensitive.

Starbucks was also good because the steam machine made a shitload of noise and covered up the conversation if you were inside and the traffic covered up the conversation if you were outside. At least here on the streets of the District.

He ate some scone and launched the crumbs off his dark blue suit and light blue tie.

A moment later a man sat down across from him. He had a Starbuck's coffee, too, but it'd been doctored up big time—almond or hazelnut, whipped cream, sprinkles. The man was weasely, Billings reflected. When you're in your forties and somebody looks at you and the word weasel is the first thing that comes to mind, you might want to start thinking about image. Gain some weight.

Have a scone.

Billings now said to Harris, "Evening."

Harris nodded then licked whipped cream from the top of his coffee carton.

Billings found it repulsive, the darting, weasely tongue. "We're at the go/no-go point."

"Right."

"Your man down south."

"Adam."

As good a code as any for Harris's contracting agent in Hermosillo, presently dogging Alonso María Carillo, AKA Cuchillo. Harris, of course, wasn't going to name him. Loud traffic on the streets of D.C. is like cappuccino machines, only loud. It masks, it doesn't obliterate, and both Harris and Billings knew there were sound engineers who could extract incriminating words from cacophony with the precision of a hummingbird sipping nectar in a hover.

"Communication is good?" A near whisper by Billings.

No response. Of course communication would be good. Harris and his people were the best. No need for a nod, either.

Billings wanted to take a bite of scone but was, for some reason, reluctant to do so in front of a man who'd killed at least a dozen people, or so the unwritten resume went. Billings had killed a number of people *indirectly* but, one on one? Only a squirrel. Accidentally. His voice now dropped lower yet. "Has he been in contact with the PIQ?"

Person in Question.

Cuchillo.

"No. He's doing the prep work. From a distance."

"So he hasn't seen, for instance, weapons or product at the compound?"

"No. They're staying clear. Both Adam and his counterpart from the D.F." Harris continued, "All the surveillance is by drone."

Which Billings had seen. And it wasn't helpful.

They fell silent as a couple at a table nearby stood and gathered their shopping bags.

Billings told himself to be a bit subtler with his questions. Harris was on the cusp of becoming curious. And that would not be good. Billings was not prepared to share what had been troubling him for the past several hours, since the new intelligence assessment came in: that he and his department might have subcontracted out a job to assassinate the wrong man.

There was now some doubt that Cuchillo was in fact head of the Hermosillo Cartel.

The intercepts Billings's people had interpreted as referring to drug shipments by the cartel in fact referred to legitimate products from Cuchillo's manufacturing factories, destined for U.S. companies. A huge deposit into one of his Cayman accounts was perfectly legal—not a laundering scam, as originally thought—and was from the sale of a ranch he had owned in Texas. And the death of a nearby drug supplier they were sure was a hit ordered by Cuchillo turned out to be a real traffic accident involving a drunk driver. Much of the other data on which they'd based the terminate order remained ambiguous.

Billings had hoped that Adam, on the ground in Sonora, might have seen something to confirm their belief that Cuchillo ran the cartel.

But apparently not.

Harris licked the whipped cream again. Caught a few sprinkles in the process.

Billings looked him over again. Yes, weasely, but this wasn't necessarily an insult. After all, a sneaky weasel and a noble wolf weren't a lot different, at least not when they were sniffing after prey.

Harris asked bluntly, "So, do I tell Adam to go forward?"

Billings took a bite of scone. He had the lives of the passengers of the bus to save . . . and he had his career to think of, too. He considered the question as he brushed crumbs. He'd studied law at the University of Chicago, where the theory of cost-benefit analysis had largely been developed. The theory was this: you balanced the cost of preventing a mishap versus the odds of it occurring and the severity of the consequences if it does.

In the Cuchillo assassination, Billings had considered two options: Scenario One: Adam kills Cuchillo. If he's not the head of the cartel and is innocent, then the bus attack happens, because somebody else is behind it. If he's guilty, then the bus incident *doesn't* happen and there'd be no bus incidents in the future. Scenario Two: Adam stands down. Now, if Cuchillo's innocent, the bus incident happens. If he's guilty, the bus incident happens and there'll be more incidents like it in the future.

In other words, the hard and cold numbers favored going forward, even if Cuchillo was innocent.

But the obvious downside was that Billings could be crucified if that was the case . . . and if he and Harris and Adam were discovered.

An obvious solution occurred to him.

Oh, this was good. He finished the scone. "Yeah, Adam's green-lighted. But there's just one thing."

"What's that?"

"Tell him however he does it, all the evidence has to be obliterated. Completely. Nothing can trace the incident back here. Nothing at all."

And looking very much like a crossbreed, a weasel-wolf, Harris nodded and sucked up the last of the whipped cream. "I have no problem with that whatsoever."

∾

Díaz and Evans were back in the apartment in a nice section of Hermosillo, an apartment that was paid for by a company owned by a company owned by a company whose headquarters was a post office box in Northern Virginia. Evans was providing not only the technical expertise but most of the money as well. It was the least he could do, he'd joked, considering that it was America that supplied most of the weapons to the cartels; in Mexico it is virtually impossible to buy or possess weapons legally.

The time was now nearly five p.m. and Evans was reading an encrypted email from the U.S. that he'd just received.

He looked up. "That's it. We're green-lighted."

Díaz smiled. "Good. I want that son of a bitch to go to hell."

And they got back to work, poring over data-mined information about Cuchillo's life: his businesses and associates and employees, household staff, his friends and mistresses, the restaurants and bars where he spent many evenings, what he bought, what he downloaded, what computer programs he used, what he enjoyed listening to, what he ate and drank. The information was voluminous; security forces here and in the U.S. had been compiling it for months.

And, yes, much of this information had to do with books.

Weaknesses . . .

"Listen to this, Al. Last year he bought more than a million dollars' worth of books."

"You mean pesos."

"I mean dollars. Hey, you turn the A.C. down?"

Evans had noticed that the late afternoon heat was flowing into the apartment like a slow, oppressive tide.

"Just little," Díaz said. "Air conditioning, it's not so healthy."

"Cold temperature doesn't give you a cold," Evans said pedantically.

"I know that. I mean, the mold."

"What?"

"Mold in the ducts. Dangerous. *That* is what I meant, unhealthy."

Oh. Evans conceded the point. He actually had been coughing a lot since he'd arrived. He got another Coke, wiped the neck and sipped. He spit Handi-wipe. He coughed. He turned the A.C. down a little more.

"You get used to the heat."

"That's not possible. In Mexico, do you have words for winter, spring and fall?"

"Ha, funny."

They returned to the data-mined info. Not only was the credit card data available but insurance information about many of the books was often included. Some of the books were one of a kind, worth tens of thousands of dollars. They seemed to all be first editions.

"And look," Díaz said, looking over the documents. "He never sells them. He only buys."

It was true, Evans realized. There were no sales documents, no tax declarations of making money by selling capital items described as books. He kept everything he bought.

He'd want them around him all the time. He'd covet them. He'd need them.

Many people in the drug cartels were addicted to their own product; Cuchillo, it seemed, was not. Still, he had an addiction.

But how to exploit it?

Evans considered the list. Ideas were forming, as they always did. "Look at this, Al. Last week he ordered a book inscribed by Dickens, *The Old Curiosity Shop*. The price is sixty thousand. Yeah, dollars."

"For a book?" the Mexican agent asked, looking astonished.

"And it's *used*," Evans pointed out. "It's supposed to be coming in, in a day or two." He thought for some moments. Finally he nodded. "Here's an idea. I think it could work . . . . We'll contact this man—" He found a name on the sheet of data-mined printouts. "Señor Davila. He seems to be Cuchillo's main book dealer. What we'll do is tell him we suspect him of money laundering."

"He probably is."

"And he'd pee his pants, thinking if we announce it, Cuchillo will . . . "Evans drew his index finger across his throat.

"Do you do that in America?"

"What?"

"You know. That thing, your finger, your throat? I only saw that in bad movies. Laurel and Hardy."

Evans asked, "Who?"

Alejo Díaz shrugged and seemed disappointed that he'd never heard of them.

Evans continued, "So Davila will do whatever we want."

"Which will be to call Cuchillo and tell him his Dickens book arrived early. Oh, and the seller wants cash only."

"Good. I like that. So somebody will have to meet him in person—to collect the cash."

"And I'll come to his house to deliver the book. His security man probably won't want that but Cuchillo will insist to take delivery. Because he's—"

"Addicted."

The Mexican agent added, "I'll have to meet him, not you. Your Spanish, it is terrible. Why did they send you here on assignment?"

The reason for sending P.Z. Evans to a conflict zone was not because of his language skills. "I like the soft drinks." He opened another Coke. Did the neck cleaning thing. He cleared his throat and tried not to cough.

Díaz said, "We'll need to get the book, though. That Dickens." Nodding at the list.

Evans said, "I'll make some calls to my people in the States, see if they can track one down."

Díaz asked, "Okay, so it is that I'm inside. What do I do then? If I shoot him, they shoot me."

"Effective," Evans pointed out.

"But not the successful plans you're known for, P.Z."

"True. No, what you're going to do is plant a bomb."

"A bomb?" Díaz said uneasily. "I don't like them so much."

Evans gestured to his computer, referring to the email he'd just received. "Instructions are nothing's supposed to remain. Nothing to trace back to our bosses. Has to be a bomb. And one that produces a big honking fire."

Díaz added, "Always collateral damage."

The American agent shrugged. "Cuchillo doesn't have a wife. He doesn't have any children. Lives pretty much alone. Anybody around him is probably as guilty as he is." Evans tapped a drone picture of the compound. "Anything and anyone inside?" A shrug. "They're just acceptable sacrifices."

❧

He liked his nickname.

Alonso María Carillo was actually honored that people thought enough of him to give him a name that sounded like it was attached to some Mafioso out of a movie. Like Joey "The Knife" Vitelli.

"Cuchillo"—like a blade, like a dagger: How he loved that! And it was ironic because he wasn't a thug, wasn't like Tony Soprano at all. He was solid physically and he was tough, yes, but in Mexico a businessman must be tough. Still, his voice was soft and, well, inquisitive sounding. Almost innocent. His manner unassuming. His temper even.

He was in the office of his home not far from the upscale Hidalgo Plaza area of the city. Though the compound was surrounded by high walls, and sported a number of trees, from this spacious room he had a view of the city's grandest mountain, Cerro de la Compana, if a thousand-foot jut of rock can be described thus.

It was quitting time—he'd been working here since six that morning. No breaks. He put his work aside and went online to download some apps for his new iPhone, which he would synchronize to his iPad. He loved gadgets—both in his personal life and in business he always stayed current with the latest technology. (Since his companies had sales reps throughout Mexico and he needed to stay in constant touch with them he used the Cloud and thought it was the best invention of the last ten years.)

Rising from his desk, declaring it the end of the day, he happened to regard himself in a mirror nearby. Not so bad for an old man.

Cuchillo was about five nine and stocky and resembled Fernandez, Mexico's greatest actor and director, in the businessman's opinion. Though he was in scores of films, Fernandez was at his peak as Mapache in *The Wild Bunch*, one of the few truly honest films about Mexico.

Looking over his face, thick black hair. Keen brown eyes. Cuchillo thought again, No, not so bad . . . The women still appreciated him. Sure, he paid some of them—one way or another—but he also had a connection with them. He could converse with them. He listened. He also made love for hours. Not a lot of 57-year-olds could do that.

"You old devil," he whispered.

Then he gave a wry grin at his own vanity and left the office. He told his maid he'd be staying at home for dinner.

And he walked into his most favorite place on earth, his library. The building was large: sixty feet by forty, and very cool, as well as carefully humidity controlled (which was ironic in Hermosillo, in the heart of the Sonoran desert, where there were two or three rainy days a year). Gauze curtains kept the sun from bleaching the jackets and leather bindings of the books.

The ceilings were thirty feet off the ground and the entire space was open, lined with tall shelves on the ground floor and encircled with levels above, which one could reach by climbing an iron spiral staircase to narrow walkways. In the center were three parallel shelves ten feet high. In the front of the room was a library table, surrounded by comfortable chairs and an overstuffed armchair and a floor lamp with a warm yellow bulb. A small bar featured the best brandy and single-malt scotches. Cuchillo enjoyed Cuban cigars. But never here.

The building was home to 22,000 titles, nearly all of them first editions. Many, the only ones in existence.

On a night like this, after a long day working by himself, Cuchillo would normally have gone out into the relatively cool evening and eaten at Sonora Steak and then gone to Ruby's bar with his friends and—of course—his security. But the rumors of this impending attack were too real to ignore and he'd have to stay within the compound until more was learned about the threat.

Ah, what a country we live in, he reflected. The most philanthropic businessman, and the most hardworking farmer, and the worst drug baron all are treated equally . . . treated to fear.

Someday it will be different.

But at least Cuchillo had no problem staying home tonight, in his beloved library. He called his housekeeper and had her prepare dinner, a simple linguine primavera, made with organic vegetables and herbs out of his own garden. A California cabernet, too, and ice water.

He turned on a small high definition TV, the news. There were several stories about the ceremony in the D.F. on Friday, commemorating the latest war against the cartels. The event would include speeches by the country's president and an American official from the DEA. More drug killings in Chihuahua. He shook his head.

In a half hour the food arrived and he sat down at the table, removed his tie—he dressed for work, even when staying home— and stuffed a napkin into his collar. As he ate, his mind wandered to the Dickens that his book dealer, Señor Davila, would be delivering tomorrow. He was delighted that it had arrived early, but pleased, too, that he was getting it for a lower price than originally agreed. The seller whom Davila had found apparently needed cash and would reduce the price by five thousand if Cuchillo paid in U.S. dollars, which he immediately agreed to do. Davila had said he would reduce his percentage of the finder's fee accordingly, but Cuchillo had insisted that he receive the full amount. Davila had always been good to him.

There was a knock on the door and his security chief, José, entered.

He could tell at once: bad news.

"I heard from a contact in the *Federales*, sir. There is intelligence about this bus attack on Friday? The tourist bus? The reports are linking you to it."

"No!"

"I'm afraid so."

"Dammit," he muttered. Cuchillo had uttered only a few obscenities in his life; this was usually the worst his language got. "*Me*? This is absurd. This is completely wrong! They blame me for everything!"

"I'm sorry, sir."

Cuchillo calmed and considered the problem. "Call the bus lines, call the security people, call whoever you have to. Do what you can to make sure passengers are safe in Sonora. You understand, I want to be certain that no one is hurt here. They will blame me if anything happens."

"I'll do what I can, sir, but—"

His boss said patiently, "I understand you can't control the entire state. But use our resources to do whatever you can."

"Yessir, I will."

The man hurried off.

Cuchillo finally shrugged off the anger, finished dinner and, sipping his wine, walked up and down the aisles enjoying the sight of his many titles.

22,000 . . .

He returned to his den and worked some more on the project that had obsessed him for the past few months: opening another auto parts fabrication plant outside of town. There was a huge U.S. automobile manufacturer here in Hermosillo and Cuchillo had made much of his fortune by supplying parts to the company. It would employ another 400 local workers. Though he benefitted from their foolishness, he couldn't understand the Americans' sending manufacturing *away* from their country. He would never do that. Business—no, all of life—was about loyalty.

At ten p.m., he decided to retire early. He washed and walked into his large bedroom, thinking again of *The Old Curiosity Shop* he would receive tomorrow. This buoyed his spirits. He dressed in pajamas and glanced at his bedside table.

What should he read now, he wondered, to lull him to sleep?

He decided he would continue with *War and Peace*, a title that, he thought wryly, perfectly described a businessman's life in Mexico.

❧

In the living room of the apartment with the complicated ownership, P.Z. Evans was hunched over his improvised workbench, carefully constructing the bomb.

The care wasn't necessary because he risked getting turned into red vapor, not yet, in any event; it was simply that the circuits and wiring were very small and he had big hands. In the old days he would have been soldering the connections. But now improvised explosive devices were plug and play. He was pressing the circuits into sheets of especially powerful plastic explosive, which he'd packed into the leather cover after slicing it open with a surgeon's scalpel.

It was eleven p.m. and the agents had not had a moment's respite today. They'd spent the past twelve hours acquiring the key items to the project, like the surgeon's instruments, electronics and a leather-bound edition of the play *The Robbers* by Friedrich Schiller, which their new partner—book dealer Señor Davila—had suggested because Cuchillo liked the German author.

Through a jeweler's loupe over his right eye, Evans examined his handiwork and made some small adjustments.

Outside their door they could hear infectious *norteño* in a nearby square. An accordion was prominent. The windows were open because the evening air teased that it was heading toward the bearable, and the A.C. was off. Evans had convinced himself he had a moldinduced cough.

Alejo Díaz sat nearby, not saying anything and seemingly uneasy. This was not because of the bomb, but because he'd apparently found the task of becoming an expert on book collecting and Charles Dickens daunting, to say the least.

Still, Díaz would occasionally look up from Joseph Connolly's *Collecting Modern First Editions*, his eyes on the bomb. Evans thought about diving to the floor, shouting, "Oh, shit! Five . . . four . . . three . . ." But while the Mexican agent had a sense of humor, that might be over the line.

A half hour later he was gluing the leather into place. "Okay, that's it. Done."

Díaz eyed his handicraft. "Is small."

"Bombs are, yes. That's what makes them so nice."

"It will get the job done?"

A brief laugh. "Oh, yeah."

"Nice," Díaz repeated uneasily.

Evans's phone buzzed with an encrypted text. He read it.

"Bait's here."

A moment later there was a knock on the door and, even though the text he'd just received had included all the proper codes, both men drew their weapons.

But the delivery man was just who he purported to be—a man attached to the Economic Development Council for the U.S. consulate in northern Mexico. Evans had worked with him before. With a nod the man handed Evans a small package and turned and left.

Evans opened it and extracted the copy of Charles Dickens's *The Old Curiosity Shop*. Six hours ago it had been sitting in a famed book dealer's store on Warren Street in New York City. It had been bought with cash by the man who had just delivered it, and its journey to Sonora had been via chartered jet.

Killing bad guys is not only dangerous, it's expensive.

The American wrapped the book back up.

Díaz asked, "So, what are the next steps?"

"Well, you—you just keep on reading." A nod toward the book in his hands. "And when you're through with that, you might want to brush up on the history of English literature in general. You never know what subject might come up."

Díaz rolled his eyes and shifted in his chair, stretching. "And while I'm stuck in school, what are you going to do?"

"I'm going out and getting drunk."

"That is not so fair," Díaz pointed out.

"And it's even less fair when I'm thinking I may get laid, too."

THURSDAY

The latter part of his plans did not happen, though Evans had come close.

But Carmella, the gorgeous young woman he met at a nearby bar, was a little too eager, which set off warning bells that she probably had designs to land a good-looking and apparently employed American husband.

In any event, tequila had intervened big time and the dance of your-place-or-mine never occurred.

It was now ten in the morning and, natch, hot as searing iron. No A.C., but Evans's cough was gone.

Díaz examined his partner. "You look awful. Hey, you know that many of Charles Dickens' most popular novels were first published serially and that he wrote in a style influenced by gothic popular novels of the Victorian era, but with a whimsical touch?"

"You're fucked if you go in talking like that."

"I going to read one of his books. Is Dickens translated into Spanish?"

"I think so. I don't know."

Evans opened an attach case he'd bought yesterday and had rigged with a false compartment. Into this narrow space he added the Schiller he'd doctored last night and sealed it. Then he added receipts, price guides, scraps of paper—everything that a book dealer would carry with him to a meeting with a collector. The Dickens, too, which was packed in bubble wrap. Evans then tested the communications app on the iPad that Díaz would have with him—it would appear to be in sleep mode, but a hypersensitive microphone would be picking up all the conversation between Cuchillo and Díaz. The system worked fine.

"Okay." Evans then checked his 9mm Beretta. He slipped it into his waistband. "Diversion's ready, device is ready. Let's do it."

They walked down to the parking lot. Evans went to a huge old Mercury—yes, a real Mercury, in sun-faded Mercury brown, with an untraceable registration. Díaz's car was a midnight blue Lincoln registered to Davila Collectable Books, which Señor Davila had quickly, almost tearfully, agreed to let them borrow.

According to the unwritten rules of times like these, the start of a mission, when either or both might be dead within the hour, they said nothing of luck, hope, or the pleasure of working together. Much less did they shake hands.

"See you later."

"*Sí.*"

They climbed in, fired up the engines and hurried out of the lot.

❧

As he drove to Cuchillo's compound, Alejo Díaz could not help but think of the bus.

The people tomorrow, the tourists, who would be trapped and burned to death by this butcher. He recalled P.Z. Evans's words yesterday and reflected that these people were also—to Cuchillo—acceptable sacrifices.

Díaz was suddenly swept with fury at what people like this were doing to his country. Yes, the place was hot and dusty and the economy staggered and it dwelt forever in the shadow of that behemoth to the north—the country that Mexicans both loved and hated.

But this land is our home, he thought. And home, however flawed, deserves respect.

People like Alonso María Cuchillo treated Mexico with nothing but contempt.

Of course, Díaz would have to keep his revulsion deeply hidden when he met Cuchillo. He was just a shopkeeper's assistant; the drug lord was just another rich businessman with a love of books.

If he screwed that up, then many people—himself included—were going to die.

Then he was at the compound. He was admitted through a gate that swung open slowly and he parked near the modest front door. A swarthy, squat man who clearly was carrying a pistol greeted him pleasantly and asked him to step to a table in the entryway. Another guard gently but thoroughly frisked him.

Then the briefcase was searched.

Díaz regarded the operation with surprising detachment, he decided, considering he might be one minute away from being shot.

The detachment vanished and his heart thudded fiercely when the man frowned and dug into the case.

Jesus . . .

The man gazed at Díaz with wide eyes. Then he grinned. "Is this the new iPad?" He pulled it out and displayed it to the other guard.

His breathing stuttering in and out, Díaz nodded and wondered if his question had burst Evans's eardrum.

"Four-G?"

"If there's a server."

"How many gig?"

"Thirty-two," the Mexican agent managed to say.

"My son has that, too. His is nearly filled. Music videos." He man replaced it and handed the briefcase back. The Schiller novel remained undiscovered.

Struggling to control his breathing, Díaz said, "I don't have many videos. I use it mostly for work."

A few minutes later he was led into the living room. He declined water or any other beverage. Alone, the Mexican agent sat with the briefcase on his lap. He opened it again and smoothly freed the Schiller and slipped it into his waistband, absently thinking about the explosive two inches from his penis. The open lid obscured prying eyes or cameras if there were any. He extracted the Dickens and closed the case.

A moment later a shadow spread on the floor and Díaz looked up to see Cuchillo walking steadily forward on quiet feet.

The Knife. The slaughterer of hundreds, perhaps thousands.

The stocky man strode forward, smiling. He seemed pleasant enough, if a bit distracted.

"Señor Abrossa," he said—the cover name Davila had given when he'd called yesterday. Díaz now presented a business card they'd had printed yesterday. "Good day. Delighted to meet you."

"And I'm pleased to meet such an illustrious client of Señor Davila."

"And how is he? I thought he might come himself."

"He sends his regards. He's getting ready for the auction of eighteenth century Bibles."

"Yes, yes, that's right. One of the few books I *don't* collect. Which is a shame. I understand that the plot is very compelling."

Díaz laughed. "The characters, too."

"Ah, the Dickens."

Taking it reverently, the man unwrapped the bubble plastic and examined the volume and flipped through it. "It is thrilling to know that Dickens himself held this very book."

Cuchillo was lost in the book, a gaze of admiration and respect. Not lust or possessiveness.

And in the silence, Díaz looked around and noted that this house was filled with much art and sculpture. All tasteful and subdued. This was not the house of a gaudy drug lord. He had been inside those. Filled with excess—and usually brimming with beautiful and marginally clad women.

It was then that a sudden and difficult thought came to Díaz. Was it at all possible that they'd made a mistake? Was this subdued, cultured man *not* the vicious dog they'd been led to believe? After all, there'd never been any hard proof that Cuchillo was the drug lord many believed him to be. Just because one was rich and tough didn't mean he was a criminal.

Where exactly had the intelligence assigning guilt come from? How reliable was it?

He realized Cuchillo was looking at him with curiosity. "Now, Señor Abrossa, are you *sure* you're the book dealer I've been led to believe?"

Using all his willpower, Díaz kept a smile on his face and dipped a brow in curiosity.

The man laughed hard. "You've forgotten to ask for the money."

"Ah, sometimes I get so caught up in the books themselves that, you're right, I *do* forget it's a business. I personally would give books away to people who appreciate them."

"I most certainly *won't* tell your employer you said that." He reached into his pocket and extracted a thick envelop. "There is the fifty-five thousand. U.S. "Díaz handed him the receipt on Davila's letterhead and signed "*V. Abrossa*."

"Thank you . . .?" Cuchillo asked, lifting an eyebrow.

"Victor." Díaz put the money in the attach case and closed it. He looked around. "Your home, it is very lovely. I've always wondered about the houses in this neighborhood."

"Thank you. Would you like to see the place?"

"Please. And your collection, too, if possible."

"Of course."

Cuchillo then lead him on a tour of the house, which was, like the living room, filled with understated elegance. Pictures of youngsters—his nieces and nephews who lived in Mexico City and Chihuahua, he explained. He seemed proud of them.

Díaz couldn't help wondering again: Was this a mistake?

"Now, come to my library. As a booklover, I hope you will be impressed."

They walked through the kitchen, where Cuchillo paused and asked the housekeeper how her ailing mother was doing. He nodded as she answered. He told her to take any time off she needed. His eyes were narrow with genuine sympathy.

A mistake . . . ?

They walked out the back door and through the shade of twin brick walls, the ones protecting him from sniper shots, and then into the library.

Even as a non-book lover, Díaz was impressed. *More* than impressed.

The place astonished him. He knew the size from the drone images, but he hadn't imagined it would be filled as completely as it was. Everywhere, books. It seemed the walls were made of them, like rich tiles in all different sizes and colors and textures.

"I don't know what to say, sir."

They walked slowly through the cool room and Cuchillo talked about some of the highlights in the collection. "My superstars," he said. He pointed out some as they walked.

The Hound of the Baskervilles by Conan Doyle, *Seven Pillars of Wisdom* by T.E. Lawrence, *The Great Gatsby* by F. Scott Fitzgerald, *The Tale of Peter Rabbit* by Beatrix Potter, *Brighton Rock* by Graham Greene, *The Maltese Falcon* by Dashiell Hammett, *Night and Day* by Virginia Woolf, *The Hobbit* by J.R.R. Tolkien, *The Sound and the Fury* by William Faulkner, *A Portrait of the Artist as a Young Man* by James Joyce, *A La Recherche Du Temps Perdu* by Marcel Proust, *The Wonderful Wizard of Oz* by Frank Baum, *Harry Potter and the Philosopher's Stone* by J.K. Rowling, *The Bridge* by Hart Crane, *The Catcher in the Rye* by J.D. Salinger, *The Thirty-Nine Steps* by John Buchan, *The Murder on the Links* by Agatha Christie, *Casino Royale* by Ian Fleming.

"And our nation's writers too, of course—that whole wall there. I love all books, but it's important for us in Mexico to be aware of *our* people's voice." He strode forward and displayed a few. "Salvador Novo, Jos Gorostiza, Xavier Villaurrutia, and the incomparable Octavio Paz. Whom you've read, of course."

"Of course," Díaz said, praying that Cuchillo would not ask for the name of one of Paz's books, much less a plot or protagonist.

Díaz noted a book near the man's plush armchair. It was in a display case, James Joyce's *Ulysses*. He happened to have read about the title last night on a rare book website. "Is that the original 1922 edition?"

"Yes, that's right."

"It's worth about $150,000."

Cuchillo smiled. "No. It's worth nothing."

"Nothing?"

His arm swept in a slow circle, indicating the room. "This entire *collection* is worth nothing."

"How do you mean, sir?"

"Something has value only to the extent the owner is willing to sell. I would never sell a single volume. Most book collectors feel this way, more so than about paintings or cars or sculpture."

The businessman picked up *The Maltese Falcon*. "You are perhaps surprised I have in my collection spy and detective stories?"

The agent recited a fact he'd read. "Of course, popular commercial fiction is usually *more* valuable than literature." He hoped he'd got this straight.

He must have. Cuchillo was nodding. "But I enjoy them for their substance as well as their collectability."

This was interesting. The agent said, "I suppose crime is an art form in a way."

Cuchillo's head cocked and he seemed confused. Díaz's heart beat faster.

The collector said, "I don't mean that. I mean that crime and popular novelists are often better craftspeople than so-called literary writers. The readers know this; they appreciate good storytelling over pretentious artifice. Take that book I just bought, *The Old Curiosity Shop*. When it first came out, serialized in weekly parts, people in New York and Boston would wait on the docks when the latest installment was due to arrive from England. They'd shout to the sailors, 'Tell us, is Little Nell dead?'" He glanced at the display case. "I suspect not so many people did that for *Ulysses*. Don't you agree?"

"I do, sir, yes." Then he frowned. "But wasn't *Curiosity Shop* serialized in monthly parts?"

After a moment Cuchillo smiled. "Ah, right you are. I don't collect periodicals, so I'm always getting that confused."

Was this a test, or a legitimate error?

Díaz could not tell.

He glanced past Cuchillo and pointed to a shelf. "Is that a Mark Twain?"

When the man turned Díaz quickly withdrew the doctored Schiller and slipped it onto a shelf just above *Ulysses*, near the drug baron's armchair.

He lowered his arm just as Cuchillo turned back. "No, not there. But I have several. You've read *Huckleberry Finn*?"

"No. I just know it as a collector's item."

"Some people consider it the greatest American novel. I consider it perhaps the greatest novel of the New World. It has lessons for *us* as well." A shake of the head. "And the Lord knows we need some lessons in this poor country of ours."

They returned to the living room and Díaz dug the iPad from the case. "Let me show you some new titles that Señor Davila has just gotten in." He supposed P.Z. Evans was relieved to hear his voice and learn that he had not been discovered and spirited off to a grave in the graceless Sonora desert.

He called up Safari and went to the website. "Now, we have—"

But his phony sales pitch was interrupted when a huge bang startled them all. A bullet had struck and spattered against the resistant glass of a window nearby.

"My God! What's that?" Díaz called.

"Get out of the room, away from the windows! Now!" José, the security man, gestured them toward the doorways leading out of the living room.

"They're bulletproof," Cuchillo protested.

"But they could try armor piercing when they realize! Move, sir!"

Everyone scattered.

෴

P.Z. Evans didn't get a chance to shoot his gun very often.

Although he and Díaz had earlier commented about Cuchillo meeting with an "accident" in a euphemistic way, in fact staging natural deaths was the preferred way to eliminate people. While the police would often *suspect* that the death of a terrorist or a criminal was not happenstance, a good craftsman could create a credible scenario that was satisfactory to avoid further investigation. A fall down stairs, a car crash, a pool drowning.

But nothing was as much fun as pulling out your long-barreled Italian pistol and blasting away.

He was about fifty yards from the compound, standing on a Dumpster behind a luxury apartment complex. There wasn't a support for the gun, but he was strong—shooters have to have good muscles—and he easily hit the window he was aiming for. He had a decent view through the glass and for his first shot aimed where nobody was standing—just in case this window happened not to be bullet proof. But the slugs smacked harmlessly into the strong glass. He emptied one mag, reloaded and leapt off the Dumpster, sprinting to the car, just as the side gate opened and Cuchillo's security people carefully looked out. Evans fired once into the wall to keep them down and then drove around the block to the other side of the compound.

No Dumpsters here, but he climbed on top of the roof of the car and fired three rounds into the window of Cuchillo's bedroom.

Then he hopped down and climbed into the driver's seat. A moment later he was skidding away.

Windows up, A.C. on full. If there was mold in car's vents he'd just take his chances. He was sweating like he'd spent an hour in the sauna.

ॐ

Inside the house, after the shooter had vanished and calm—relative calm—was restored, Cuchillo did something that astonished Alejo Díaz.

He ordered his security chief to call the police.

This hardly seemed like the sort of thing that a drug baron would do. You'd think he'd want as little attention—and as little contact with the authorities—as possible.

But when a Hermosillo police captain, along with four uniformed officers, arrived twenty minutes later, Cuchillo was grim and angry. "Once again, I've been targeted! People can't accept that I'm just a businessman. They assume because I'm successful that I'm a criminal and therefore I deserve to be shot. It's unfair! You work hard, you're responsible, you give back to your country and your city . . . and still people believe the worst of you!"

The police conducted a brief investigation, but the shooter was, of course, long gone. And no one had seen anything—everyone inside had fled to the den, bedroom or bathroom, as the security chief had instructed. Díaz's response: "I'm afraid I didn't see much, anything really. I was on the floor, hiding." He shrugged, as if faintly embarrassed by his cowardice.

The officer nodded and jotted his words down. He didn't believe him, but nor did he challenge Díaz to be more thorough; in Mexico one was used to witnesses who "didn't see much, anything really."

The police left and Cuchillo, no longer angry but once more distracted, said goodbye to Díaz.

"I'm not much in the mood to consider Señor Davila's books now," he said, with a nod to the iPad. He would check the website later.

"Of course. And thank you, sir."

"It's nothing."

Díaz left, feeling even more conflicted than ever.

You work hard, you're responsible, you give back to your country and your city . . . and still people believe the worst of you . . .

My God, was he a murderous drug baron or a generous businessman?

And whether Cuchillo was guilty or innocent, Díaz realized he was stabbed by guilt at the thought that he'd just planted a bomb that would take the life of a man at his most vulnerable, doing something he loved and found comfort in: reading a book.

෴

An hour later Cuchillo was sitting in his den, blinds closed over the bulletproof windows. And despite the attack, he was feeling relieved.

Actually, *because* of the attack, he was feeling relieved.

He had thought that the rumors they'd heard for the past few days, the snippets of intelligence, were referring to some kind of brilliant, insidious plan to murder him, a plan that he couldn't anticipate. But it had turned out to be a simple shooting, which had been foiled by the bullet proof glass; the assassin was surely headed out of the area.

Jos knocked and entered. "Sir, I think we have a lead about the attack. I heard from Carmella at Ruby's. She spent much of last evening with an American, a businessman, he claimed. He got drunk and said some things that seemed odd to her. She heard of the shooting and called me."

"Carmella," Cuchillo said, grinning. She was a beautiful if slightly unbalanced young woman who could get by on her looks for the time being, but if she didn't hook a husband soon she'd be in trouble.

Not that Cuchillo was in any hurry for that to happen; he'd slept with her occasionally. She was very, very talented.

"And what about this American?"

"He was asking her about this neighborhood. The houses in it. If there were any hotels nearby, even though earlier he'd said he was staying near the bar."

While there were sights to see in the sprawling city of Hermosillo, Cuchillo's compound was in a nondescript residential area. Nothing here would draw either businessmen or tourists.

"Hotel," Cuchillo mused. "For a vantage point for shooting?"

"That's what I wondered. Now, I've gotten his credit card information from the bar and data-mined it. I'm waiting for more information but we know for a fact it's an assumed identity."

"So he's an operative. But who's he working for? A drug cartel from *north* of the border? A hit man from Texas hired by the Sinaloans? . . . The American government?"

"I hope to know more soon, sir."

"Thank you."

Cuchillo rose and, carrying the Dickens, started for the library.

He stopped. "José?"

"Sir?"

"I want to change our plans with the bus."

"Yes sir?"

"I know I said I wanted safe haven for all bus passengers in Sonora on Friday, that nothing should happen to the passengers here."

"Right, I told the men to wait to attack until it crossed the border into Sinaloa."

"But now, tell the men to hit a bus *here* tomorrow morning."

"In Sonora?"

"That's right. Whoever is behind this *must* know that I won't be intimidated. Any attempts on my life will be met with retribution."

"Yes sir."

Cuchillo looked as his security man carefully. "You don't think I should be doing this, do you?" He encouraged those working for him to make their opinions known, even—especially—differing opinions.

"Frankly, sir, not a tourist bus, no. Not civilians. I think it works to our disadvantage."

"I disagree," Cuchillo said calmly. "We need to take a strong stand."

"Of course, sir, if that's what you want."

"Yes, it is." But a moment later he frowned. "But wait. There's something to what you say."

The security man looked his boss's way.

"When your men attack the bus, get the women and children off before you set it on fire. Only burn the men to death."

"Yes sir."

Cuchillo considered his decision a weakness. But José had a point. The new reality was that, yes, sometimes you *did* need to take public relations into account.

❦

At eight p.m. that evening Cuchillo received a call in his library.

He was pleased at what he learned. One of his lieutenants explained that a shooting team was in place and would assault a large bus as it headed along Highway 26 west toward Bahia de Kino tomorrow morning.

They would stop the vehicle, leave the men on board, then wire shut the door and douse the bus in petrol and shoot anybody who tried to leap from the windows.

The communications man on the shooting team would call the press to make sure they arrived for video and photos before the fire was out.

Cuchillo thanked the man and disconnected, thinking of how much he was looking forward to seeing those news accounts.

He hoped the man who had shot at him would be watching the news, too, and would feel responsible for the pain the victims would experience.

Glancing up from his armchair, he happened to notice that a book was out of order.

It was on the shelf above the case containing the *Ulysses*.

He rose and noted the leather spine. *The Robbers*. How had a Schiller gotten here? He disliked disorder of any kind, particularly in his book collection. One of the maids, perhaps.

Just as he plucked the volume from the shelf, the door burst open. "Sir!"

"What?" he turned quickly to Jos.

"I think there's a bomb here! That man with the book dealer, Davila; he's fake. He was working with the American!"

His eyes first went to the Dickens but, no, he'd flipped through the entire volume and there'd been no explosives inside. The assassins had simply used that as bait to gain access to Cuchillo's compound.

Then he looked down at what he held in his hand. The Schiller.

"What is it, sir?"

"This book . . . It wasn't here earlier. Abrossa! He planted it when I gave him the tour." Cuchillo realized that, yes, the book was heavier than a comparable book of this size.

"Set it down! Run!"

"No! The books!" He glanced around at the library.

22,000 volumes . . .

"It could blow up at any moment."

Cuchillo started to set it down, then hesitated. "I can't do it! You get back, José!" Then still holding the bomb, he ran outside, the security guard remaining loyally beside him. Once they were to the garden, Cuchillo flung the Schiller as far as he could. The men dropped to the ground behind one of the brick walls.

There was no explosion.

When Cuchillo looked he saw that the book had opened. The contents—electronics and a wad of clay—colored explosives—had tumbled out.

"Jesus, Jesus."

"Please, sir. Inside now!"

They hurried into the house and got the staff away from the side of the house where the box lay in the garden. José called the man they used for making their *own* bombs. He would hurry to the house and disarm or otherwise dispose of the device.

Cuchillo poured a large Scotch. "How did you find this out?"

"I got the data-mined information on the American in the bar, the one who was drinking with Carmella. I found records that he was making calls to the book dealer. And he used his credit card to buy electronic parts at a supplier in town—the sort of circuits that are used in IEDs."

"Yes, yes. I see. They threatened Davila to help them. Or paid the bastard. You know, I suspected that man, Abrossa. I suspected him for a moment. Then I decided, no, he was legitimate."

Because I wanted the Dickens so much.

"I appreciate what you did, José. That was a good job. Would you like a drink, too?"

"No, thank you, sir."

Still calm, Cuchillo wrinkled his brow. "Considering how the American tried to kill us—and nearly destroyed a priceless collection of books—how would you feel if we instructed our people on Highway 26 *not* to get the women and children off before setting fire to the bus?"

José smiled. "I think that's an excellent suggestion, sir. I'll call the team."

∾

Several hours later the bomb had been slipped into a steel disposal container and taken away. Cuchillo, the engineer explained, had unwittingly disarmed it himself. The panicked throw had dislodged the wires from the detonator, rendering it safe.

Cuchillo had enjoyed watching the bomb-disposal robot—the same way he liked being in his parts manufacturing operation and his drug synthesizing facilities. He enjoyed watching technology at work. He had always wanted the *Codex Leicester*—the DaVinci manuscript that contained the inventor's musings on mechanics and science. Bill Gates had paid $30 million for it some years ago. Cuchillo could easily afford that, but the book was not presently for sale. Besides, such a purchase would draw too much attention to him, and a man who has tortured hundreds to death and—in the spirit of mercy—painlessly shot perhaps a thousand, does not want too many eyes turned in his direction.

Cuchillo spent the rest of the night on the phone with associates, trying to find more details of the two assassins and any associates they might have, but there was no other information. He'd learn more tomorrow. It was nearly midnight when finally he sat down to a modest dinner of grilled chicken and beans with tomatillo sauce.

As he ate and sipped a very nice cabernet, he found himself relaxed and curiously content, despite the horror of what might have happened today. Neither he nor any of his people had been injured in the attack. His 22,000 volumes were safe.

And he had some enjoyable projects on the horizon: killing Davila, of course. And he'd find the name of the person masquerading as Abrossa, his assistant, and the shooter who'd fired the shots—a clumsy diversionary tactic, he now realized. Probably the American. Those two would not die as quickly as the book dealer. They had destroyed an original Friedrich Schiller (albeit a third printing with water damage on the spine). Cuchillo would stay true to his name and would use a knife on them himself—in his special interrogation room in the basement below his library.

But best of all: he had the burning bus and its scores of screaming passengers to look forward to.

FRIDAY

At one a.m. Cuchillo washed for bed and climbed between the smooth sheets, not silk but luxurious and expensive cotton.

He would read something calming to lull him to sleep tonight. Not *War and Peace.*

Perhaps some poetry.

He picked up his iPad from the bedside table, flipped open the cover and tapped the icon to bring up his e-reader app. Cuchillo, of course, generally preferred traditional books for the most part. But he was a man of the 21st century and found e-books were often more convenient and easier to read than their paper forebears. His iPad library contained nearly a thousand titles.

As he looked at the tablet, though, he realized he must have hit the wrong app icon—the forward camera had opened and he found he was staring at himself.

Cuchillo didn't close the camera right away, however. He took a moment to regard himself. And laughed and whispered the phrase he'd used to describe himself earlier, "Not so bad, you old devil."

❧

Five hundred yards from Cuchillo's compound, Alejo Díaz and P.Z. Evans were sitting in the front seat of the big Mercury. They were leaning forward, staring at the screen of Evans's impressive laptop computer.

What they were observing was the same image that Cuchillo happened to be basking in—his own wide-angle face—which was being beamed from his iPad's camera to the laptop via a surveillance app that Evans had loaded. They could hear the man's voice too.

You old devil . . .

"He's in bed, alone," Evans said. "Good enough for me." Then he glanced at Díaz. "He's all yours."

"*Sí?*" asked the Mexican agent.

"Yep."

"*Gracias.*"

"*Nada.*"

And without any dramatic flair, Díaz pressed a button on what looked like a garage door opener.

In Cuchillo's bedroom, the iPad's leather case, which Evans had stuffed with the potent incendiary explosive last night, detonated. The explosion was far larger than the American agent had expected. Even the bullet-proof windows blew to splinters and a gaseous cloud of flame shot into the night.

They waited until it was clear the bedroom was engulfed in flame—and all the evidence of the attack was burning to vapors, as they'd been instructed to do by Washington—and then Díaz started the car and drove slowly through the night.

After ten minutes of silence, looking over their shoulders for police or other pursuers, Díaz said, "Have to say, *amigo*, you came up with a good plan."

Evans didn't gloat—or act shy with false modesty, either. It *was* a good plan. Data-mining had revealed a lot about Cuchillo (this was often true in the case of targets like him—wealthy and, accordingly, big spenders). Evans and *Díaz* had noted not only his purchases of collectable books, but his high-tech acquisitions too: an iPad, an e-reader app and a number of e-books, as well as a leather case for the Apple device.

Armed with this information, Evans duplicated the iPad and filled the case with the deadly explosive. *This* was the actual weapon that Díaz smuggled into the compound and swapped with Cuchillo's iPad, whose location they could pinpoint thanks to the finder service Evans had hacked into. With Díaz inside, holding the iPad to show Davila's latest inventory of books, Evans had fired into the windows, scattering everyone and giving his partner a chance to slip into the bedroom and switch the devices. He'd fired into that room's windows, too, just in case Díaz had not been alone there.

The bullets would also serve a second purpose—to let Cuchillo and his security people believe the shooting was the assault they'd heard about and lessen their suspicion that another attack was coming.

Lessen, but not eliminate. The Knife was too sharp for that.

And so they needed a second misdirection. Evans let slip fake information about himself—to Carmella, the beautiful woman who was part of Cuchillo's entourage at Ruby's Bar (phone records revealed he called her once or twice a month). He also fed phony data-mined facts that suggested he and Díaz might have snuck a bomb into the library. He'd hollowed out a copy of Schiller's *The Robbers*—Sorry, Fred—and filled it with real explosives and a circuit, but failed to connect the detonators.

Cuchillo would know his library so well it wouldn't take much to find this out-of-place volume, which Díaz had intentionally planted askew.

After finding this device, they would surely think no more threats existed and not suspect the deadly iPad on Cuchillo's bedside table.

Díaz now called José, the security chief for the late drug baron, and explained—in a loud voice due to the chief's sudden hearing loss—that if any bus attacks occurred he would end up in jail accompanied by the rumor that he had sold his boss out. As unpopular as Cuchillo had been among the competing cartel figures, nothing was more unpopular in a Mexican prison than a snitch.

The man assured them that there would be no attacks. Díaz had to say goodbye three times before the man heard him.

A good plan, if a bit complicated. It would have been much easier, of course, simply to get a real bomb into the library and detonate it when drone surveillance revealed Cuchillo inside.

That idea, however, hadn't even been on the table. They would never have destroyed the library. Aside from the moral issue—and P.Z. Evans *did* have his standards—there was the little matter of how such a conflagration would play in the press if word got out about the identity of the two agents who'd orchestrated it and who their employers were.

You can kill drug barons and their henchmen with impunity; 20,000 destroyed classics were not acceptable sacrifices. That was the sort of mar from which careers do not recover.

In a half hour they were back at the hotel and watching the news, which confirmed that indeed Alonso María Carillo, known as Cuchillo, the suspected head of the Hermosillo Cartel, was dead. No one else had been injured in the attack, which was blamed on a rival cartel, probably from Sinaloa.

The news, Evans was surprised to note, wasn't the lead story, which Cuchillo probably would have taken hard. But, in a way, it was his own fault; he'd contributed to the ubiquity of the drug business in Mexico, which made stories about death in the trade unnewsworthy.

Evans supposed it was something like book collecting: the bigger the print run for first editions, the less the interest, the lower the value.

He shut the set off. They decided to get a little dinner and a lot of tequila—though definitely not at Sonora Steak or Ruby's bar, Cuchillo's favorite hangouts. They'd go somewhere across town. They'd probably be safe; the Hermosillo Cartel had been neutralized. Still, both men had their weapons underneath their untucked shirts. And extra magazines in their left pockets.

As they walked to the big old Mercury, Díaz said, "You should have seen all those books in the library. I never saw so many books in my life."

"Uhn," Evans said, not particularly interested.

"What does that mean, that sound? You don't *like* books?"

"I like books."

The Mexican agent gave a fast laugh. "You no sound like you do. You read at all?"

"Of course I read."

"So, what do you read? Tell me."

Evans climbed into the passenger seat and counted three pickup trucks pass by before he answered. "Okay, you want to know? The sports section. That's all I read."

Díaz started the car. "*Sí*, me too."

Evans said, "Could we get that A.C. going, Al? Does it *ever* cool off in this goddamn town?

II

Pronghorns of the Third Reich

C. J. Box

As HE DID every morning, Paul Parker's deaf and blind old Labrador, Champ, signaled his need by burrowing his nose into Parker's neck and snuffling. If Parker didn't immediately throw back the covers and get up, Champ would woof until he did. So he got up. The dog used to bound downstairs in a manic rush and skid across the hardwood floor of the landing to the back door, but now he felt his way down slowly, with his belly touching each step, grunting, his big nose serving as a kind of wall bumper. Champ steered himself, Parker thought, via echo navigation. Like a bat. It was sad. Parker followed and yawned and cinched his robe tight and wondered how many more mornings there were left in his dog.

Parker glanced at his reflection in a mirror in the stairwell. Six-foot-two, steel-gray hair, cold blue eyes, and a jaw line that was starting to sag into a dewlap. Parker hated the sight of the dewlap, and unconsciously raised his chin to flatten it. Something else: he looked tired. Worn and tired. He looked like someone's old man. Appearing in court used him up these days. Win or lose, the trials just took his energy out of him and it took longer and longer to recharge. As Champ struggled ahead of him, he wondered if his dog remembered *his* youth.

He passed through the kitchen. On the counter was the bourbon bottle he had forgotten to cap the night before, and the coffee maker he hadn't filled or set. He looked out the window over the sink. Still dark, overcast, spitting snow, a sharp wind quivering the bare branches of the trees. The cloud cover was pulled down like a window blind in front of the distant mountains.

Parker waited for Champ to get his bearings and find the back door. He took a deep breath and reached for the door handle, preparing himself for a blast of icy wind in his face.

Lyle and Juan stood flattened and hunched on either side of the back door of the lawyer's house on the edge of town. They wore balaclavas and coats and gloves. Lyle had his stained gray Stetson clamped on his head over the balaclava, even though Juan had told him he looked ridiculous.

They'd been there for an hour in the dark and cold and wind. They were used to conditions like this, even though Juan kept losing his focus, Lyle thought. In the half-light of dawn, Lyle could see Juan staring off into the backyard toward the mountains, squinting against the pinpricks of snow, as if pining for something, which was probably the warm weather of Chihuahua. Or a warm bed. More than once, Lyle had to lean across the back porch and cuff Juan on the back of his skull and tell him to get his head in the game.

"What game?" Juan said. His accent was heaviest when he was cold, for some reason, and sounded like, "*Wha' gaaaame?*"

Lyle started to reach over and shut Juan up when a light clicked on inside the house. Lyle hissed, "Here he comes. Get ready. *Focus.* Remember what we talked about."

To prove that he heard Lyle, Juan scrunched his eyes together and nodded.

Lyle reached behind him and grasped the Colt .45 1911 ACP with his gloved right hand. He'd already racked in a round so there was no need to work the slide. He cocked it and held it alongside his thigh.

Across the porch, Juan drew a .357 Magnum revolver from the belly pocket of the Carat hoodie he wore.

The back door opened and the large blocky head of a dog poked out looking straight ahead. The dog grunted as it stepped down onto the porch and waddled straight away, although Juan had his pistol trained on the back of its head. It was Juan's job to watch the dog and shoot it dead if necessary.

Lyle reached up and grasped the outside door handle and jerked it back hard.

Paul Parker tumbled outside in a heap, robe flying, blue-white bare legs exposed. He scrambled over on his hands and knees in the snow-covered grass and said, "Jesus Christ!"

"No," Lyle said, aiming the pistol at a spot on Parker's forehead. "Just us."

"What do you want?"

"What's coming to me," Lyle said. "What I deserve and you took away."

A mix of recognition and horror passed over Parker's face. Lyle could see the fear in the lawyer's eyes. It was a good look as far as Lyle was concerned. Parker said, "Lyle? Is that you?"

What could Lyle want, Parker thought. There was little of significant value in the house. Not like Angler's place out in the country, that book collection of Western Americana. But Lyle? He *was* a warped version of Western Americana . . .

"Get up and shut the hell up," Lyle said, motioning with the Colt. "Let's go in the house where it's warm."

Next to Parker, Champ squatted and his urine steamed in the grass.

"He don' even know we're here," Juan said. "Some watch dog. I ought to put it out of its misery." *Meeserie.*

"Please don't," Parker said, standing up. "He's my bird dog and he's been a great dog over the years. He doesn't even know you're here." Lyle noticed Parker had dried grass stuck to his bare knees.

"You don't look like such a hotshot now without your lawyer suit," Lyle said.

"I hope you got some hot coffee, mister," Juan said to Parker.

"I'll make some."

"Is your wife inside?" Lyle asked.

"No."

Lyle grinned beneath his mask, "She left you, huh?"

"Nothing like that," Parker lied. "She's visiting her sister in Sheridan."

"Anybody inside?"

"No."

"Don't be lying to me."

"I'm not. Look, whatever it is . . ."

"Shut up," Lyle said, gesturing with his Colt, "Go inside slowly and try not to do something stupid."

Parker cautiously climbed the step and reached out for the door Lyle held. Lyle followed. The warmth of the house enveloped him, even through his coat and balaclava.

Behind them, Juan said, "What about the dog?"

"Shoot it," Lyle said.

"Jesus God," Parker said, his voice tripping.

A few seconds later there was a heavy boom and simultaneous yelp from the back yard, and Juan came in.

Paul Parker sat in the passenger seat of the pickup and Lyle sat just behind him in the crew cab with the muzzle of his Colt kissing the nape of his neck. Juan drove. They left the highway and took a two-track across the sagebrush foothills eighteen miles from town. They were shadowed by a herd of thirty to forty pronghorn antelope. It was late October, almost November, the grass was brown and snow from the night before pooled in the squat shadows of the sagebrush. The landscape was harsh and bleak and the antelope had been designed perfectly for it: their brown and white coloring melded with the terrain and at times it was as if they were absorbed within it. And if the herd didn't feel comfortable about something— like the intrusion of a 1995 beat-up Ford pickup pulling a rattletrap empty stock trailer behind it—they simply flowed away over the hills like molten lava.

"Here they come again," Juan said to Lyle. It was his truck and they'd borrowed the stock trailer from an outfitter who got a new one. "They got so many antelopes out here."

"Focus," Lyle said. He'd long since taken off the mask—no need for it now—and stuffed it in his coat pocket.

Parker stared straight ahead. They'd let him put on pajamas and slippers and a heavy lined winter topcoat and that was all. Lyle had ordered him to bring his keys but leave his wallet and everything else. He felt humiliated and scared. That Lyle Peebles and Juan Martinez had taken off their masks meant that they no longer cared if he could identify them, and that was a very bad thing. He was sick about Champ.

Lyle was close enough to Parker in the cab that he could smell the lawyer's fear and his morning breath. Up close, Lyle noticed, the lawyer had bad skin. He'd never noticed in the courtroom.

"So you know where we're going," Lyle said.

"The Angler Place," Parker said.

"That's right. And do you know what we're going to do there?"

After a long pause, Parker said, "No, Lyle, I don't."

"I think you do."

"Really, I . . ."

"Shut up," Lyle said to Parker. To Juan, he said, "There's a gate up ahead. When you stop at it I'll get Paul here to come and help me open it. You drive through and we'll close it behind us. If you see him try anything hinky, do the same thing to him you did to that dog."

"Champ," Parker said woodenly.

"*Ho-kay,*" Lyle said.

Juan Martinez was a mystery to Parker. He'd never seen nor heard of him before that morning. Martinez was stocky and solid with thick blue/black hair and he wore a wispy gunfighter's mustache that made his face look unclean. He had piercing black eyes that revealed nothing. He was younger than Lyle, and obviously deferred to him. The two men seemed comfortable with each other and their easy camaraderie suggested long days and nights in each other's company. Juan seemed to Parker to be a blunt object; simple, hard, without remorse.

Lyle Peebles was dark and of medium height and build and he appeared older than his 57 years, Parker thought. Lyle had a hard narrow pinched face, leathery dark skin that looked permanently sun and wind-burned, the spackled sunken cheeks of a drinker, and a thin white scar that practically halved his face from his upper lip to his scalp. He had eyes that were both sorrowful and imperious at the same time, and teeth stained by nicotine that were long and narrow like horse's teeth. His voice was deep with a hint of country twang and the corners of his mouth pulled up when he spoke but it wasn't a smile. He had a certain kind of coiled menace about him, Parker thought. Lyle was the kind of man one shied away from if he was coming down the side-walk or standing in the aisle of a hardware store because there was a dark instability about him that suggested he might start shouting or lashing out or complaining and not stop until security was called. He was a man who acted and dressed like a cowpoke but he had grievances inside him that burned hot.

Parker had hoped that when the trial was over he'd never see Lyle Peebles again for the rest of his life.

Parker stood aside with his bare hands jammed into the pockets of his coat. He felt the wind bite his bare ankles above his slippers and burn his neck and face with cold. He knew Juan was watching him closely so he tried not to make any suspicious moves or reveal what he was thinking.

He had no weapons except for his hands and fists and the ball of keys he'd been ordered to bring along. He'd never been in a fist-fight in his life, but he could fit the keys between his fingers and start swinging.

He looked around him without moving his head much. The prairie spread out in all directions. They were far enough away from town there were no other vehicles to be seen anywhere, no buildings or power lines.

"Look at that," Lyle said, nodding toward the north and west. Parker turned to see lead-colored clouds rolling straight at them, pushing gauzy walls of snow.

"Hell of a storm coming," Lyle said.

"Maybe we should turn back?" Parker offered.

Lyle snorted with derision.

Parker thought about simply breaking and running, but there was nowhere to run.

It was a standard barbed-wire ranch gate, stiff from disuse. Wire loops from the ancient fence post secured the top and bottom of the gate rail. A heavy chain and padlock mottled with rust stretched between the two. "You got the keys," Lyle said, gesturing with his Colt.

Parker dug the key ring out of his pocket and bent over the old lock. He wasn't sure which key fit it, or whether the rusty hasp would unsnap. While he struggled with the lock, a beach-ball-sized tumbleweed was dislodged from a sagebrush by the wind and it hit him in the back of his thighs, making him jump. Lyle laughed.

Finally, he found the right key and felt the mechanism inside give. Parker jerked hard on the lock and the chain dropped away on both sides.

"Stand aside," Lyle said, and shot him a warning look before he put his pistol in his pocket and leaned against the gate. The way to open these tight old ranch gates was to brace oneself on the gate side, thread one's arms through the strands until the shoulder was against the gate rail and reach out to the solid post and pull. The move left Lyle vulnerable.

Parker thought if he was prepared to do something and fight back, this was the moment. He could attack Lyle before Juan could get out of the pickup. He felt his chest tighten and his toes curl and grip within his slippers.

Lyle struggled with it. "Don't just stand there," red-faced Lyle said to Parker through gritted teeth, "Help me get this goddamned thing open."

Parker leaned forward on the balls of his feet. He considered hurtling himself like a missile toward Lyle, then slashing at the man's face and eyes with the keys. He could tear Lyle's gun away, shoot Lyle, and then use it on Juan. That's what a man of action would do. That's what someone in a movie or on television would do.

Instead, the lawyer bent over so he was shoulder-to-shoulder with Lyle and his added bulk against the gatepost was enough that Lyle could reach up and pop the wire over the top and open it.

Back inside the pickup, they drove into the maw of the storm. It had enveloped them so quickly it was astonishing. Pellets of snow rained across the hood of the pickup and bounced against the cracked windshield. The heater blew hot air that smelled like radiator fluid inside the cab. Parker's teeth finally stopped chattering but his stomach ached from fear and his hands and feet were cold and stiff.

Juan leaned forward and squinted over the wheel, as if it would help him see better.

"This is the kind of stuff we live with every day," Lyle said to Parker. "Me and Juan are out in this shit day after day. We don't sit in plush offices taking calls and sending bills. This is the way it is out here."

Parker nodded, not sure what to say.

"The road forks," Juan said to Lyle in the backseat, "Which way do we go?"

"Left," Lyle said.

"Are you sure?"

"Goddamit, Juan, how many years did I spend out here on these roads?"

Juan shrugged and eased the pickup to the left. They couldn't see more than fifty feet in any direction. The wind swirled the heavy snow and it buffeted the left side of the pickup truck, rocking the vehicle on its springs when it gusted.

Parker said, "When this is over and you've got whatever it is you want, what then?"

Lyle said, "I'm still weighing that one, counselor. But for now just let me concentrate on getting to the house."

"It would he helpful to know what you've got in mind," Parker said, clearing his throat. Trying to sound conversational. "I mean, since I'm playing a role in this I can be of better service if I know your intentions."

Lyle backhanded the lawyer with his free hand, hitting him hard on the ear. Parker winced.

"Just shut up until we get there," Lyle said. "I heard enough talking from you in that courtroom to last the rest of my pea-pickin' life. So just shut up or I'll put a bullet into the back of your head."

Juan appeared to grimace, but Parker determined it was a bitter kind of smile.

Lyle said to Parker, "You got the keys to that secret room old Angler has, right? The one he never let anybody into? The one with the books?"

"How far?" Juan asked. They were traveling less than five miles an hour. The snow was so thick, Parker thought, it was like being inside a cloud. Tall sagebrush just a few feet from the road on either side looked like gray commas. Beyond the brush, everything was two-tone white and light blue.

"What's in the road?" Juan asked, tapping on the brake to slow them down even further.

Parker looked ahead. Six or seven oblong shadows emerged from the whiteout. They appeared suspended in the air. They looked like small coffins on stilts.

The pickup inched forward. The forms sharpened in detail. Pronghorn antelope—part of the same herd or from another herd. A buck and his does. They stood braced into the storm, oblivious to the truck. Juan drove so close to them Parker could see snow packed into the bristles of their hide and their goat-like faces and black eyes. The buck had long eyelashes and flakes of snow caught in them. His horns were tall and splayed, the hooked-back tips ivory colored.

"Fucking antelope," Lyle said. "Push 'em out of the way or run right over them."

Instead, Juan tapped the horn on the steering wheel. The sound was distant and tinny against the wind, but the pronghorns reacted; haunches bunching, heads ducking, and they shot away from the road as if they'd never been there.

Parker wished he could run like that.

"Few miles," Lyle said. "We'll pass under an archway. I helped build that arch, you know."

"I didn't know that," Juan said.

"Me and Juan," Lyle said to Parker, "We've worked together for the past what, twelve years?"

Juan said, "Twelve, yes. Twelve."

"Some of the shittiest places you could imagine," Lyle said. "All over the states of Wyoming and Montana. A couple in Idaho. One in South Dakota. Most of those places had absentee owners with pricks for ranch foremen. They're the worst, those pricks. They don't actually own the places so for them it's all about power. You give pricks like that a little authority and they treat the workingman like shit. Ain't that right, Juan?"

"*Eees* right."

Parker thought: *It's like we're the only humans on earth.* The world that had been out there just that morning—the world of vistas and mountains and people and cars and offices and meetings—had been reduced for him to just this. Three men in the cab of a pickup driving achingly slow through a whiteout where the entire world had closed in around them. Inside the cab there were smells and weapons and fear. Outside the glass was furious white rage.

There was a kind of forced intimacy that was not welcome, Parker thought. He'd been reduced to the same level as these two no-account ranch hands who between them didn't have a nickel to rub together. They had guns and the advantage, Parker thought, but they were smart in the way coyotes or other predators were smart in that they knew innately how to survive but didn't have a clue how to rise up beyond that. He knew that from listening to Lyle testify in court in halting sentences filled with poorly chosen words. And when Lyle's broken down ninety-eight-year-old grandfather took the stand it was all over. Parker had flayed the old man with whips made of words until there was no flesh left on his ancient bones.

Lyle likely couldn't be reasoned with-he knew that already. No more than a coyote or a raven could be reasoned with. Coyotes would never become dogs. Likewise, ravens couldn't be songbirds. Lyle Peebles would never be a reasonable man. He was a man whose very existence was based on grievance.

"This is getting bad," Juan said, leaning forward in his seat as if getting six inches closer to the windshield would improve his vision. *Thees.*

Parker gripped the dashboard. The tires had become sluggish beneath the pickup as the snow accumulated. Juan was driving more by feel than by vision, and a few times Parker felt the tires leave the two-track and Juan had to jerk the wheel to find the ruts of the road again.

"We picked a bad day for this," Juan said. *Thees.*

"Keep going," Lyle said. "We been in worse than this before. Remember that time in the Pryor Mountains?"

"Si. That was as bad as this."

"That was *worse*," Lyle said definitively.

There was a metallic clang and Parker heard something scrape shrilly beneath the undercarriage of the truck.

"What the hell was that?" Lyle asked Juan.

"A T-post, I think."

"Least that means we're still on the road," Lyle said.

"*Ay-yi-yi,*" Juan whistled.

"We could turn around," Parker said.

"We could," Juan agreed. "At least I could follow our tracks back out. As it is, I can't see where we're going."

"We're fine, Godammit," Lyle said. "I know where we are. Keep going. We'll be seeing that old house any time now."

Parker looked out his passenger window. Snow was sticking to it and covering the glass. Through a fist-sized opening in the snow, he could see absolutely nothing.

He realized Lyle was talking to him. "What did you say?"

"I said I bet you didn't expect you'd be doing this today, did you?"

"No."

"You're the type of guy who thinks once a judge says something it's true, ain't you?"

Parker shrugged.

"You thought after you made a fool of my grandpa you were done with this, didn't you?"

"Look," Parker said, "we all have jobs to do. I did mine. It wasn't personal."

Parker waited for an argument. Instead, he felt a sharp blow to his left ear and he saw spangles where a moment ago there had been only snow. The voice that cried out had been his.

He turned in the seat cupping his ear in his hand.

Lyle grinned back. Parker noticed the small flap of skin on the front sight of the Colt. And his fingers were hot and sticky with his blood.

"You say it ain't personal, lawyer," Lyle said. "But look at me. *Look* at me. What do you see?"

Parker squinted against the pain and shook his head slowly as if he didn't know how to answer.

"What you see, lawyer, is a third-generation loser. That's what you see, and don't try to claim otherwise or I'll beat you bloody. I'll ask you again: what do you see?"

Parker found that his voice was tremulous. He said, "I see a working man, Lyle. A good-hearted working man who gets paid for a hard day's work. I don't see what's so wrong with that."

"Nice try," Lyle said, feinting with the muzzle toward Parker's face like the flick of a tongue from a snake. Parker recoiled, and Lyle grinned again.

"That man fucked over my grandpa and set this all in motion," Lyle said. "He cheated him and walked away and hid behind his money and his lawyers for the rest of his life. Can you imagine what my grandpa's life would have been like if he hadn't been fucked over? Can you imagine what my life would have been like? Not like this, I can tell you. Why should that man get away with a crime like that? Don't you see a crime like that isn't a one-shot deal? That it sets things in motion for generations?"

"I'm just a lawyer," Parker said.

"And I'm just a no-account working man," Lyle said. "And the reason is because of people like you."

"Look," Parker said, taking his hand away from his ear and feeling a long tongue of blood course down his neck into his collar, "maybe we can go back to the judge with new information. But we need new information. It can't just be your grandfather's word and his theories about Nazis and . . ."

"They weren't just theories!" Lyle said, getting agitated. "It was the truth."

"It was so long ago," Parker said.

"That doesn't make it less true!" Lyle shouted.

"There was no proof. Give me some proof and I'll represent you instead of the estate."

Parker shot a glance at the rearview mirror to find Lyle deep in thought for a moment. Lyle said, "That's interesting. I've seen plenty of whores, but not many in a suit."

"Lyle," Juan said sadly, "I think we are lost."

The hearing had lasted less than two days. Paul Parker was the lawyer for the Fritz Angler estate, which was emerging from probate after the old man finally died and left no heirs except a disagreeable out-of-wedlock daughter who lived in Houston. From nowhere, Benny Peebles and his grandson Lyle made a claim for the majority of the Angler estate holdings. Benny claimed he'd been cheated out of ownership of the ranch generations ago and he wanted justice. He testified it had happened this way:

Benny Peebles and Fritz Angler, both in their early twenties, owned a Ryan monoplane together. The business model for Peebles/ Peebles Aviation was to hire out their piloting skills and aircraft to ranchers in Northern Wyoming for the purpose of spotting cattle, delivering goods, and transporting medicine and cargo. They also had contracts with the federal and state government for mail delivery and predator control. Although young and in the midst of the Depression, they were two of the most successful entrepreneurs the town of Cody had seen. Still, the income from the plane barely covered payments and overhead and both partners lived hand-to-mouth.

Peebles testified that in 1936 they were hired by a rancher named Wendell Oaks to help round up his scattered cattle. This was an unusual request, and they learned Oaks had been left high-and-dry by all of his ranch-hands because he hadn't paid them for two months. Oaks had lost his fortune in the crash and the only assets he had left before the bank foreclosed on his 16,000-acre spread were his Hereford cattle. He'd need to sell them all to raise $20,000 to save his place, and in order to sell them he'd need to gather them up. The payments to Peebles/Peebles would come out of the proceeds, he assured them.

Benny said Fritz was enamored with the Oaks Ranch—the grass, the miles of river, the timber, and the magnificent Victorian ranch house that cost Oaks a fortune to build. He told Benny, "This man is living on my ranch but he just doesn't know it yet."

Benny didn't know what Fritz meant at the time, although his partner, he said, always had "illusions of grandiosity," as Benny put it.

Fritz sent Benny north to Billings to buy fence to build a massive temporary corral for the cattle. While he was gone, Fritz said, he'd fly the ranch and figure out where all the cattle were.

Benny returned to Cody four days later followed by a truck laden with rolls of fence and bundles of steel posts. But Fritz was gone, and so was the Ryan. Wendell Oaks was fit to be tied. Bankers were driving out to his place from Cody to take measurements.

Three days later, while Benny and some locals he'd hired on a day-rate were building the corral, he heard the buzz of an airplane motor. He recognized the sound and looked up to see Fritz Angler landing the Ryan in a hay meadow.

Before Benny could confront his partner, Fritz buttonholed one of the bankers and they drove off together into town. Benny inspected their monoplane and saw where Fritz had removed the co-pilot seat and broken out the interior divides of the cargo area to make more space. The floor of the aircraft was covered in white bristles of hair and animal feces. It smelled dank and unpleasant.

The next thing Benny knew, sheriff's deputies descended on the place and evicted Wendell Oaks. Then they ordered Benny and his laborers off the property by order of the sheriff and the bank and new owner of the ranch, Fritz Angler, who had paid off the outstanding loan balance and now owned the paper for the Oaks Ranch.

The arch appeared out of the snow and Juan drove beneath it. Parker was relieved to discover how close they were to the ranch house, and just as frightened to anticipate what might come next.

Lyle was wound up. "That mean old German son-of-a-bitch never even apologized," he said heatedly from the backseat. "He used the airplane my Grandpa owned half of to swindle our family out of this place, and he never even said sorry. If nothing else, we should have owned half of all this. Instead, it turned my family to a bunch of two-bit losers. It broke my Grandpa and ruined my dad and now it's up to me to get what I can out of it. What choice do I have since you cheated us again in that court?"

"I didn't cheat you," Parker said softly, not wanting to argue with Lyle in his agitated state. "There was no proof . . ."

"Grandpa told you what happened!" Lyle said.

"But that story you told . . ."

"He don't lie. Are you saying he lied?"

"No," Parker said patiently. "But I mean, *come on*. Who is going to believe that Fritz Angler trapped a hundred antelope fawns and flew them around the country and sold them to zoos? That he sold some to Adolf Hitler and flew that plane all the way to Lakehurst, New Jersey and loaded a half-dozen animals on the Hindenburg to be taken to the Berlin Zoo? I mean, come on, Lyle."

"It happened!" Lyle shouted. "If Grandpa said it happened, it fucking happened."

Parker recalled the skeptical but patient demeanor of the judge as old Benny Peebles droned on at the witness stand. There were a few snickers from the small gallery during the tale.

Juan shook his head and said to Parker, "I hear this story before. Many times about the plane and the antelopes."

Parker decided to keep quiet. There was no point in arguing. Lyle spoke with the deranged fervor of a true believer, despite the outlandishness of the tale.

Lyle said, "Look around you. There are thousands of antelope on this ranch, just like there were in 1936. Angler used the plane to herd antelope into a box canyon, where he bound them up. Grandpa showed me where he done it. Angler loaded them into the Ryan and started east, selling them all along the way. He had connections with Hitler because he was German! His family was still over there. They were a bunch of fucking Nazis just like Angler. He knew who to call.

"He sold those fawns for $100 to $200 each because they were so rare outside Wyoming at the time. He could load up to 40 in the plane for each trip. He made enough cash money to buy airplane fuel all the way to New Jersey and back and still had enough to pay off Wendell Oaks' loan. He did the whole thing in a plane co-owned by my Grandpa but never cut him in on a damned thing!

"Then he started buying other ranches," Lyle said, speaking fast, spittle forming at the corners of his mouth, "then they found that damned oil. Angler was rich enough to spend thousands on lawyers and thugs to keep my Grandpa and my dad away from him all those years. Our last shot was contesting that old Nazi's estate—and *you* shut us out."

Parker sighed and closed his eyes. He'd grown up in Cody. He despised men who blamed their current circumstances on past events as if their lives were preordained. Didn't Lyle know that in the West you simply reinvented yourself? That family legacies meant next to nothing?

"I can't take this ranch with me," Lyle said. "I can't take enough cattle or vehicles or sagebrush to make things right. But I sure as hell can take that damned book collection of his. I've heard it's worth hundreds of thousands. Ain't that right, Parker?"

"I don't know," Parker said. "I'm not a collector."

"But you've seen it, right? You've been in that secret room of his?"

"Once." Parker recalled the big dark room with floor-to-ceiling oak bookshelves that smelled of paper and age. Fritz liked to sit in a red-leather chair under the soft yellow light of a Tiffany lamp and read, careful not to fully open or damage the books in any way. It had taken him sixty years to amass his collection of mostly leather-bound first editions. The collection was comprised primarily of books about the American West and the Third Reich in original German. While

Parker browsed the shelves he had noted both volumes of *Mein Kampf* with alarm but had said nothing to the old man.

"And what was in there?" Lyle said. "Did you see some of the books I've heard about? Lewis and Clark's original journals? Catlin's books about Indians? A first edition of Irwin Wister?"

"Owen Wister," Parker corrected. "*The Virginian.* Yes, I saw them."

"Ha!" Lyle said with triumph. "I heard Angler brag that the Indian book was worth a half million."

Parker realized two things at once. They were close enough to the imposing old ranch house they could see its Gothic outline emerge from the white. And Juan had stopped the pickup.

"Books!" Juan said, biting off the word. "*We're here for fucking books? You said we would be getting his treasure.*"

"Juan," Lyle said, "his books are his treasure. That's why we brought the stock trailer."

"I don't want no books!" Juan growled, "I thought it was jewelry or guns. You know, *rare* things. I don't know nothing about old books."

"It'll all work out," Lyle said, patting Juan on the shoulder. "Trust me. People spend a fortune collecting them."

"Then they're fools," Juan said, shaking his head.

"Drive right across the lawn," Lyle instructed Juan. "Pull the trailer up as close as you can get to the front doors so we don't have to walk so far."

"*So we can fill it with shitty old books,*" Juan said, showing his teeth.

"Calm down, amigo," Lyle said to Juan. "Have I ever steered you wrong?"

"About a thousand times, amigo."

Lyle huffed a laugh, and Parker watched Juan carefully. He didn't seem to be playing along.

Lyle said, "Keep an eye on the lawyer while I open the front door." To Parker, he said, "Give me those keys."

Parker handed them over and he watched Lyle fight the blizzard on his way up the porch steps. The wind was ferocious and Lyle kept one hand clamped down on his hat. A gust nearly drove him off the porch. If anything, it was snowing even harder.

"*Books*," Juan said under his breath. "He tricked me."

The massive double front doors to the Angler home filled a gabled stone archway and were eight feet high and studded with iron bolt heads. Angler had a passion for security, and Parker remembered noting the thickness of the open door when he'd visited. They were over two inches thick. He watched Lyle brush snow away from the keyhole and fumble with the key ring with gloved fingers.

"Books are not treasure," Juan said.

Parker sensed an opening. "No, they're not. You'll have to somehow find rich collectors who will overlook the fact that they've been stolen. Lyle doesn't realize each one of those books has an *ex libre* mark."

When Juan looked over, puzzled, Parker said, "It's a stamp of ownership. Fritz didn't collect so he could sell the books. He collected because he loved them. They'll be harder than hell to sell on the open market. Book collectors are a small world."

Juan cursed.

Parker said, "It's just like his crazy story about the antelope and the Hindenburg. He doesn't know what he's talking about."

"He's *crazy*."

"I'm afraid so," Parker said. "And he sucked you into this."

"I didn't kill your dog."

"*What*?"

"I didn't kill it. I shot by his head and he yelped. I couldn't shoot an old dog like that. I like dogs if they don't want to bite me."

"Thank you, Juan." Parker hoped the storm wasn't as violent in town and that Champ would find a place to get out of it.

They both watched Lyle try to get the door open. The side of his coat was already covered with snow.

"A man could die just being outside in a storm like this," Parker said. Then he took a long breath and held it.

"Lyle, he's crazy," Juan said. "He wants to fix his family. He don't know how to move on."

"Well said. There's no reason why you should be in trouble for Lyle's craziness," Parker said.

"Mister, I know what you're doing."

"But that doesn't mean I'm wrong."

Juan said nothing.

"My wife . . ." Parker said. "We're having some problems. I need to talk to her and set things right. I can't imagine never talking to her again. For Christ's Sake, my last words to her were, 'Don't let the door hit you on the way out.'"

Juan snorted.

"Please . . ."

"He wants you to help him," Juan said, chinning toward the windshield. Beyond it, Lyle was gesticulating at them on the porch.

"We can just back away," Parker said. "We can go home."

"You mean just leave him here?"

"Yes," Parker said. "I'll never breathe a word about this to anyone. I swear it."

Juan seemed to be thinking about it. On the porch, Lyle was getting angrier and more frantic. Horizontal snow and wind made his coat sleeves and pant legs flap. A gust whipped his hat off, and Lyle flailed in the air for it but it was gone.

"Go," Juan said.

"But I thought . . ."

"Go now," he said, showing the pistol.

Parker was stunned by the fury of the storm. Snow stung his face and he tried to duck his head beneath his upraised arm to shield it. The wind was so cold it felt hot on his exposed bare skin.

"Help me get this goddamned door open!" Lyle yelled. "I can't get the key to work." He handed Parker the keys.

"I don't know which one it is any more than you do," Parker yelled back.

"Just fucking try it, counselor!" Lyle said, jabbing at him with the Colt.

Parker leaned into the door much as Lyle had. He wanted to block the wind with his back so he could see the lock and the keys and have room to work. He tried several keys and none of them turned. Only one seemed to fit well. He went back to it. He could barely feel his fingers and feet.

He realized Lyle was shouting again.

"Juan! Juan! What the hell are you doing?"

Parker glanced up. Lyle was on the steps, his back to him, shouting and waving his arms at the pickup and trailer that vanished into the snow. Faint pink tail lights blinked out.

At that moment, Parker pulled up on the iron door handle with his left hand while he turned the key with his right. The ancient lock gave way.

Parker slammed his shoulder into the door and stepped inside the dark house and pushed the door shut behind him and rammed the bolt home.

Lyle cursed at him and screamed for Parker to open the door.

Instead, Parker stepped aside with his back against the cold stone interior wall as Lyle emptied his .45 Colt at the door, making eight dime-sized holes in the wood that streamed thin beams of white light to the slate-rock floor.

He hugged himself and shivered and condensation clouds from his breath haloed his head.

Parker roamed through Angler's library, hugging himself in an attempt to keep warm and to keep his blood flowing. There were no lights and the phone had been shut off months before. Muted light filtered through gaps in the thick curtains. Outside, the blizzard howled and threw itself against the old home but couldn't get in any more than Lyle could get in. Snow covered the single window in the library except for one palm-sized opening, and Parker used it to look around outside for Lyle or Lyle's body but he couldn't see either. It had been twenty minutes since he'd locked Lyle out.

At one point he thought he heard a cry, but when he stopped pacing and listened all he could hear was the wind thundering against the windows.

He started a fire in the fireplace using old books as kindling and had fed it with broken furniture and a few decorative logs he'd found in the great room downstairs. Orange light from the flames danced on the spines of the old books.

He wanted a fire to end all fires that would not only warm him but also act as his shield against the storm and the coming darkness outside.

After midnight Parker ran out of wood and he kept the fire going with Angler's books. Mainly the German language volumes. The storm outside seemed to have eased a bit.

As he reached up on the shelves for more fuel, his fingers avoided touching the copies of *Mein Kampf*. The act of actually touching the books terrified Parker in a way he couldn't explain.

Then he reasoned that if books were to be burned, *Mein Kampf* should be one of them. As he tossed the volumes into the flames, a loose square of paper fluttered out of the pages onto the floor.

Parker bent over to retrieve it to flick it into the fire when he realized it was an old photograph. The image in the firelight made him gasp.

Parker ran down the stairs in the dark to the front door and threw back the bolt. The force of the wind opened both the doors inward and he squinted against the snow and tried to see into the black and white maelstrom.

"Lyle!" he shouted to no effect. "Lyle!"

AUTHOR'S NOTE

The story is fiction but the photograph is not.

In 1936, in one of the odder episodes of the modern American West, Wyoming rancher and noted photographer Charles Belden did indeed catch pronghorn antelope fawns on his ranch and deliver them to zoos across the nation in his Ryan monoplane, including a delivery to the German passenger airship LZ 129 *Hindenburg* in Lakehurst, New Jersey, bound for the Berlin Zoo.

The photograph appears courtesy of the Charles Belden Collection, American Heritage Center, University of Wyoming.

I can find no information on the fate of the pronghorn antelope. They would have arrived shortly after the conclusion of Adolf Hitler's '36 Olympics.

—CJB, 2011

III

The Book of Virtue

Ken Bruen

M Y OLD MAN:
       Tough.
Cruel.
Merciless.
And that was on the weekends when he was happy. If a psycho could do happy.
His cop buddies said,
"Frank, Frank is just intense."
Right.
Other kids go,
"My dad took me to the Yankees."
Mine, he took out my teeth.
With intensity.
The horrors of peace. He bought the farm when I was seventeen. My mom, she took off for Boise, Idaho.
Hell of another sort.
They buried my father in the American flag. No argument, he was a patriot.
I played
"Another one bites the dust."
He'd have hated Queen to be the band.
His inheritance?
A book.
Rich, huh?

My father died horribly. A slow, lingering, eat-your-guts-in-pieces cancer. His buddies admired my constant vigil.

Yeah.

I wanted to ensure he didn't have one of those miraculous recoveries. His last hour, we had an Irish priest who anointed him, said,

"He will soon be with God."

The devil, maybe. With any luck.

He was lucid in his last moments. Looked at me with total fear.

I asked,

"Are you afraid?"

He nodded, his eyes welling up. I leaned close, whispered,

"Good, and, you know, it will get worse."

A flash of anger in those dead brown eyes, and I asked,

"What are you going to do, huh? Who you going to call, you freaking bully?"

The death rattle was loud and chilling. The doctor rushed in, held his hand, said,

"I am so sorry."

I managed to keep my smirk in check. He was buried in a cheap box, to accessorize his cheap soul. A week after, I was given his estate.

The single book.

Mind you, it was a beautiful volume, bound in soft leather, gold leaf trim. Heavy, too.

And well thumbed.

I was puzzled. My old man, his reading extended to the sports page in *The Daily News*.

But a book?

WTF?

On the cover, in faded gold was,

Virtue.

Like he'd know any damn thing about that.

Flicked through it

???

In his spidery handwriting, it was jammed with notes. The first page had this:

"You cannot open a book without learning something."

. . . Confucius.

I put the book down.

"Was he trying to educate himself?"

The schmuck.

My cell shrilled.

Brady, my boss. He muttered,

"Sorry about your old man."

Yeah. Yada, yada.

Did the sympathy jig for all of two minutes. Then,

"Grief in the club last night."

The outrider here being

"The hell where you?"

And, unsaid,

"So your old man bought the farm. You're supposed to ensure the club runs smooth."

The Khe San, in midtown.

Home to:

Wise guys

Cops

Strippers

Low lifes

Skels

Power trippers

Politicians.

All R and R-ing in a place of uneasy truce.

My job: to maintain smooth and easy vibe. I didn't ask if they checked their weapons at the door but did try to keep a rack on the rampant egos. I had an assistant—in truth a Mack 5 would have been the biz—but, lacking that, I had—

Cici.

A weapon of a whole deadly calibre.

Brady was a Nam wanna-be, like Bruce in his heyday, a dubious tradition begun by John Wayne with the loathsome Green Berets. Rattle on enough about a lost war and it gave the impression you were there. Sure to be shooting, Brady played "Born in the USA" like his own personal anthem. That he was from the Ukraine seemed neither here nor deceptive there.

I ran the club, and well.

Was taught by the best, my best friend, Scotty, but more of that later.

Had learned to walk the taut line between chaos and safety that growing up with a bully equips you to do. When your mother takes a walk early, you lose any semblance of trust. My old man, second generation Mick, was as sentimental as only a fledging psychopath can be. His MO was simple:

Beat the living shit out of your child, play the suck-heart songs:

"Danny Boy"

"Galway Bay"

"Molly Malone"

Sink a bottle of Jay.

Weep buckets for your own miserable self.

What they term the "Constellation of Disadvantage."

Booze, mental illness, violence.

But books?

Never.

So what the hell was this beautifully bound edition about? I opened another page at random.

Got

"A book must be an ice axe

To break

The seas

Frozen inside our soul."

I was rattled.

If he could quote that, and, Jesus wept, have applied it to his own self, where the fook did that leave my dark finished portrait of him?'

Resolved to run it by Cici.

She was

Brady's babe, in every sense.

Twenty five years of age with the experience of fifty, and all of them dirty.

And ruthless.

Concealed behind a stunning face, she had that rarity, green eyes, and a mouth designed by a *Playboy* deity.

She was a simple girl at heart, really.

All she wanted really was a shitload of cash.

And, like, before the spring.

Her beauty was of that unique stop-you-dead variety.

Worse, she knew it.

Used it.

Sure, I was banging her. If you live a cliché, then that's the most lame of all. But, see, I could talk to her, I think. And,

Get this:

She read.

Our club catered to the young punks, reared on the movies *Casino* and *Wise Guys*.

They spoke a mangled Joe Peschi, convoluted by snatches of Travis Bickle.

Books? Nope.

They didn't know from kindle to *National Enquirer*. But Cici, she'd have a book running alongside her vegetarian Slurpee. Her latest was titled, *Ethics of the Urban Sister*.

I shit thee not.

So, she seemed to know stuff. Couple that with an old soul glint in her amazing eyes and you had, what?

Sensuality with knowledge.

Late February, New York was colder than my old man's eyes.

An hour before the club opened, we were having the usual hassle:

Chef on the piss

Waitresses on the whinge

And a mega tab from an old guy in one of The Families who no one had the *cojones* to ask,

"Yo, fook head, you want to like, settle your freaking bill?"

Translate

Me.

As in having to ass kiss and somehow get some major green from the dangerous bastard.

Cici was down with the young guns' lingo,

Was explaining to me the essence of

"Too school for cool."

And the extreme irrationality of adding NOT to a statement. Like

"I'm happy."

Dramatic pause,

Then,

"Not."

Fook on a bike.

But the word that annoyed me beyond coherent belief was the universal reply to seemingly any situation.

Like

"Your wife was killed."

". . . Whatever!"

Or, even good news:

"You won the State Lottery."

They go

". . .Whatever."

Drives me ape shit.

My old man was dead five months then. Okay, five months and change.

So, I counted. You betcha. Joy can be measured.

Cici had, in a drunken moment, told me that Brady kept a mountain of coke, and a ton of cash, in his apartment. She was laying down the seed of a plan.

Scotty had been dead three months.

We cherished the hour before Brady showed. Cici had taken my music faves on board. We had a ritual down. She'd ask,

"Caf Corretto?"

Basically the Italian version of a pick me up. Caffeine with Jameson.

The tunes: U2, with "Bad."

The Edge proving he was indeed the owner of the driving guitar.

Lorena McKennet, with "Raglan Road."

Vintage regret. The Irish legacy.

The Clash, with "London Calling."

Because they rock, always.

Gretchen Peters' "Bus to San Cloud."

Pining in beauty.

We were midway along when the door whipped open and Brady blasted in. Heavy-set, muscle and fat in contention. A squashed-in face with eyes that never heard of humor.

His opener:

"Turn off that shit."

Meant we'd have

"Born in the USA."

Ad nauseum.

And add ferocity.

His crudity always managed to reach new depths of offense.

Like,

"Bitch, the office. I need servicing."

Cute, huh?

Scotty.

My best and, in truth, only friend.

The ubiquitous *them*, whoever the fook they be, say,

"The difference between one friend and none is infinite."

Scotty was the manager of Khe Shan before me. I was taken on as his assistant. I'd been fiercely pressured by my father to follow his footsteps—heavy, brutal, as they were and join the NYPD.

Yeah, right, like hell.

I went to business college at night. Learned that school teaches you one thing: Greed rocks.

I wanted to rock.

I had a job during the day stocking shelves. And,

Get this:

Carrying customers' bags to their cars. All I ever, Christ ever, needed to know about humiliation, being almost literally invisible.

Until,

A Friday, carrying mega-freight for a guy in his forties, driving a Porsche. Dressed casual, but rich. His casual gear wasn't from Gap, unless he owned the branch, and he had that permanent tan that drives New Yorkers nuts.

Envy? Oh, yeah.

And his shoes, those Italian jobs that mock,

"Sucks being poor."

I managed to finally get his heavy bags in the car. He never looked at me, flipped me a buck. I said,

"You're fooking kidding."

He turned, levelled the bluest eyes outside of Hollywood, laughed, said,

"You're the help, be grateful."

One thing genetics bestows: I've a temper.

My fist bunched instantly and he clocked it, asked,

"How dumb are you, T?"

T?

He pulled out a hundred,

"This stir your mojo?"

I gave him the look, the one that goes,

"Keep fooking with me and see how that pans out."

Two things happened that changed my life.

One, I decked him.

Two, my boss saw me do it, rushed out, picked the dude up, muttered profuse, insincere apologies, pledging,

"His ass is so fired."

The guy rubbed his chin, dismissed my boss with a curt,

"Let me have a word."

Asked,

"What are you going to do now, job wise?"

The hundred was still crumpled in his hand, a trickle of blood leaking from his mouth. I fessed up.

"Don't know."

He assessed me anew, then,

"You like clubs, as in nightclubs?"

"Sure, what's not to like?"

"You want to work in The Khe?"

That's how famous/infamous it was. Didn't even need its full title.

Was he kidding?

"Are you kidding?"

No.

Straight up.

He was El Hombre. The guy who transformed it from a seedy mediocrity to the exclusive joint it was. He turned towards the Porsche, said,

"Be there this evening, six sharp. Wear black pants, a clip-on tie, white shirt, and shoes that fly."

My mind was playing catch up, badly. I asked,

"Clip-on?"

"Yeah, the client wants to pulp you, he goes for the tie, every predictable time."

I couldn't help it. I stared at the vanishing Franklin. He laughed.

"For punching your new boss, you're fined the hundred."

As the Porsche went into its beautiful rev, I shouted,

"What's T?"

"T . . . is for Trash."

Later, I would discover the reason for the

Unflappable

Laid back

Luded

Vibe he had.

A blend of Klonapin and Tequila. Keeps not only the demons at bay but awarded a chill of the emotions as outrider.

I duly showed up at the club and muddled through for the next few weeks. Learned the biz the hard way, by mostly screwing up. Scotty was from South Detroit, not so much street wise as street lethal. Steered me through the delicate art of handling the wise guys, as in, if they didn't pick up their tabs, let it slide until the club owner decided to act. He warned,

"If you're told to ask for payment directly, get yourself a very large gun."

Added,

"If you don't adapt to thinking outside the box, you'll be in one."

Right.

Scotty had earned a shit-load of cash, from, as he put it,

"Creative stealing."

Creative, I could do.

We began to hang out on our Sundays, the only day the club closed. I coerced him into coming to Shea Stadium. I didn't convert him from a Yankees fan, but I did get him to at least appreciate Reyes.

Scotty had taken on my choice of Jameson. Our final Sunday, he'd taken me to a pub he frequented, The Blaggard, West 39th Street, between Fifth and Sixth Avenues. They had Guinness on tap. What more recommendation could you need? Scotty looked more tense the more he knocked back, said,

"Brady is connected to the Russian gangs."

One thing I'd absorbed fast was those mothers made the Italians seem tame. And were regular customers. Always with the incredible dames. They carried a built-in smirk, the one that whispered,

"Fook with me, we'll bury you."

I believed.

He asked me,

"You ever see the Korean movie, *I Saw the Devil*?"

Nope.

I didn't do Oriental unless it was a hooker. Scotty laughed, said,

"You're a piece of work, but hear this: if I disappear, you can be sure, Brady is behind it."

What?

I went,

"What?"

He explained.

He claims to be American as cover for his gang ties. The cocksucker is from Minsk . . . fooking Minsk, yah believe it?

Scotty was so ultra cool, so in freaking control, I couldn't imagine anyone getting the jump. As if he read my thoughts, he added,

"Brady has a small country's money in his apartment. I know because he showed me. The fook is a showboat, almost daring me to rip him off."

I was saturating this, a silence of foreboding over us. Scotty said,

"If, if, you have to step up, and I'm in the wind, amass a pension, then take Brady out before he buys you the farm."

I was so immersed with my father's book that I put this rap down to the Jay. Changing the subject, I told him about my "inheritance."

He laid a mess of twenties on the counter, to the bar lady's delight. No wonder they liked him—and they did. He knocked back his last shot, said,

"Some men, they think if they can give the impression of goodness despite being a first class son of a bitch, then they have rewritten the book of their life."

Deep, huh?

I wasn't buying, asked,

"That's what you figure my father tried to do?"

He stood, shucked on his shearling coat, a cool three thousand bucks worth, looked at me, with something like warmth, said,

"Oh, yeah, his very own *Book of Virtue*."

We walked down Fifth, a wind blowing across our backs like the dead prayer of despair. We stopped at the intersection and Scotty hailed a cab, turned to me, registering my expression of alarm as he raised his arms, and laughed. Asked,

"What, you think I'm going to give you a hug?"

Paused.

"One thing I learned about the Micks: they don't do affection."

I regret very little of the life I've lived, not even the heavy crap, but oh, Sweet jaysus, why didn't I at least say,

"Thanks for being my buddy and hey, you know, you needn't worry, I've got your back."

I didn't.

Didn't have his back, either.

And that's a true Micked pity.

Monday was one of those stunning New York days. A bright, sunny afternoon, cold but crisp. Reason you never left.

Ever.

Scotty didn't show up for work. Two days later, they fished his beaten body out of the East River.

I had literally read in *The Book of Virtue*, as I now termed the book,

"When the incredible happens, add credible to your account."

Brady was in hyper spirits that evening, dancing around, treating the mob factions to champagne, was almost civil to me.

Like that would last.
It didn't.

He sneered at me,
"Scotty has moved on."
And, as if it was a real award,
"You're the new boss."

Did I start checking on Scotty's death then?
Nope, I was too busy amassing my own fortune.
Months trickled by, I read my father's book, went to bed,
frequently with Cici.
Did her sleeping with Brady bother me?
Take a flying guess.
Was near the end of *The Book of Virtue* and read,
"What warehouse of the soul awaits me now?"
I muttered,
"As long as it's hot as hell."
Thought,
Scotty, where were you when I needed you?
Conscious of . . .
"Where was I when he went in the East River?"
And the days moved on until Brady began his dismantling of me.
With an awareness of unpaid tabs circulating in the club.

Brady had literally grabbed my arm, hissed,
"Get the tabs settled."
I tried, adding as much steel as I dared.
"Scotty would have dealt discreetly with this."
He gave me a sneer of such malevolence, like he was crowing,
said,
"Pity he didn't learn to swim."
Dancing away, he threw,

"D'Agostino owes me, that's what you need to get your focus with."

Meaning, the old Mafiosi whose running bill was getting seriously out of hand. I asked,

"You really want to mess with him?"

He gave his crooked grin, all malice and spite, said,

"I won't be."

Pause.

"You will."

Then added,

"Before Tuesday."

My father's cop buddies were like a vile extension of him. Save for one, Casey. Yeah, second generation of cop and Mick. Almost a caricature.

Boozy

Hard ass

Harp-ed

If Gene Hackman were Irish, he'd be Casey. But he treated me good.

Very.

After my father passed, he'd said,

"You ever need anything . . ."

So.

So met with him, in an Irish bar off Madison Square Garden. He was dressed in a thick offwhite Aran Island sweater, heavy pea jacket, tweed cap, as if he were auditioning for a part in *Mick Does New York*. A shock of wiry white hair and hands that could cover Manhattan and you had the essence of the Irish NYPD legacy. It wasn't that these guys took life as it came. Hell, no. They grabbed it by the throttle, kicked its ass, and, if that failed, they beat the living shit out it.

Casey had the end booth, shielded from prying eyes, though you'd need some *cojones* to stare at Casey. He welcomed,

"I got you a Jay, lad. Sit yer own self down."

The Jay was at least a double, no ice, heaven forbid. Those Micks weren't hot on blasphemy. He didn't reach over and ruffle my hair but the vibe was there. Even if I reached eighty, I'd always be "the kid" to these dinosaurs.

I knew the drill: get some shots down, then approach the subject in a creep-up-on-it fashion. If you were in a hurry, park it elsewhere. Casey ordered a side of fries and a bunch of pickled eggs. He ordered, I swear, by pounding the table, just once. And, you guessed it, offered/commanded,

"Dig in."

Those old timers, the book in their lives was,

"Book 'em, Danno."

Once we had the ritual drinks in, eggs demolished, he leaned back, asked,

"How you holding up, kiddo?"

I lied, said okay, then asked,

"You know anything about Brady, my boss at Khe Shan?"

He sighed. The guy could have sighed for the entire U. S. Shook his huge head, said,

"Piece of shite, connected to the Russian mob. Animals."

Paused.

Gave me the cool slow appraisal, fine-honed in nigh twenty years of staring down the enemy. *Enemy* covered just about the whole planet save cops and family.

He asked,

"This about the schmuck they pulled out of the East River?"

You might ridicule these throw-back nigh vigilante cops but Holy shit, they were on the ball. You didn't trawl the five boroughs for two decades and be stupid.

I advised, if quietly,

"He was my buddy."

Casey snorted and, when you have a Jameson shooter half way to your lips, it's doubly effective, but he never spilled a drop. Drained it, crashed it down on the table with,

"Never had you down as a bollix, much less a stupid one."

I did the smart thing: shut the hell up. Dense silence over us and . . . few things more lethal than a brooding silent Mick. He finally said,

"Lemme educate you, son. Scotty was well known to the Detroit PD, but a slick fook, so they never nailed him. He headed west, hooked up with Brady, another piece of work who'd adopted an Irish name to make him thug-friendly. They made a lot of cold cash and ploughed it into the club to make it seem legit. The past year, Scotty began to make inroads into his own crew to oust Brady."

Paused.

"You get the picture?"

Yeah.

Then he added,

"Brady will let you run the club for a year, tops, then whack you and bring in some other naïve schmuck."

I excused me own self, headed for the restroom, ordered up a fresh batch of the Jay, and punched the wall, hurt the living crap out of me hand. On my return, I changed tack, asked,

"You ever have my old man down for a reader?"

We clinked shots, downed them, and Casey answered,

"No way. You kidding?"

I told him about *The Book of Virtue* and he let a low whistle, said,

"Me, I never was much for no book learning."

Sounding like he was in a bad Western.

We mulled it over, then he went,

"My mother, Lord rest her and all the bad Caseys, she used to sing a Yeats poem, yeah, *sing* it. All I got is,

"The world is more full of weeping than we can understand."

God is good; he didn't sing it. I hadn't enough Jay to ever endure that. Then he leaned over, put his large hand on my shoulder, said,

"Frank had his faults but, deep down, he was a decent guy."

I felt the bile rise, spat,

"Oh, like, *he meant well?*"

He sat back, stunned by my venom, tried,

"Jaysus, Tommy, c'mon, he loved you."

I said,

"That weeping world . . . *Frank* caused his fair share."

And that was the end of the chat.

He warned me to watch my back, and to call if I needed anything.

I got out of there, had a moment of vague regret that I'd busted his balls, then thought, "He was my Dad's buddy, so the hell with him."

My father's book

Was diverted by a note on the binding. Read,

"Sewn binding, the strongest yet the most expensive. The pages are sewn into the book manually with a sewing machine."

Followed by a note, in my father's hand,

"Check out Moleskin diaries, used by Hemingway and Chatwin."

Now I was seriously perplexed.

Too, the oddest thing, just holding the book, it gave me the strangest sensation of, hell, I'm slow to admit this,

Peace?

WTF?

I went online, put in,

www.realbooks.com

Trawled through a ton of sites until I found one dealing exclusively with the physical qualities of a book, not the contents.

Read long-winded boring passages about the creation of a book, the printing, art of binding, and muttered,

"Bibliophiles."

Come the final Wednesday of the virtue saga.

The last page of my father's book had passages of two poems, Francis Thompson's *The Hound of Heaven* and Cafavvy's *Alexandria*. The gist being, he'd been pursued all his life in dread and terror and, secondly, no matter what he did, he couldn't escape his life, as if you fooked up in one place, so you would always do.

If cops were secretly reading this stuff in their leisure time, no wonder they ate their guns.

Cici had the day off and came to my apartment, the top floor of a brownstone that I lavished my savings on. She had a mouth on her, kidding I ain't. She asked,

"How much are you ripping off from the club?"

A lot.

I said,

"As if I would."

She let that slide.

Gave me the hot look.

It burned.

Followed with a blast of white radiance.

After, I had one of my rarest cigs and, God forgive me, one supplied by Cici.

Virginia Slims.

Not too macho. She pulled on one of my faded denim shirts. I had it longer than I had sense. Looked good, looked in heat. Trailing smoke, she went to mix up a batch of Vodka Spritzers.

Most appetites nigh sated, she picked up my dad's book, asked,

"You read?"

What?

Like I was a dumb bastard?

Hello.

She flicked through it, said,

"Now there's a word."

I followed her to the main room, an XL Yankees T-shirt on, asked,
"What's that?"
She read,
"*Schadenfreude*."
I asked,
"The hell does that mean?"
She pulled a battered dictionary from my battered book collection,
found the entry, intoned,
"A pleasure taken from another's misfortune."
Looked at me,
Added,
"Brady."
Got my vote.
Handed me a glass of the freshly blended batch, it tasted,
Cold
Good and
Like
Hope.
As artificial as that.
And as long lasting.
I said,
"Or my old man."
She sat lotus style on the sofa, looked at me for a long beat.
Then,
"We need to deal with Brady."
Sure.
How?
I asked,
"How?"
She took a deep gulp of her drink, her eyes watching me over the
rim of the glass. And,
"We need to cash his check."
No dictionary needed for that.

"I wanted to develop a curiosity that was oceanic and insatiable as well as a desire to learn every word in the English language that didn't sound pretentious or ditzy."

Pat Conroy.

My Losing Season.

I was beginning to understand that my old man had used his book in a vain attempt at catching an education. Was that admirable? Weighed it against the terror he'd inflicted on me all his miserable life.

Time was running out on my supposed plea to the Mafioso to ask him to settle his tab. No doubt, if I did, he'd see it as the ultimate diss and, man, this was a guy who beat a busboy to pulp for standing too close while the psycho was getting up from a meal—a meal, of course, that he didn't pay for.

Too, the schmuck, horror, never, like, not *ever*, left a tip.

Enough reason right there to whack his tight ass. I owned an illegal Browning Nine. You run my kind of club, you need to pack more than attitude.

Cici had it down.

Brady rented a fook pad on West 45th Street, between Madison and Fifth Avenues. Friday afternoons, he liked Cici to come by and . . . entertain him. She had a key and gave me a copy.

Oh, and a shit-load of coke. Said,

"Scatter it around the bedroom, make it look like a dope gig gone south."

Cici would have a very high profile lunch with some friends, alibi ensuring. Me, I had none and that itself is its own defense.

The gun was untraceable. I'd literally found it a year ago, shoved down behind a seat in the VIP section.

Friday, coming up to noon, I felt calm. Removing Brady would be a downright freaking joy and, in some odd way, like a lash back at me old man. I dressed casual, not sure of the dress code for murder. Old jeans, a battered windbreaker, Converse sneakers that had always been a size too small. Walk in the blood and the cops, gee, they'd have a footprint.

It went like clockwork.

Brady had laughed when I let myself in. He was nose deep in candy, lolling on a sofa, rasped,

"Jesus, never thought you had the *cojones* to attempt a burglary."

Why wasn't he alarmed?

The coke had fried his brain . . . too out there to be alarmed.

Put one in his gut first, let him whine a bit, chalk up serious payback . . . but all fine things must end so added three to his dumb head.

All she wrote.

I then scattered the coke like fragile snow around his pad.

Found the money in a suitcase.

Yeah, believe it, a suitcase.

Enough cash to launch two new clubs.

Got the hell out of there.

Discreetly.

Next day, the cops arrived.

I kid thee not.

Two detectives, one surly and the other surlier. Bad cop by two.

The latter asked,

Pushing a book at me,

"This yours?"

"My dad's book!"

Before I could protest, the first added,

"If it has your fingerprints?"

They had a warrant and found the suitcase in jig time.

Cici.

The bitch.

I did of course try to implicate her but her alibi was solid. More than.

My lawyer was very young, up to speed with the current kid jargon. Said, "You don't have to worry."

Looked at the cop's book, of evidence, added

"Not."

I sat back in the hard prison metal chair, looked at him, said slowly,

"What . . .

   the . . .

      fook . . .

        ever."

IV

The Book of Ghosts

Reed Farrel Coleman

QUEENS, NEW YORK, 2011

Having survived three years in five concentration camps, Jacob Weisen knew death as one twin knows another. But that period of his schooling had come to a close seventy years ago. Now there remained but one last thing to learn of death, and that lesson would come soon enough. Weisen neither feared death-he had seen it in all its permutations so that he understood there was a kind of peace in it-nor welcomed it-he had fought too hard to live during his years in hell to give into it simply because he was a tired old man.

"What are you thinking about, Zaydeh?" asked Leah, Weisen's granddaughter, noticing the sour expression on his face.

"Dying."

"Oy, not this again."

"One day, Totty, the rain will come. It will lift me up like an oil spot off the gutter and wash me into the sewer. One day I will be here, then I will be gone. No one should mourn an oil spot and that is all we are . . . less, maybe."

"Zaydeh, please stop it. I hate it when you get this way," she said, as she drove out of Kennedy airport and onto the Van Wyck Expressway.

"You hate that I talk the truth?"

"Your truth, Zaydeh, not everyone's."

He pushed back the arm of his jacket, rolled up his shirt sleeve, and tapped his gnarled index finger to the sagging skin of his forearm and the faded numbers tattooed there. "No, Totty, not my truth, *the* truth. I have seen the truth of oil spots and ashes: here one day, gone the next, and then forgotten. And once you're forgotten . . . there is no return."

"Not all are forgotten," she said, her voice impatient. "There's you and your friend Isaac Becker. You two won't be forgotten. The both of you will be tied to *The Book of Ghosts* forever."

The Book of Ghosts, indeed! What a load of dreck, he thought. While Leah was correct about them being bound together, Jacob Weisen had no more been a friend to Isaac Becker than a spider to a fly. It was then, for fear of letting the endless years of pent-up bile and guilt pour out of him in one furious rush, that he decided to keep his mouth clamped shut until they reached the auction house. Many, many, decades had passed since he'd been forced to learn to hold his tongue in the face of unrelenting atrocity. In a world where speaking up got you nothing but a bullet or "delousing," self-imposed silence was an essential survival skill. Lying, too, became second nature. Lying was a particularly effective skill at Birkenau in the anteroom of the gas chamber.

"*Remember your hook numbers so you can collect your clothing after your shower,*" was a lie he had learned to utter quickly and with conviction in many different languages: Yiddish, German, Russian, Ukrainian, Polish, Hungarian, Czech, Dutch . . . the list was long. Jacob still woke up some nights with that polyglot lie on his lips.

One of the guards, Heilmann, a real bastard with coal for a heart and a face like a plane crash, used to repeat the same joke to Jacob after each group of the dead was carted to the ovens. "You Jews must have such terrible memories. Your people never come back for their clothes. I wonder where they have all gotten to?" And each time, Heilmann would laugh—each laugh a little stab wound. He wondered why he should be thinking of Heilmann after all these years. Would he finally start bleeding from the thousand little stab wounds?

So it was no small irony that Jacob Weisen's failure to just keep his mouth shut and that his most foolish and unnecessary fabrication had caused his life after the war to be haunted by Isaac Becker and his accursed book, the book for which the idiot Becker—with Jacob's complicity—had sacrificed his life. And as Weisen grew older, the taste of irony grew more bitter in his mouth-so bitter that he could have choked on it. He *was* choking on it now as Leah drove down the Long Island Expressway, the skyline of Manhattan and the prospect of the rare book auction looming before him. And as they did, he asked himself the same question he had asked himself a thousand, ten thousand, a million times in the wake of the camp's liberation at the hands of the Red Army. Why? Why: three letters, one syllable, a single sound, but the most complex question in the universe when it came to the human heart. Why didn't he just keep his trap shut when the Jewish resettlement agency people came to interview him in the hospital? Why spin the tale of Isaac Becker and *The Book of Ghosts* when he might have gotten to America anyway?

He was not without answers, reasonable answers, ones that sometimes let him sleep the whole night through. He wanted no part of the Soviets. He had witnessed their barbarity first-hand and thought them not much better than the Nazis. He had no desire to build a new life in the ruins and gloom of a blood-soaked Europe, nor did he have the zeal to fight the British for a homeland in Palestine. America. He wanted a new world in which to make something of the shreds of whatever remained of himself. Jacob Weisen thought if he could just make himself seem heroic—the Americans, he knew, had a weakness for heroes—he might stand a better chance of making it across the Atlantic. So he took the facts and spliced them with lies and embellishments to create the myth of his salvation. Only now, with Manhattan but minutes away, it felt much more like damnation.

"Your name is Jacob Weisen." The ravenhaired American woman from the agency had read from his request form. She was actually quite beautiful, delicate, and spoke passable Yiddish. "It says here you want to be resettled in the United States or Canada."

"United States only. See, I wrote the United States there for my second choice too, but they crossed it out and made me write Canada."

She smiled in spite of herself. "Why America only, Jacob?" she asked, giving him the opening he'd been hoping for.

And thus Weisen told the story of how his brave childhood friend, Isaac Becker, the storyteller—" Even the SS men called him that"—had written a book during his year and a half in Birkenau and the other Auschwitz satellite camps. That Becker's book was a novel featuring a protagonist known only as the Gypsy.

"You see, in the book," Jacob explained to the American woman, "the Gypsy is visited by the ghosts of the people he knew in the camps before they were gassed. The ghosts tell their stories to the Gypsy who commits them to memory to tell to the world if he himself should survive. Isaac never told me the book's title, but I came to think of it as *The Book of Ghosts*."

"This is fascinating, Jacob, but I don't see how this relates to you or your request for resettlement in the United—"

Weisen cut her off, continuing his tale. "You see, because Isaac was such a wonderful storyteller, he sort of became the personal property of Oberleutnant Kleinmann. He was Kleinmann's pet and it was Kleinmann who gave Isaac the writing tablet and pen in the first place so he could write down his stories. What that bastard Kleinmann didn't know was that Isaac was really using the tablet to write *The Book of Ghosts*. He only pretended to be reading stories from the book to placate the Nazi pig. In exchange for the stories, the lieutenant kept Isaac from the showers. The charade worked until Isaac told a story Kleinmann was so taken with that he demanded to have the tablet back from Isaac and to keep it for his own. Isaac protested for a time, but what choice did he have, really? In the end, he gave the book to Kleinmann who just glanced at it, saw that the first page had some Hungarian on it, and locked it in his desk drawer."

"Still, as captivating as this all is, I don't understand how it helps your cause," she said, although the quiver in her voice betrayed her words.

"Poor Isaac came to me, frantic, explaining the situation and how he feared our whole barracks might be punished for his indiscretion. 'If they think you all knew about the book and didn't tell them,' he said, 'who knows how they will punish you?'"

The woman was hooked, so much so that she reached across the table for Jacob's hand. "Please, tell me what happened next?"

"Under cover of darkness, Becker and I snuck back to Kleinmann's little office where the book was hidden. We were prying open the lock when Kleinmann caught us in the act. I stabbed the monster through the neck with a piece of sharpened glass. Here," Jacob whispered, reaching out and touching the soft white skin of the American's neck, "but not before he had wounded Isaac in the leg. I wanted to stay, to help my friend, but he wouldn't hear of it. All he could think about was the book. 'Save yourself,' he said, 'and smuggle the book out of here no matter what it takes. The world must know what happened in this place.' I did as he asked. I wrapped the book in some fabric and rubber sheeting I had bartered for with one of the guards. The next morning I slipped the package into a wagon of ashes headed for one of the nearby farms I heard was owned by a man in the Polish resistance. Did you know the Poles used our ashes as fertilizer? We were no use to them alive, but dead . . ."

"Oh, my God!" she gasped, tears running down her cheeks. "And Becker, what happened to Isaac Becker?"

"Tortured, then crucified. Took him three days to die and they left his body for everyone to see as the birds gnawed at him."

"The book. What became of the book?" She wanted desperately to know.

Jacob Weisen shrugged his broad shoulders. "It could be plowed beneath the soil in some Polish farmer's field or it could be anywhere. I fear we will never know." Jacob could have left it at that, but didn't. He was so encouraged by the woman's touch, her tears, and her beauty, that he took one step too far. "So you see—I'm sorry, I have been impolite. What is your name?"

"Ava, Ava Levinsky," she said, blushing slightly.

"So you see, Miss Ava Levinsky, I must go to America and tell this story to our people. They will see pictures of the camps, but they will never know the horrors like us few surviving Jews of Europe. The book is gone, but our people in America must know we did not all die like sheep, that some of us kept our pride. They must know of poor Isaac's bravery and his book. Remember, he told me before I left him there next to Kleinmann's body, 'The world must know what happened in this place.'"

And so was born the legend of Isaac Becker and the myth of *The Book of Ghosts*. The truth of it was something else altogether, but there was no one left to dispute Weisen's version of history. The last member of his barracks died of typhus the day before the Red Army marched into the camp and none of the SS henchmen who managed to avoid justice or death in the aftermath of the war was apt to come forward to set the record straight. So Jacob Weisen was granted his wish and only a few months later had his new American life.

Settled into a one-bedroom apartment on the ground floor of a Victorian house on Foster Avenue in Brooklyn, commuting to 32nd Street in the city where he worked as a cutter in the *schmatte* trade, the garment business, he might very well have lived out a quiet, productive life as a simple man. Maybe he would have taken a wife, had some children, but maybe not. To put more distance between himself and his past, he had begun to call himself Jack Wise and had even gone to a lawyer to start the process of legally changing his name. It all could have turned out very differently had someone else interviewed him at the hospital after the war.

When he was lonely, which was all the time, he had thoughts of the beautiful American girl with the passable Yiddish and the silken black hair who had been instrumental in making his new life a reality. He remembered the warmth and softness of her hand as she caressed his and the feel of her lovely white skin when he brushed his fingers against her neck. Sometimes he repeated her name in his head like a lullaby as he rode the noisy, crowded subway to work and then home to his spare apartment. *Miss Ava Levinsky . . . Miss Ava Levinsky . . . Miss Ava Levinsky . . .* There were weak moments when he considered hiring an investigator to track her down. But no, he thought, little good would come of it. Whatever they might've had would have been built on the wet sand of his lies.

Then one glorious spring Sunday morning, as he did every Sunday morning, Jack Wise went fishing off the pier in Coney Island, the Parachute Jump shooting up into the cloudless blue skies at his back. Fishing was something he did without regard to the weather. The camps had hardened him to the weather: hot and cold, wet or dry. He would get up with the sun, ride the subway into Sheepshead Bay or to the end of the line at Coney Island, and drop his line. Fishing was his only indulgence, the solitary joy he allowed himself that remained beyond of reach of his sometimes suffocating guilt and the horrors he had left behind in Poland. Sunday mornings were the only times he could ever fully get the stink of burning human flesh out of his head and nostrils.

That Sunday was particularly beautiful—a light breeze off the ocean, the scent of Nathan's fries mixing with the salt air, the sound of children laughing—and he would have remembered it even if he hadn't snagged a shark and attracted a crowd when he yanked it out of the water. He posed for pictures, holding his catch, for what seemed an hour, but was only a few minutes. Then, when he tossed the beast back to King Neptune, the crowd evaporated and the other fishermen went back to their own poles. Jack went back to his.

And then he heard her voice. "Jacob Weisen!"

He fought very hard to ignore it, to pretend it was his mind playing tricks, but he knew it was her. He squeezed his eyes shut and prayed—it was the first time he'd prayed since God went deaf in 1933—for her to go away. His heart had a very different prayer.

"Jacob," she repeated, only this time she grabbed his bicep.

He could not fight the fight any longer. His heart's prayer was answered because its petition was made to a flawed and lonely man, not to an aloof God.

"Miss Ava Levinsky," he said, turning to see the face he had dreamed of for three years. For a brief moment, his heart sank. "It is still *Miss* Levinsky, yes?"

"Yes, but not for long, I hope."

"We will just see about that, young lady," he said, leaning over and kissing her softly on the mouth.

And with that kiss, he reopened the door to Isaac Becker, *The Book of Ghosts*, and a life of haunting. He knew that instead of explaining his name change and about how he had so quickly moved from the sweatshop floor to the showroom of Beckerman & Sons Fine Menswear, that he should have confessed his sins to her right then and there. Even as he stared at her, disbelieving his good fortune, he recited the confession in his head.

Listen, Miss Ava Levinsky, let me tell you something about the man you just kissed. He's a liar, a murderer, a hypocrite. Remember that story he told you about his friend and the book? Well, some of it was true. There was a book, and this liar had known Isaac Becker since they were children in the same tiny German town on the Polish frontier, but they were enemies, not friends. They hated one another, fiercely, from the moment they met. He always thought Becker was a dreamer and a fool. Becker thought him artless and calculating. When they found themselves in the camp together, their mutual loathing only intensified. This man you're going to marry, he was the barracks' enforcer and murdered men with his bare hands for stealing rations or informing for the SS. On the other hand, he facilitated with his lies the deaths of more of his own people than half the Nazis they hung at Nuremberg. Oh, Becker was no saint, either, Miss Levinsky. He was a gifted storyteller, yes, but to escape work on the ash heap, he made a deal with Kleinmann. For each story he would tell Oberleutnant Kleinman, Becker got time off and extra food rations. Those extra rations had to come from somewhere. Some days, it meant a little less for everybody else. More often, it meant one or two additional dead Jews.

The bit about Kleinmann keeping the writing tablet—that much was true as well. But this man, this liar standing before you, he didn't go with Isaac Becker to retrieve the book. That would have been an act of insanity. No, Becker went on his own. It was Becker, not the liar, who stabbed Oberleutnant Kleinmann in the liver, not in the neck, with the sharpened glass. This man you just kissed, you know what he did? He turned Becker in for some extra crusts of bread and rat meat soup. And yes, there was a Gypsy, but he was not the hero of Becker's book. The Gypsy was a prisoner from another barracks who kept himself alive by consorting with the SS, by smuggling things in and out of the camp. It was the Gypsy who put the book in the ash cart. As to the actual contents of the book, this liar, this murderer, he has no idea. It could have been a book of recipes or poetry or Hungarian curse words for all he knew. The Book of Ghosts! There were so many ghosts they couldn't have fit in all the books in all the world. And yes, Becker was tortured and crucified and the birds did eat his eyes out.

He told her none of it, instead feeding her a line about how he'd been wrong back in Poland, that he found he had no taste for talking about his time in the camps. "That's why I changed my name, why I am working so hard to become an American," he said. "The past is gone. Let it remain buried with the dead."

Ava seemed satisfied with his explanation. She had certainly dealt with enough survivors during her time overseas for the agency to know that very few people were anxious to tell their stories. She never once mentioned Becker or the book during their abbreviated courtship. It was only after too many glasses of champagne that she finally let something slip. Ava was talking to Jack's boss, Mr. Beckerman, at the wedding reception when the other shoe dropped.

"A survivor! Jackie! Who knew?" asked Beckerman. "He doesn't say to me a word about it."

"He never told you about *The Book of Ghosts*?"

"Never a word."

"It's what we talked about the first time we met. He was still in the hospital over there," she said. "His name was Jacob then and . . ."

Even from across the reception hall, seeing the look on Mr. Beckerman's face, Jack knew he was screwed. Two days after he returned from his honeymoon in Niagara Falls, Jack Wise was summoned into the boss' office.

"Listen, Jackie, your wife told me already the story about the book and I told it to my rabbi and you shouldn't know from his reaction. He was on *shpilkes*, on pins and needles," old Beckerman said in his heavily accented English. "He's a wise man, Jackie, my Rabbi Greenspan. He says you must share the story of your friend and the book. He says no matter how much pain it brings you to talk about it, to not share it with your people is a scandal, a *shanda*. The rabbi asked me to talk sense to you. He has called a special meeting of the temple brotherhood for a week from Sunday and he wants you to speak to us to tell us the story."

Jack didn't bother protesting. He had known this day would come sooner or later and there was a practical part of his decision. Mr. Beckerman put a roof over his head and food on his table. If surviving the camps taught him anything at all, it was never to be cavalier about shelter and food. To disappoint his boss would also be professional suicide. Besides, he loved the old man. So he went and he spoke but, to his relief, it pretty much stopped there. Over the course of the next year, he had the occasional request from this Jewish group or that to repeat the myth and he did. It wasn't until the *Forward* got hold of the story that the legend of the heroic storyteller Isaac Becker, his boyhood friend Jacob Weisen, and *The Book of Ghosts* spread. It didn't take long for the New York tabloids and the *Times* to run with it.

What could Jack Wise do? He couldn't unscramble the eggs of his lies. And having once been caught in the momentum of history, he understood there was no swimming against its tide. So, he figured, if everyone else was going to swim with the tide, he would swim with it too, as far as it would take him, which, as it happened, was very far. Playing it for all it was worth, he went back to using the name Jacob Weisen and accepted every paying speaking engagement he could land, including ones in Argentina and the newly established state of Israel. The money helped because Ava was pregnant with their first child and they were saving to buy a house on Long Island. Even Mr. Beckerman cooperated, giving Jacob all the time off he needed. But by 1952, with no witnesses to corroborate or challenge his story and with no book unearthed, his life settled back into a happy and largely uneventful routine. Ava was again pregnant. David, their three-year-old, was a terror. They had their ranch house in Wantagh and Jacob rode the Long Island Railroad to work five days a week instead of the subway.

Oswiecem (Auschwitz), Poland, 1946

Bronka Kaczmarek had nothing to lose and everything to gain in trying to get the hell away from the family farm outside Oswiecim. The Nazis, as kind of a farewell to the neighborhood, had murdered her parents and older brother while she lay hidden in the hayloft, listening to the *pop, pop, pop* of the Walther. Not a week later, a squad of Red Army soldiers had filled the void left by the fleeing Germans and announced their arrival by stealing Bronka's last cow—a pathetic-looking animal—and by raping her more or less continuously for two days running. If their treatment of her was any indication, it seemed to Bronka that the Russians hated the Poles almost as much as they hated the Germans. In any case, she had had enough of them both. One monster, she thought, but for tailoring, was much like another.

Over the course of the last eight months, she had sold everything that wasn't nailed down to neighboring farmers or on the black market. She had taken her time so as not to arouse suspicion. It was probably an unnecessary precaution because now that Poland had been swallowed up by the Bolsheviks and private property was deemed a capitalist folly perpetrated by the masses, everyone was scrambling to survive. Desperation, not wheat, was the biggest cash crop in Poland after the war. The only thing Bronka hadn't sold was the thing she wished she had never seen: the little package wrapped in the tatters of striped pajamas, a Jew's striped pajamas. How did she know? Because although the yellow star was missing, its six-pointed silhouette remained. She didn't much like Jews nor did her father, but her father was a superstitious man. He had pulled her aside one day shortly after the ash cart had come from the camp and shown her the package.

"What is it, Papa?"

"It is one of *their* secret things," he whispered as if the animals were listening.

"Maybe it's money or some of their diamonds. Let me have it. I will untie the knot and look."

He pulled it to his chest. "No, Bronka, never!" He crossed himself and spit on the ground. "Now that I have taken it, we will be cursed if we do not protect it. Yes, they killed Christ, but they are God's Chosen. They have powers."

She laughed at her father. "Powers! Power to what, to make blue smoke out of the sky? Chosen for what, to be slaughtered like cattle?"

Her father slapped her so hard across the face that the imprint of his thick fingers marked her left cheek for days. She hated that the slap was now her most enduring memory of her Papa, but because the package meant so much to him, it had become her only way to hold onto her father. Since she possessed neither the inclination toward deep thought nor the time to ponder the universe, Bronka Kaczmarek sewed the package into the lining of her coat and left Oswiecem forever under cover of darkness in the rear of a potato truck.

As it wasn't in Bronka's nature to let irony take purchase in her thoughts, she didn't waste time worrying about the fact that she found herself, two years later, in West Berlin, married to a British man named Daniel Epstein. Daniel, a wiry, handsome man who worked for the BBC World Service, was nominally Jewish and didn't ask Bronka to convert. In fact, he didn't ask much of her at all. She was more a housekeeper than a wife to him—a kiss farewell in the morning and one when he arrived home in the evening—and that suited her well enough. After those two days with the Russians, the thought of a man—handsome and well-mannered or not—inside her made her break out in a cold sweat. And so it went for three years until the morning Bronka was crushed beneath the wheels of a potato truck outside the local market. Wherever her eternal soul might be, even Bronka must have appreciated the irony in her deliverance.

When Daniel was going through his wife's things, he found the coat Bronka had worn the night she left Oswiecem buried in the back of a closet. If he hadn't patted down the pockets to see if she had left anything of value in them, the remainder of Jacob Weisen's life might have been spent in relative peace. But Daniel Epstein *did* pat down the pockets and he *did* find the tatter-wrapped package sewn into the lining of the threadbare coat. Although he had no idea of what to make of it, he knew someone who might. Yes, he knew him quite well.

After several years back in the States, Max Baumgarten, an army intelligence officer during the war—translating captured documents, mostly—had been assigned to Berlin as a correspondent for the *Herald Tribune*. He loved everything about the job, including his ability to scratch a particular kind of itch out of the sight of prying eyes. Unlike Daniel, Max felt no need to take on a bride for cover, but the British had that peculiar need to keep up appearances. Hell, Daniel even played the dutiful husband in the aftermath of Bronka's death, refusing to "see" Max until a proper and respectful period of mourning had been observed. So it was a surprise, a happy surprise, when the week after the Polish peasant was buried, Max picked up the phone and Daniel was on the other end.

They set a time to meet at "their" flat. They kept this place for their trysts, renting it under a false name and paying monthly in cash. Even seven years after the war, pounds or dollars talked loud and kept questions to a minimum. They had the place until the end of the month. After that, Max didn't see the need to keep it any longer, not now that Daniel's Polish peasant was dead. Max arrived early: setting up candles, icing down a bottle of pre-war vintage Veuve Cliquot, and setting out an iced tin of pearl black caviar, sour cream, and thinly sliced and toasted pieces of baguette. When Daniel showed up carrying a package wrapped in pajama tatters, Max's lustful intentions evaporated. Max could barely contain himself. "Holy shit! It's *The Book of Ghosts*."

Daniel crooked his head like a confused puppy. "What?"

"Did Bronka tell you where she was from in Poland?" Max answered the question with his own.

"Well, at first, no. I suppose even she was embarrassed. But one night after one too many vodkas, she confessed to me that she grew up on a farm-"

"—near Oswiecem," Max finished his lover's sentence.

"How could you possibly know that?"

"When I was back home after the war, my parents schlepped me to some cockamamie lecture at my old temple from a guy who was an Auschwitz survivor. He told some wild tale about his friend and how they murdered an SS lieutenant and smuggled a book out of Birkenau in a cart of victims' ashes that the local farmers used as fertilizer. To my amazement, it was a pretty fascinating story, but I thought it was just a load of horseshit. You know, a lot of survivors have this terrible guilt and they feel like people, other Jews especially, blame them for being too sheep-like, as if these poor people marched happily into the ghettos and then the showers. So I figured this guy dreamed up this story to relieve his own guilt and to defend the people he watched die at the hands of the Nazis. I guess I was wrong."

"It would appear so. Shall we open it?"

Max clutched his hand around Daniel's. "No. Let me check a few things out about its potential value and historical significance. We don't want to do anything that might damage it. We'll store it here for safekeeping," Max said, taking the package. "Plus, when you get home, try and find anything in Bronka's papers that connect her to her family and farm in that area. Provenance is critical."

Daniel was so thrilled at the idea of being a part of history, as opposed to flitting around at its edges, that he dispensed with proper mourning etiquette and dropped to his knees.

Wantagh, Long Island, NY, 1952

Ava had taken David to visit his grandparents in Scarsdale and Jacob Weisen had just settled in to read the paper after returning from his Sunday morning fishing excursion to Twin Lakes when the bell rang. There wasn't anything particularly ominous in the sound of the bell or the hour or the time of year and Jacob was always invigorated by fishing, so he was almost jaunty as he got up to answer the bell. That all changed when the short, rotund figure in an ill-fitting suit and a squashed down fedora on the other side of the storm door announced he was Karl Olson from the *Herald Tribune*.

"What can I do for you, Mr. Olson?"

"You got me wrong, Mr. Weisen, or is it Mr. Wise?"

"Weisen."

"Like I say, you got me wrong. It's what I, or rather, my paper, can do for you."

"You're not making sense to me, Olson."

Olson had been a journalist long enough to spot the signs of withdrawal and he couldn't afford to lose Weisen, so he went to plan B. He opened a thin folder he carried in his left hand, removed an 8" x 12" photograph, and held it up to the screen on the storm door.

"Do you recognize the item in the photograph, Mr. Weisen?"

He didn't have to say a word, for Olson had his answer as Weisen's eyes grew big and shock flashed across his face like sheet lightning. And for the first time since he fainted during his second shift removing bodies from the gas chamber, Jacob Weisen nearly swooned.

Then, quickly recovering, Jacob said, "I was in shock there for a second. Excuse me."

"So, you think it's—"

"Isaac's book, *The Book of Ghosts*? I know that's the answer you want, but I cannot say for certain," he lied. "It's been eight years. Eight years I have spent fighting a war with myself between remembering and forgetting. Besides, anyone, any unscrupulous person who has heard me talk of the book, would know just how to make such a thing seem real. Look, Olson, even now I'm sure there are hundreds, thousands of those dreadful striped pajamas around. In my talk, I always discuss just how I wrapped the book in black rubber sheeting I got from this bastard guard named Heilmann. I then wrapped that in a layer of fabric," Weisen gestured with his hands as if neatly folding invisible fabric. "The fabric came from the pajamas of a poor barracks mate who had died in his sleep that same night. I used a long strip of sleeve fabric to hold the bundle tight together and tied a strong knot." He made the motions of tying a knot, even wincing, as he tugged at the ends of the invisible strip. "So, you see, anyone could have made a fake."

In spite if his equivocation, there was no doubt in Jacob's mind that this was the book, for he had, in fact, wrapped it exactly as he had just described before giving it to the Gypsy to smuggle out of the camp in the ash wagon. The one detail he had always left out—the silhouette of the six-pointed star—was clearly visible in the photograph. Seeing it brought all the horror back to him. He swore he could smell the stink of the ovens on the package in the picture.

"You'll have to excuse me, Olson. You can understand how even seeing a photograph of such a thing is disturbing to a man who went through what I went through."

The survivor doth protest too much, thought the reporter, but decided not to directly confront Weisen. Instead, he asked, "Why would someone want to do that, make a fake, I mean?"

Jacob shrugged. "Why does anyone make a hoax? For a sick joke maybe. To profit somehow? To discredit? I wouldn't know. Where is the thing, anyway?"

"In West Berlin."

"Curious. And how did it get to be there?"

Olson said, "I don't know all the particulars, but apparently a woman brought it with her when she fled Poland several years ago."

"A woman?"

"Yeah, she grew up on a farm outside Auschwitz."

There was that sheet lightning again. "And who has the package?" Jacob asked, his voice brittle.

"I'm afraid I can't divulge that information to you, Mr. Weisen. I just need you to conform to me that this might actually be *The Book of Ghosts*."

Once again, Jacob was caught in his own web of lies. He needed to stall, to have a moment to think. "And what, you're gonna write a story about it?"

"Not yet," Olson said. "At the moment I'm only fact checking. For now, I just need to know it's not an obvious fake. My guess is that sooner or later, you'll be asked to authenticate it."

"Sooner or later?"

This guy's playing for time, Olson thought, which only cemented the opinion he'd reached seeing Weisen's reaction to the photograph. Still, he was a reporter and his opinions and impressions counted for only so much. He needed to hear Weisen say the words, so he prodded, "I'm sorry, Mr. Weisen. You haven't answered my question. Is it an obvious fake?"

"No," Jacob heard himself say, "not an obvious one. But I'm not saying it's the—"

"Thank you, sir," Olson cut him off, already turning his back on Weisen. "I've got all I need for now."

West Berlin, Federal Republic of Germany, 1952
JW confirms package probably authentic—Olson

The person manning the teletype machine in the *Herald Tribune* office the day Olson's cryptic message to Max Baumgarten arrived was a man named Ernst Flesch, the same man who had sent Max's original inquiry note to the New York bureau. Flesch had a small burn scar on the underside of his left arm near his armpit. The burn hadn't occurred during the war, but immediately in its wake. Many men in both the Federal Republic of Germany—West Germany—and the German Democratic Republic—East Germany—bore such scars. In retrospect, it was foolish of them to burn themselves in this manner as the resulting scar marked them as certainly as the thing they were so desperate to obliterate: their Waffen-SS blood group tattoo.

That a former member of the Waffen-SS was manning the teletype that day might not have been so terrible a thing had Max Baumgarten been a little more like his lover Daniel. The reserved and cautious Daniel would never give such a note to the teletype operator to send. He would have done it himself, but Max, in spite of his work in army intelligence, often did careless things. Even still, few, maybe no other former SS man, would have understood the implications of the messages sent between Max Baumgarten and Karl Olson.

It was Max's misfortune, however, that Corporal Ernst Flesch had served for a short time at Birkenau under a certain Oberleutnant Kleinmann, an officer who had treated him well. It was Flesch who, in the wake of Kleinmann's murder, had driven the railroad spikes into the cross through the wrists and ankles of Isaac Becker. Flesch ripped the message out of the machine, crumpled it into a ball, and tossed it into the trash.

The rest was almost as easy as that: Getting Baumgarten's address, gaining entrance by saying he had an important message from New York, garroting the Jew with a length of piano wire held tightly between his gloved hands. Only when another man stepped out of the lavatory, wet from a shower, did things get a little complicated, but not so much that Flesch couldn't handle it. The man almost seemed more embarrassed by his nudity in front of a stranger than shocked by Baumgarten's lifeless body on the floor before him. By the time the nude man regained his wits, it was too late. Flesch slammed the heel of his gloved right palm into the base of the nude man's nose, breaking it. Daniel reeled blindly, falling to the floor. Flesch grabbed his old Walther, put a pillow around the pistol, held the pillow to the man's face, and squeezed the trigger. Flesch held his breath, waiting to see if any of the neighbors would react. None did. There were no shouts to call the police, no shrieks, no running feet in the hallway, no banging at the flat door. Ernst Flesch exhaled and calmly set about tossing the apartment, even checking the undersides of all the drawers and emptying out all the food canisters. He repeated this same process later that evening at Daniel Epstein's flat, but neither search produced the package.

Wantagh, Long Island, New York, 1952

As is often the case, an action taken with one purpose in mind leads to its exact opposite. And so it was with Ernst Flesch's handiwork. The double homicide got big headlines in the West Berlin papers, even bigger ones and more play in the London and New York papers.

Of course, the nature of the relationship between Max Baumgarten and Daniel Epstein was only alluded to and then obliquely, but it didn't take a genius to read between the lines. Yet the story had legs—long, powerful legs thanks to Karl Olson and the mood of the times. His story about the possible connection between *The Book of Ghosts* and the double homicide in West Berlin got picked up by every newspaper from New York to Yorkshire, from Pekin, Illinois, to Peking, China. Anyone who hadn't heard of Isaac Becker, Jacob Weisen, and the book knew about it now.

After his time in Birkenau, this period of Weisen's life was by far the worst. Even after the initial flurry of activity in the wake of Karl Olson's story, Jacob had no peace. With the Cold War in bloom, the Rosenberg executions pending, and Red paranoia spreading like the common cold, the story of *The Book of Ghosts* took a bizarre twist. Seemingly overnight, the legend went from something heroic and life affirming to something vaguely evil and suspect. There were all sorts of theories about how Isaac Becker was really a Soviet spy and that the book was full of coded secrets. That when they liberated all the Auschwitz camps, the Russians had enlisted Weisen as a spy. That the book was a lie perpetrated by the Russians to make Americans doubt the sincerity of their new allies, the West Germans. None of it made a lick of sense or held up under any kind of scrutiny, but what did that matter in 1952?

The worst part for Weisen was when the investigator from the House Un-American Activities Committee showed up at his house to interview him and his wife. It was bad enough that this preppy asshole came into his home, asking questions not so different than a Gestapo or KGB interrogator might have asked, but what really infuriated Jacob was that this prig hounded Ava as well.

"Levinsky, that's your maiden name, is it not, Mrs. Weisen?" He didn't wait for an answer. "You're the daughter of Saul Levinsky, the lawyer who represents the grocery workers union. Is that correct?

"Yes and yes."

"Were you aware that the head of the union is alleged to of have ties to the New York Socialist Workers Committee?"

"No."

"Do you think your father is aware of these allegations?"

Ava was cool. "You'd have to ask my father, I suppose."

And so it went. Jacob kept his answers short and nearly bit through his tongue in frustration because, in spite of his anger, the investigator's unfounded insinuations and thinly veiled anti-Semitism, Jacob knew he had been the one to bring this down on their heads. He, and he alone, was responsible. Nothing ever came of the allegations, but rumors and whispers were enough to ruin people in those days, especially Jews who spoke with foreign accents. After all, who needs the truth when you've got demagoguery on a grand scale?

Jacob and Ava Weisen were luckier than most in that they weren't ruined. In fact, Olson's story did far more damage than HUAC ever could. Now that the legend of *The Book of Ghosts* was out there for the world to know and the pictures Max Baumgarten had snapped of the tattered package were in wide circulation, Jacob had very little peace. Jewish groups raised funds to hire investigators to look for it. The Federal Republic of Germany, as an act of atonement and as a gesture to the people of Israel, had agents on its trail. It was rumored that the Israeli government had assigned some Mossad agents from the Nazi hunter squads to search for the book. For a moment there, it seemed that every adventurer, freelance reporter, and foreign government on the planet was out searching for the damned thing. And of course, they all wanted to interview Jacob Weisen. Worse still were the constant rumors of the book's whereabouts. *The Book of Ghosts* had been transformed from a lie into a combination of the Holy Grail and the Maltese Falcon. With every report, every rumor, came a knock on Weisen's front door or a ring of his phone.

Yes, there were whole months, years sometimes, when the activity would slow to a trickle and Jacob and Ava could enjoy their children and, eventually, their grandchildren. The damned book, however, was never completely out of their lives and each time an escaped Nazi was captured—the year Eichmann went on trial was hell—or a Holocaust-related movie like *The Pawnbroker*, *Schindler's List*, *Shoah*, *Marathon Man*, *The Odessa File*, *The Boys From Brazil* or even *The Producers* was released, Jacob was forced back into the hell of his own making. The Internet only made things worse. By then, at least, he had retired and they'd moved down to Boynton Beach. After Ava passed in 2002, Jacob Weisen had a brief period where he was practically Zen about the whole affair. He could not undo things. What was done was done, but it wasn't done, not by a long shot.

Berlin, Federal Republic of Germany, 2009

At first they assumed Al Qaeda was responsible for the bomb blast because the center of the powerful explosion was just meters away from a subway entrance. It was only the next day, after the rescue teams had pulled the survivors from the ruins of the old building and pieces of the device were collected that it was determined the blast was actually a long time in the making. The five-hundred-pound bomb had likely been dropped from the belly of a B-17 or B-24, been paved over, and laid dormant beneath the sidewalk for more than six decades. When the demolition and cleanup crews came to sort through the rubble, the fuse was lit to another type of dormant bomb. For in the piles of bricks, twisted metal, splintered wood, and plaster dust was a package wrapped in the tatters of concentration camp pajamas. In the report issued after a court-ordered investigation, a tentative link was established between *The Book of Ghosts*, Bronka Kaczmarek, and Daniel Epstein, who was murdered shortly after Kaczmarek's own death. During an interview, the lead investigator said he was certain that the destroyed building had contained a flat that had once been rented by Daniel Epstein and Max Baumgarten. His best guess was that the book had been hidden beneath a floor board or behind a closet wall, but he had no way of knowing for certain. What was known for sure was that none of the dozens of people who had rented the flat since had ever stumbled onto the package.

Manhattan, New York City, 2011

They had arrived, finally, and so had judgment day. Quinby's Auction House had someone waiting at the curb to help Jacob Weisen into the building, but the stooped, white-haired man rejected the offer with a curt snap of his head and a grunt.

"Zaydeh, please be polite," Leah chided.

"Forgive an old man," he said, admiring the willowy blonde who had been sent to see to him.

"Of course, Mr. Weisen. Please, if you will follow me."

And as the blonde held the door for them, another Quinby's employee went to park their car.

This wouldn't be the first time Jacob would see the package since it was unearthed in Berlin two years ago. No, he had been flown into Berlin to authenticate it and, he supposed, he could have ended his eternal nightmare by telling yet another lie. All he had needed to say was, "It's a fake. A good one, but a fake."

He had planned to say it, meant to say it right up until he said, "That's the package I put in the ash wagon in 1944." He was too near death, too accustomed to the chaos he had made of his life, to lie about it now. Besides, like everyone else, he was curious to see what that idiot Isaac Becker had sacrificed his life for all those years ago. He recognized the silhouette of the star immediately and his heart raced at the sight of it. And though it had been sixty-five years since it had been put it in the cart, he swore the thing still smelled like ashes.

Preservationists, historians, museum curators, religious leaders, and survivors disagreed about how to handle the find. Some argued the package should be carefully opened, with each of the component parts—the garment wrapping, the rubber sheeting, and the book itself—sent to undergo further analysis and preservation. Some argued that to divide the package up would be to destroy its value and historical significance. Still others claimed that to do anything at all to the package would ruin its spiritual nature. But the German government held that the decision was not rightly theirs to make. An intensive search was made to find the closest living blood relative of Isaac Becker. After nearly a year, a second cousin of Becker's, a Hyman Jablonsky, who, at twelve was sent with his family to Treblinka and survived, was found living in the Midwood section of Brooklyn. Although he had never met his cousin Isaac and had never heard the legend of *The Book of Ghosts*, it was determined that he was the book's rightful owner.

Jablonsky had a similar nature to his cousin. A man of humble means, Jablonsky needed to profit from the sale of the package, but he also understood its multi-layered significance. So it was arranged that any party to the bidding had to agree in advance of the auction to a strict set of stipulations concerning the future handling of the package. Small swaths of the wrapping, rubber sheeting and a page from the book itself had to be donated to Yad Vashem, the Israeli Holocaust Memorial, the Holocaust Museum in Washington, D.C., to the Auschwitz Museum in Poland, and to the German Holocaust Memorial for permanent display and for six months each year, the package should be on display at museums and memorials around the world. It was further stipulated that upon the new owner's death that *The Book of Ghosts* would be sold, at a prearranged figure, to Yad Vashem.

The main room of Quinby's was abuzz. The media were there in force as were diplomats from the United States, Israel, Germany, and Poland. Curators from the Holocaust memorials and museums were there too. All the bidders were present as well. In order to prevent any possible sale to Holocaust deniers, hate groups, or other types who might be motivated to break the terms of the sale and destroy the package, phone bidding was disallowed. A specially designed air-tight glove box—not dissimilar to the kind used when handling plutonium—with the package inside its Plexiglas walls, was on display. It had been agreed that the package should be unwrapped immediately following the sale. Expert linguists were on hand to read from the book. Yet in this room full of statesmen and dignitaries, the wealthy and the wise, it was Jacob Weisen's entrance that caused the greatest stir. First one person applauded, then another, and another, and another still, until everyone was on their feet and the room rang with applause. The old man was overcome, but only he understood why. He excused himself for a minute and went into the men's room.

He ran cold water into the sink basin, dipped his face into it, and when he stood up he saw his younger self looking back at him from the mirror. Isaac Becker—black holes where his eyes had been, blood pouring from his stigmata—was standing over his right shoulder.

"Yes, Becker," Jacob spoke into the mirror, nodding his head, "I know what must be done."

With that he reached into his pocket. When he was done drinking water out of his cupped hands, Jacob returned to the main room. There he took his seat in between the glove box and Leah. The bidding, which started at two million dollars, took much less time than he expected. When the price was at five million, Jeffrey Meyer, who ran several hedge funds and who personally owned large blocks of stock in many of the world's largest companies, went all in and indicated he was willing to go to twelve million. When the other bidders balked, the package went to him.

"Sold!" proclaimed the auctioneer, striking her gavel on the rostrum.

Jacob, on increasingly unsteady legs, stood for pictures next to Meyer and the glovebox and then sat down. The moment he had dreaded for over sixty years was here. An eerie hush fell over the crowded room as the preservationist stepped forward and slid her hands into the gloves. These gloves were rather more soft and supple than the type used to handle hazardous materials. With fine, delicate instruments already in the box, the preservationist carefully untied the knot in the long shred of pajamas used to bind the package together. Next she removed the rubber sheeting to expose the book that Isaac Becker thought so precious he had been willing to sacrifice himself. The crowd literally gasped. Through heavy-lidded eyes, Jacob Weisen recognized it immediately. A little frayed at the edges, a little worse for wear, perhaps, but the book indeed. That the book was in there was no surprise, of course. The package had been x-rayed and scanned in Germany long before things had come to this. The scans were so sensitive that they even detected fragments of Becker's writing, but nothing comprehensible.

Ever so carefully, the preservationist pulled back the cover and the linguists stepped forward as the faded writing on the first page was exposed. The writing was projected onto a large screen behind the rostrum and on TV monitors for the audience.

"Hungarian, definitely Hungarian," Jacob Weisen heard someone say as he began slipping away. His eyes fluttered as the vial of pills he'd swallowed in the men's room was now taking full hold of him. Death was no more than a few heartbeats away.

"What does it say?" a media type cried out.

"*The Ghost Book*," said the linguist.

Jacob Weisen shook his head at the irony of it all. So, it wasn't a book of poetry or of recipes or colorful Hungarian curse words. He not sure how to feel about the truth buried in his sixty plus years of lies. He wouldn't have time to figure it out. Jacob Weisen pitched forward, already dead. Some there claimed he was smiling.

V

The Final Testament

Peter Blauner

THE DOCTOR'S HANDS were trembling as he took the clutching end of the clothes-pin and put it in his mouth. On some days, there was no other way to negotiate past the pain that caused his jaws to lock up. Carefully, he pushed the head of the pin past his lips, up to his gums, and then tried to wedge it between his clenched teeth.

Fighting back tears, he began to bargain. A dull, persistent throb he could accept if he could stay off the morphine and maintain a clear mind. The occasional hot skewer up through the cheekbone could be borne, even as his eyes blurred with tears. What he quietly feared was overwhelming, incapacitating anguish that would render him finally useless and put the work of his life at a permanent end.

It was autumn of 1938 and the news on the radio was not good. The Germans had crossed the border into Austria in March, meeting no resistance. He had tried to tell himself that this could be lived with. But then had come the introduction of the racial laws and the decrees that all Jewish assets were assumed to be improperly acquired and therefore subject to confiscation without advance notice. When they burned his books in the street, he joked about the progress of civilization. "In the Middle Ages, they would have burned me."

But then Nazis had shown up at the offices of the publishing company he owned, aiming a gun at his son and confiscating the financial ledgers. Soon after, the Gestapo had come to his home in Vienna without an appointment, leaving Berggasse 19 with six thousand schillings in cash. After that, he had no choice but to call upon favors from foreign friends in high places so that he could find another country that would accept him and the rest of the family should they manage, by some miracle, to be able to flee Austria with a few remaining assets.

Now he was in London and Hitler's troops had overrun Poland. On the radio, the Fuhrer was demanding the Czechs leave the Sudetenland. Back in Austria, brownshirts were swinging clubs and breaking windows of stores owned by Jews. The doctor's relatives who could not get out were being threatened, robbed and beaten on the street almost every week. Such things could not be controlled or reliably contained anymore. At the same time, the cancer in his own body was spreading. He'd recently lost much of his upper palate and right cheek to radical maxiofacial surgery. To block off the space left open between his mouth and the nasal cavity, he'd been forced to wear a large dental prosthesis he called "the monster," which caused constant irritation and made it difficult for him to talk. His speech, never euphonious, had become labored, nasal, and unpleasant even to his own ears.

He refused to take anything stronger than aspirin for the pain. He was eighty-two years old. The manuscript for his last and most dangerous book—the contemplation of which terrified and excited him at times—sat two-thirds finished on his desk. He knew he would not be able to complete it with a fogged mind. Yet some distraction was required to endure the discomfort and continue his writing.

He took the clothes-pin out of his mouth and turned it around, using the thin slat of a pincer to pry open a larger space between the prosthesis and his lower jaw. Then he jammed a Reina Cubana cigar into the aperture, struck a match, lit it, and lay back on the couch where his patients like Dora and the Rat Man had disclosed their darkest and most troubling secrets.

It had been years since he smoked regularly—the disease had been ravaging him since the 1920s—and he knew his daughter Anna would be furious to find him with a cigar in hand. But what other pleasures were left to an old man in a strange country?

True, the Nazis had surprised him by unexpectedly releasing some of the furniture and books from his Vienna study after he paid the exorbitant taxes and duties demanded. He took a measure of solace as he looked around. The famous couch was against a wall, covered by velvet pillows and a Persian blanket with byzantine designs as rich and complex as the dreams of the patients who used to lie upon it. Just behind the head was the green tub-like chair where he would sit sideways, out of the patient's sight, taking notes. On the walls were some of the pictures from back home: the carved mountainside temple of Abu Simbel, the depiction of Oedipus interrogating the sphinx, the photographs of certain dear friends. The mantles, bookshelves, and even his desktop were engulfed by pieces from his massive collection of Egyptian antiquities—Osiris, Isis, and figurine of the warrior goddess—but a special place of honor was accorded to the small statue of the Greek goddess Athena, whose calm thoughtful expression reminded him of his beloved daughter Anna.

Even among these familiar possessions, he had spent too many hours lately depressed and lost to himself in this room. But now, as he took his first puff, he became the master of his mood once more, magisterial and wise, the heady aroma in his nostrils, and blue smoke going down into his lungs summoning memories of better days. Yes, sometimes, a cigar was not just a cigar.

"Father, what are you doing?" Anna was in the doorway.

"Let me be."

She came toward him, with her hand out. His beloved daughter. Gaunt, too wise for her own good, and still unmarried at forty-three. He worried for her, especially the degree of repression revealed by his own analysis of her. But she was his joy and hope for the future. The last and most capable of his six children. Her keen and incisive mind was the most like his own, and he strongly believed that one day she would become an estimable psychoanalyst in her own right. When it was time to flee Austria, she had handled the most troublesome details. More important, she was the only person he trusted to help him put the prosthesis into his aching mouth every day and to continue his life's work after he was gone.

"Where did you get that from anyway?" She reached for the cigar.

"That annoying Mr. Dali who came to visit the other day," the doctor confessed. "His paintings leave me cold. But the cigars he brought are superb so far."

"If you're smoking one of them now, you must be even more insane than he is. You're a doctor who doesn't listen to his own physician. Aren't you sick enough?"

"Yes, I'm sufficiently sick. But if you want me to live longer, let me finish this cigar."

"Don't be ridiculous." She plucked it from between his withered fingers. "They'll cut the rest of your jaw out if you keep doing this."

"Better to cut off the whole head and be done with it." He muttered between clenched teeth.

"Anyway, you have a visitor."

"Is there an appointment?"

With the dislocation and lack of sleep these days, his grasp of his schedule wasn't what it once was.

"No. And I'm not at all sure you should see him."

"Who is it?"

"Anton Sauerwald."

He'd been sitting in his desk chair with its stark totem-like back, with one leg slung over an arm. At once, he came to attention.

"Sauerwald from Vienna?"

"The same."

He watched her sweetly protuberant eyes and slightly lopsided mouth for a hint of a smile.

"He's downstairs right now."

The doctor stroked the white beard that had become more of a chore to trim lately. "What does he want?"

"He wouldn't tell me." Her words came out in an uncharacteristic rush. "He insisted he must speak to you in private. He says it's a matter of great concern. I'm surprised they even let him in the country."

"Some of the English still think appeasement is possible," the doctor muttered. "They don't know enough about aggressive urges."

"I've told him to leave already but he's very persistent. He politely requested that I at least tell you he was here and mentioned that you both knew Josef Herzig."

"Show him in," the doctor sighed, waving away the lingering dragons of smoke in the air.

"Are you sure?"

"Shall I ask twice?"

Anna looked in distaste at the smoldering cigar between her fingers and left the room. He listened to the strain of polite conversation in the foyer and the singing of birds in the garden. A heavy tread on the stairs caused a slight tightening of his stomach. He wished she hadn't taken the Cubana with her.

"Dr. Freud?"

The man before him was in his thirties, of medium build, with blond hair and blue-gray eyes. He wore a dark wool suit, narrow at the waist and broad in the shoulders, probably the handiwork of one of Vienna's finest tailors provided at a steep coerced discount. His nose was reddish and waxy-looking as if he'd scrubbed at it too vigorously. Under his arm, he carried a brown leather attaché case, bulging at the seams.

"Pardon me if I don't get up," the doctor said through gritted teeth, and passed a hand to indicate the length of his slowly atrophying body.

"I understand." Sauerwald nodded curtly. "May I take a seat?"

Freud nodded toward a plain wooden chair near the bookcase. Instead Sauerwald took the doctor's own plush green chair behind the head of the couch.

"Do you know who I am?" Sauerwald asked, turning the chair so he could look straight at Freud.

"I have heard your name."

"I'm sure you have." Sauerwald put the leather case flat on his lap. "Years ago, I was a student of Dr. Herzig's at the University of Vienna."

"Herzig was a good man and a fair card player," Freud said, parceling out his words judiciously. "You are a chemist then."

"Yes, I had my own laboratory in Vienna before I was hired by the government."

"Ah . . ."

"Of course, this was a few years ago, when one had to wear one's Fatherland Front pin on the outside of the lapel and the swastika on the inside. The National Socialists were considered to be a terrorist group then, setting off bombs all over Vienna. My job was to work with the police, analyzing the contents of the material that was used in these explosions. Which I did very well, you see. Because thanks to our friend Dr. Herzig, I have learned to cultivate the virtues of patience, observation, and careful planning."

Freud put a hand over his mouth, revealing nothing by his expression. Never betraying that he'd had heard stories before he'd left Vienna. That, in fact, the reason Sauerwald was so efficient at dismantling these devices and determining the content of explosives was that he'd created them himself in his own laboratory the day before. Patience, observation, and careful planning.

"But you did not come here to talk about ordnance," Freud said matter of factly.

"No, *herr professor*, you are right." Sauerwald patted the case on his lap. "We have even more urgent matters to discuss. I know you have heard my name more recently because I am a member of the National Socialist Party now. I am one of those given the task of liquidating illegal Jewish assets and turning the profits over to the Reich. And I have been assigned to take a special interest in you and members of your family."

"I see."

"As I'm sure you remember, Dr. Freud, members of the party came to your publishing office and your home in Vienna to conduct a thorough investigation and confiscate the relevant records."

State-sanctioned thuggery. The doctor grimaced as the prosthesis dug into his badly-damaged soft palate, under pressure from the tongue he was trying to restrain. Not only had Nazi criminals come to the publishing office and stuck a gun in his son Martin's stomach while rifling the safe and stealing every coin they could find. Then they had come to his house down the street and taken six thousand Austrian schillings as their due. But worst of all, the Gestapo had detained his precious Anna for questioning, leaving her father pacing the floor, smoking cigar after cigar, unable to speak or eat, as he fretted that she'd been taken to the camp in Dachau that people were starting to talk about. When she was finally returned to him, exhausted but intact, he'd wept and sworn he would use whatever strength he'd left in his cancer-ravaged body to get them out of Austria.

"What you may not know," Sauerwald said, "is that I personally went to your publishing office after these oafs trampled though, and I looked for all things they might have missed."

"As I recall, there wasn't much left." Freud fidgeted in the swivel chair before his office desk.

"To the contrary, these idiots were so busy stuffing their pockets with money that they missed what was most valuable on the premises. Your books and papers."

Freud said nothing, adjusting his spectacles and staring intently.

"I must confess that even though I'd heard Professor Herzig speak highly of you, I had never actually read your work before." Sauerwald rubbed the palms of his well-manicured hands over the surface of the attaché case, warming to his subject now. "As I said, most of my training has been in the field of chemistry, so this business of suppressed desire and hidden aggression had not much interested me before. But as I read through your papers, I found a world that I had not known about before. You are the great discoverer of people's secrets, *herr professor*. Aren't you?"

"Some people have said that." Freud shrugged. "But I find it a crude and reductive description of psychoanalysis."

"Do you?" Sauerwald thrust his lower lip in a mock-pout. "Well, I believe I have discovered some of your secrets, Dr. Freud."

Freud took a small sharp breath and cold stinging air passed through a small gap in the roof of his mouth.

"I'm not sure I understand," he said.

Sauerwald pulled several pieces of paper out of the leather case on his lap.

"These are letters of correspondence to banks in Zurich, Paris, and London. You have been sending money overseas for years. This is entirely illegal."

The doctor said nothing.

"You could have been detained from leaving Austria and your whole family could have been imprisoned," Sauerwald said, his voice rising in stentorian admonition. "It was a clear act of disloyalty that could have been punished."

The doctor tried to use the tip of his tongue to shift the prosthesis to a more comfortable position as the cords of his throat tensed.

"You should have been prosecuted to the full extent of the law." Small white flecks of spittle flew from Sauerwald's lips. "You profited from the neuroses of the bourgeois class when our nation was starving. You violated racial laws restricting Jewish parasitism. You committed acts of treason by diverting this money from the national treasury."

As he spoke, Sauerwald slapped the top of the attaché case, which continued to bulge as if a heavy item was still inside. His complexion became rough and spongy, and his voice began to crack.

"Your age and fame are no excuses," he continued. "You should be dangling from the end of a hangman's rope with your family beside you, instead of living out your days in comfort with your beloved statues and pictures around you, and your daughter brewing tea for you in the kitchen. I could have stopped you from leaving at any time and made sure your life ended in agony without adequate medical care. And my superiors in the party would have thanked me by advancing my career."

"But you did not," Freud observed quietly.

"No. I did not."

Sauerwald exhaled and relaxed his hands, allowing the normal color to return to his face.

"I was given back my passport and allowed to board the Orient Express with my family," the doctor noted, taking care to articulate each word despite the prosthesis. "I am in another country, safe from 'the hangman's rope,' as you call it. My wife is with me, my children are secure. But you continue to speak as if I had reason to fear you. Why?"

"Dr. Freud, you still have four sisters living in Austria," Sauerwald replied. "Don't you?"

"Yes."

"For the moment, they are safe and free. But I promise you, under the Reich, that will not last."

The doctor looked away, his eyes gliding past all his other rescued antiquities as he thought of his spinster sister Dolfi. An old maid who had devoted her life to caring for their mother. Freud's jaw ached and dampness spotted the corner of his right eye as he sniffed deeply.

"So what is it exactly that you came here to discuss?" he asked.

"I wish to talk to you about books, Dr. Freud." Sauerwald crossed his ankles, settling in more comfortably.

"*Books?*"

"Yes, the books that you are writing and the books that you will publish. Of course, you are much more experienced than I am in this realm, Dr. Freud. So I believe we can help each other."

"How can that be?"

"If I may?" The corners of Sauerwald's eyes crinkled as he put down the leather case and stood up. "I've been looking at a pile of papers sitting on your desk as we've been speaking. They appear thick enough to be the body of a manuscript."

Freud did not turn. He knew exactly what page was on top.

"Would I be right in assuming that this is the doctor's latest book?" Sauerwald asked, starting to cross the room.

"It might be," Freud grunted.

"Then this would be the long-awaited Moses book, wouldn't it?"

Sauerwald was standing less than a foot from him now, hovering vampirishly over Freud's desk, staring at the pages written in longhand through hours of excruciating pain.

"It might be," Freud said, refusing to meet Sauerwald's eye or acknowledge that this guest in his house had transgressed by coming into such close physical proximity with his private work area.

"You've been working on this for some time, haven't you?" Sauerwald let his fingertips lightly brush the curled corner of a page. "I read the excerpts in *Imago*."

Freud looked askance. "I am surprised that high-ranking members of the Nazi party subscribe to obscure journals for psychoanalysts."

"You're forgetting that I am a doctor and scientist myself, herr Freud." Sauerwald pursed his lips as if insulted. "And I am not quite a high-ranking member of the party. At least not yet. But as I said, I have taken a keen interest in your work since going through your papers."

"I should be flattered, then," Freud said drily, still refusing to look at him, even as the flowery smell of Sauerwald's cologne made him cringe inwardly and caused his eyes to water.

There was a soft ripple of paper as Freud realized that the guest was now turning pages.

"You are a very brave man, Dr. Freud. You've said many things other people were afraid to say in the course of your work."

"Some of my critics think that they should never have been said."

"Yes, of course." Freud turned his head just enough to see the visitor nodding and turning pages more quickly. "The ego and the unconscious. The unhealthy repression of sexual urges. The fixations with anal and oral functions. The death drive. Few people would have dared to think of such things, let alone commit them to paper."

"Perhaps so."

A thatch of blond hair fell over Sauerwald's ruddy brow, and he swiped it away in a state of growing excitement.

"But up until now, you have never been afraid to publish any of it. I've read *Totem and Taboo*, *The Interpretation of Dreams*, *Future of an Illusion*, and *Essays on the Theory of Sexuality* . . ."

"I hope you paid for all of them, instead of borrowing library copies," Freud interrupted.

Sauerwald gave a hoarse barking laugh. "Yes, I've also read *The Joke and Its Relation to the Unconscious*. Amazing. Fantastic stuff. Only you would have been daring enough to write it."

"Or be foolish enough to write it," Freud said, aware of a stiffening throughout his body.

"But you have not published this Moses book yet."

"It's not finished."

"No?"

He turned and saw his guest pick up the pages, weigh them in his hand, and return to the chair behind the head of the couch. Then Sauerwald donned a pair of glasses, crossed his long legs, and began to read more closely.

"Are you are forgetting that I've been in your office and seen your notes?" Sauerwald asked evenly, pushing the center-piece up his nose. "You see, I know you have been working on this Moses book for years. This is actually much of the same material I saw back in Vienna. The book was finished long ago. But you have not published it. What is the reason?"

"I think the only one who can say when a book is truly done is the author."

"You are lying and we both know it." Sauerwald gave him a glacial stare. "You have not published this book because you're afraid to do so in this lifetime."

"I've heard the Nazis were working on a number of scientific breakthroughs," Freud broke in. "I didn't realize mind-reading was one of them. Perhaps you'll render psychoanalysis obsolete without having to kill me personally."

"I don't blame you for being frightened of your own book." Sauerwald ignored him and held up a page. "Your thesis is a highly disturbing one. If you had simply stated your theory that Moses was not a Jew, but an Egyptian, that would be enough to cause an uproar."

"What do you want, Mr. Sauerwald?"

"*Doctor* Sauerwald. I studied medicine and law at the university, so I am due that respect as much as you are. And may I remind you, Dr. Freud, we were speaking of your sisters before."

Freud cupped a hand over the lower half of his face, his jaw almost exploding with pain as he clenched it. "Yes," he said, between his teeth. "I have not forgotten."

Sauerwald took another page from the top of the manuscript and put in on the bottom. "It's a blasphemous notion, but you don't stop there," he said blandly. "You assert that if Moses existed, then he was almost surely a follower of the pharaoh Akhenaten."

"Correct." Freud nodded calmly as the image of Munch's screamer flashed in his head.

"And this pharaoh was the first monotheist, the individual who insisted on destroying images of all the other great Egyptian gods in favor of worshipping just the one sun god."

"I am not the first to suggest something like that. Greater scholars have put forth similar theories."

"But you go much further than anyone before you." Sauerwald reached for the figurine of Neith on a nearby shelf, but then thought better of it. "You say that after Akhenaten died and Egypt went back to its many old gods, this Moses, the gentile, *this fanatic*, sets out into the desert with a ragtag group of Hebrew followers, where he convinces them to join up with the wandering cult of a violent volcano god to form a new heretic religion."

Freud steepled his fingers, choosing his words as carefully as a sculptor choosing his stone. "Yes, I believe it's possible that is what happened, but I never claimed to be an historian or an archeologist. I'm just an old man speculating."

"Of course, doctor, that is what you do in analyzing the human mind. You speculate. You conjecture. You make an educated guess. And as your fame and status suggest, you have very often been right."

" 'Often' is not the same as *always*," Freud demurred. "I have been spectacularly wrong more than once."

"Don't be modest." Sauerwald took several more pages from the top of the manuscript and placed them on an old mahogany side-table. "We're coming to the best part. The murder mystery."

Freud tried to shift the pressure from the right side of his jaw to the left, lest the remains of his fragile face collapse from the way he was grinding his teeth.

"Are you under the impression you were reading Sherlock Holmes?"

"Not at all. I know I am reading a book by Sigmund Freud. Because no one else could have written it. In the midst of this scholarly work, you have posited something even more astonishing. You accuse your own people of one of the greatest crimes in all of history. "

Freud tried to swallow, but his salivary glands would not cooperate. "You misunderstand my work."

"I don't think I do, *herr professor*." Sauerwald tapped the pages with a shiny fingernail. "You say the Jews killed their own prophet and then covered up the crime. You state this with absolute clarity and boldness in your writing. You say the strictures of this severe new religion were too much for these wandering Hebrews. And so they rebelled and murdered their leader. And then buried him somewhere in the sands of the Sinai desert, where his bones would never be found. And that generations later, the unexpiated guilt of this sin rose up in their souls and led them to proclaim Moses's one god as their own and conveniently forget the fact that they had murdered Moses for saying the exact same things many years before. It's brilliant and original. Only you could have written it, Dr. Freud. And I can see why you've been so afraid to publish it."

Freud winced and sniffed. Hating the fact that this swine was half-right. Just the other day, his neighbor, the great Jewish Bible scholar Abraham Shalom Yehuda had stopped by and, just on the basis of the relatively tame *Imago* excerpts, pleaded with Freud not to publish this scandalous Moses book. His voice had joined with the letters the doctor had received from Jews in America, who had heard rumors of the text and begged him to suppress it. Especially now, when the world was on the brink of war, and recent events in Germany suggested that their tribe in Europe would soon be threatened with annihilation.

"*Sauerwald* . . ."

The name sounded like a curse, a damp and swampy thing laden with foul-smelling funguses.

"I find it hard to believe that you traveled all the way from Vienna to London in order to speak to me about a book that has not yet gone to press."

"*Yet?* " The visitor's nostrils flared. "Is this deliberate or one of the famous slips you accuse others of making?"

"I *do* intend to publish this book." Freud jabbed an unsteady finger into the air. "I've spent my life saying things that most people in polite society think should never be said. Why would I stop now?"

Sauerwald stooped his shoulders and offered his palms. "Because some people think you would be giving support to enemies of your race?"

Freud cleared his phlegm-ravaged throat and glared. "You are mistaken. The point of my book is not to discredit the religion of my people. It is to consider the distinctive characteristics of the Jewish people and to try to understand how they might have evolved over time."

"But you must recognize that some people would use your book as justification for staying out of a war to save Jews," Sauerwald said, goading him shamelessly.

"You give me far too much credit for being influential." Freud shook his head, refusing the bait. "I very much doubt this slender volume you're holding would change anyone's mind about anything."

"An author is often the worst judge of how a book will be received." Sauerwald chuckled and rocked back so that his feet left the floor. "I applaud your decision to go ahead, nevertheless. Is there a publication date?"

"It needs to be translated and copy-edited in several languages. My American publisher expects to have it out by spring next year."

"*Wunderbar.* " Sauerwald's smile faded as quickly as a flashbulb dimming. "Excuse me, Dr. Freud. But I would like now to ask an impertinent question."

"*Now* you are worried about manners?"

"It's no secret that your health has deteriorated greatly in the last few months, and that you have been suffering greatly." The visitor thinned his liver-colored lips. "Do you expect to be alive by the time your book comes out?"

Several seconds of silence passed. Birds began to sing, trying to fill the empty space, and then stopped. A toilet flushed somewhere in the house. A baby cried out on the street.

His life's work had been the study of raw emotion. He had made a habit of measuring and analyzing his own responses with as much detachment as possible. But, for an instant, he became a child of the Vienna streets, broiling with scarlet rage as his meek father had a beautiful new fur hat knocked from his head by a Jew-hating brute and failed to retaliate with appropriately unrestrained violence.

"That is an ugly and inhuman thing to say," he said quietly. "If not for my sisters, I would demand that you leave my home now"

"But you know you will not."

"What is it you want then? For God's sake, *out with it already*."

Sauerwald sat back and laced his hands behind his head, tauntingly. "I would like you to help me become an author."

"Are you serious?"

"I have never been more serious." The visitor undid the snaps of his attaché case and took out a slender volume with a brown leather cover and gold lettering on the spine. "I took this manuscript to one of the finest bookbinders in Vienna and paid for the work out of my own pocket."

And probably took your money back after you had him arrested, Freud thought grimly.

Sauerwald smiled, the skin as tight as a sausage casing over his features, then put the attaché case aside and stood up. He crossed the room with a brisk ebullient stride and handed the book to Freud.

The doctor took it and placed it on his lap, closing his eyes for a moment to collect himself. "This is a book you wrote?"

"In a manner of speaking." Sauerwald nodded.

"Are you asking me to read it and offer a critique?"

"Both more than that and less than that."

"I don't understand." Freud blinked.

"Open the cover."

With stiff gnarled fingers, Freud did as he was asked and his eye glanced over a title rendered in fourteen point Garamond type: *The Theft of the Birthright*. But then his eye found the author's byline and his heart stopped for a good half-second.

"What do you mean by this?" He looked up, translucent whorls and eddies floating before his eyes.

"You should be even more flattered."

"I should be flattered that my name is on a book that I did not write?"

"Most writers would be delighted to have someone else produce their work for them." Sauerwald waggled his eyebrows roguishly. "I would expect you to say thanks."

Freud's hands shook as he began to turn the onion-skin pages quickly, looking for thoughts and words that he might recognize as his own. Like most writers, he was the most fervid admirer and the fiercest critic of his own prose, and was always pleased when he detected his own influence on the work of others. But here was a book that claimed to have him as an author, and its style was appalling. Barbaric phrases and sentiments abounded from every paragraph. "*These so-called holier-than-holy chosen people . . . A pattern of mendacious deceptive audacity repeated audaciously throughout the tortured course of history . . . The most monstrous of all lies told with the cleverness of ants . . . the sanctimonious legitimacy of parasitic larceny . . .*"

"This is work that you're trying to pass off as mine?" Freud closed the cover and set the book down on the edge of his desk, a wave of dizziness and nausea causing him to pitch forward a little in his creaking chair. "Why would you do such a thing?"

Sauerwald had returned to the green seat behind the head of the couch. "I'm merely taking up what you suggested in your Moses book and bringing it to its logical conclusion. I'm saying what even you, *herr professor*, lacked the nerve to say."

"Which is what?"

"That this entire religion, this entire race, this entire *culture*— as some people insist on calling it—is based on an even greater lie than the murder of a prophet and its concealment. It begins with an astonishing act of fraud and bad faith, and only gets worse from there."

Freud's fingers grappled among themselves, trying to select a single digit to grip as a cigar substitute. "Explain yourself."

"It would be far better if you would take the time to read it. I'm quite proud of it."

"Spare me the effort. As you say, I'm an old man. And I'm sure you can summarize the contents."

Sauerwald sighed, a look of unmistakable disappointment tilting down the corners of his mouth. "Well, if you insist . . ." He huffed. "I tried to the best of my abilities to emulate your style and mimic your methodology. Like yourself, I take the Bible as my source material, then I put it on the couch like a patient and dissect it without fear or favor."

"I do not *dissect* patients." Freud moved his tongue around inside his mouth, trying to rid himself of the taste of decay. "I analyze them."

"A fine distinction, but not important here." Sauerwald smirked. "I began with an origin myth that takes place long before this Moses legend. You are familiar, of course, with the story of Abraham in the Book of Genesis?"

"I suppose this will concern the attempted sacrifice of the son Isaac." Freud shifted restlessly. "I've already written about some of these themes in *Civilization and Its Discontents* . . ."

"Please don't try to anticipate. I really do wish you would approach this book with an open mind. We begin before that primal scene you describe. When Abram—as he was called then—leaves the land of Ur with his barren and disagreeable wife Sarah and sets out for Canaan. Somehow they wind up in Egypt, where in a burst of shameful cowardice Abram lies to the pharaoh and says that Sarah is his sister because he fears he will be killed otherwise. Instead the pharaoh discovers the truth and treats both of them honorably."

"A curious section, but I wouldn't make too much of it." Freud shrugged.

"Except that it sets a pattern that continues and escalates. A few chapters later, after God has promised Abram that he will make a great nation of his descendants and award them the land from the

Nile to the Euphrates, he has a son. Only it's not born from Sarah, who is still barren. But from an Egyptian handmaiden named Hagar who gives birth to Ishmael, a strong capable boy and a worthy heir."

"Yes, I'm familiar with this narrative." Freud rolled his hand with barely constrained disgust. "Get to your point."

"By all lights, this first-born should be a true descendant in the line of prophets," Sauerwald said, enjoying—*no! luxuriating*—in the sound of his voice. "Instead, the authors trump up this preposterous tale about the child's mother ridiculing Sarah as an excuse to cast mother and child out into the desert. Somehow they survive and become acknowledged as the progenitors of the great Arab tribes. Meanwhile, Sarah finally manages to have a child of her own, this Isaac, who somehow supplants his half-brother in the line of succession—"

"Everyone knows this, Sauerwald. There's no need to rub my face in it . . ."

"Please, *herr professor*, you're interrupting yourself." Sauerwald sat back and placed his hands on his stomach. "In this next section of your book, which is handled with great élan if I don't say so myself, you demonstrate that this proclivity for dishonesty and larceny continues down through the bloodlines. Isaac has two sons. Esau, who is strong and hairy, and Jacob, who is weak and shiftless. By law, Esau, the first-born, should inherit all his father's land. Instead, Jacob conspires to trick his brother out of his birthright. Jacob goes to Esau when he knows his older brother is exhausted and hungry from working the fields and then fools his sibling into trading away his rightful due for a bowl of porridge. He compounds this injustice later, by going to his blind father on his deathbed and disguising himself with furry gloves to simulate Esau's hairy hands so he can cheat his brother out of a father's final blessing. Then down through the ages, the tribes of Esau become the people of Edom, who become part of the Arab race and . . ."

"Oh, for God's sake." Freud pounded the arms of his chair, losing patience. "What is your point?"

"To show the true nature of things. To undermine this patently false Zionist narrative and reveal its true psychological underpinnings. In your terms, the Jews try to conceal the guilt for their own historic crimes, but they give clues in spite of themselves."

Freud's entire body had started to shake, but he tried to keep his voice steady. "In other words, you hope to give support to anti-Semites all over the world, and discourage the allies from getting involved in the war."

"Really, I implore you to read your own tome." Sauerwald pointed to the book on Freud's lap. "It's quite scintillating, if I may say so. You make a very cogent argument and support it with voluminous scholarship. I spent more than twelve months doing the research and marshaling my sources. I've spoken to some of the most important archeologists and theologians in all of Austria and Germany. I've studied ancient texts and compared translations . . ."

"I'm sure you made half of them up yourself," Freud said.

"If I did, I wouldn't be the first," Sauerwald riposted. "And do you honestly believe most readers bother with footnotes?

"You actually believe that I would publish such a book under my own name?" Freud said fiercely, creating an unexpected shock of pain by the sudden movement of his jaw.

"I'm sure you would not find it difficult to place it. Your authority goes far beyond the field of psychiatry now. I read in the newspaper that you were recently given the honor of signing the charter book for the Royal Society of England—your name inscribed beneath Newton's and Darwin's . . ."

Freud winced, the memory of the Society's secretaries coming to his house to present the ledger personally souring and turning gray behind his eyes.

"Why would anyone take this seriously coming from me?" he argued. "I am not a historian or a Bible scholar."

"No, but you are truly one of the most respected eminences on the continent," Sauerwald spoke over him. "In the world, in fact.

Anything you write would command attention from an international audience and have instantly credibility."

"*Sauerwald*." Freud mustered the strength to slam a gavel-like fist on his desk. "The world is on the brink of war. Jews like myself are being robbed, persecuted, and even murdered under the color of law on the streets and in the houses of every country where your party holds sway. Do you honestly think I would aid in hurting the cause of my own people?"

"I believe you would do what you needed to do to protect your sisters."

"And so that is the choice you give me? Save my sisters or put my name on a book intended to defame and harm the race that I belong to?"

"It would appear so." A tiny smile tugged at the corner of Sauerwald's mouth and as his hands rested on his belly, two fingers flexed with a hint of playfulness. "If you insist on putting it that way"

Freud sank down in his seat, seething at his own helplessness. At the betrayal of his body. At the betrayal of his countrymen back home. At the betrayal of the European allies. At the betrayal of humanity at large for allowing people like Sauerwald to spread such lies in the service of further German atrocities. He began to breathe more heavily, as if he was starting to suffocate under the accumulating weight of history. This would not do. His chin began to wag from side-to-side, an involuntary old man tremor turning into a deliberate headshake.

Almost without conscious decision, he took the book off his lap and set it aside on his desk. Then he picked up his fountain pen, the implement of his trade, which he'd used to take notes on his famous patients. He brandished it, like a cowboy in one of the American movies he so deplored, strapping on his gun one last time, and reached for a notepad. Then he narrowed his eyes and tried to imagine Sauerwald stretched on the couch, instead of sitting in his green chair.

"Sauerwald, tell me something," he said. "What is your purpose in writing this book?"

"Dr. Freud, I think I've been very clear about my motives."

"Have you?" Freud touched his pen to the corner of a blank notebook page. "To write a book of any kind is a serious undertaking, requiring a great commitment of time and effort. I'm interested why you chose to write about these particular themes in a book that you've put my name on. The betrayal of Ishmael, the theft of Esau's birthright . . ."

"Very clever." Sauerwald interrupted. "Perhaps you are onto something."

"How so?"

"You mentioned that this book could be construed as helping our war effort." Sauerwald's Adam's apple bobbed behind the tight red knot of his necktie. "But it could be said that it was written with an eye toward the future as well. And I believe the future belongs to the Arabs."

"The *Arabs?*"

"Of course." Sauerwald offered his palms like a waiter showing an expensive wine list. "Everyone else will be focused on the war here in Europe for the next few years. Eventually, though, the conflict will move to the Allies' colonial holdings in North Africa, where the Arab population is substantial. And where there is oil. And whoever controls the oil to feed the tanks and airplanes will win the war."

"Excuse me, Sauerwald." Freud picked the book off his desk again, where it had been sitting among his collection of totems and figurines. "But how would a fraudulent volume about ancient prophets possibly be of any benefit to twentieth-century Germans in the Middle East?"

"The leaders of these Arab countries will appreciate the attack on their blood enemies, the Jews, and support us in gratitude."

Freud nodded twice, and then bowed his old bald head, as if he was resigned to the logic. The rumors about Sauerwald were undoubtedly true, he now realized. This was a man who could design bombs for the Nazis and then take credit for defusing them for the police the next day.

"But there is one obvious flaw in all this, isn't there?" Freud said. "How will this supposed Arab appreciation for an attack on the Jews redound to you and the Germans if the name on the title page belongs to an old Jewish doctor?"

Sauerwald crossed his arms in front of his chest and raised his chin proudly. "Dr. Freud, if you would only take the time to open this book and read it more closely, you would see there is an acknowledgments page. You give effusive thanks to your invaluable colleague and successor, Dr. Anton Sauerwald, without whom this final testament would not have been written. Through diplomatic channels, the Arabs will be made aware of the true authorship and then they will show their gratitude appropriately."

Freud stared at his visitor for a long time without speaking. The quality of light changed in the room as the sun shifted. A clock chimed on the parlor floor. He heard the fluff of bedsheets as his wife changed the linens across the hall, and the tread of Anna's feet as she came up the stairs. A few stray pellets of water hit the windows behind him, and then began to land sequentially on the grass and peonies below, an English rain turning torrential on the garden.

"Sauerwald," he said. "I believe you misunderstand yourself even more severely than you misunderstand my Moses book."

"What do you mean?" Sauerwald's narrow shoulders went back into the upholstery of Freud's green chair.

"You say you have read my writing extensively. So did it never occur to you as you were creating this forgery that you were fixating on stories like Abraham's denial of Ishmael and Isaac's mistaking Jacob for Esau?"

"These are the stories in the Bible, Dr. Freud. I didn't create them."

"But you *chose* to focus on them. Narratives about fathers and sons." Freud made another note on his pad, to deliberately draw the guest's attention. "Does that not strike you as curious?"

"What are you driving at, *herr professor?*"

"You did not write this book for the Fatherland." Freud reached over and tapped the leather cover with his crooked aged finger. "You did not write it for the Arabs either. In fact, you did not write it for the war effort at all."

"Then why do *you* think I wrote it, Dr. Freud?" Sauerwald tried to affect a grin as his arms stayed wrapped tight around his chest.

"Isn't it obvious?" Freud shrugged. "You mentioned my great friend Dr. Josef Herzig from Vienna. You call yourself my successor. Is it that hard to imagine you see us both as father figures?"

Sauerwald shook his head. "I already had a father, *herr professor.* This is absurdly reductive."

"It's not surprising you would say that." Freud turned another page in his notebook and continued to scribble. "Most people are unaware of their own true motives. You are just an extreme example. It's plain that you come here seeking approval and absolution from me . . ."

"*Herr professor*, this is nonsense." Sauerwald raised his voice, as his pant cuffs hiked up showing pale shins and black garters holding up his socks. "You cannot psychoanalyze me like one of your neurotic patients. I have the advantage here. I hold the cards, as you might have told Dr. Herzig. Your sisters' fate is in my hands."

"Is it really?" Freud lifted the tip of his pen from the page and held it up for effect. "Didn't you tell me earlier in this conversation that you are not a high-ranking member of the Nazi party?"

"Yes, I said that, but I was being modest." Sauerwald looked down and uncrossed his ankles. "Everyone knows I am in good favor with our leaders and my star is shining brightly in Berlin."

"Then why are you in London, trying to blackmail an old man with cancer?"

Freud picked up the book that Sauerwald had brought and tossed it down onto the carpet between them. It landed on its side with a muffled thud and splayed open, with a couple of its pages spilling out. So much for Vienna's finest bookbinder.

"Dr. Freud, that was a mistake." Sauerwald's face began to turn bright red.

"Spare me, please." Freud shook his head. "Your promise to protect my sisters is meaningless. Even if you were sincere, you do not have the power to do anything for them."

"You don't know that." Sauerwald puffed up in the seat.

"Herr Sauerwald, I will die very soon," Freud slowly lifted his eyes from the book on the floor. "You will die sometime after that. Probably not in as much pain, which is as good a proof as any that there is not a just and fair God. And long after we are both gone, there will still be good and bad men. And good and bad books. There will be people with characteristics of the Jews and those who hate them. What we do and say here today won't matter. So throw your stupid book away when you leave here. Don't disturb the forests any further by causing trees to be cut down for the paper to print such nonsense. Submit to the dust."

Sauerwald stood up abruptly and snatched the book off the floor. He closed it carefully, wiped the cover with his palm and then hugged it tightly to his chest.

"You should not say such things, *herr professor.*"

"Why? Do you still insist I should fear you?" Freud closed his notebook and put down his pen. "I'm an old man at the end of his life. My immediate family is safe here in England with me. And my sisters are beyond your control. So why exactly should I not say such things?"

"Because they are not the truth." Sauerwald's voice cracked like an adolescent's before he caught himself. "I mean to say, they are not the whole truth. Yes, it's a fact; I cannot save your sisters. But I did save you."

"Excuse me?"

"I speak honestly now." Sauerwald's eyes had begun to brim. "You cannot dismiss me so easily. Without my help, you and your family never would have gotten out of Vienna alive. I made it possible to get back your passports. I could have had you all arrested for stashing money in foreign banks and sent to the work camps, where you would have surely died horrible deaths. You would not have had the chance to finish your Moses book. I could have wiped you all out and—yes—advanced my career to the very top of the hierarchy with just one phone call."

"Maybe so . . ."

"And my good deeds continued even after you were gone." Sauerwald pointed to objects around the room, his voice rising close to a hoarse shout. "All these beloved possessions that comfort you in this terrible time? I was the one who arranged to have them sent to you. Your books. Your rugs. The rare antiquities you have arranged just so. Your photographs and paintings. The chair you're sitting in. I could have withheld them from you. Just as I could have withheld the passports for your most precious possessions, your children, your legacy . . ."

In his high dudgeon, Sauerwald failed to notice that Anna was standing in the doorway, alarmed. Freud looked at her sternly, forbidding her to enter or interrupt.

"I could have denied you all of that." Sauerwald shook a fist. "I could have made your final days a misery, to my own lasting benefit. But I did not."

"And why didn't you?" Freud looked up at him with quiet owlish curiosity.

Sauerwald's fist fell to his side. "I'm not entirely sure," he said haltingly. "I've asked myself the same question several times." He gathered himself up and took a deep breath, as if to deliver a speech he'd practiced to himself. "The Fuhrer, who of course knows best, realizes that the Fatherland is in a state of siege. The Jews, due to their internationalist leanings and their tendency toward individualistic behavior, cannot form a reliable part of the population. Thus they have to be eliminated. This might be deplored, but the end justifies the means. This does not mean, however, that an individual should not be permitted to alleviate individual hardship in selected cases."

"Perhaps that's true." Freud opened a desk drawer. "Some aspects of human behavior cannot be explained by any theory. They are mysteries that cannot be solved. And sometimes, a cigar is just a cigar."

He took out a new Cubana Reina and stuck it in the corner of his mouth, defying Anna to stop him.

"And in that case, there is nothing more for us to say to each other. Goodbye, Sauerwald."

"Goodbye." Sauerwald turned to leave, his shoulders sagging as he saw Freud's daughter had witnessed the end of the exchange.

"And Sauerwald, one more thing."

"What, *herr professor?* "

Freud gestured with his unlit cigar at the loose pages on the floor. "Don't forget to take the rest of your book with you."

Background note: Anton Sauerwald was a true historical figure. He was a former student of Freud's good friend Dr. Josef Herzig, who was later assigned by the Nazi party to oversee the confiscation of assets from the Freud family's publishing venture. Sauerwald did, in fact, discover that Freud was circumventing the law under occupation by transferring those assets to foreign banks. However, despite, his own good standing as a member of the Nazi party, he did not alert his superiors. Instead, he made it possible for Freud to escape with family members to England, where Freud died on September 23, 1939.

Sauerwald went on to serve as a technical expert in the Luftwaffe as part of the Nazi war effort. He was arrested by the Allies and sent to an American prisoner of war camp, then released in June, 1945. He was re-arrested several months later at the insistence of Harry

Freud, a nephew of the famous doctor, then serving as an officer in the American army. Sauerwald was accused of abusing his position as a trustee to rob the Freud family of valuable assets, including cash, manuscripts, artwork and books. His trial lasted eighteen months, with Sauerwald held in detention throughout. He was released when Sigmund Freud's daughter Anna wrote a letter to the court, declaring that the Nazi officer had helped her family. Sauerwald later moved to the Tyrol and died in Innsbruck in 1970.

VI

What's in a Name?

Thomas H. Cook

ALTMAN HAD NEVER seen New York dressed so gaily. Bunting hung from every window, and Broadway was decked out in various elaborations of red, white and blue. There'd been an enormous parade earlier in the day, and it had left a festive atmosphere in its wake, people laughing and talking and in a thousand different ways expressing the joy they felt at what this day—November 11, 1968, the 50th Anniversary of Armistice Day—had commemorated.

Altman, himself, could hardly believe the day had actually come. Fifty years since the Great War had ended, and the unlikely predictions of a few cock-eyed optimists had proven true. It really had been "the war to end all wars."

As he walked toward the little bookstore where he was to give his talk, it struck him that he'd never have thought it possible that the world would remain at peace for five decades after that odious treaty his native Germany had been forced to sign in that humiliating little railway car near Compiegne on what had been fatefully recorded as "the eleventh hour of the eleventh day of the eleventh month" of 1918.

At the time, Altman could not have imagined that this treaty, with its many dreadful provisions, would actually put an end to war in Europe. Nor had he been alone in his doubts. The great economist, John Maynard Keynes, no less, had predicted that a second world war would inevitably result from this sorry peace, one that had saddled Germany with an impossible burden of reparations. In fact, it had been the resulting inflation, with its consequent social chaos, that had urged Altman to leave Germany and come to America, abandon impoverished, defeated Berlin for bountiful, victorious New York. To leave that world behind had been his goal in coming to America, and now, on this splendid anniversary of fifty years of world peace, he felt certain that he'd truly escaped it.

For that reason, it was with complete confidence that his life had been the result of his own wise decisions that Altman entered the bookstore where he was to speak, and after a few pleasantries to the audience, began his talk.

He'd finished it only a few minutes later, exactly as planned, and just in time to conclude with his customary summation.

"Therefore, despite the magisterial splendor of the language Thomas Carlyle employed in his great book, *The Hero in History*," Altman said, "his theory that the course of history can be changed by a single human being simply isn't true." He felt quite satisfied with the thoroughly convincing argument he'd made against Carlyle. Not bad, he thought, for a man who was simply a rare book dealer who specialized in books and manuscripts in his native tongue, particularly those written just after the Great War, when Germany had seemed on the brink of economic and social collapse, a dangerously spinning maelstrom from which anything might have emerged.

Even better, the attendance was greater than he'd expected given the 50th Anniversary Armistice Day parties that were no doubt planned for this particular evening. In light of those festivities, Altman had hardly expected anyone to show up for his talk, despite the fact that the History Bookstore catered to a well-educated audience.

"Roman history would have followed the same course without Caesar," Altman added now, "and France would have followed the same course without Napoleon."

He thought of his vast collection of books and manuscripts, a bibliophile's dream, shelves and shelves of works from the most famous to the most obscure writers. How thoroughly he'd searched through them, not in order to disprove Carlyle, but to support his theory that a great man could change the world. But in the end he'd come to the opposite conclusion.

"A nation may look for a hero who can restore its optimism and revitalize its faith in itself," Altman said. "But history is made by great forces, not great men." He smiled. "This is the conclusion to which I have come after many, many years of study." He paused, then said, "Any questions?"

There were a few, all of them intelligent, and Altman answered them graciously, and even with a bit of humor.

"All right, well, thank you for coming," Altman said after the last of them had been addressed.

With that the members of his audience began to pick up their belongings.

He'd expected them all to have trundled off into the evening by the time he'd returned his notes to his briefcase, but as he glanced up, he saw that one of them remained, an old man, quite pale, with white hair, who sat staring at him fixedly and a little quizzically.

Perhaps, Altman thought, there'll be one final question.

He was right.

"Mr. Altman," the old man said. "It was very interesting, your talk."

The old man remained where Altman had first seen him, seated third chair from the aisle in the second row. He was dressed in dark blue trousers, with a shirt that was a lighter shade of blue. There was something disheveled about him, a sense of buttons in the wrong holes, of trouser legs with uneven cuffs, but it was the slight tremor Altman now noticed more than anything else about the poor fellow. It was in his head and in his hands, and it made him look quite frail, as if precariously holding on to life, like an autumn leaf.

"I'm glad you found my remarks interesting," Altman said.

The old man smiled shyly. "I would like to have a great many books, as you do," he said, "but I am on a pension."

"I understand," Altman said, then made his way up the aisle, his mind on the chicken salad sandwich waiting for him at the diner on 83rd and Broadway, a treat he allowed himself despite his doctor's warnings about mayonnaise.

"Do you remember the *Realschule*? In Linz?"

Altman stopped dead, astonished by the question. "The *Realschule* in Linz?"

The old man struggled to his feet. "You were a student there before the Great War."

"Yes, I was," Altman told him.

He had not thought of the *Realschule* in a great many years. Why should he? He'd come to America a few years after the war, a journey funded by his wealthy Berlin parents despite their objections to his "go West young man" argument for leaving Germany and moving to the New World. It was a position Altman had found ridiculous in its patriotism, his father's feeling that despite the horrible times being endured by Germany in the wake of the Great War, its "noble sons" should remain and rebuild the homeland.

"I was there also," the old man said in a voice that was little above a whisper. "At the *Realschule*."

"Really?" Altman said. "After the Great War, there can't be many of us left now, can there?" He shook his head. "Such a slaughterer of young men, that war."

The old man nodded, and the wave of straight white hair that lay across his brow drooped slightly. "Slaughter," he murmured, "yes."

There was something disturbing about this old man, and for that reason, Altman felt a curious urge to get away from him. In addition, that chicken salad sandwich was calling to him powerfully. And yet, he also felt called to engage this poor fellow a little longer. Evidently they'd been in school together, and clearly this unfortunate and apparently infirm old gentleman had not had an easy life, a fact that seemed to waft up from him, like an odor.

"Did you like the *Realschule*?" Altman asked.

The old man shook his head.

"Why not?" Altman asked, since he'd loved his time at the *Realschule*, even fell in love there, this girl of his dreams now rising to his consciousness after so many years, blond, with radiant blue eyes, still a vision to him.

"I was not treated well," the old man said.

Altman could find no way to respond to this, and so merely stared silently at the luckless fellow whose conversation was still keeping him from his sandwich, this spectral figure, pale as a ghost, a phantom so frail he appeared insubstantial, his hat trembling in his oddly shaped fingers.

"There was a bully," the old man added.

And indeed this unfortunate fellow did look like one of life's perennial victims, bullied not just in the schoolyard, but no doubt forever after that, bullied on the factory floor, or in the lumberyard, bullied, as it were, by the stars above, always the one at the back of the line, the one who gets the cold soup, and even that, spilled upon him. What was the word those awful Polish Jews who'd worked in his father's factory had had for such a creature? Ah, yes, Altman thought: *schlemazel*.

"I'm sorry to hear it," Altman said, "My own experience at the *Realschule* was quite pleasant."

"You were smart," the old man said.

Altman waved his hand as if to bat away such flattery despite the fact that he quite enjoyed being remembered in such a way. But then, he had been smart, hadn't he? In fact, he still was.

"I was not smart," the old man said.

And so even nature had proved a bully to this poor fellow, Altman thought, proved a bully by shortchanging him in the critical matter of intelligence. He'd been shortchanged in height as well, and from the look of him, the crumpled gray hat, the threadbare jacket, he'd never known success in any venture. What an unfortunate wretch, Altman thought, and for the first time in a long time, calculated his own good fortune, born into a wealthy family, able to pursue his intellectual interests without fear of want, a man now living contentedly among his many books and manuscripts. His life, he decided, had been good.

"I did not distinguish myself in my studies," the old man said. He smiled sadly. "I have never distinguished myself." He shrugged. "Well, maybe a little during the Great War."

The old man's brown eyes were somewhat milky and the whites were faintly yellow. This is not a well man, Altman told himself. Even in health, shortchanged.

"Were you in the Great War, Ziggy?" the old man asked.

Ziggy!

Altman had not been called Ziggy since his school days in, yes, the *Realschule* in Linz. His father and all his relatives had called him Ziegfried then, but after coming to America, he'd switched first to Franz, then to Franklin, and it was by this name, Franklin Altman, that he'd been known ever since: Franklin Altman on his marriage license, on his business cards, on . . . everything. Ziegfried, and most certainly Ziggy, had, like so many things from his past, simply disappeared.

"Yes, I was in the war," Altman said proudly, despite the fact that he'd never actually seen combat. His superior intelligence had served him well in that department, too, so that he'd worked in Berlin throughout the conflict, a pampered member of the Intelligence Service who'd never so much as seen a trench or fired a rifle.

"You fought on the side of the Fatherland, of course," the old man said.

What an odd remark, Altman thought. Of course he'd fought— well, at least in a matter of speaking—but certainly on the German side. He looked at the old man sternly, wondered if he'd just been insulted.

"Of course on the side of the Fatherland," Altman answered with only a slight hint of offence at the question.

"I was wounded twice," the old man said, "and gassed at Ypres."

Altman thought of the many dead, the dreadful way they'd died: shot to ribbons, blown to bits, buried alive in the muddy expanse of No Man's Land. "In Flanders Field the poppies grow," he recited by way of giving homage to these fallen comrades. "Between the crosses row on row."

It was obvious that this poor fellow had never heard this well-known verse, and yet he seemed deeply moved by it.

"So many died," he said. Then, after a pause, he added, "You were in the Intelligence Service."

"Yes, I was," Altman said. "How did you know?"

"There was a picture after the war," the old man answered. "All of you got medals. You were in the picture. I remembered you from the *Realschule*. You were standing next to the Kaiser."

Altman vividly recalled that proud moment, all of the members of the Intelligence Service High Command on the steps of the Reichstag, proud even in defeat. It was the last time the old aristocracy had seemed intact, and he suddenly felt an unmistakable nostalgia for the ease and elegance of his former life, the great houses and the balls, a Germany not yet burdened with reparations or afflicted with runaway inflation, not yet the suffering object of French and British revenge.

"We needed to believe in ourselves, we Germans," the old man said in the melancholy way, as Altman observed, of the vanquished.

"Indeed, we did," Altman agreed, and suddenly felt a powerful kinship with this former countryman. As if urged toward him by the pull of their shared blood, he offered his hand. "So, we are old soldiers then, you and I."

The old man did not take the offered hand.

"In Ypres we were trying to get behind the British lines," he said. "It was a secret plan, through a tunnel. When we came out, we were supposed to be behind the lines." He stopped suddenly, as if by machine gun fire. "But they were waiting there, the British."

"Waiting?" Altman asked hesitantly.

"They knew we were coming," the old man explained. "They shot at us on all sides." His eyes grew tense. "They shot Max. Gerhardt, too. Good boys, those two. Bavarian farm boys."

Altman watched him with a sudden wariness, as if, step by step, he were being led down a dark corridor. "War is terrible," he said after a moment.

"Betrayal is terrible," the old man said. "To be stabbed in the back by one of your own."

"One of your own?" Altman asked, now lowering his hand since it appeared the old man either had not seen him offer it or had declined the offer. "Why do you say that?"

"Because someone in the Intelligence Service sent us into the tunnel," the old man answered.

"How do you know that?"

"They were the only ones who knew about the mission," the old man answered. "It was a secret to everyone but them."

"So you think one of my colleagues betrayed you," Altman said tensely. "That is a terrible accusation."

"No one else knew," the old man said. He shook his head and lowered his voice slightly. "Good Bavarian boys," he said, almost to himself. "Poor boys." His melancholy lay like a black veil across his face. "So much time has passed since those dark days," he said.

"And we have both grown old." Altman said and again offered his hand. "Old comrades in arms."

This time, the old man took Altman's hand and shook it weakly.

"Fifty years now," Altman added as he started to withdraw his hand from the old man's grip. "Fifty years and . . ."

"You went to England," the old man interrupted, squeezing his fingers more tightly around Altman's hand as he did so. "After the war."

Cautiously, Altman nodded. Why did talking to this poor fellow make him feel as if he were walking across a minefield? He was small and sick. What could he do to a man of Altman's robust health and mountainous build? And yet, there was something fearsome about him, some dark energy. Inside this old man, he thought, there is a fiery core.

"And you started to collect rare books," the old man added as he finally released Altman's hand.

"Yes," Altman said.

The old man smiled. "You became a bibliophile. That is the word, yes? You were always good with words. Back at the *Reaschule*, you were always reading."

"Was I?"

"English, always reading English," the old man said. "You are also maybe an Anglophile?"

Before Altman could answer, the old man laughed. "So many big words I have now." He chuckled softly, though it seemed to Altman that it was less a laugh than a disguised rebuke.

"At the *Realschule*, I was always good with speaking," the old man said. "I wanted to be a debater, but the bully stopped me."

"Who was this bully?" Altman asked. "I don't remember a bully. I never saw anyone physically attack a . . ."

The old man stepped back slightly. "Oh, it was not physical," he said. "It was all with words. You would understand this, since you are a bibliophile. You would understand the power of words, yes? You collect words, isn't that so? You collect words in books."

"I do," Altman said cautiously, as if he were being accused of having such an interest, one he'd never thought it necessary to defend. And yet this old man did make him feel defensive. Suddenly, he thought he knew why.

"Am I the bully?" he asked. "Did I bully you in some way?"

"No, never," the old man said softly, then with a curious darkening of his tone. "I was invisible to you."

There it was again, Altman thought, a vague accusation. "I'm sorry if I . . . never noticed you."

And it was clear that Altman hadn't noticed this poor fellow. In fact, even now he found that other than those of his closest friends, he couldn't recall any of his fellow students at the *Realschule*. He remembered the faces of certain boys and girls, but that was all. Save for Magda, of course. He would always remember Magda.

"I would not have expected you to notice me," the old man said softly. "You were from a fine family. For you, the *Realschule* in Linz was just . . ." He looked at Altman to finish his sentence.

"Temporary," Altman said. "I was only sent there for a year while my father arranged our family's move to Vienna."

"Where you stayed until the war?"

"Yes, and where my father stayed even after the war," Altman said. "At least for a few years."

"Your family moved to Vienna, yes," the old man said. "This was mentioned at the time." He smiled. "And so, of course, the *Realschule* was for you something—as you say—temporary."

"Still, I'm sorry," Altman told him. "So do forgive me for not recalling you."

"Of course," the old man replied.

"Good night, then," Altman said.

With that, he started to move on down the aisle, but in a movement far quicker than Altman would have expected from such a pale and sickly old gentleman, the man again grabbed his hand.

"We both still have our German accents, Ziggy," he said.

"Time cannot obliterate everything," Altman told him as he gently pulled his hand free.

"And never the things of youth," the old man agreed. "The things that made us. Particularly our crimes, yes?"

"Our crimes?" Altman asked, then added, "Yes, I suppose so."

The man suddenly appeared embarrassed. "Forgive me for troubling you, Zig . . ." he stopped, straightened himself like a low ranking soldier before an officer, then said, "Herr Altman."

"No trouble at all," Altman said, then moved on down the aisle, empty seats on both sides. At the end of it, and for a reason he could not fathom, he stopped and turned back toward the front of the room, where the old man now sat, facing forward, peering at the lectern, his shoulders drooping beneath a jacket that was not only threadbare, as Altman had previously observed, but perhaps a size too big, something purchased at a thrift store, no doubt, so that he abruptly felt a seizure of pity for this old fellow, so lonely, as it seemed, at the end of an unfortunate life. Might he have known some modest glory, Altman asked himself, had history turned his way? Might he have loved beautiful women, had accomplished children, felt the reverence of the few, if not the adulation of the multitude?

He glanced at the clock that hung on the opposite wall and suddenly considered the passage of his own life. He was a widower, with children in distant cities, a man with a solitary evening before him. Normally he would have gone back to his apartment to work on his catalogue, a large collection of books and manuscripts written after the Great War, the works of those who'd known the fire and thunder of battle, along with the great unrest that had followed the Peace of Versailles, some of which he'd cited this very night during his talk on Carlyle. As a way of spending the remainder of his evening, he did not find this in the least off-putting. Still, would it be so bad to indulge this other old man, this compatriot—though admittedly at a distance—of those ancient, sanguinary fields, for a little while, perhaps find a way to suggest to the poor fellow that he was not so lacking in distinction as he so clearly thought himself? Earlier, he'd had a vaguely unsettling sense that the old man was accusing him of something, but none of that remained. Now all he felt was pity.

"Have you had dinner?" he blurted with a suddenness that surprised him.

The old man had resumed his seat, his head deeply bowed. He did not move or in any other way respond to Altman's questions. Could it be that this unfortunate old gentleman had simply been unable to imagine himself being asked to dinner by the distinguished "Herr Altman? If so, how very, very sad, Altman thought.

And so he strode back to where the old man sat, his hands folded over his lap as if in stern guardianship of the package in his lap. A rectangular package, as Altman observed, wrapped in cheap brown paper and tied with a string.

A manuscript!

Ah, so that was what had brought this unfortunate man out into the rain, Altman thought, he has a manuscript he no doubt thinks valuable. It would have no value at all, of course. As a collector, he'd been approached untold times by people clutching books and manuscripts they felt valuable, then untied this same gray string and drawn back this same brown paper only to find . . . a tattered, forty-year-old edition of *Doctor Faustus,* or the nearest thing imaginable to a book club edition of Heinrich Heine. And yet these poor, ignorant souls had held on to their "precious" treasures either lovingly or avariciously. It was often hard to tell which.

But not now, not with this fellow. It was clear that in his case, it was love. Altman could see it in the gentle way his gnarled fingers curled around the corners of the manuscript, his index fingers moving softly back and forth, as if he were comforting an infant. In fact, he had never seen anyone touch a book with such tenderness. It was as if, through his fingers, the old man were singing it a lullaby.

"Excuse me?" Altman said softly.

The old man looked up.

"I was thinking we might have dinner together," Altman said.

"Dinner . . . together?"

"Yes," Altman said. "I've a favorite place a few blocks from here. They make a wonderful chicken salad sandwich."

The old man peered at him hesitantly. "I am a pensioner," he reminded him.

"Oh, don't worry about that," Altman said expansively. "Dinner will be on me. Think of it as payment for the effort you made in coming out into the rain, coming to a bookstore and sitting through my poor remarks."

"Oh, no," the old man protested. "I found your remarks quite persuasive."

"Please, let's have dinner," Altman said cheerfully, then added an unexpectedly poignant truth, "Sometimes I grow tired of eating alone."

"I wouldn't want to impose upon your time," the old man said hesitantly.

"Oh, no, not at all," Altman said.

"Well, if you're sure," the old man said, then pressed the package to his chest and began to rise. "If you're sure I'm not imposing."

"Not at all, I assure you."

Altman saw that the poor fellow was having trouble getting to his feet, and so he reached over and tucked his hand under his shoulder.

"Easy does it," he said with a quick laugh. "Old bones are not easily commanded, are they?" He reached for the package, thinking that it might be easier for the old man to get to his feet without it, but rather than release it, he clung to it all the more tightly.

"It's all right," the old man said, "I'm used to carrying it."

"Really?" Altman asked. "You carry it everywhere?"

"It is the only thing I ever . . . created," the old man said.

Ah, so I was right, Altman thought, it *was* a lullaby.

Altman watched as the man drew on the black raincoat he'd earlier hung over the back of his chair. It was frayed at the sleeves and worn in the shoulders, proof once again that the poor fellow was of little means, so that Altman suddenly felt quite proud of himself for asking this old schoolmate to dinner, whoever he was. They were different certainly, he thought, and yet they'd both fled the ravages of postwar Germany, then helplessly watched as misfortune after misfortune had fallen upon their native land.

"To the right," he said to one who now seemed truly his fellow countryman, "the restaurant is only a couple of blocks away."

The rain had briefly fallen during Altman's talk, and the sidewalk was still wet and slippery. As they walked, Altman noticed that the old man had a slight limp.

"From the war?" he asked.

"No," the old man answered. "My job. My legs were broken on my job."

"Where did you work?"

"The shipyards," the old man answered. "The Brooklyn shipyards."

"What was your job?"

"I loaded cargo."

"And something fell on you?" Altman asked.

"A big crate," the old man said. "Of guns. It was marked 'Steel Rods,' but the crate was full of guns. Hundreds of guns. Cartons of ammunition, too."

"Going where?"

"Palestine."

"Ah, yes," Altman said. "So much trouble there."

They reached the corner, where they were stopped by the traffic signal.

"I told the shipyard master," the old man continued, "and some people came and they took the guns away." He shrugged. "I'm sure they just sent them in another crate."

"Have you found other guns?"

The old man looked up and smiled softly. "They are always going there," he added. "To the Jews."

Altman nodded. He was well versed in the region's current troubles. After all, they'd been going on for over fifty years, and there was no solution in sight. Each year brought more conflict, a struggle that he suspected would never find resolution.

The light turned and the two of them moved forward, Altman at a pace far slower that he would normally have taken, the man limping along beside him. He could not imagine living such a life, and this made it all the more important for him to give this poor chap a decent dinner and some kindly conversation.

They reached the restaurant a few minutes later. Everyone knew Altman and made a great fuss over him, something that clearly impressed the old man.

"I'm a regular," Altman explained demurely.

"It's nice to be noticed," the old man said.

To live so unheralded a life seemed infinitely sad to Altman, never to be appreciated, never to be spoken to with respect or honored in any way. There is a sorrow in smallness, he decided, a pain that goes with being just another bit of microscopic plankton in a sea of green. He knew better than to give any hint of his pity, however, and so he cheerfully opened the menu though he, as well as the entire staff, knew exactly what he'd order.

Once he'd ordered it, he handed the waiter the menu.

"And what about you?" he said to his guest.

The enormous menu lowered to reveal a face veiled in perplexity.

"I don't know," the old man said, then looked again, and after a moment ordered what Altman recognized was the single cheapest item available.

"Only a split pea soup?" he asked. "That's all you want?"

The old man nodded.

"All right, then," Altman said to the waiter, "A split pea soup for my good friend here."

When the soup came it was clear to Altman that the old fellow was hungry. Perhaps he should have guessed as much from the slightness of his frame, the loose hang of his skin. He had seen hunger before and so he found it odd, and perhaps even a bit disturbing, that the plenty of his years in America had caused him to forget the ghostly look of it, the sallow cheeks, the hollow eyes, the way the old man couldn't keep from taking two bites at a time of the bread that came with the soup, quickly wiping his mouth, then taking two more. *Fressen* was the German word for it: to eat like an animal.

"You were right," the old man said. "The food here is good."

Altman nodded. "They have great wiener schnitzel, too," he said, "and I sometimes have a Reuben sandwich. My doctor tells me that I shouldn't have pastrami, but I like it, and at a certain age, what's the point of being strict with oneself? We all end up dead in the end, isn't that so?"

"Yes, we all end up dead," the old man agreed. He sipped from his spoon, a loud slurp after which he seemed to see himself in Altman's eyes, see himself as hungry, and because of his hunger, pathetic. Slowly, he returned the spoon to the bowl and with a slow, sad movement, drew an errant wave of white hair back and away from his forehead. "We all end up dead in the end, yes," he repeated, "and after that, we cannot make amends."

"Amends for what?" Altman asked.

"As I said before, for our crimes," the old man answered.

Altman glanced at the package that now rested beside him in the booth they'd taken by the window and wondered if it was confessional. There had been such want after the Great War that he'd heard tales of murder, even of cannibalism. Could it be that this poor soul had . . .?

No, Altman told himself, you are being melodramatic. Still, the very presence of the man's manuscript worked like a question mark in his soul, a door he could not stop himself from cautiously prying open.

"It's a manuscript, isn't it?" he asked with a nod toward the package.

The old man nodded.

"Is it . . . about you?"

The old man nodded again, clearly disinclined to discuss it further, so that Altman decided to go in a different direction.

"It was hard to make your way after the war, yes?" he asked.

"Very hard," the old man said. He looked at Altman with a curious passion, one laced with what seemed a host of old angers. "It was terrible, what was done to us."

"Yes, terrible," Altman said. "Truly terrible. We were treated as monsters, a people who could commit any atrocity. They had made up these stories of the Hun. The British mostly, but the Americans, too. And the French. Terrible, terrible lies."

"All of them lies," the old man said in a kind of snarl that both surprised and alarmed Altman with its barely contained fury. "The land of Beethoven. The land of Goethe." He seemed overwhelmed with ire. "Killing babies. That's what they said in their lies. Killing women and old people. That is what they said we did."

"Exactly," Altman said. "Things no civilized people would do."

The old man looked away, his attention once again drawn to the world beyond the window. He seemed to be working very hard not to explode. Then, after a moment, his gaze drifted back to Altman. "Your uncle was an English teacher," he said. "At the *Realschule*. I was in his class."

"Really?"

"He was a very good teacher," the old man said.

Altman sat back slightly. "I'm quite sorry to say so, but I still can't quite recall you from those days."

"You were younger," the old man said. "I had to leave the *Realschule* the same year that you came to it."

"So, we were never actually classmates?"

The old man shook his head. "My name would mean nothing to you," he said. "I saw you at school. That is all. In the playground or the hallway. Sometimes walking with your uncle." His smile was thin, but not without warmth. "I admired you. Everyone said you were very smart. In math. In English." With a trembling hand he reached for the spoon, then drew back, as if afraid of humiliating himself again. "In everything." He glanced again toward the window, lingered a moment, then returned his attention to Altman. "I am seventy-nine," he said.

"I'm seventy-five," Altman said. "But there really isn't much difference at our age, is there? We're just two old men, you and I."

The old man smiled but something in his eyes remained mirthless, so that he seemed to drift in a sea of bad memories, perhaps nightmarish ones. He had no doubt sought refuge in America as so many had done through the decades, Altman thought. But clearly, he'd found something considerably less than the Promised Land. Life was unfair, that was the long and the short of it, Altman decided. He remembered a Latin phrase his father had taught him, something written by Horace: *Mutato nomine de te fabula narratur: You need but change the name and this story is about you.* How true, he thought now as he briefly recalled his own journey out of the whirlwind.

The old man seemed almost to read Altman's thoughts, or at least divine the direction of them.

"I could not make my way after the war," he said. "It was chaos, and everywhere a new trouble. I am sure you recall those times."

"Vividly, I'm afraid."

The old man's eyes grew cold. "It is dangerous to humiliate a people. A people can be like a cornered animal."

Altman nodded. "That is true. And so they look for a hero, which is what I was speaking about tonight. A great leader. But a hero can't change the history of a nation."

The old man nodded. "We were looking for such a person," he said. "It is true that we were looking. But you are right as you said in your talk. It would not have mattered. It is the great forces that matter, not one person." He smiled.

"So smart, Herr Altman, to know such things."

Altman tried not to react to such flattery.

"I'm not a Marxist," he said, "but Marx was right about one thing. It is great forces that determine great events. A man is carried on the stream of history. He cannot direct that stream or change its course."

"This is true," the old man said. He smiled, but it was a dark smile, laced with something that seemed to teeter on the edge of bitterness. "As a young man, I had great hopes for myself," he said in the sad tone of a small, insignificant man admitting to having once had some great dream for himself.

It was a tone that touched Altman's heart with such force that he reached out and patted the old man's hand.

"Of course," he said. "We all have such hopes in our youth."

"But from your talk I have learned that nothing—not a man or a book or anything else—can change history," the old man said. "Little things change little things, that is all. Like those Bavarian boys. Someone whispered into someone's ear, or maybe sent a cable, and it was over for them." He looked at Altman tensely. "They were small, and a small thing took them away."

Altman again felt uncomfortably in the old man's sites.

"And a bully at school can only change the one he bullies," the old man added.

"History is nothing but the accumulation of such things," Altman said with complete confidence. "It is made by millions of small actions by small people who are themselves responding to great forces."

The old man was clearly not inclined to dispute the point with which he'd already expressed agreement, and so, as a matter of simple politeness, Altman changed the subject.

"So, after you left the *Realschule* in Linz, what did you do?" he asked.

The old man shrugged. "Nothing until I got older. And then I only changed my name."

Altman was relieved that the old man had now drawn his fingers away from the package and seemed quite abruptly to be a different track entirely. "Why did you do that?" he asked.

"Because I hated my father," the old man answered. "I had always hated him, but I was like other boys, I felt I should respect him, obey him. You know how we Germans are. We obey. It is what we do best."

"So it must have been hard for you, changing your name," Altman said. "I mean, to be so disrespectful of one's father."

"Very hard," the old man said. "It is not easy to deny your father, even when your father is a cruel man."

"So, you took a different name?" Altman asked.

"Yes," the old man said. "I took my grandmother's name. She was very kind, very warm. I wanted the name of someone kind and warm." He seemed to drift back to that distant time. "I wanted this name to comfort me because things had not gone well for me. I had no home. Living on scraps. Living in rags. It is terrible not to know when you will eat again, when you will wash again. It is terrible and you can go mad. Perhaps I went a little mad."

"After the war we all felt as if we no longer had a home," Altman said. "Everything was shattered."

"Did you go mad?" the old man asked bluntly.

"No," Altman said.

"Were you poor?"

"No, not poor."

"Your father helped you?"

"Yes," Altman answered, and felt weakened by that answer, pampered by that answer. Not just luckier than this old man, but unfairly, and thus grotesquely so. "Yes, he helped me."

"How did he help you?"

"He helped me get to America," Altman answered.

"How did he do that?"

"Well, there was something left after the war," Altman told him cautiously. "Some . . . money."

"But German money was worthless after the war."

Even more cautiously, Altman said, "There was other money."

"Other money?"

"Pounds," Altman said. "Francs. Dollars."

"The victor's money," the old man said. "Your father had a lot of that?"

"Some," Altman admitted. "Enough."

"Enough for you to leave Germany and come here, to America?" Altman nodded.

The old man peered at him for a long time before he spoke again. "I could not leave Germany," he said. "Except for a little while, in Austria."

"Well, we thought of Austria as Germany, didn't we?" Altman asked. "The Pan-Germanic peoples. At least that was what the slogans said."

The old man nodded. "I remember the slogans."

"Austria," Altman whispered softly, now caught up in the history of his own life. "My father had business there. I was thinking of being in this business, but I wasn't cut out for it." He felt a tense chuckle break from him. "I was always more the scholarly type. I wanted to teach at the university, to write books." He shrugged. "But more than anything, I wanted to collect them. Especially German books."

"The call of the Fatherland," the old man whispered.

He was staring into the empty bowl of his soup, his gaze curiously intense, as if he were reading a lost future there.

"The call of the Fatherland," Altman repeated. "That's quite well put." He smiled. "Perhaps you should have been a writer."

The old man's fingers crawled over to the package, then spread over it like the legs of a spider. "I have only this."

"And you say that you have had it for a long time?" Altman asked.

"I wrote it after the war," the old man said. "It reminds me of what I was."

Altman suddenly felt a spike of dread move through him, sharp and tingling, like an electric charge. Once again, he thought of the old man's mention of crime, and once again he wondered if the book was a confession of some unspeakable act.

"It is about the way things were in our country," the old man said. A dark sparkle came into his eyes. "You remember how they were, I'm sure."

Altman did indeed remember how things had been in Germany after the war, the rise of extreme parties, the street fighting, a country coming apart at the seams.

"Germany was headed for an abyss," Altman said. "Communists and fascists attacking each other. The twin plagues. At the time, the direction seemed clear, and it was a very scary one."

"Is that why you left?" the old man asked. "Because you were afraid of what might happen?"

"Yes," Altman admitted.

"I left because of Elsa," the old man said.

"Elsa?"

"She was so sweet," the old man added. "So kind to me. She worked in the hotel." He looked at Altman knowingly. "You know what that means?"

"I do, yes," Altman answered.

"She was murdered."

"Murdered?" Altman asked.

"They said it was a rich man," the old man said. "A rich man who lived in Vienna."

"I see."

"It made me very angry that so sweet a girl should be murdered."

"No doubt," Altman said cautiously, now once again unaccountably tense in the old man's presence, like a man who suddenly sees a snake in the tall grass.

"A Jew," the old man added. "The rich man from Vienna."

Altman felt a wave of relief. He'd wondered if the old man had somehow thought his father the murderer. But luckily, he thought

Elsa's murderer a Jew, which certainly removed his father from the list of suspects.

The old man nodded toward the package. "It's all in there. How I felt in those days."

"So your book is a memoir?" Altman asked, now hoping to get away from the disturbing subject of a poor, heart-of-gold prostitute murdered by a sinister and stereotypically wealthy Jew.

"It is, yes," the old man answered. "No one wanted to publish it. They said I had a silly name. Which is true. It held me back in those days after the war. You can't rise in the world if you have a silly name."

Altman felt the normal urge to ask what this name was, but he could see that it still embarrassed the old man. "Well, at least things got better," he said. "Germany came out of the darkness . . . unscathed." He looked at the manuscript, the way the old man's hand was now stroking it gently. "So," he said, "your book."

The old man said nothing, his sadness so deep, his disappointment so fathomless, Altman once again felt a wave of pity sweep over him.

"I'd like to read it," he said as he nodded toward the package. "Would you mind? You've said that has to do with Germany after the Great War, and I collect that sort of material. I plan to place my collection in an archive at some point. The collection of these . . . documents will be my legacy." He sat back and smiled broadly at being able to offer the old man a little sliver of immortality. "Your manuscript would have a permanent place in history."

The old man looked at the manuscript as if offering a long goodbye before his hand suddenly swept out dismissively, a gesture that suggest that at long last he had decided it had no value. "Take it then," he said. He picked up the manuscript and handed it to Altman. "I have no use for it."

"I shall treasure it," Altman said. "Thank you."

"You are most welcome," the old man said. He began to put on his raincoat. "Well, good night," he said and with those words, struggled to his feet, then reached into his pocket.

"No, please," Altman told him quickly. "It's my pleasure." He patted the manuscript softly. "Payment for this gift you have made to history."

The old man appeared quite touched by Altman's remark. "Perhaps my life might have some use, after all," he said softly as he got to his feet.

"By the way, what's your name?" Altman asked.

Rather than answer, the old man simply waved his hand as if to dismiss himself from Altman's interest, or the world's.

"It is a silly name," he said.

With that he drew on his coat with trembling hands, then with a soft nod, bid Altman good night.

Altman watched as the old fellow moved shakily down the aisle, then out into the night, the chill, the suddenly returning rain, all of which bestowed a deeper fragility upon his figure so that he seemed to Altman much like man himself, weak against the great forces that are arrayed against him, the ravages of time no less strong and ultimately overwhelming than vast social and economic forces no "hero"—Carlyle's magisterial language not withstanding—could alter or affect. Even so, one thing remained clear, this old man, along with millions of others, could have had it much worse. He'd fully expected it to get much worse on the day he left Germany. Most everyone had felt the same. The predictions had been terrible. That Germany would fall under the hand of dictatorship, that there would be yet another great war, one that, like the first, would engulf all of Europe, the whole world. He offered the forces of history a soft, appreciative smile, for they'd been kinder to the world than anyone had expected all those years go.

Still captured in the warm glow of that smile, Altman glanced down at the manuscript, then, on an impulse, untied the string and read the title page: *Mein Kampf* by *Adolph Schicklgruber*.

He smiled again.

Schicklgruber?

It was true what the old man said, Altman thought, it was indeed a silly name. But it wouldn't have mattered if he'd had a different one. The old man had hoped to change the world, but no single man could shape history. Only great forces could do that.

He glanced down at the manuscript again, smiled at the name. The old man had clearly blamed it for all his failure. He shook his head at so absurd an idea, for after all, he asked himself as he reached for his coat, what's in a name?

VII

Book Club

Loren D. Estleman

CHIEF DOCKERTY KNEW the shadiest spot in New Mexico wasn't the Santa Rita copper mine in Silver City. It was right there in the town of Good Advice, and it belonged to Avery Sharecross' bookshop.

Sharecross had established it, years before many of the residents were born, in a three-hundred-year-old mission that had been by turns a community theater, a Salvation Army shelter, a home for armadillos, and a place for juvenile delinquents to smoke cigarettes and listen to rock and roll. Its walls were adobe, three feet thick, its few windows just large enough to shoot Indians from inside without attracting too many arrows from outside. During its empty period, it had been as dark and mossy—feeling as a cave. Sharecross had managed to make it darker still by installing towering bookcases and stocking them with volumes, some the same vintage as the building, with narrow passages between the cases. Generations of children had dared one another to approach the place after dark, when the ghosts of William Shakespeare and Mark Twain prowled among the stacks (or during the day, when the proprietor did the haunting); none accepted. Even at high noon, a visitor needed a flashlight to explore the place without running into Thackeray or Gibbon and cracking a tooth.

Fortunately for the chief's new bridge, the bookseller had suspended trough lights from the distant ceiling, with chain switches for the convenience of browsers, who were requested by hand-lettered cardboard signs posted throughout the store to turn them off when they moved from one aisle to the next. The fluorescent tubes flickered and buzzed when activated and spilled watery illumination onto many centuries of literature, but not quite as far as the plank floor, which was heaped with books on both sides of the passages, narrowing the avenues even further. Dockerty groped his way forward with his feet to avoid kicking them over.

The cases were ancient, built of old-growth oak from the East, and gray with the accumulation of dust that had worked its way deep into the grain. Although the proprietor was scrupulous with a duster so that none of his patrons would shun the place to keep from smearing his best suit or her new dress, the pulverized bones of prehistoric buffalo and extinct Indian tribes that made up the Santa Fe Trail would not be prevented entrance, either to the shop or Chief Dockerty's nostrils.

Sneeze. Blow nose. Creep forward. Repeat.

A reader of bulletins and arrest reports exclusively, he hadn't visited the place often, and not in months. He had only a vague memory of the layout, and Sharecross' regard for his customers did not extend to sparing them the annoyance of the occasional dead end: Aisles that were open at both ends alternated with those whose exits were sealed with perpendicular bookcases, and as the bookseller was constantly rearranging his stock and changing how it was displayed, even a Daniel Boone would find himself retracing his footsteps and muttering all the way.

But it was a Tuesday, and therefore a lucky one for the chief of the Good Advice Police Department (five officers, three of them part-timers). That was the day the book club gathered to drink iced tea, eat lemon cookies, and talk about Plot, Theme, and Character. All he had to do was follow the murmur of voices.

"Well, I hated it. Six hundred pages about dancing bears and a boy biting a dog."

This was "Uncle Ned" Scoffield, whose ninety-nine-year-old voice cracked as air whistled through his dentures.

"It isn't just about that, Ned. Garp's a tragic hero."

Birdie Flatt: retired after forty years when the phone company yanked out the old switchboard. Dockerty knew her shrill tones from every call he'd placed when he was a patrolman new to the force.

Someone else snorted. That would be Carl Lathrop, head of the town council, who overrode hecklers at meetings by way of his expressive nasal passages. "He's a cartoon character. Not every book is *Wuthering Heights.*"

"The dancing bear's a symbol, folks," said another man whose voice the chief couldn't peg right away. "Irving's making a point about the folly of human nature."

Ned put in another two cents' worth. "Symbols, shmymbols. Leave it to a newspaperman to like a book about a boy biting a dog."

That made the other man Gordon Tolliver, the publisher of *The Good Adviser*, a weekly, popularly believed to have been founded by Horace Greeley. At fifty, he'd be the youngest member of the club.

There followed a lively exchange of views, simultaneous and pierced through by Birdie's stridor.

"Friends, friends," Sharecross' reedy tenor quieted the tumult. "This is a literary discussion, not professional wrestling. Ned: There's a great deal more to *The World According to Garp* than a boy biting a dog, which you'd know if you'd read past the opening chapters instead of just counting the pages.

Miss Flatt: He's not quite a figure of tragedy, because the book is intended as a black comedy, and you can't have both on the same stage at the same time. Neither is he a cartoon character, Carl; he's too fleshed-out for that. Gordon, it pains me to tell you that the dancing bear is just a dancing bear. There's one in nearly every book Irving's written. It's his trademark, like Poe's gloomy tarn and Ayn Rand's monologues."

"Next time, let's read Louis L'Amour," said Uncle Ned. "His dogs don't get bit and his bears don't do the polka."

"Let's mix it up a bit. Each of you pick a book, and we'll compare their various merits and shortcomings next week. Don't forget to mark it in the ledger before you go."

Dockerty emerged from the literary labyrinth just as the group was rising from its folding chairs. Sharecross, who'd been holding court from behind his massive desk, as old and gray as the bookshelves—*hell, as old as him*, thought the chief—got up from his wooden swivel to greet his visitor. The others nodded greetings, each preoccupied with his or her quest among the stock.

"A pleasant surprise, Chief. Have I persuaded you to join us at last? An experienced criminologist will be invaluable when we take up Ed McBain."

The bookseller resembled a caricature of the trade: gaunt, with hair of a gray to match his shelves straggling to his collar, thick spectacles, and limbs like bent pipe cleaners, his knees and elbows trying to gnaw through the rusty black woolen suit he wore even when the temperature topped a hundred. Now that he thought about it, Dockerty had never seen the man sweat. If someone fetched him a hard blow, his pores would release only dry air and desiccated bindings.

"I'm a cop, not a detective," the chief said. "That's your specialty."

"I've been a bookseller longer than I was a detective. Back then, DNA stood for Do Not Arrest. The captain had a blind spot where his son was concerned."

In the beginning, Dockerty had had trouble picturing this elderly scarecrow collaring and interrogating suspects. Any Hollywood studio would have cast him as the absentminded ascetic in some musty archive. Then he'd Googled Sharecross' name, and spent twenty minutes reading commendations and looking at pictures of him shaking hands with a U.S. attorney general, an FBI director, and the graduating class at the New York Police Academy. In one shot, with a chestful of medals and a police commissioner placing a ribbon around his neck ending in yet another decoration, his dress uniform appeared to be wearing him rather than the other way around. Even back then he'd looked like an assistant professor employed by a not-very-distinguished university. Twenty years into his own career, the chief had learned the first lesson of police work: Don't judge a man by his appearance.

"I'm not here to join your book club, Avery. It's official business."

Sharecross raised his voice a decibel. "I don't have that one in stock, but I'm attending an estate sale in Albuquerque next week. I'll look for it."

Dockerty was confused, then aware of Lathrup, the last book club member present, letting himself out the door. When it shut behind him, jangling the copper bell attached to it, the bookseller said, "The city council has a right to discuss police business, but I assume you'd rather keep it off the table this early in the investigation."

The chief nodded, embarrassed that he hadn't thought of it himself. "It's Lloyd Fister."

"Lloyd's my best customer. What's happened?"

"Accident, I hope, though it looks like murder."

"Dear me."

Not the usual response from an experienced detective. But then, Sharecross wasn't your usual detective.

Lloyd Fister had been born in Good Advice, the fifth generation in his family to first see the light in the rambling Victorian pile on the hill overlooking the town. His great-great-grandfather had brought the railroad and, with it, prosperity, to the town and himself. Rather than desert when the local economy went into decline a hundred years later, Lloyd had stayed on, using a great deal of his inheritance to build one of the finest book collections in private hands. His interest ran toward the history of the Southwest, and Sharecross had been instrumental in helping him stock his shelves. Their friendship had survived the onslaught of the Internet; rather than consign his search for rare and obscure titles to a soulless electronic machine,

Fister preferred to continue a relationship that had outlasted his own marriage, which had ended in widowhood many years before.

"I'll print out these pictures at the station." Andy Barlow, the deputy chief, gestured with the digital camera in his hand. "I got every angle."

"Okay. Tolliver will be all over you for a print soon as he hears about it. I'll decide which he can put in the paper. I don't want this showing up on the front page."

As he spoke, Dockerty inclined his head toward the sheet-covered figure on the floor.

"He'll turn that rag into a tabloid if he gets half a chance." Barlow left.

Apart from the number and variety of volumes present, Fister's private library bore no resemblance to the bookshop where he had acquired so many of its titles. Mahogany bookshelves, intricately carved by a long-dead Mexican artisan, walled its seven hundred square feet all the way to the twelve-foot ceiling, holding several thousand volumes bound in leather, buckram, and parchment, all upright and level, with spaces left here and there for future acquisitions which now would never be made. A ladder made of the same wood stood against one wall, fitted into a ceiling track that allowed it to be moved into position to retrieve books from the upper shelves. The collector's desk, of mahogany also, contained a banker's lamp and more books in stacks, and an armchair upholstered in maroon full-grain leather stood in each corner beside a tall reading lamp. The air smelled pleasantly of paper and leather in various stages of genteel decay.

In fact, the only thing untidy about the room was the corpse under the sheet.

Sharecross knelt and lifted the sheet with a half-hopeful expression, as if it might not be his old friend and fellow bibliophile lying there with a cracked skull. He let the sheet fall back into place and rose, his knees creaking and disappointment on his emaciated face.

"His housekeeper called us," Dockerty said. "She found him about an hour ago when she came in to clean. It broke her up bad. Doc Simms has her under sedation."

"Poor Greta. She doesn't sleep here, does she?"

"She lives with her sister in town. She wasn't here when it happened; the Doc swears to that. He figures Fister was dead at least two hours when he examined him. Blunt-instrument trauma's probably cause of death, but he won't swear to it till the autopsy. I wanted you to see the body before I had it taken away."

"No need. I took your word for it—he's dead." Sharecross walked around the room, looking up toward the top of the shelves, where various objets d'art stood in the space between them and the ceiling.

"We thought of that," Dockerty said. "Maybe one of those doodads fell off and hit him on the noggin. But there wasn't any on the floor, and the angle's all wrong. He was hit on the back of the head with something hard and heavy enough to cave in the skull. Whoever did it didn't leave it behind."

"I wasn't looking for what killed him."

"Then, what . . .?"

The bookseller stepped back to the body, placing the toes of his shoes in line with the soles of Fister's. "He stood here, a few yards inside the door. Either someone was waiting, possibly hidden behind the door, or it was someone he knew and trusted, at least not to attack him. The blow was struck from behind and he fell forward onto his face. Tell me if you think I'm wrong. I'm a bit rusty, I'm afraid."

Rusty as a brand-new Swiss watch, the chief thought. "Works for me. I sure hope it was someone hiding behind the door, a burglar passing through. I wouldn't want to think we've got a murderer living here."

"They have to live somewhere. What about that?" He pointed.

Dockerty followed the angle of his finger, but all he saw was a shelf about nine feet from the floor. He said so.

"There's a space between those two books."

"There's spaces all over. I guess he didn't want to have to rearrange the whole library to make room for a new book. I'll be goldarned if I can figure out his system, but he must've had one. Mr. Fister was tidy about everything."

"He arranged them chronologically, beginning with the earliest Spanish explorations all the way up to recent changes made by the state legislatures. But as you see, the spaces he left are wider, to accommodate several books at a time. This gap is approximately the width of two books of ordinary width, or perhaps one large one. It's the only example in the room, and it suggests a book's missing."

"Maybe it belongs to one or two of the books on the desk."

"No, I looked at those. They're reference works, common to the book trade. I have them as well. They're consulted so often it only makes sense to keep them handy rather than constantly be climbing the ladder to retrieve them; certainly not from a shelf so high up. I'm sure you know where I'm heading."

"Well, robbery's a motive I can wrap my head around. You think he surprised somebody while he was stealing the book that belonged there?"

"If Lloyd came back unexpectedly, trapping the thief in the library, forcing him to hide behind the door and strike him just after he came in, that certainly suggests itself. It could just as easily be someone he knew; the moment he turned his back, the thief hit him, then stole the book."

"I like the first theory, and not just because I don't want the killer to be one of ours. It makes it an act of desperation, not planning. He might have wanted just to knock him out so he could make his escape."

Sharecross took off his glasses to wipe them with a handkerchief. Unlike the case with most nearsighted men, his eyes looked sharper when they were naked; he resembled an old and seasoned eagle.

"The only thing that argues against it is: What became of the weapon? It wasn't one of the objects in this room. I hardly think, having eliminated the threat to his freedom and acquired what he came for, he'd stop to put the weapon back. If, on the other hand, he brought it with him, it becomes a coldblooded act."

"Fingerprints."

"I was trained to think like a murderer. I'd wipe them off rather than take the chance of being seen on the street carrying a bronze vase or a marble bust."

"DNA."

"Possibly. As I said, I'm far from current." He hooked on his spectacles. "Wasn't Lloyd interviewed recently by a television crew?"

"Yeah. Big to-do when a network van rolls into a town this little. Some kind of reality show like Hoarders, only high-end: rich collectors. It was what you call a pilot, hoping to become a series."

"Not an unlikely procession. In many cases, the only difference between a wealthy bibliomaniac and somebody's mother-in-law living in an apartment full of old newspapers and empty pop bottles is the size of the investment."

"Sort of a nutjob *Lifestyles of the Rich and Famous*."

Sharecross looked pained.

"I'd hate to see that adjective applied to Lloyd. The reason I brought it up . . ."

"For once we're neck-and-neck. I'll see about getting that TV footage and we'll compare it to the crime scene. If the picture's sharp enough, we'll see what was in that gap—if Mr. Fister didn't overhaul the library in the meantime."

"I doubt it. It looks the same as the last time I visited him, and as we've discussed, he had the foresight to prevent an extensive reorganization." The bookseller's tone was wistful.

"Cheer up, Avery. One morning you'll hop out of bed, rarin' to give your place a good old-fashioned spring cleaning."

"That's the pep-talk I've been giving myself for thirty years."

"I can't believe it. I can't sleep nights thinking I'll be murdered in my bed."

"Don't concern yourself, Birdie," said Uncle Ned. "It ain't as if everybody in town ain't dreamt about it as long as they knew you."

Carl Lathrup used his gavel. "That's enough of that, Ned. Miss Flatt has the floor."

"She ought to take a mop to it now and again. I been stepping in the same wad of Billy Fred Muster's gum since I voted last."

Billy Fred, chewing in the back row of chairs in the crowded town hall, shook his head. "That's a lie, you old coot. Lincoln's been dead since before gum was invented."

"Pipe down, the both of you." Birdie gave her girdle a mighty tug. "We used to have a nice safe town to raise our children in. The last week alone, the murder rate's gone up a hundred percent."

"That's because last week it was zero," Chief Dockerty pointed out. He stood near the door with his thumbs hooked inside his Sam Browne belt, his belly pushing out around them.

Lathrup pointed the gavel his way. "Since you feel like talking, Chief, maybe you can bring this special session up to date on the progress of your investigation."

"Mr. Sharecross and me—"

"And *I*," corrected Neil Bonn, principal of the elementary school and a substitute English teacher.

"Well, Mr. Bonn, I didn't know you was putting your heads together when I wasn't present." Dockerty grinned. "Mr. Sharecross and I are expecting an express package from ZBC headquarters in New York City sometime today. The program director's sending us a DVD of that TV pilot they shot in Mr. Fister's library back in March. With any luck, it'll tell us what book the killer stole."

"And what good will *that* do, I'd like to know?" asked Birdie. "While I'm at it, what's the purpose of inviting a shopkeeper into a homicide investigation? My nephew Roy, the Eagle Scout"—she stared around the room over the tops of her half-glasses, while the title sank in—"has a badge in tracking, and would seem to me the more appropriate choice, this incident being apparently beyond the talents of the police force we all pay taxes to support."

Dockerty untucked one of his thumbs to rest that hand on his sidearm; not that he had any intention of blowing Birdie Flatt out from under her Dolly Parton wig. "Apart from his background, which we all seem to keep forgetting, Mr. Sharecross knows books. Once we've established *which* book Mr. Fister was killed for, he'll be able to narrow down the suspects to those collectors who specialize in that particular area. Even if the killer wasn't one of them, they'd be the ones he'd approach to sell the item. I'll be talking to them all."

"I hope you're right, Chief." Gordon Tolliver, publisher of *The Good Adviser*, rose to his considerable height. "I'd like to feature some good news for a change; something more diverting than Sherm McDonough's quest for pre-Colombian Indian arrowheads."

"As opposed to pre-Colombian *European* arrowheads," put in Neil Bonn, who taught American History in a pinch.

"Go ahead, make fun." Sherm McDonough left off plucking cockleburs from his socks to address the congregation. "I've got an offer of a thousand bucks from the Smithsonian for a Clovis point I found up on Superstition Overlook."

Lathrup rapped the podium. "We're drifting away from the reason for this gathering. Where *is* Avery Sharecross?"

"Oh, he's busy," Dockerty said. "Nobody ever accused Avery of laziness and sloth."

"Busy doing what?" pressed the head of the council. "Sifting through clues, analyzing evidence, interrogating suspects? The citizens of Good Advice have a right to know how their trust is being invested."

The chief returned his thumb to his belt, shifted his weight from one foot to the other. "I can't answer for him right this minute, but when I talked to him this morning he was rearranging his inventory according to the Dewey Decimal System, whatever that is."

"There!" Sharecross gripped Andy Barlow's shoulder, making the deputy chief wince. He hadn't much more flesh in that area than the bookseller had in his whole body—which Chief Dockerty could lose from his middle without anyone noticing.

Andy hit PAUSE. The picture on the computer monitor in Dockerty's office froze.

"Can you zoom in?" Sharecross asked.

"Sure." Andy played an adagio on the keys. The shelf in question filled the screen.

"We lucked out there." Andy reached back to knead his bruised flesh. "Not all of the TV networks have gone over to Blu-Ray. Ten years ago this would've been on videotape, and good luck identifying the printing on the spine from Mrs. O'Leary's cow."

Sharecross shushed him, sliding his thick spectacles down to the tip of his long nose, back up to the bridge, and back down halfway, like a Chinese cleric manipulating beads on an abacus. At length he straightened, returning them to their customary place.

"Something?" Chief Dockerty was a patient man, but he and the bookseller seemed to live in parallel universes where the value of time fluctuated like foreign currency.

"*L'Exploration d'Descubrimientos en Nuevo Espano*. Gentlemen, I'm dumbfounded."

"Me, too," Dockerty said. "I don't know if you're speaking Latin or Swahili."

"Castilian Spanish, in which I assure you I am no expert. Roughly translated, it's *The Exploration of Discoveries in New Spain*; published, if memory serves, in Madrid in 1545."

Dockerty whistled. "Anything that old's got to be worth something."

"Not necessarily. Age is not a factor in evaluating a book; if it were, every ancient family Bible in North America would be worth thousands, but no one ever throws them away so they're common as clothespins.

"Nor is rarity, although this particular item certainly qualifies. I doubt more than ten copies were issued, handset in wooden type for the court of Philip II of Spain. Condition is often a factor, but not in this case: Missing its covers, and even significant pages from the text, would hardly affect its value. Demand, gentlemen; that thing that drives capitalism tips the balance in this circumstance. I know of ten billionaires who would bid energetically against one another to lay hold of *L'Exploration* in any condition and, from what I see here, this copy is complete, and as close to pristine as you're ever likely to find."

"This is a murder investigation, not a meeting of your book club. Come to the point this side of when they invented gunpowder."

"Actually, the *Conquistadors* were well-equipped in that—"

"Avery!"

"Sorry. If I were the murdering kind, I would certainly give it proper consideration in this case. This book was written by Hernando Cortez, conqueror of Mexico. Considering the paucity of copies and the stature of the individuals to whom it was presented, it's more than likely Cortez delivered them in person. He would have held this book in his hands."

Dockerty slid his Stetson to the back of his balding head.

"I don't see it myself, but I can understand where some folks might covet it at whatever the cost. Give me a list of those folks and I'm on the way."

"I'll get right on it. Verne Platt knows his way around the computer at the library. He can Goggle—"

"Google," corrected Andy.

"He can Google the title and find out who's most interested. This could make your career, Chief. The suspects must have access to millions in cash."

"I like my career as it is. Nice town, decent wages, four acres I can grow sunflowers and entertain my grandchildren, when we have 'em. Be a nicer place with one less murderer in it."

"You're a good man, Chief."

"You sell him this book?"

"I wish I had; I could have retired, if I hadn't already from the police department. He must have found it on the Net, despite his distrust of it, or on one of his buying trips. I'm surprised he didn't share the discovery with me. Half the fun of collecting is rubbing other collectors' noses in your best acquisitions."

"Maybe he'd just got it."

"Which may narrow the field further, to others who were interested at the same time. How about the autopsy?"

"Busted skull, extensive brain damage, death close to instant as I guess it ever comes. Doc Simms has the Latin, for the record. Leather fibers in the cavity—left by the weapon, most like; if Fister was wearing a leather cap at the time, it hasn't turned up."

"I doubt Lloyd owned anything as casual as a cap. His taste ran to three-piece suits and a freshly blocked felt fedora. Sap?"

"I hate to think it. It means the killer came prepared."

"I never put it aside. Lloyd was sane as a carpenter's level, but he'd do anything to guard his collection."

"Including fight to the death?"

"Including that. Love is the strongest motive of all."

"Well, it's a big book and he was killed in broad daylight. Maybe someone saw whoever it was lugging it away."

"At almost a thousand pages, each of them thick parchment, it would be heavy as well. Those clasps are solid iron, to reinforce the binding." He pointed at the thick horizontal ridges on the top and bottom of the spine of the book onscreen. "If he left on foot, he'd be one tired man—or woman, if she's built for it—by the time he got where he was going. Perhaps someone saw somebody who looked worn-out so early in the day."

"Could be. Andy took pictures of the driveway, but the only tread marks there belonged to Fister's Land Rover, which is still in the garage. If it was a sneak thief, he wouldn't want to advertise his coming with the sound of a motor."

"If it was a sneak thief," Sharecross said. "Call it an old cop's hunch, but I've got a sinking feeling it was someone we know."

Deputy Chief Barlow rapped on the frame of Dockerty's door, which had remained open as long as he'd had the office. "We got a ping on that door-to-door," Barlow said. "Gordon Tolliver saw something."

Dockerty dumped his half-eaten Big Mac back into the sack and wiped his hands. "Go ahead, Andy. Keep me in suspense. I'm just the guy who fights the council for your annual pay raise."

"I was wondering who to thank for that extra dime an hour. If you let me finish, I would've told you he's waiting outside."

"Prod him in. I don't know why we even had this conversation."

Tolliver entered, ducking his head from instinct. The top of the doorway gave him two inches' clearance, but it was a tall doorway. At the half-century point he looked in good shape, no extra fat, and a fine head of brown hair.

"I didn't think anything of it until Andy told me you were looking for a man who looked tired and might have been carrying a large object," said Tolliver, folding himself into a captain's chair. "I was taking down last week's front page from the window. A small-town newspaper tradition, Chief. The point is to tease people into paying to read the stuff you jump to an inside page."

"I wondered about that. It always seemed to me the opposite, plastering your wares out in full sight for free."

"No danger of that, Chief. Ever since I left my old newspaper job, it's been my dream to publish my own. It's a challenge, especially today, with the Internet and all. I struggle to keep myself in paper and ink."

Dockerty nodded sympathy, resisting the urge to strangle the rest of the story out of him. You had to be a diplomat in Good Advice, where you kept running into the same people day after day. "Tell me what you told Andy."

"I'd just peeled off the tape when I saw a man hurrying past the window. He was red and panting, as if he'd run a long way, and carrying something under one arm."

"What was it?"

"I didn't see. It was on the side opposite the window."

"Anything else? A sap?"

"What's a sap?"

"A blackjack, but not that necessarily. Some kind of blunt object that might be used to crack open a man's skull."

"I saw nothing like that."

"Sure?"

"Someone running around town swinging a bludgeon would leave an impression, don't you think?"

"You'd be surprised what folks don't notice. They can't all be eagle-eyed journalists. Recognize him?"

"I'd never seen him before, and I like to think I know everyone in town. It's part of my job."

"Know him again?'

"I think so."

Officer Floyd Debner, a part-timer, had studied art at the University of New Mexico. He listened to Tolliver's description and sketched a rat-faced man with bulging eyes, his mouth hanging open to show a set of teeth only an orthodontist could love. Dockerty had copies made for distribution. He showed Avery Sharecross the original.

The bookseller climbed down from a wobbly stepladder to accept the drawing. His corduroy jacket was smeared with sooty dust; he'd been reorganizing the shop for a week but the chief couldn't see that he'd made a dent in the chaos.

"The story checks," Dockerty said, as Sharecross studied the sketch. "The newspaper's halfway between Fister's house and the bus station. The killer wouldn't hang around town a minute longer than he had to."

"That's logical. This man would attract notice." He slid his glasses back up to the bridge of his nose. "Does he look familiar?"

"He does, but I'll be goldarn if I can place him."

"Was it at the Gaiety Theater, possibly?"

"Why the Gaiety?"

"Orville Potts, the manager, has a weakness for crime films. Many of them feature Steve Buscemi."

He snatched back the picture and stared. "I'll be—"

"Have you heard back on fingerprints?"

"Got the results from the state police lab this morning. I'm glad we took yours. I was able to eliminate those, and a couple of other sets belonging to folks who knew Fister well enough to visit. We're working on the rest."

"You dusted the library ladder?"

"First thing, seeing as how high up that book was shelved. All we got was Fister's."

"Gloves?"

"They leave marks, too, not that they're unique, like fingerprints." He shook his head. "And he didn't wipe it down, neither, or we wouldn't have found Fister's."

Sharecross looked at a wall calendar featuring a cartoon caterpillar wearing spectacles. He might have been peering into a mirror. "This is Wednesday, isn't it?"

"Comes around every week about this time. Why?"

"*The Good Adviser* comes out today. I think I'll go down and buy a copy."

"Why? It'll just be full of this case, with that picture on the front page. You won't learn anything there you don't already know."

"I agree."

The rodent features he'd just been looking at stared at him through the tall window beside the door to the newspaper office, on the ground floor of a false-front building as old as statehood: PUBLISHER IDENTIFIES KILLER read the headline on the front page taped to the plate glass.

"Avery! What brings the owl out of his barn?" The publisher got up from his desk to shake the visitor's hand. He towered over the bookseller.

"The quest for information; an experienced journalist like yourself shouldn't find that unusual, and you know more than most. Didn't you mention once you wrote a book column before you came here?"

"*The El Paso Times.* The feature was discontinued. I was told there weren't enough readers interested in books. Does that sound oxymoronic?"

"Stupid's more appropriate. Did you ever visit Lloyd Fister's mansion?"

"Quite recently. He was kind enough to grant me an interview about his TV appearance. Tragically, he was killed before I could run the article."

"Have you ever been fingerprinted?"

"Odd question. As a matter of fact—no, I haven't. I wasn't in the military and I don't own a firearm. I'm happy to say I've never been arrested."

"Well, never's a long time. It eliminates one of the sets of prints the police couldn't identify. Did you discuss Fister's collection?"

"Am I a suspect?"

"I don't have the authority to judge, but I am helping out Chief Dockerty. I'm interviewing everyone who had contact with Fister just before his death."

"I see. Yes, he did show me some of his prize acquisitions."

"Was one of them *L'Exploration d'Descrubrimiento en Nuevo Espano*?"

"I couldn't say offhand. He had some Spanish titles, but I don't understand the language. It may be in my notes."

"Don't trouble yourself to look for them. It's a large book, bound in morocco leather, with iron clasps on the spine. You'd remember it if he showed it to you, I'm sure."

"It doesn't ring a bell."

"It's missing. The police are operating on the theory it was stolen."

"That would explain why I didn't see it. Perhaps he sold it."

"Doubtful. Lloyd spent his life building that collection. He wouldn't be likely to break it up. How tall are you, Gordon?"

"That's rather a personal question."

"And yet not an unusual one for you, I imagine. You stand out in a crowd."

"I'm six-foot-seven."

"As tall as that. No wonder Fister's prints were the only marks on the ladder in his library. You wouldn't even have to stand on tiptoe to take down the book."

The publisher stiffened, adding to his height. "Please leave. I won't have my character assassinated in a building I pay rent on."

"One of your many expenses. They must have been on your mind when he showed you the latest addition to his library. The book being so old and rare, naturally he wouldn't let you handle it; but being familiar with the book trade, you knew it was valuable.

"The nearest telephone was downstairs. Perhaps it rang and he went down to answer it, leaving you alone in the room. Whatever the interruption was, it wasn't long enough for you to stash the book where you could retrieve it on your way out. Did you hear him coming and duck behind the door?"

"I'm warning you, Sharecross. I'll throw you out."

"Violence would be an option in your case. It was when you panicked and struck Fister on the back of the head, with the book you were holding."

"Okay." Tolliver reached down, gathered the bookseller's lapels in both fists, and lifted him off his feet.

"Put him down!"

The voice was Chief Dockerty's. He stood in the doorway with his feet spread and his revolver clasped in both hands, the barrel pointed at the publisher's sternum.

Tolliver hesitated. All the tension went out of him then. He lowered Sharecross to the floor.

"Dear me." Sharecross brushed at his wrinkled lapels.

"Hands on your head, Tolliver!"

"No need for that," said the bookseller. "He doesn't own a gun. I think he told the truth about that. His weapon of choice is the very thing he committed murder to own."

Dockerty shook his head and laid Sharecross' signed statement on his desk. "I never heard anything like it, the stolen property doubling as the weapon in a homicide."

"It was pure impulse. Had he been thinking, he wouldn't have risked damaging it. It's tragic, but fortunate for posterity, that those clasps were harder than Lloyd's head." He nodded toward the evidence on the desk, a volume as big as a hefty dictionary, clamped in iron.

"How'd you know Tolliver was lying about the stranger?"

"It was a hunch, as I said. He lacked imagination—people who look for symbols in books like *Garp* often do—or he'd have come up with a description that didn't belong to a well-known actor. The unused ladder started me thinking the thief had to be tall enough to reach a shelf nine feet from the floor."

"He might've gotten away with it if he weren't so interested in throwing us off the track."

"Not really. The only other copy of *L'Exploration* known to exist is in the Library of Congress. He couldn't try to sell Fister's without implicating himself. No imagination, and too volatile for reason."

"They'll cure him of that in prison. Meanwhile, what do we do with the book?"

Sharecross looked uneasy. "It mustn't languish in a non-climate-controlled evidence room through the trial and inevitable appeals. I keep my rarer stock in a properly maintained storage room in Santa Fe. I'm offering it to the justice system indefinitely, without charge."

"You're a civilian. That would constitute ownership. No judge would allow it."

Sharecross' face fell.

Dockerty stood. "Get up and raise your right hand."

"Whatever for?"

"I'm swearing you in as an officer with the Good Advice Police Department and putting you in charge of homicide evidence."

The bookseller rose with a smile. "All of it?"

"Every last volume."

VIII

Death Leaves a Bookmark

William Link

TROY PELLINGHAM HADN'T read a book since college. He had better things to do with his life, but so far none of these had turned out to be profitable. The irony was that his uncle, Rodney Haverford, was an antiquarian who dealt in rare books, having an exclusive shop on Melrose Avenue. Uncle Rodney was so snooty, so nose-in-the-air, that Troy jokingly wondered how he blew it. The old man was healthy as an ox, was in his eighties, and never had suffered a head cold. This presented Troy with a problem.

His uncle always dressed in Saville Row bespoke clothing, imported from London: heavy tweeds with vests and watch fob pockets, even on sizzling summer days. And he never seemed to sweat. Perspiration would be unseemly to the old snob, something only blue collar laborers were forced to endure. Or other members of the lower class who worked with their hands.

Of course Uncle Rodney had a trust fund, set up by his father, whom Troy's late mother had once told him was another snob.

Genetically, Rodney was cut from the same bolt of disdain. Like father, like son, both elitist snots who might wipe their fingers with a scented hankie after shaking hands with someone below their status.

Troy had degradingly flattered his uncle, licked his posterior daily and twice on Sunday. He always metaphorically got on his knees to the wealthy, especially if he knew he could inherit some of their vast riches when they croaked in a comfortable bed.

The only family Uncle Rodney had left were a niece by marriage and his nephew Troy. The niece, Marcella, was attractive and spent money as if she could always print more because she knew the printing press was her uncle. Uncle Rodney and Marcella had formed a close relationship during the summers she and her mother had stayed with him when she was a child. Later she came to live with Rodney in his Beverly Hills home while studying at UCLA. Their bond remained so strong that she stayed on after college.

Once the old man had learned that Troy was no book worm, and was a failure in his business endeavors, he wrote the lad off as if he were a bad investment. He had even threatened to cut him out of his will, but Troy knew for a fact that he hadn't gotten around to it yet and probably wouldn't. After all, to Uncle Rodney, family ties were sacrosanct.

Troy also knew he wasn't going to allow the old snob to die peacefully in his comfortable bed, surrounded by sycophantic doctors and nurses, all with greedy, outstretched hands. That would take too long. Now, how was he going to work it? That was the question. Since all his business plans had gone awry, he knew that this undertaking couldn't. It had to be the most carefully well-thought-out scheme of his life. He had heard that some mystery books had beautifully worked-out murder plots, but he was no reader. He had once thought that he could pretend to read a book but he knew his uncle would ask him some well-chosen questions and prove him to be a liar.

Rodney seemed to dote on Marcella. She was a little flighty and self-centered, but Troy didn't mind splitting Uncle Rodney's fortune with her. Perhaps they would wind up married and he would then have it all. Stop dreaming, he cautioned himself. You're still a long way from driving a Rolls and flinging money around like confetti. First he needed a fool-proof plan.

His uncle had him working in his bookstore, wrapping books to send out to book lovers here and in Europe, going to the post office to mail them, keeping things tidy, and overseeing new purchases. Uncle Rodney had reduced him to a gofer, a member of the same working class that he despised. Lately, as Troy worked in the store, he found himself trying to come up with a murder plan. One that would require an air-tight alibi, something that couldn't be picked apart. He thought, jokingly, that maybe the old man was the perfect person to work the plan out for him.

As it turned out, serendipitously, he didn't need a plan at all.

It was a slow afternoon, Uncle Rodney reading at his desk in the back of the store. Troy didn't know what the hell to do with himself. He could only stare out at the few passers-by on the street, most looking as bored as himself.

Scanning the store while his uncle was engrossed, he noticed that there was a small space behind the large bookcase on the west wall. The bookcase held a random collection of large art books, crime novels, and some law books. God, what a mess. He would have to reorganize all of those next. If he slipped behind the bookcase and his uncle came looking for him, he might . . .

But that meant he had to have a lot of strength in his arms and shoulders, and he had stopped going to the gym because of his money problems. Suppose someone came in at the wrong moment? It just might be worth it, though.

On an impulse, he closed the blinds on the street door and moved into the space behind the tall bookcase. God, am I really going to do this?

He gathered his inner strength and then called out: "Uncle Rodney!"

Querulous: "What do you want?"

"Could you please come here a moment?"

He could hear the old man's footsteps moving toward the front of the store. Annoyed: "Where the devil are you?"

Troy stood behind the bookcase placing both arms and his strongest leg behind it. It was the most difficult thing he had ever attempted in his soft life. He got the bookcase to move—and then with a push, it toppled over on the old man. The clatter could probably be heard in the adjoining stores and on the street.

He moved out immediately. He looked down through the empty shelves and saw the old man still twitching, just barely alive. He'd better finish the job and be damn quick about it!

He anxiously looked around. Several large art books were laying splayed open on the floor. He reached down to grab the heaviest one and almost dropped it. Fumbling again, he picked it up and closed the covers. This would do nicely. Death of a bookseller, ironically by one of his own books, he thought. Then he battered the old man's head through the space between two of the shelves. Satisfied now that he was dead, he wiped off the blood and his prints on the front and back covers of the volume with his handkerchief. And also the spine, just in case. He threw the book down on the floor, right next to his victim's head. He would have to remember to get rid of the handkerchief later.

He stood still, out of breath, listening for a moment, hoping against hope that the clatter went unnoticed and that nobody was too near-by. Then he took a deep breath. Held it for a bit. Waited. Frozen. Thank God there was still no response from anyone outside.

Knowing he hadn't left any prints on the back of the bookcase, he grabbed two parcels that had to be mailed, and ran to the back door of the store.

Outside now in the small parking lot, he moved past Rodney's Rolls and jumped into his own car, an eleven-year-old Dodge. Only one car had come down the alley, but he had turned away just in the nick of time. He was flying on the wings of luck and there was no better carrier, not even FedEx!

As he sailed down Melrose on the way to the post office, he saw in his mind's eye his future. It was lit up like neon. Uncle Rodney's money, all millions of it, and half of it would be his. And who knew what his future would be with Cousin Marcella? It was about time he got married, anyway.

At a Dumpster far away from the bookstore he threw away the bloody handkerchief, covering it with the accumulated trash.

There was nothing that night on the tube about his uncle's "strange accident." Marcella called around eleven, worried to death that Uncle Rodney had not returned yet to the house. She had called the store but all she got was his answering machine. "Should I call the police?" she asked him.

"Definitely. Why didn't you call me earlier?"

"I thought . . . I thought that maybe he had dinner and gone off with a friend to have a drink. Oh, God, Troy, something like this has never happened before!"

"Call the police. You want me to come over?"

She hesitated. "Well . . . yes. Why don't you?"

"Be right there."

He hung up, combed his hair, and put on his best sport jacket. With Marcella in a very vulnerable mood, maybe this was just the time to be sympathetic and slowly start a relationship. A romantic one.

My, what a greedy pig you are, he thought with an inner smile. Half a fortune isn't good enough for you? You want the whole damn pie with a good-looking young woman serving it? Yes. I do.

The Rodney mansion was a Georgian Colonial, conforming to Rodney's expensive and elegant tastes. Another asset that would be his and his cousin's. It was all dark except for a light leaking through the blinds in the living room.

Marcella had been crying, her eyes red, but that didn't obscure her beauty. She had almost snow-white blonde hair left long, the way Troy preferred. Blue eyes and a pale provocative mouth that started rumblings in his lower region. A very nice piece, indeed.

He gave her a hug, his hands just lingering a beat around her slim body. Smallish breasts, but that was fine. He was not a big breast man.

"Did you talk to the police?" he said, still holding her.

"Yes. They've sent somebody over to the store in case he's still there, working late."

"But you said you called him there."

She broke slowly away from him, trying to regain her composure. "I know. But Uncle Rodney sometimes doesn't answer if he's in the middle of something. You know that from working there."

"Yes, you're right."

She sat down on a plush, comfortable davenport. He joined her, keeping a safe, chaste distance. He had been wrong: this was not the proper time to approach her. But somehow, as never before, she had whet his appetite. She was wearing jeans and a simple gray pullover. In Troy's mind, she could have been in a bare-shouldered evening gown and he probably wouldn't have been turned-on more.

He had begun to tell her to stop worrying when the doorbell rang. She jumped up to get it.

The guy who walked in was nothing special, to say the least. He introduced himself with a badge as Lieutenant Columbo. He was wearing a raincoat that seemed to have endured a million rainstorms, and he seemed to be a bit bowlegged as he walked further into the room.

"Have you found our uncle?" Troy asked. Marcella was still standing.

Columbo hesitated, his expression darkening over. "I don't have good news," he said finally, looking at Marcella. She was stunned into silence.

"What is it?" Troy asked, his voice intentionally muted.

"We found Mr. Haverford in his bookstore. A big bookcase had fallen on him . . ."

"Good God!," Troy cried out. He was on his feet now, an arm around Marcella, who was staring in shock at the cop.

"I hate to say this," Columbo said, "but there was something additional."

Troy felt Marcella's body tighten with tension.

"Someone had bashed his head in with one of the books," Columbo added. "I'm really sorry to have to tell you this." He looked sorry, as if it had happened to his own uncle.

Marcella shuddered and collapsed into Troy's arms. God, he thought, what a lovely bundle. Her Chanel perfume floated up his nostrils like the fragrance of a garden of summer roses. He had to physically restrain himself from cupping her rear.

"Lieutenant . . . I don't know what to say . . ." He tried to exhibit a deep grief, but he knew not to lay it on with a cement-worker's trowel.

Columbo said, "We can't do much at this time of night. All the other stores are long closed. What's your name, sir?"

"Troy Pellingham." He nodded at Marcella: "Marcella and I are distant cousins." He didn't mention he had been working in the bookstore. This guy would find that out in the morning.

Columbo took some time trying to locate his notebook, finally coming up with it in his back trouser pocket. He started jotting something down. Probably our names, Troy thought. He could feel Marcella beginning to tremble. "Marcella dear," he said softly. "I think you better sit down."

He guided her back to the davenport, helped her sit down, her head lowered as if she didn't want to hear any more horrible news.

Columbo had closed his notebook, having trouble finding an empty pocket to put it back in. "I think that's all," he said, the dark look on his face again. "I know how you both must feel, and I have to tell you again I hated coming here to tell you this."

Troy nodded. "That's very good of you, lieutenant . . . Costello, was it?"

"Columbo," Columbo said. He shuffled a little toward the door, stumbling a little, glancing back at Marcella. He wasn't bowlegged, but his legs seemed tired as if he had been on his feet all day. "You better be sure the young lady gets to bed as soon as I leave."

"Yes, lieutenant, I will."

"Do you know if there are any sleeping pills in the house? She might need one tonight."

"No, I don't, but I'll certainly check."

Columbo was at the door. "Then I'll say goodnight to both of you."

"Goodnight, lieutenant," Troy said. Marcella murmured something that was impossible to hear.

Columbo went out, and Troy sat down on the davenport, keeping his distance again from his cousin.

That guy seems a pushover, he thought. But you never know with these cops. He had never dealt with one before, but maybe, just maybe, he had lucked out with this forgetful guy. He had a premonition it was going to be a very interesting experience.

He finally led Marcella to the stairs. "Do you want me to help you go up?" he said.

A weak smile. "No, I can manage it. When will I see you?"

"Tomorrow. I'll call and make sure you're up and okay."

He chanced a light kiss on her cheek. She didn't mind, giving him another weak smile. Then she slowly mounted the stairs.

The next morning Troy called his cousin and found out she was feeling "okay." He said he would be over, take her out for lunch if she was up to it.

He hung up the phone and it rang immediately. It was the cop, Columbo.

"Could you meet me down at your uncle's store?" he asked.

"When?"

"As soon as possible."

Troy hesitated. "I promised my cousin I would take her out to lunch. It's important that I do that."

Columbo said, "I understand, sir. But I'm afraid this has to come first. Can you tell her you'll pick her up a little later?"

Irritation curled his words. "I guess. I certainly hope I can help you."

"You never know, sir. I'll be waiting for you at the store; I'm there now."

"Okay." Best to play along with this bird. He called Marcella and told her he'd be delayed, helping the cop with his investigation. She understood. What a doll, he thought.

A half hour later he joined Columbo at the bookstore. There were other plainclothes people poking around, probably a forensic team. The bookcase was still on the floor, the book he had used on Rodney was now on the old man's desk.

"Any clues?" he asked Columbo.

He had half a dead cigar in one hand. "The book on the desk was used by the killer to bash your uncle's head in after the bookcase fell on him."

Troy made himself wince. "How awful!"

"Yeah, not pretty. The killer pushed it over on him. That's the only explanation."

"Any prints on its back?" A very safe question.

"Nah. Nothing so far. The murderer no doubt wiped them off."

Troy took time to supposedly mull this over. "You already dusted the book?"

"Yeah. We're waiting for that new electronic gadget for finding prints that hasn't come into our jurisdiction yet."

"No kidding. Gee, the whole world's going electronic these days."

Columbo nodded, vaguely.

"What kind of a book was it?"

"A big, fat, art book. But I think he just picked a book at random, didn't notice what it was."

Troy knew that was true—it just had to be big and heavy. He took a look back at the art book lying on the desk, placed there by the forensics guy. It was Rene Magritte's *Catalogue Raisonne, Volume I.* "Well, you know about these things, lieutenant. You've probably investigated a lot of murders like this."

Columbo frowned. "A book case falling on a victim? Nah, never. This is a new one on me . . . Oh, by the way, Mr. Pellingham . . ."

"What's that?" He braced himself.

"You didn't tell me you were working here." It was a neutral statement, seemingly nothing behind it.

"I'm sorry. After you announced last night what had happened, we were both in shock. I don't think Marcella or I had a clear thought in our heads."

"How long had you been working here?"

"About a year. My uncle was getting old and needed some help mailing packages, keeping the place clean, organizing things, dealing with clients, various stuff like that."

Columbo was scratching the back of his neck. "That reminds me. Where were you when this thing happened? I know you couldn't have been here, but just where were you?"

He knew he was well prepared for the question. "I guess at the post office, mailing some books out to some of the collectors. Dayton, Ohio. Bangor, Maine. Places like that."

Scratch. Scratch. "And what time do you think you left for the post office?"

"I probably left here around three or so. You can always check at the post office."

"If you're wondering, I'm trying to figure out a time when the murderer came in here. He sure didn't want you around."

Troy nodded, his expression dead sober. "Hell, no, I'm sure he didn't. Anything else I can tell you?"

"The blinds on the door to the street," Columbo said, not looking back at them.

"What about the blinds?" Now there was a question that came from the bleachers. What was it with him?

"I'm not here to annoy you, sir, but the blinds were closed when we got here."

Hell. He had forgotten to open the damn blinds before he high-tailed it out. "The murderer undoubtedly closed them before he did his dirty work. He certainly didn't want anyone on the street looking in."

"That's what I thought too, Mr. Pellingham. Just wanted to check with you." He hesitated, thinking. "But you know . . ."

This guy was starting to drive him crazy. But at least he wasn't scratching his damn neck any more. "What?"

"If he was smart he probably went out that back door. If he went out the front somebody might've remembered him leaving."

"Makes sense. Now anything else before I pick up my cousin?"

Columbo pursed his lips, reflecting again. "No, can't think of anything else I wanted to ask you."

Troy quickly turned away and was about to head for the rear door when Columbo said, "Oh, just more thing, sir."

"What's that?"

"We gotta get your prints before you leave."

"They're all over the store; after all, I worked here."

"I know that, sir, but we have to separate yours from others, just in case the killer was a little careless and left us one." Columbo was staring guilelessly at him.

"Okay, but please make it fast. My cousin's in a shaky condition and I want to get her out in the world, get some fresh air, before she breaks down again."

"Excellent idea, getting her out. I promise it won't take a minute."

One of the plainclothesmen took his prints and Troy was out of there.

He picked Marcella up at the mansion and took her to Spago in Beverly Hills. She seemed a lot better than before, with her careful makeup and stylish getup. He had requested a table near the back wall so they could have a private conversation.

"What do you suggest I have?" she asked, looking candidly at him over her menu. He was taken again by her beauty.

"Everything on the menu's great, the salads, the fish, chops, whatever you're in the mood for."

She told him she would have the North American plaice, a fish Troy had never heard of.

The prescient waiter was there at almost that instant. "What can I get you two?" he asked.

Troy ordered for both of them, deciding on a steak for himself.

"Very good," the waiter said. "How would you like that steak done, sir?"

"Ah, medium rare."

"May I get you some starters?"

Troy looked at Marcella, who shook her head no.

"Not today," Troy told him.

"Very good." The waiter melted away in the crowded restaurant.

"You seem much better," Troy said to her.

"I guess I am. A good night's sleep cures a lot. But I'll never get over Uncle Rodney's death. Murder, I *should* say."

"Neither will I," he lied. "What do you think about this Lieutenant Columbo? Is he up to the job?"

"I only spent a few minutes with him. How did you size him up?"

Troy shrugged. "Hard to tell, never having had any dealings with cops before. I guess he's par for the course. Sort of disorganized, though, forgetful. Did you see how he couldn't find a pocket to put his notebook in? And the way he shuffled around like he didn't know what to do. If he's in charge of finding Uncle Rodney's murderer, God forbid, I wouldn't want to take any bets."

She smiled. "That's not very encouraging."

"Well, we'll find out, won't we?" He wanted to reach across and take her hands, but he resisted the impulse. "Let's just have a nice meal and try to forget what happened for a little while."

She nodded in confirmation.

When their food arrived, they were silent as they ate.

The waiter suddenly appeared as they finished. "May I tempt you with some desserts?"

Again Marcella shook her head.

"Some other time," Troy said.

"Very good, sir. I hope you enjoyed your meal."

Troy nodded. "We did. We'll be back soon."

Pleased, the waiter drifted away.

"How about a drive?" Troy asked her. "It'll keep you away from the house for a few hours, take your mind off things."

She mulled this over. Then: "Yes, let's do it. Change of scenery."

He drove them out to the ocean, turning north up the Pacific Coast Highway. "You want to go as far as Santa Barbara?" he asked her.

"No. Maybe half-way and then turn back."

"You're the boss, Boss."

At approximately the half-way point, he turned around and headed back.

"Who would kill Uncle Rodney?" she mused.

"Good question. I don't think he had any enemies."

Her hand rested near her side and he noticed she hadn't applied any polish on her nails. "People, his customers, really liked him. He was always fair in his business dealings, as far as I know."

"We don't know everything," he said. "Some people you treat fair and they still have problems with you."

"How would you know, Troy? You never ran a successful business, did you?" She smiled to take some of the sting out of it.

What was she getting at? "No, but I goddamn tried. And I did deal with some people you could never please."

"But now you're going to come into a lot of money when the estate is cleared."

What the hell was she getting at? Did she think he had murdered Rodney? "So are you. But it's a hell of a way to inherit, wouldn't you say?"

"If I remember, Uncle Rodney never thought you tried hard enough."

"Well, he never said anything to me." But he had. Many times. Luckily, Marcella hadn't been present at any of those. But why was she bringing this stuff up?

He decided to take the deer by the antlers or whatever the hell the saying was. "Why are you bringing this up now?"

"No reason. Just seems you got lucky when Uncle Rodney died. The inheritance, I mean."

"I'm not even sure I'm in his will. He certainly never mentioned anything about it."

She lowered the window slightly and the wind was not kind to her hair. "I think he had millions. How does it feel to maybe becoming a multi-millionaire?"

"I haven't the slightest idea. But if he left some money to me, I do know I would get rid of the payments on this old rattle-trap. First things first, though."

She smiled to herself. She removed a scarf from her handbag and tied it around her blowing hair. Making her look even more adorable, he noted.

He decided to show her some balls: "What about you, Marcella? Did *you* ever have a paying job in your life?"

The question didn't seem to disturb her in the least. "No, I haven't. I was a pampered brat ever since Uncle Rodney took care of me. And that, of course, was Uncle Rodney's choice. We loved each other."

"Pretty soft life," he said, looking over at her. Better not over-do this, he thought. How the hell am I going to make her fall in love with me? Seems all she wanted to do was pick on him.

"Yes. Pretty soft. I've had a life wrapped in cotton-wool. But that's the way he wanted it. I majored in political science in college and that prepares you for nothing."

He met her eyes. "Did Rodney think you'd meet some rich young man who would sweep you off your feet? You are quite beautiful, you know."

Her smile brightened. "Why thank you, Troy. I never thought you noticed."

"I've got two eyes, don't I?"

"Do you think you could fall in love with me?"

Jesus, she was really putting him on the spot. "What makes you think I'm not already in love with you? That I was in love with you ever since you were no taller than a toadstool."

"I never knew that," she said. It was hard to tell if she was sincere or not.

"Well, now you know."

"How come you never told me this before?"

"Because I'm good at hiding things." Like committing murder, he thought.

"I'm really surprised."

He was having trouble keeping his eyes on the road and also glancing at her. She looked like she had more color in her face. God, was he turning her on?

"Well, now you know," he said, dangerously taking his eyes off the road again for a quick moment to look at her. "So what are we going to do about it? Do you feel anything for me?"

"You know you're quite handsome," she said. Her slight teasing tone had vanished. "Want to call each other's bluff?"

"What do you mean?" He could feel his heart jumping.

"We could stop and take a motel room. Just for the afternoon."

My God, was she kidding? Was this really happening to him? Much earlier, he had thought his lucky star had disappeared somewhere in the firmament.

There was a row of motels on the side facing the ocean. "Take your pick," he said.

"Any one's as good as another. Let's try this one right here."

He waited until a few speeding cars had passed before he swung into the motel's driveway.

"I'll see if they have a room," she said, getting out of the car.

He waited, his pulse racing. Was this his day or not? Sometimes Lady Luck smiled when you weren't even looking.

She came out of the manager's office and gave him a thumbs-up. He drove into one of the empty stalls and parked.

He practically floated out of the car like he was on a magic carpet.

She had a key with a tag and she opened door number four. He followed her in, breathing deeply. If she couldn't read his surging desire she was both blind and deaf.

The room was typical with moldy green drapes open to the highway and a double bed with a bleached-out russet bedspread. But who gave a damn?

She closed the drapes and pulled the bedspread and blanket to the foot of the bed. The sheets looked fresh and clean.

Before he knew it, she was pulling off her sweater and shucking off her skirt. Off came her bra and panties and he was so impressed with her gleaming nudity that he wondered if he could perform. He found out almost immediately.

It was a half hour of fabulous sex. She even had a condom in her handbag! He totally forgot where he was as he enjoyed her opulent body.

When it was over, he lay back on the bed exhausted. What he really wanted now was a cigarette, even though he had given them up years ago. He was happily astonished when she removed a pack of cigarettes and a lighter from that horn of plenty, her handbag. She shook out a cigarette and handed it to him.

He stuck the cigarette in his mouth. "My God," he said, "did you plan all this? Knowing men always want a cigarette after sex?"

She only smiled, lighting his cigarette. Then she was lying next to him on the sheet, staring at him with those depthless blue eyes.

"I think you did," he said, giving her a large smile in return.

"Do you know what *I* think?" she said.

"No. What?"

"I think you put Uncle Rodney out of his pain." The smile hadn't lost its strength.

"What? Jesus, that's a terrible thing to say. I liked the old man. I could never do something like that."

"No? Not even to split all his millions?"

He sat up on one arm, staring back at her. "No! Absolutely not! I wouldn't have the guts to pull something off like that." *I wouldn't have the guts? What a stupid thing to say.*

"Sure you would. We just made love, Troy. You're a very strong guy, even down there. "She poked a playful finger at him.

"Well, I didn't. That cop will find the real killer and it certainly won't be me."

"You're a little flushed, baby. What brought that on?"

He poked her gently in both breasts. "You did, *baby*. You could arouse a dead man, and you know it."

"Maybe I could. Never tried it."

"Well you sure got me aroused again."

Now she raised herself on her arm. "When we're having a serious conversation?"

"It's not serious. It's stupid. Get that crazy idea out of your pretty head that I did it. Columbo will undoubtedly nab the murderer."

"I thought you said the jury was out on him."

"Maybe he's a little shrewder than we think. As I said, I have no experience with cops. How do we know he won't come up with the killer?"

She was grinning. "The killer just gave me one of the best lays I've ever had."

"I'm not the goddamn killer! Got that?"

She was putting her bra back on, and he was unfortunately losing sight of those lovely breasts. Maybe they would do this again even if she thought he was the murderer. And it seemed she really did, damn it.

She was slipping into her panties, one gorgeous leg at a time, which was driving him insane again. They *had* to have another session; that was imperative. Should he admit he did it? He had the strong impression that she didn't care one way or another. God, how he had misjudged her! Little Miss Innocent with a condom in her handbag.

It was like she was reading his mind: "I don't care if you killed the old bastard. He kept me penned up in that house for years when I could've been out doing what we just did. Now I've got my freedom and I love it."

"I know what you mean."

She was silent, staring at him again. Suddenly, she began firing a bunch of questions. "Is there anything Columbo could find? And what about that book you used? Are you sure you wiped all your prints off? Answer me. You did, didn't you?"

"Yes, of course I did."

She looked at him and smiled with satisfaction.

Christ, now he had admitted it. Wait a minute, could he backtrack? How could he have done that? She could get the truth out of a politician. "Now wait a minute, just, uh, wait a minute here."

It was truly established now that he had done it, Troy thought. Had the cop gotten her to wring out a confession from him? No way. He was positive about that, although he knew now she was as tricky as he was and maybe even more cunning.

Silence.

"Do you know when we're going to find out about the will?" she asked.

"No."

She was into herself now, thinking. "You know, you could strangle me now and get all the money. Have you thought of that?"

"Are you serious? Of course not."

"When I checked in I put the wrong license number and phony names when I filled out the form. They only saw *me* in the office.

And I noticed no one passed by the window to check out your car and license plate."

He was astonished again. "You mean while we were making love?"

"When else? That didn't mean I wasn't having the time of my life. I'm a multi-tasker, Troy-boy."

He shook his head. "You're really something. My hat's off to you."

Sexy smile: "You had more off than your hat a short while ago."

"You got me there. Should we drive back?"

"No. Let's drive over to a seafood restaurant on the ocean and have another good meal. Great sex gets my taste buds flowing."

He swung off the bed and began to get dressed. "Wonderful idea. Maybe by the time we get back we'll be revved up for another gitgo."

"Hmmm. Sounds yummy."

The following morning, Columbo received a message from Marcella that she wanted to see him at her uncle's house.

He drove over from the station not sure what to expect. Had she come up with an enemy or enemies of the deceased? His own investigation hadn't come up with anything so far, but they had just started.

She answered his ring herself. She looked much more composed than before, wearing a jaunty blouse and full skirt. Quite a good-looking young lady.

She took him into the living room and pointed him to a chair. "Beautiful day," she said.

"Beautiful. Just why did you want to see me?"

"My cousin just confessed to me."

His bland expression stayed in place. "To the murder of your uncle?"

"What else?"

"He confessed"—snapping his fingers—"just like that? Or did you have to pry it out of him?"

"We made love, lieutenant. So afterwards he was in a vulnerable condition. Besides, the fool trusted me."

Columbo thought this over. "You made love. Were you in the habit of doing that with him?"

"No. First time. He was adequate but I let him think he was the king of seducers. You men are so easy to manipulate. He was so turned on he wanted to do it again. Right away."

Columbo kept his eyes on her—not very hard to do. "Why are you telling me this?"

"Because I loved my uncle and I want his murderer brought to justice. Even if it's my own cousin. That's not too hard to understand, is it?"

Columbo's scrutiny grew deeper. "No, not at all, particularly with all that money at stake. I can see why you might want your cousin out of the way."

"You mean the inheritance? You mean I want it all instead of just half?"

"Yeah. That's exactly what I was implying."

"Did anyone ever tell you have very penetrating eyes, lieutenant?"

"I think my wife did, once. But why don't you answer my question."

"What was the question again?"

"Are you turning him in for the money? So you can get it all instead of just half?"

"To be honest, that could be part of it. In fact, it could be a large part of it. And I don't want him to get away with killing my uncle. That is a definite no-no in my book."

"Book," he mused. "And your uncle was murdered with a book."

"Why are you complicating things?" she asked. "I'm handing him to you on a silver platter and you're bringing up a book. I guess Troy was right about you."

"About what?"

"That you're no great shakes at what you do. You think that's true?"

Columbo shrugged. "Different people have different opinions about me. All in the game."

"And you really don't care what people say about you?"

"I guess not. I just do my job as I see it."

She wasn't satisfied, obviously getting annoyed with his lackadaisical manner. "You don't believe he actually confessed to me?"

Columbo began opening the buttons on his raincoat. "Oh, I believe that's a strong possibility. Although I think you're a pretty devious person. I mean, you told me yourself how you manipulated him into confessing."

"So why aren't you out of here questioning the hell out of him?"

Columbo clasped the fingers of both hands around his raised knee. "Because it's not that easy. He might have confessed to you, and he might not have, but why would he confess to me? This is what we call a 'he said, she said' situation. I guess you don't have anything on tape, do you? Or anyone to corroborate it?"

"You think I carry a mini-recorder around in my handbag just in case somebody might confess to me?"

Columbo smiled. "Silly question. I'm sorry. Although you did engineer the tryst, you might also have thought to have a recorder with you."

Her laugh was this side of sarcastic. "And another thing, lieutenant. Do you make love to your wife with other people standing around to corroborate it?"

Got him. She saw a faint flush rising from his neck to the roots of his hair. She knew instantly that she had caught him off balance and she delighted in the moment.

"Oh, no, no, no way! Sorry again. But I had to check because you never know in certain situations."

Now she laughed just a laugh. "So you're not going to question him? Is that it?"

"Oh, I'll question him all right. But he might say you were in it with him." Short beat. "And maybe you were."

Unfazed by his supposition, she said, "Don't worry, I can handle him. How long are you going to be clasping that knee?"

"Oh, yeah, you're right," he said, lowering his leg to the ground. "I get so tied up with stuff I sometimes forget what I'm doing."

She couldn't help looking amused. "Okay. You know he'll deny ever having that postcoital conversation with me. So what are you going to do when he does?"

"Keep plugging."

"And what exactly does that mean?"

Columbo got to his feet. "It means I've gotta come up with something that'll stick. And I've got to do it before either one of you gets half of your uncle's money."

She was interested. "And why is that?"

"Because then either one or both of you can buy the best defense counsel in the country. The D.A. doesn't like going up against people like that. Do you blame him?"

"Yes, I do. He wants everything nice and easy so he won't be late for dinner? That's not my idea of a perfect, hard-working civil servant."

Columbo shrugged again. "Well, that's what we've got. I thank you for telling me all this. I really do."

She got up too. "My pleasure. If I need any help fending Troy off, I'll let you know."

Columbo wasn't finished. "I guess if you're the guilty party you would've had somebody else do it for you. A hitman, a friend, maybe even a cousin."

"What, and leave myself open to blackmail? Do you really think I'm that stupid?"

"Oh, no, no, miss, believe me, I don't." He edged toward the door. "Have a nice day."

And he was off, unbuttoned, flapping raincoat and all.

Around three that afternoon, Troy was in Columbo's office. He had received a message after lunch that the cop wanted to see him again.

"What is it this time, lieutenant?" he asked.

"I was talking to your cousin."

Troy tightened up. "Oh?"

"She told me something very interesting about you. That you had confessed to the murder after you two had sex."

Troy covered up his anger at the betrayal with a big smile. "That's right, I did."

Columbo looked surprised. "You did?! You admit you were the perp?"

Troy appeared perfectly relaxed in his chair. "That's what she wanted to hear more than anything else after our love making. So I took the hint and indulged her. I suddenly understood that it was to be a sex game with her. That's what she wanted, a sex game, and that's what she would get. It was a great ploy to make sure she would keep coming back for more. Apparently, the thought that I had killed my uncle seemed to intrigue and titillate her. A little sick, perhaps, but not criminal."

Columbo looked surprised. "Boy, oh boy, oh boy, that is really something. That is a good one. And I gotta say that's a new one on me. I never heard that used for slipping out of a bear-trap before. You two are really two pieces of work."

Columbo secured both his hands on the desk and leveraged himself to a standing position. "Guess what? I don't think it was a lie at all, Mr. Pellingham. She suspected you were the killer and you admitted it. Either that or she convinced you to kill your uncle."

Troy stamped an angry foot on the floor. "Screw you. It was a lie to get her on her back some more, maybe plenty more. Now let's see the color of your evidence if you've got any—which I know you don't."

"That kind of arrogance can get you in a lot of trouble, sir."

He was not to be deterred: "I'm still waiting to see your evidence. So quit stalling."

Columbo picked up a sheet of paper from his blotter. "You think I'd accuse you of murder just as a lark?"

Troy leaned back in the chair as if someone had pushed him. "I'm still waiting." His voice had lost some of its conviction.

"You pushed that bookcase over on your uncle and when that didn't do the job, you bludgeoned him to death with that book."

"Can the suppositions. They'd get you laughed out of court."

Columbo looked down at the sheet of paper. "This lab report isn't a supposition."

"So what's in the goddamn report? This better be good."

Columbo tossed the report back on his desk. "It was the murder book that gave you away."

Angry disbelief: "What?"

"You see, you wiped your prints off the cover. But you still left a print on the book."

"*Where?*"

Columbo picked a book up from his desk. "You see on the side where all the edges of all the pages are lined up perfectly in a block?"

He saw—and he could feel the sweat crawling in his palms.

"That's why I had your prints taken. There was a fair to middling partial print on those lined up edges. When the pages are flipped through, the print vanishes." He riffled through the pages. "When the book is closed, when you used it as a weapon, you inadvertently left your print on the tight block of pages." He picked up a volume from his desk. "Here, try it with this one."

Troy hesitantly reached out for the book and Columbo handed it to him. He looked at the block of page edges, but said nothing.

"Take a look at the title," Columbo said, punching in an extension on his phone.

Troy did. *The California Penal Code.* He looked up at Columbo, his face a grim mask now.

"You'll have plenty of time to read it after you're sent up for twenty years for Murder One." He said to the receiver when someone picked up: "Come on in, Pagano. I want you to make the arrest."

Troy flung the heavy book back on the desk.

"Now your sexy, ruthless cousin will get all of your uncle's fortune," Columbo added.

"The little bitch," he mumbled.

"She knew you did it, Mr. Pellingham, but she didn't have our expert lab."

"Or you," he said bitterly.

Columbo shrugged with his usual modesty. "Or me."

IX

The Book Thing

Laura Lippman

Tᴇss Mᴏɴᴀɢʜᴀɴ ᴡᴀɴᴛᴇᴅ to love the funky little children's bookshop that had opened just two years ago among the used bookstores that lined Twenty-Fifth Street in North Baltimore. There was so much to admire about it—the brightly painted miniature rockers and chairs on the converted sun porch, the mynah bird who said "Hi, Hon!" and "Hark, who goes there!" and—best of all— "Nevermore."

She coveted the huge Arnold Lobel poster opposite the front door, the one that showed a bearded man-beast happily ensconced in a tiny cottage that was being overtaken by ramshackle towers of books. She appreciated the fact that ancillary merchandise was truly a sideline here; this shop's business was books, with only a few stuffed animals and Fancy Nancy boas thrown into the mix. Tess was grateful that gift-wrapping was free year-round and that the store did out-of-print book searches. She couldn't wait until her own two-year-old daughter, Carla Scout, was old enough to sit quietly through the Saturday story hour, although Tess was beginning to fear that might not be until Carla Scout was a freshman in college. Most of all, she admired the counterintuitive decision to open a bookstore when so many people seemed to assume that books were doomed.

She just thought it would be nice if the owner of The Children's Bookstore actually *liked* children.

"Be careful," the raven-haired owner growled on this unseasonably chilly October day as Carla Scout did her Frankenstein stagger toward a low shelf of picture books. To be fair, Carla Scout's hands weren't exactly clean, as mother and daughter had just indulged in one of mother's favorite vices, dark chocolate peanut clusters from Eddie's grocery. Tess swooped in with a napkin and smiled apologetically at the owner.

"Sorry," she said. "She loves books to pieces. Literally, sometimes."

"Do you need help?" the owner asked, as if she had never seen Tess before. Tess's credit card begged to differ.

"Oh . . . no, we're looking for a birthday gift, but I have some ideas. My aunt was a children's librarian with the city school system."

Tess did not add that her aunt ran her own bookstore in another part of town and would happily order any book that Tess needed—at cost. But Tess wanted this bookstore, so much closer to her own neighborhood, to thrive. She wanted all local businesses to thrive, but it was a tricky principle to live by, as most principles were. At night, her daughter asleep, the house quiet, she couldn't help it if her mouse clicked its way to online sellers who made everything so easy. Could she?

"You're one of those, I suppose," the woman said.

"One of—?"

The owner pointed to the iPad sticking out of Tess's tote. "Oh . . . no. I mean, sure, I buy some digital books, mainly things I don't care about owning, but I use the reading app on this primarily for big documents. My work involves a lot of paper and it's great to be able to import the documents and carry them with me—"

The owner rolled her eyes. "Sure." She pushed through the flowery chintz curtains that screened her work area from the store and retreated as if she found Tess too tiresome to talk to.

Sorry, mouthed the store's only employee, a young woman with bright red hair, multiple piercings and a tattoo of what appeared to be Jemima Puddleduck on her upper left arm.

The owner swished back through the curtains, purse under her arm. "I'm going for coffee, Mona, then to the bank." Tess waited to see if she boarded a bicycle, possibly one with a basket for errant nipping dogs. But she walked down Twenty-Fifth Street, head down against the gusty wind.

"She's having a rough time," said the girl with the duck tattoo. Mona, the owner had called her. "You can imagine. And the thing that drives her mad are the people who come in with digital readers— no offense—just to pick her brain and then download the electronic versions or buy cheaper ones online."

"I wouldn't think that people wanted children's books in digital."

"You'd be surprised. There are some interactive Dr. Seuss books— they're actually quite good. But I'm not sure about the read-to-yourself functions. I think it's still important for parents to read to their kids."

Tess blushed guiltily. She did have *Hop on Pop* on her iPad, along with several games, although Carla Scout so far seemed to prefer opening—and then deleting—her mother's e-mail.

"Anyway," Mona continued, "it's the sudden shrinkage that's making her cranky. Because it's the most expensive, most beautiful books. *Hugo*, things like that. A lot of the Caldecott books, but never the Newberys, and we keep them in the same section. Someone's clearly targeting the illustrated books. Yet not the truly rare ones, which are kept under lock-and-key." She indicated the case that ran along the front of the counter, filled with old books in mint condition: *Elouise Goes to Moscow*, various Maurice Sendak titles, *Emily of Deep Valley*, Eleanor Estes's *100 Dresses*, a book unknown to Tess, *Epaminondas and His Auntie*, whose cover illustration was deeply un-PC.

Tess found herself switching personas, from harried mom to a professional private investigator who provided security consultations. She studied her surroundings. "All these little rooms—it's cozy, but a shoplifter's paradise. An alarm, and a bell on the door to alert you to the door's movement, but no cameras. Have you thought about making people check totes and knapsacks?"

"We tried, but Octavia got the numbers confused and when she gets harried—let's just say, it doesn't bring out her best."

"Octavia?"

"The owner."

As if her name conjured her up, she appeared just like that, slamming back through the door, coffee in hand. "I always forget that the bank closes at three every day but Friday. Oh well. It's not like I had that much to deposit."

She glanced at Mona, her face softer, kinder. She was younger than Tess had realized, not even forty. It was her stern manner and dyed black hair that aged her. "I can write you a check today, but if you could wait until Friday . . ."

"Sure, Octavia. And it's almost Halloween. People will be doing holiday shopping before you know it."

Octavia sighed. "More people in the store. More distractions. More opportunity." She glanced at Carla Scout, who was sitting on the floor with a Mo Willems book, "reading" it to herself. Tess thought Octavia would have to be charmed in spite of herself. What could be more adorable than a little girl reading, especially this little girl, who had the good sense to favor her father, with fair skin and thick dark hair that was already down to her shoulders. Plus, she was wearing a miniature leather bomber jacket from the Gap, red jeans and a Clash T-shirt. Tess had heard "She's so adorable" at least forty times today. She waited for the forty-first such pronouncement.

Octavia said: "She got chocolate on the book."

So she had. And they already owned *Don't Let the Pigeon Drive the Bus*, but Tess would just have to eat this damaged copy. "I'll add it to my other purchases when I check out," Tess said, knowing it was folly to try to separate Carla Scout from any object that was keeping her quiet and contented.

"I understand you've been having some problems with theft?"

"Mona!" Owner glared at employee. Tess would have cowered under such a glance, but the younger woman shrugged it off.

"It's not shameful, Octavia. People don't steal from us because we're bad people. Or even because we're bad at what we do. They do it because they're opportunistic."

"A camera would go far in solving your problems," Tess offered.

Octavia sniffed. "I don't do gadgets." She shot another baleful look at Tess's iPad, then added, with slightly less edge: "Besides, I can't afford the outlay just now."

Her honesty softened Tess. "Understood. Have you noticed a pattern?"

"It's not like I can do inventory every week," Octavia began, even as Mona said: "It's Saturdays. I'm almost certain it's Saturdays. It gets busy here, what with the story time and more browsers than usual—often divorced dads, picking up a last-minute gift or just trying desperately to entertain their kids."

"I might be able to help—"

Octavia held up a hand: "I don't have money for that, either."

"I'd do it for free," Tess said, surprising herself.

"Why?" Octavia's voice was edged with suspicion. She wasn't used to kindness, Tess realized, except, perhaps, from Mona, the kind of employee who would sit on a check for a few days.

"Because I think your store is good for North Baltimore and I want my daughter to grow up coming here. To be a true city kid, to ride her bike or take the bus here, pick out books on her own. *Betsy-Tacy, Mrs. Piggle-Wiggle, The Witch of Blackbird Pond*. Edward Eager and E. Nesbit. All the books I loved."

"Everyone wants to pass their childhood favorites on to their children," Octavia said. "But if I've learned anything in this business, it's that kids have to make their own discoveries if you want them to be true readers."

"Okay, fine. But if I want her to discover books, there's nothing like browsing in a store or a library. There are moments of serendipity that you can't equal." She turned to her daughter just in time to see—but not stop—Carla Scout reaching for another book with her dirty hands. "We'll take that one, too."

Back on Twenty-Fifth Street, Carla Scout strapped in her stroller, Tess was trying to steer with one hand while she held her phone with another, checking e-mails. Inevitably, she ran up on the heels of a man well-known to her, at least by sight.

She and Crow, Carla Scout's father, called him the Walking Man and often wondered about his life, why he had the time and means to walk miles across North Baltimore every day, in every kind of weather, as if on some kind of mission. He might have been handsome if he smiled and stood up straight, but he never smiled and there was a curve to his body that suggested he couldn't stand up straight. When Tess bumped him, he swung sharply away from her, catching Tess with the knapsack he always wore and it was like being hit with a rock. Tess wondered if he weighed it down to help correct his unfortunate posture.

"Sorry," Tess said, but the walking man didn't even acknowledge their collision. He just kept walking with his distinctive, flatfooted style, his body curving forward like a C. There was no bounce, no spring, in Walking Man's stride, only a grim need to put one foot in front of the other, over and over again. He was, Tess thought, like someone under a curse in a fairy tale or myth, sentenced to walk until a spell was broken.

Before her first Saturday shift at the bookstore, Tess consulted her aunt, figuring that she must also see a lot of "shrinkage" at her store.

"Not really," Kitty said. "Books are hard to shoplift, harder to resell. It happens, of course, but I've never seen a systemic ongoing plan, with certain books targeted the way you're describing. This sounds almost like a vendetta against the owner."

Tess thought about Octavia's brusque ways, Mona's stories about how cranky she could get. Still, it was hard to imagine a disgruntled customer going to these lengths. Most people would satisfy themselves by writing a mean review on Yelp.

"I will tell you this," Kitty said. "Years ago—and it was on Twenty-Fifth Street, when it had even more used bookstores—there was a rash of thefts. The owners couldn't believe how much inventory they were losing, and how random it was. But then it stopped, just like that."

"What happened then? I mean, why did it stop? Did they arrest someone?"

"Not to my knowledge."

"I should probably check with the other sellers on the street, see if they're noticing anything," Tess said. "But I wonder why it's happening *now*."

"Maybe someone's worried that there won't be books much longer, that they're going to be extinct."

It was clearly a joke on Kitty's part, but Tess couldn't help asking: "Are they?"

The pause on the other end of the phone line was so long that Tess began to wonder if her cell had dropped the call. When Kitty spoke again, her voice was low, without its usual mirth.

"I don't dare predict the future. After all, I didn't think newspapers could go away. Still, I believe that there will be a market for physical books; I just don't know how large it will be. All I know is that I'm okay—for now. I own my building, I have a strong core of loyal customers, and I have a good walk-in trade from tourists. In the end, it comes down to what people value. Do they value bookstores? Do they value books? I don't know, Tess. Books have been free in libraries for years and that didn't devalue them. The Book Thing here in Baltimore gives books away to anyone who wants them. Free, no strings. Doesn't hurt me at all. For decades, people have bought used books from everywhere-from flea markets to the Smith College Book Sale. But there's something about pressing a button on your computer and buying something so ephemeral for 99 cents, having it whooshed instantly to you. Remember *Charlie and the Chocolate Factory?*"

"Of course." Tess, like most children, had been drawn to Roald Dahl's dark stories. He was another one on her list of writers she wanted Carla Scout to read.

"Well, what if you could do what Willie Wonka did—as Dahl fantasized—reach into your television and pull out a candy bar? What if everything you wanted was always available to you, all the time, on a 24/7 basis? It damn near is. Life has become so a la carte. We get what we want when we want it. But if you ask me, that means it's that much harder to identify what we really want."

"That's not a problem in Baltimore," Tess said. "All I can get delivered is pizza and Chinese—and not even my favorite pizza or Chinese."

"You're joking to get me off this morbid school of thought."

"Not exactly." She wasn't joking. The state of food delivery in Baltimore was depressing. But she also wasn't used to hearing her ebullient aunt in such a somber mood and she was trying to distract her, as she might play switcheroo with Carla Scout. And it worked. It turned out that dealing with a toddler, day in and day out, was actually good practice for dealing with the world at large.

The Children's Bookstore was hectic on Saturdays as promised, although Tess quickly realized that there was a disproportionate relationship between the bustle in the aisles and the activity at the cash register.

She also noticed the phenomenon that Mona had described, people using the store as a real-life shopping center for their virtual needs. She couldn't decide which was more obnoxious—the people who pulled out their various devices and made purchases while standing in the store, or those who waited until they were on the sidewalk again, who hunched over their phones and eReaders almost furtively as if committing a kind of crime. They were and they weren't, Tess decided. It was legal, but they were ripping off Mona's space and time, using her as a curator of sorts.

At the height of the hubbub, a delivery man arrived with boxes of books, wheeling his hand truck through the narrow aisles, losing the top box at one point. He was exceedingly handsome in a preppy way—and exceedingly clumsy. As he tried to work his way to the back of the store, his boxes fell off one, two, three times. Once, the top box burst open, spilling a few books onto the floor.

"Sorry," he said with a bright smile as he knelt to collect them. Except—did Tess see him sweep several books off a shelf and into a box? Why would he do that? After all, the boxes were being delivered; it's not as if he could take them with him.

"Tate is the clumsiest guy in the world," Mona said with affection after he left. "A sweetheart, but just a mess."

"You mean, he drops stuff all the time?"

"Drops things, mixes up orders, you name it. But Octavia dotes on him. Those dimples . . ."

Tess had not picked up on the dimples, but she had a chance to see how they affected Octavia when the delivery man returned fifteen minutes later, looking sheepish.

"Tate!" Octavia said with genuine delight.

"I feel so stupid. One of those boxes I left—it's for Royal Books up the block."

"No problem," Octavia said. "You know I never get around to unpacking the Saturday deliveries until the store clears out late in the day."

He looked through the stack of boxes he had left, showed Octavia that one was addressed to Royal Books and hoisted it on his shoulder. Tess couldn't help noticing that there wasn't any tape on the box; the top had been folded with the overlapping flaps that people used when boxing their own possessions for a move. She ambled out in the street behind him, saw him put the box on his truck—then drive away, west and then north on Howard Street, completely bypassing Royal Books.

He looks like someone, Tess thought. *Someone I know, yet don't know. Someone famous?* He probably just resembled some actor on television.

Back inside the bookstore, she didn't have the heart to tell Octavia what she suspected. Octavia had practically glowed when she saw Tate. Besides, Tess had no proof. Yet.

"So, did you see anything?" Octavia asked at day's end.

"Maybe. If there was anything taken today, it was from this shelf." Tess pointed to the low one next to where the box had fallen, spilling its contents. Mona crouched on her haunches and poked at the titles. "I can't be sure until I check our computer, but the shelf was full yesterday. I mean—there's no Seuss and we always have Seuss."

"If you saw it, why didn't you say something?" Octavia demanded, as peevish as any paying customer. "Or *do* something, for God's sake."

"I wasn't sure I saw anything and I didn't want to offend . . . a potential customer. I'll be back next Saturday. This is a two-person job." Life is unfair. Tess Monaghan, toting her toddler daughter in a baby carrier, was invisible to most of the world, except for leering men who observed the baby's chest-level position and said things like "Best seat in the house."

But when Crow put on the Ergo and shouldered their baby to *his* chest, the world melted, or at least the female half did. So he stood in the bookstore the next Saturday morning, trying to be polite to the cooing women around him, even as he waited to see if he would observe something similar to what Tess had seen the week before. Once again, Tate arrived when story hour was in full swing, six boxes on his hand truck.

No dropped box, Crow reported via text.

Damn, Tess thought. Maybe he was smart enough to vary the days, despite Mona's conviction that the thefts had been concentrated on Saturdays. Maybe she was deluded, maybe—

Her phone pinged again. *Taking one box with him. Says it was on cart by mistake. I didn't see anything, tho. He's good.*

Tess was on her bike, which she had decided was her best bet for following someone in North Baltimore on a Saturday. A delivery guy, even an off-brand one working the weekends, had to make frequent stops, right? She counted on being able to keep up with him. And she did, as he moved through his route, although she almost ran down Walking Man near the Baltimore Museum of Art. Still, she was flying along, watching him unload boxes at stop after stop until she realized the flaw in her plan: How could she know which box was the box from the Children's Bookstore?

She sighed, resigned to donating yet another Saturday to The Children's Bookstore.

And another and another and another. The next four Saturdays went by without any incidents. Tate showed up, delivered his boxes, made no mistakes, dropped nothing. Yet, throughout the week, customer requests would point out missing volumes—books listed as in-stock in the computer, yet nowhere to be found in the store.

By the fifth Saturday, the Christmas rush appeared to be on and the store was even more chaotic when Tate arrived—and dropped a box in one of the store's remote corners, one that could never be seen from the cash register or the story-time alcove on the converted sun porch. Tess, out on the street on her bike, ready to ride, watched it unfold via Facetime on Crow's phone, which he was holding at hip level. The action suddenly blurred—Mona, taken into Tess's confidence, had rushed forward try and help Tate. Tate brushed her away, but not before Carla Scout's sippee cup somehow fell on the box, the lid bouncing off and releasing a torrent of red juice, enough to leave a visible splotch on the box's side, an image that Crow captured and forwarded in a text. Tess, across the street, watched as he loaded it, noted the placement of the large stain.

It was a long, cold afternoon, with no respite for Tess as she followed the truck. No time to grab so much as a cup of coffee, and she wouldn't have risked drinking anything because that could have forced her to search out a bathroom.

It was coming up on four o'clock, the wintry light beginning to weaken, when Tate headed up one of the most notorious hills in the residential neighborhood of Roland Park, not far from where Tess lived. She would have loved to wait at the bottom, but how could she know where he made the delivery? She gave him a five-minute head start, hoping that Tate, like most Baltimore drivers, simply didn't see cyclists.

His truck was parked outside a rambling Victorian, perhaps one of the old summer houses built when people would travel a mere five to fifteen miles to escape the closed-in heat of downtown Baltimore. Yet this house, on a street full of million-dollar houses, did not appear to be holding its end up. Cedar shingles had dropped off as if the house were molting, the roof was inexpertly patched in places, and the chimney looked like a liability suit waiting to happen. The delivery truck idled in the driveway, Tate still in the driver's seat. Tess crouched by her wheel in a driveway three houses down, pretending to be engaged in a repair. Eventually, a man came out, but not from the house. He had been inside the stable at the head of the driveway. Most such outbuildings in the neighborhood had been converted to new uses or torn down, but this one appeared to have been untouched. A light burned inside, but that was all Tess could glimpse before the doors rolled shut again.

That man looks familiar, she thought, as she had thought about Tate the first time she saw him. *Is he famous or do I know him?*

The man who walked to the end of the driveway, she realized, was Walking Man. No backpack, but it was clearly him, his shoulders rounding even farther forward without their usual counterweight.

He shook the driver's hand and Tess realized why she thought she had seen Tate before—he was a handsomer, younger version of Walking Man.

Tate handed Walking Man the box with the red stain. No money changed hands. Nothing changed hands. But even in the dim light, the stain was evident. The man took the box into the old stable and muscled the doors back into place.

Tess was faced with a choice, one she hadn't anticipated. She could follow Tate and confront him, figuring that he had the most to lose. His job was on the line. But she couldn't prove he was guilty of theft until she looked inside the box. If she followed Tate, the books could be gone before she returned and she wouldn't be able to prove anything. She had to see what was inside that box.

She texted Crow, told him what she was going to do and walked up the driveway without waiting for his reply, which she supposed would urge caution, or tell her to call the police. But it was only a box of books from a children's bookstore. How high could the stakes be?

She knocked on the stable door. Minutes passed. She knocked again.

"I saw you," she said to the dusk, to herself, possibly to the man inside. "I know you're in there."

Another minute or so passed, a very long time to stand outside as darkness encroached and the cold deepened. But, eventually, the door was rolled open.

"I don't know you," Walking Man said in the flat affect of a child.

"My name is Tess Monaghan and I sort of know you. You're the—"

She stopped herself just in time. Walking Man didn't know he was Walking Man. She realized, somewhat belatedly, that *he* had not boiled his existence down to one quirk. Whoever he was, he didn't define himself as Walking Man. He had a life, a history. Perhaps a sad and gloomy one, based on these surroundings and his compulsive, constant hiking, but he was not, in his head or mirror, a man who did nothing but walk around North Baltimore.

Or was he?

"I've seen you around. I don't live far from here. We're practically neighbors."

He stared at her oddly, said nothing. His arm was braced against the frame of the door—she could not enter without pushing past him. She sensed he wouldn't like that kind of contact, that he was not used to being touched. She remembered how quickly he had whirled around the day she rolled her stroller up on his heels. But unlike most people, who would turn toward the person who had jostled them, he moved away.

"May I come in?"

He dropped his arm and she took that as an invitation—and also as a sign that he believed himself to have nothing to fear. He wasn't acting like someone who felt guilty, or in the wrong. Then again, he didn't know that she had followed the books here.

The juice-stained box sat on a work table, illuminated by an overhead light strung from the ceiling on a long cable. Tess walked over to the box, careful not to turn her back to Walking Man, wishing she had a name for him other than Walking Man, but he had not offered his name when she gave hers.

"May I?" she said, indicating the box, picking up a box cutter next to it, but only because she didn't want him to be able to pick it up.

"It's mine," he said.

She looked at the label. The address was for this house. Cover, should the ruse be discovered? "William Kemper. Is that you?"

"Yes." His manner was odd, off. Then again, she was the one who had shown up at his home and demanded to inspect a box addressed to him. Perhaps he thought she was just another quirky Baltimorean. Perhaps he had a reductive name for her, too. Nosy Woman.

"Why don't you open it?"

He stepped forward and did. There were at least a dozen books, all picture books, all clearly new. He inspected them carefully.

"These are pretty good," he said.

"Good for what?"

He looked at her as if she were quite daft. "My work."

"What do you do?"

"Create."

"The man who brought you the books . . ."

"My younger brother, Tate. He brings me books. He says he knows a place that gives them away free."

"These look brand-new."

He shrugged, uninterested in the observation.

Tess tried again. "Why does your brother bring you books?"

"He said it was better for him to bring them, than for me to get them myself."

Tess again remembered bumping into Walking Man on Twenty-Fifth Street, the hard thwack of his knapsack, so solid it almost left a bruise.

"But you still sometimes get them for yourself, don't you?"

It took him a while to formulate a reply. A dishonest person would have been thinking up a lie all along. An average person would have been considering the pros and cons of lying. William Kemper was just very deliberate with his words.

"Sometimes. Only when they need me."

"Books need you?"

"Books need to breathe after a while. They wait so long. They wait and they wait, closed in. You can tell that no one has read them in a very long time. Or even opened them."

"So you 'liberate' them? Is that your work?"

Walking Man—William—turned away from her and began sorting through the books his brother had brought. He was through with her, or wanted to be.

"These books weren't being neglected. Or ignored."

"No, but they're the only kind of books that Tate knows how to get. He thinks it's all about pictures. I don't want to tell them they're not quite right. I make do with what he brings, and supplement when I have to." He sighed, the sigh of an older brother used to a sibling's screw-ups. Tess had to think that Tate had done his share of sighing, too

"William—were you away for a while?"

"Yes," he said, flipping the pages, studying the pictures, his mind not really on her or their conversation.

"Did you go to prison?"

"They said it wasn't." Flip, flip, flip. "At any rate, I got to come home. Eventually."

"When?"

"Two winters ago." It seemed an odd way to phrase it, pseudo-Native American stuff, affected. But for a walking man, the seasons probably mattered more.

"And this is your house?"

"Mine and Tate's. As long as we can pay the taxes. Which is about all we can do. Pay the taxes."

Tess didn't doubt that. Even a ramshackle pile in this neighborhood would have a tax bill of at least $15,000, maybe $20,000 per year. But did he actually live in the house? Her eyes now accustomed to the gloom, she realized the stable had been converted to an apartment of sorts. There was a cot, a makeshift kitchen with a hot plate, a mini fridge, a radio. A bathroom wasn't evident, but William's appearance would indicate that he had a way to keep himself and his clothes clean.

Then she noticed what was missing: *Books.* Except for the ones that had just arrived, there were no books in evidence.

"Where are the books, William?"

"There," he said, after a moment of confusion. Whatever his official condition, he was very literal.

"No, I mean the others. There are others, right?"

"In the house."

"May I see them?"

"It's almost dark."

"So?"

"That means turning on the lights."

"Doesn't the house have lights?"

"We have an account. Tate said we should keep the utilities, because otherwise the neighbors will complain, say it's dangerous. Water, gas and electric. But we don't use them, except for the washer-dryer and for showers. If it gets really cold, I can stay in the house, but even with the heat on, it's still cold. It's so big. The main thing is to keep it nice enough so no one can complain."

He looked exhausted from such a relatively long speech. Tess could tell that her mere presence was stressful to him. But it didn't seem to be the stress of *discovery*. He wasn't fearful. Other people made him anxious in general. Perhaps that was another reason that Walking Man kept walking. No one could catch up to him and start a conversation.

"I'd like to see the books, William."

"Why?"

"Because I—represent some of the people who used to own them."

"They didn't love them."

"Perhaps." There didn't seem to be any point in arguing with William. "I'd like to see them."

From the outside, Tess had not appreciated how large the house was, how deep into the lot it was built. Even by the standards of the neighborhood, it was enormous, taking up almost every inch of level land on the lot. There was more land still, but it was a long, precipitous slope. They were high here, with a commanding view of the city and the nearby highway. William took her through the rear door, which led into an ordinary, somewhat old-fashioned laundry room with appliances that appeared to be at least ten to fifteen years old.

"The neighbors might call the police," William said, his tone fretful. "Just seeing a light."

"Because they think the house is vacant?"

"Because they would do anything to get us out. Any excuse to call attention to us. Tate says it's important not to let them do that."

He led her through the kitchen, the lights still off. Again, out-of-date, but ordinary and clean, if a bit dusty from disuse. Now they were in a long shadowy hall closed off by French doors, which led to a huge room. William opened these and they entered a multi-windowed room, still dark, but not as dark as the hallway.

"The ballroom. Although we never had any balls that I know of," he said.

A ballroom. This was truly one of the grand old mansions of Roland Park.

"But where are the books, William?" Tess asked.

He blinked, surprised. "Oh, I guess you need more light. I thought the lights from the other houses would be enough." He flipped a switch and the light from overhead chandeliers filled the room. Yet the room was quite empty.

"The books, William. Where are they?"

"All around you."

And it was only then that Tess realized that what appeared to be an unusual, slapdash wallpaper was made from pages—pages and pages and pages of books. Some were only text, but at some point during the massive project—the ceilings had to be at least 20, possibly 30 feet high—the children's books began to appear. Tess stepped closer to inspect what he had done. She didn't have a craft-y bone in her body, but it appeared to be similar to some kind of decoupage—there was definitely a sealant over the pages. But it wasn't UV protected because there were sun streaks on the wall that faced south and caught the most light.

She looked down and realized he had done the same thing with the floor, or started to; part of the original parquet floor was still in evidence.

"Is the whole house like this?"

"Not yet," he said. "It's a big house."

"But William—these books, they're not yours. You've destroyed them."

"How?" he said. "You can still read them. The pages are in order. I'm letting them live. They were dying, inside their covers, on shelves. No one was looking at them. Now they're open forever, always ready to be read."

"But no one can see them here either," she said.

"I can. You can."

"William is my half-brother," Tate Kemper told Tess a few days later, over lunch in the Paper Moon Diner, a North Baltimore spot that was a kind of shrine to old toys. "He's fifteen years older than I am. He was institutionalized for a while. Then our grandfather, our father's father, agreed to pay for his care, set him up with an aide, in a little apartment not far from here. He left us the house in his will and his third wife got everything else. My mom and I never had money, so it's not a big deal to me. But our dad was still rich when William was young, so no one worried about how he would take care of himself when he was an adult."

"If you sold the house, you could easily pay for William's care, at least for a time."

"Yes, even in a bad market, even with the antiquated systems and old appliances, it probably would go for almost a million. But William begged me to keep it, to let him try living alone. He said grandfather was the only person who was ever nice to him and he was right. His mother is dead and our father is a shit, gone from both of our lives, disinherited by his own father. So I let William move into the stable. It was several months before I realized what he was doing."

"But he'd done it before, no?"

Tate nodded. "Yes, he was caught stealing books years ago. Several times. We began to worry he was going to run afoul of some repeat offenders law, so grandfather offered to pay for psychiatric care as part of a plea bargain. Then, when he got out, the aide watched him, kept him out of trouble. But once he had access to grandfather's house . . ." He shook his head, sighing in the same way William had sighed.

"How many books have you stolen for him?"

"Fifty, a hundred. I tried to spread it out to several places, but the other owners are, well, a little sharper than Octavia."

No, they're just not smitten with you, Tess wanted to say.

"Could you make restitution?"

"Over time. But what good would it do? William will just steal more. I'm stuck. Besides . . ." Tate looked defiant, proud. "I think what he's doing is kind of beautiful."

Tess didn't disagree. "The thing is, if something happens to you— if you get caught, or lose your job—you're both screwed. You can't go on like this. And you have to make restitution to Octavia. Do it anonymously, through me, whatever you can afford. Then I'll show you how William can get all the books he needs, for free."

"I don't see—"

"Trust me," Tess said. "And one other thing?"

"Sure."

"Would it kill you to ask Octavia out for coffee or something? Just once?"

"Octavia! If I were going to ask someone there out, it would be—"

"Mona, I know. But you know what, Tate? Not everyone can get the girl with the duck tattoo."

The next Saturday, Tess met William outside his house. He wore his knapsack on his back, she wore hers on the front, where Carla

Scout nestled with a sippee cup. She was small for her age, not even twenty-five pounds, but it was still quite the cargo to carry on a hike.

"Are you ready for our walk?"

"I usually walk alone," William said. He was unhappy with this arrangement and had agreed to it only after Tate had all but ordered him to do it.

"After today, you can go back to walking alone. But I want to take you some place today. It's almost three miles."

"That's nothing," William said.

"Your pack might be heavier on the return trip."

"It often is," he said.

I bet, Tess thought. He had probably never given up stealing books despite what Tate thought.

They walked south through the neighborhood, lovely even with the trees bare and the sky overcast. William, to Tess's surprise, preferred the main thoroughfares. Given his aversion to people, she thought he would want to duck down less-trafficked side streets, make use of Stony Run Park's green expanse, which ran parallel to much of their route. But William stuck to the busiest streets. She wondered if drivers glanced out their windows and thought: Oh, the walking man now has a walking woman and a walking baby.

He did not speak and shut down any attempt Tess made at conversation. He walked as if he were alone. His face was set, his gait steady. She could tell it made him anxious, having to follow her path, so she began to narrate the route, turn by turn, which let him walk a few steps ahead. "We'll take Roland Avenue to University Parkway, all the way to Barclay, where we'll go left." His pace was slow by Tess's standards, but William didn't walk to get places. He walked to walk. He walked to fill his days. Tate said his official diagnosis was bi-polar with OCD, which made finding the right mix of medications difficult. His work, as William termed it, seemed to keep him more grounded than anything else, which was why Tate indulged it.

Finally, about an hour later, they stood outside a building of blue-and-pink cinderblocks.

"This is it," Tess said.

"This is what?"

"Go in."

They entered a warehouse stuffed with books. And not just any books—these were all unloved books, as William would have it, books donated to this unique Baltimore institution, the Book Thing, which accepted any and all books on one condition: They would then be offered free to anyone who wanted them.

"Tens of thousands of books," Tess said. "All free, every weekend."

"Is there a limit?"

"Yes," Tess said. "Only ten at a time. But you probably couldn't carry much more, right?" Actually, the limit, according to the Book Thing's rather whimsical website, was 150,000. But Tess had decided her aunt was right about people according more value to things they could not have so readily. If William thought he could have only ten, every week, it would be more meaningful to him.

He walked through the aisles, his eyes strafing the spines. "How will I save them all?" William said.

"One week at a time," Tess said. "But you have to promise that this will be your only, um, supplier from now on. If you get books from anywhere else, you won't be allowed to come here anymore. Do you understand, William? Can you agree to that?"

"I'll manage," William said. "These books really need me."

It took him forty-five minutes to pick his first book, *Manifold Destiny*, a guide to cooking on one's car engine.

"Really?" Tess said. "That's a book that needs to be liberated?"

William looked at her with pity, as if she were a hopeless philistine.

"He spent five hours there, selecting his books," Tess told Crow that evening, over an early supper. Crow worked Saturday evenings, so they ate early in order to spend more time together.

"Did you feel guilty at all? He's just going to tear them apart and destroy them."

"Is he? Destroying them, I mean. Or is he making something beautiful, as his brother would have it? I go back and forth."

Crow shook his head. "An emotionally disturbed man with scissors, cutting up books inside his home, taking a walk with you and our daughter, whose middle name is Scout. And you didn't make one Boo Radley joke the entire time?"

"Not a one," Tess said. "You do the bath. I'll clean up."

But she didn't clean up, not right away. She went into her own library, a cozy sunroom lined with bookshelves. She had spent much of her pregnancy here, reading away, but even in three months of confinement she barely made a dent in the unread books. She had always thought of it as being rich, having so many books she had yet to read. But in William's view, she was keeping them confined. And no one else, other than Crow, had access to them. Was her library that different from William's?

Of course, she had paid for her books—most of them. Like almost every other bibliophile on the planet, Tess had books, borrowed from friends, that she had never returned, even as some of her favorite titles lingered in friends' homes, never to be seen again.

She picked up her iPad. Only seventy books loaded onto it. *Only.* Mainly things for work, but also the occasional self-help guide that promised to unlock the mysteries of toddlers. Forty of the seventy titles were virtually untouched. She wandered into Carla Scout's room, where there was now a poster of a bearded man living in a pile of books, the Arnold Lobel print from The Children's Bookstore. A payment/gift from a giddy Octavia, who didn't know how Tess had stopped her books from disappearing, and certainly didn't know that her crush had anything to do with it. During Carla Scout's bedtime routine, Tess now stopped in front of the poster, read the verse printed there, then added her own couplet. "It's just as much fun as it looks/To live in a house made of books."

It's what's in the book that matters. Standing in her daughter's room, which also had shelves and shelves filled with books, Tess re-membered a character in a favorite story saying that to someone who objected to using the Bible as a fan on a hot summer day. But she could no longer remember which story it was.

Did that mean the book had ceased to live for her? The title she was trying to recall could be in this very room, along with all of Tess's childhood favorites, waiting for Carla Scout to discover them one day. But what if she rejected them all, insisting on her own myths and legends, as Octavia had prophesied? How many of these books would be out of print in five, ten years? What did it mean to be out of print in a world where books could live inside devices, glowing like captured genies, desperate to get back out in the world and grant people's wishes?

Carla Scout burst into the room, wet hair gleaming, cheeks pink.

"Buh," she said, which was her word for book, unless it was her word for ball or, possibly, balloon. "Buh, p'ease."

She wasn't even in her pajamas yet, just her diaper and hooded towel. Tess would have to use the promise of books to coax her through putting on her footed sleeper and gathering up her playthings. How long would she be able to bribe her daughter with books? Would they be shunted aside like the Velveteen Rabbit as other newer, shinier toys gained favor? Would her daughter even read *The Velveteen Rabbit*? William Kemper suddenly seemed less crazy to Tess than the people who managed to live their lives in houses that had no books at all.

"Three tonight," Tess said. "Pick out three. Only three, Carla Scout. One, two, three. You may have three."

They read five.

Author's note: The Book Thing is a very real thing and its hours and policies are as described here. The Children's Bookstore on 25th Street is my invention, along with all characters.

X

The Scroll

Anne Perry

THE EARLY WINTER evening was drawing in. In the antiquarian bookshop well away from the High Street in Cambridge, Monty Danforth sat in his room at the back, working on unpacking and cataloguing the books and papers from the last crate of the Greville Estate. Most of it was exactly what he would have expected: the entire works of Dickens and Thackeray, Walter Scott and Jane Austin, all in leather-bound editions; many of the Russian novelists, similarly bound; *Gibbon's Decline and Fall of the Roman Empire*, Churchill's *History of the English Speaking People*. There were also the usual reference books and encyclopaedias, and some rather more interesting and unusual memoirs and books on travel, especially around the Mediterranean. He did not think much of it would re-sell easily, and it would take rather a lot of space to store it.

The owner of the shop, Roger Williams, was not well and staying at his house further north east, towards the wide, flat fen country. He might decide to auction the whole shipment off in one job lot.

Monty peered into the bottom of the crate to make sure he had everything out of it. There was something rather like an old biscuit drum on one side. He reached in and picked it up. It was too heavy to be empty. He pried the lid off and looked inside. There was definitely something there, but it was hard to make it out.

He took it over to the light and flicked on the switch. A yellow glow filled the room, leaving the corners even more shadowed. There was what looked like an old scroll inside the tin. He teased it out gently and put it on the table right under the light bulb. He unrolled it an inch or two at a time, and stared. There was writing on it, patchy, faded, in several places illegible. He tried to make out words, but it was very definitely not English, even of the very oldest sort. The letters were more like the little he had seen of Hebrew.

He touched the texture of it experimentally with his finger tips. It was soft, smooth and had not the dry fragile feeling of paper, more like vellum. There were several blanks on it, and other places where the words were half-obscured by smudges, or erased altogether.

According to what he had been told, the Greville family had travelled extensively in the Middle East in the nineteenth century and early twentieth. They could have found this scroll anywhere: Egypt, Mesopotamia, Palestine, Jordan, or what was now Israel.

Just in case it really did have some value, he should photocopy it. That could be useful to get a translation, without sending the original.

He stood up and took it over to the machine. He pressed the switch and it came to life. Very carefully he unrolled the first half of the scroll and laid it on the glass, then closed the lid. He pressed it for one copy. The paper rolled out onto the tray.

He picked it up to check it for clarity. It was blank, apart from a couple of smudges.

That was silly. He tried again, with the same result. He checked the ink, the paper, the settings, and tried a third time. Still nothing.

He took the scroll out and tried it with an old letter from a customer.

Perfect, every detail beautifully clear. It was not the machine. Just as well that, as always, he had his mobile phone with him; the camera in it was really rather good. Digital, of course, and you could check immediately on the result, and print it off on the computer later, if you wished.

He took a photograph of a customer's letter, then looked at it on the screen. It was perfect. Taking two books to hold down the ends and keep the scroll flat, he took the photograph. In the viewfinder it was perfect also, every line and smudge was there. He clicked the exposure once, twice, three times, taking the whole length. Then he looked at it. The first exposure was blank, so was the second, and the third. The vellum was clear, even to the shadows it cast on the table where the edges were torn or curled, but there was no writing on it whatsoever.

Monty blinked and rubbed his eyes. How was it possible? What had he done wrong?

He was still staring at it when he heard the shop's bell ring. It startled him, although he thought the moment after that it was not extraordinary for a lover of rare books or prints to call after hours. Sometimes it was convenient for someone who could not leave their work during the day. Quite often it was the desire to examine in privacy whatever it was that interested them. But they made appointments. Was there someone coming whom he had forgotten?

The bell rang again. He put the scroll back in the tin out of sight, then he went to the door and looked out through the glass. On the step was an old man, stooped, grey-haired, his face lined by time and from the look of him, perhaps also grief. Beside him was a child of perhaps eight years old. Her face was fair-skinned, blemishless, her hair soft and with the lamplight on it, its gold looked almost like a halo. She was staring straight back at Monty through the glass.

He opened the door. "Good evening. May I help you?" he asked.

The child gave him a shy smile and moved closer to the old man, presumably her grandfather.

"Good evening, sir," the old man replied. "My name is Judson Garrett. I am a collector of rare books and manuscripts. I believe you have just come into possession of the books from the Greville estate? Am I in the right place?"

"Yes, indeed," Monty answered. "But we've only just got it. It's not catalogued yet and so we can't put a price on it. The books are in very good condition. In fact, honestly, I'd say a good many of them haven't even been read."

Garrett smiled and his dark eyes were full of sadness. "It is the case with too many books, I fear. Old leather, fine paper are all very well, but it is the words that matter. They are the wealth of the mind and the heart."

Monty stepped back, holding the door open. "Come in, and we can discuss the possibilities."

"Thank you," Garrett accepted, stepping in, closely followed by the child.

Monty closed the door behind them and led the way to Roger Williams' office where matters of business were discussed. He turned the light on, making the bookshelves and the easy chairs leap to a warmth and inviting comfort.

"Please sit down, Mr. Garrett. If you give me your particulars, I'll pass them on to Mr. Williams, the owner, and as soon as we know exactly what we have, we can discuss prices."

The old man did not sit. He remained just inside the door, his face still cast in shadows, the little girl at his side, her hand holding his. There was a weariness in his face as if he had travelled too far and found no rest.

"There is only one item I'm interested in," he said quietly. "The rest does not concern me and you may do with it as you wish."

"Really?" Monty was surprised. He had seen nothing of more than slight worth. "What is the item?"

The old man's eyes seemed to look far away, as if he could see an infinite distance, into another realm, perhaps into a past beyond Monty's imagination. "A scroll," he replied. "Very old. It may be wrapped in some kind of protection. It is written in Aramaic."

Monty felt a chill run through him as if he had been physically touched by something ice-cold. The child was staring at him. She had clear, sky-blue eyes and she seemed hardly to blink.

Monty's first instinct was to deny having found the scroll, but he knew that the old man was already aware of it. It would be ridiculous to lie, perhaps even dangerous. He drew in a deep breath.

"I don't have the authority to sell the scroll, Mr. Garrett, but I will pass on your interest to Mr. Williams as soon as he comes back. If you leave a contact number or address with me, perhaps an email?"

"I shall return, Mr. Danforth," the old man replied. "Please do not consider selling it to anyone else before you give me an opportunity to bid." His eyes on Monty's were steady and so dark as to be almost black. His expression was unreadable.

The child tugged on his hand and her small fingers seemed to tighten on his even further.

"The scroll is of great value," the old man continued. "I hope you appreciate that?"

"No one else is aware of it yet," Monty assured him. "It isn't actually listed in the papers, and I only discovered it . . . maybe half an hour ago. May I ask how you heard it was there?"

The very faintest of smiles flickered on the old man's face, and vanished again before Monty was sure whether it was amusement or something more like regret. "Many people know it is here," he said very quietly. "They will come and offer you many things for it . . . money, but other things as well. Be very careful what you do with it, Mr. Danforth . . . very careful indeed. There is power in it you would be wise to leave."

Again Monty felt the coldness brush by him again, touching him to the bone.

"What is it?" he said huskily.

The old man drew in his breath as if to answer him. The child tugged at his hand again, and he sighed and changed his mind. He looked steadily at Monty, and there was long experience and a knowledge of evil and of pain in his eyes.

"Be careful, Mr. Danforth. It is a dangerous responsibility you are about to take upon yourself. Perhaps you have no other honourable choice. That I understand. But it is a heavy weight. There is destruction and delusion in what you are about to pick up. Do nothing without great thought."

Monty found himself gulping, swallowing as if there were something in his throat. "How do I contact you, Mr. Garrett?"

"You do not need to. I shall come back." He shook the child's hand off him impatiently and turned towards the door, pushing it open.

Monty followed him to the street entrance. He opened it and the old man walked through, the child on his heels. The street beyond was shadowed, the nearest lamp was apparently broken. When Monty looked again there was no one there.

Monty locked the door this time, not just the latch but the deadbolt as well, and went back to his room. He opened the tin again and took out the scroll. The vellum was soft to his fingers, almost warm. Was it as ancient as the old man had said? Aramaic? Perhaps from the time of Christ?

If that were so, then it could be any of a number of things, real or imagined. How did it come to be in the Greville estate? In their travels could they have found something like the Dead Sea Scrolls?

It was far more likely that they had been sold a fake. How difficult was it to make something of that nature? Or even to find an old scroll which might have been nothing more interesting than instructions to build a house, or lists of a cargo shipped from one port to another? Business writings abounded, just as domestic pottery far outweighed vases for ornament or the worship of gods.

He unrolled it on the table and weighed down both ends, putting it directly under the light. It was not very long, perhaps a thousand words or a little more. That was a lot for a cargo list, and there were no drawings or diagrams on it, so any kind of a plan seemed unlikely.

He peered at it, looking for patterns, repetitions, anything that would give him a clue as to what it was. It was the Hebrew alphabet, which he was vaguely familiar with, but Garrett had said it was Aramaic.

He really had very little idea of what he was doing, and no chance at all of actually reading it, yet he found it almost impossible to look away. Was this some passionate cry of the soul from the tumultuous times of Christ? An account of power and sacrifice, of agony and resurrection?

Or was it simply somebody's laundry list which had chanced to survive, principally because nobody cared enough to steal it?

Monty's imagination created pictures in his mind, men in long robes, sandals, dusty roads, whispers in the dark, blood and pain.

The light flickered and the shadows in the corners of the room moved, wavering and then righting themselves again. He half-expected someone to materialize out of the air, the darkness to come together, intensify and take form. Who could it be? Mephistopheles— to tempt an all too fragile Faust? With what? Forbidden knowledge?

"Don't be so damn silly!" he said aloud. "It's a power brown out! All you need to do is make sure your computer's backed up!" He had always had a weird imagination, a sensitivity to the presence of evil. He told the most excellent ghost stories to the great entertainment of his friends. He was known for it, even loved. People liked to be given a frisson of fear, just enough to get the adrenalin going.

His best friend, Hank Savage, a pragmatic scientist, teased him about it, although even he conceded that evil was real, just not supernatural. No angels, no devils, just human beings, some with rather too much excitability and a tendency to blame others for their own faults. Who easier to blame than the devil?

Monty picked up the scroll and rolled it tight, the vellum soft under his fingertips. Perhaps it was not all that old after all. It certainly wasn't dried up or likely to crack. He put it back in the tin, and then placed the whole thing in the safe, just as a precaution.

It was time he went home and had some supper, and a nice, prosaic cup of tea, or two, strong and with sugar.

The following morning was Saturday and his presence was not necessary at the bookshop. The rest of the Greville estate could wait until Monday. Monty really needed to see Hank Savage and ask his opinion. It would be perfectly sane and logical. There would be no emotional silliness in it, no heightened imagination.

He found Hank pottering in his studio at the back of his lodgings. It was a large attic room with excellent light where Hank enjoyed his hobby of cleaning up and framing old drawings and prints which he bought, often as job lots at auctions. He made a certain amount of money at it, which he gave away. His purpose was the relaxation he gained, and the triumph now and then of finding something really lovely.

He put down the blade with which he was cutting matt for a drawing and regarding Monty with wry affection.

"You look like hell, Monty. What's happened?" he asked cheerfully. Clearly Monty looked worse than his restless night justified.

"Came across an old scroll," Monty answered, sitting sideways on the edge of a pair of steps piled with papers. Hank was a scientist and his mind was exquisitely ordered. His rooms were correspondingly chaotic.

"How old?" Hank was irritatingly literal. He was tall, rather too thin, with dark hair and mild blue eyes. Monty had brown eyes, and to put it in his own words, not tall enough for his weight.

"I don't know. It's in Aramaic, I think, and I can't read it." Monty was highly satisfied with the sharp interest in Hank's face. "It's on vellum," he added for good measure. "I found it in a biscuit tube at the bottom of the last crate of books from the Greville estate."

"What is it listed as?" Hank asked, abandoning the framing altogether and giving Monty his entire attention.

"It isn't listed at all. I tried to photocopy it. Nothing came out."

"Maybe your printer's broken? I don't suppose it would be a very good idea to take it anywhere else, if it really is as old as you think. Photograph it, until you get someone in to fix the copier," Hank replied.

"I tried to photograph it. It didn't come out." Monty remembered the strange chill he had felt at the time. "And before you suggest it, there's nothing wrong with my camera. Or with the copier either, actually. They both work fine on anything else."

Hank frowned. "So what's your explanation? Other than gremlins."

"I don't have one. But within half an hour or so of my finding the thing, the oddest old man turned up, with his granddaughter aged about eight, and offered to buy it."

"How much?" Hank asked dubiously. "You didn't sell it, I trust?"

"No, of course I didn't!" Monty said tartly. "I hid it before I even let them in. But you didn't ask the obvious question!"

"Who was he?"

"No! How did he know what it was and that I had it?" Monty said with satisfaction. "I didn't tell anyone and I certainly didn't show anyone."

"Didn't Roger know?" Hank was now both puzzled and very curious.

"Roger wasn't there. He's away sick. Has been for several days."

"Well what did this old man say?"

"His name is Judson Garrett, and he wouldn't leave any address or contact. He just said not to sell it to anyone else, and that it could be very dangerous."

Hank's eyebrows rose. "A threat?"

"Actually it sounded rather more like a warning," Monty admitted, remembering the old man's face and the power of darkness and pain in it.

"Did he say why he wanted it?" Hank was still turning it over in his mind.

"No. But he said others would come after it, but he didn't give any idea who they would be."

"Did you look at this scroll, Monty?"

"Of course I did!" He took a breath. "Do you want to see it?"

"Yes, if you don't mind, I really do." There was no hesitation in Hank's voice, no fear, none of the apprehension that Monty felt. There were times when Hank's total sanity irritated him intensely, but now it was comforting, even a kind of safety from the shadows in his own mind.

At the bookshop Monty opened the safe and took out the biscuit drum. The scroll was exactly as he had placed it. It felt the same to the touch as he pulled it out, dry and slightly warm. He unrolled it on the table for Hank to examine.

Hank looked at it for a long time before finally speaking.

"I think it's Aramaic, alright, and from the few words I can recognize here and there, it seems to be during the Roman occupation of Jerusalem. It could be the time of Christ. I see quite a lot of first person grammar, so it might be someone's own account of what they did, or saw . . . a kind of diary. But I don't know enough to be certain. You need an expert on this, Monty, not only to translate it but to date it and authenticate it. But before you do any of that, you must call Roger and tell him what you have. Have you tried again to get a copy?"

"No. Use your phone if you like," Monty suggested. "See if it's any better. You're pretty good technically."

Hank gave him a quick glance, sensing the difference between 'technically' and 'artistically'. But he did not argue. He took his cell phone out of his pocket, adjusted the settings, looked through the view finder and took three separate photographs. He went back to the first one to look at it, frowned, turned to the second, then the third. He looked up at Monty.

Monty felt the chill creep over his skin.

"Nothing," Hank said quietly. "Blank."

"I'll call Roger," Monty grasped for the only useful thing he could do. He picked up the telephone and dialled Roger Williams' number. He let it ring fifteen times. There was no answer.

He tried again the following day, and again Roger did not pick up. Monty was busy cataloguing the rest of the books from the Greville

estate when he became aware of someone standing in the doorway
watching him. He was round-faced, broad-browed and smiling
benignly, but there was a gravity in his dark eyes, and a very definite
knowledge of his own importance in his posture. He was dressed in
a clergyman's cassock and he had a purple vestment below his high,
white collar.

Monty scrambled to his feet. "I'm sorry, sir," he apologized
awkwardly. "I didn't hear you come in. Can I help you?"

The man smiled even more widely. "I'm sure you can, Mr. Danforth."

Monty felt a sudden stab of alarm like a prickle on his skin, a
warning of danger. This prince of the church knew his name, just
as the old man of the previous evening had done. He had not
questioned it at the time, but he did now. It was Roger's name on
the door and on the company letterhead. Monty's name appeared
nowhere. And why had they not assumed he was Roger? Wouldn't
that be the natural thing to do?

"You have me at a disadvantage, Your Grace," he said rather
crisply. "I am quite sure I would remember if we had met."

The man smiled again. "I'm sure you would. And yet you greeted
me correctly, and with courtesy. There is no need as yet for us to
go beyond that. I imagine you also know why I am here. You are
not only knowledgeable on books of all types, Mr. Danforth, and
an intelligent man, you are also, I believe, unusually sensitive to the
power of evil, and also of good."

Monty was flattered, and then frightened. He was an excellent
raconteur and could tell ghost stories which held his audience of
friends spellbound . . . for an evening's entertainment and fellowship.
That was hardly something to spread beyond his own circle, which
did not include bishops of any faith, Catholic or Protestant. His
friends were largely academics like Hank, or else students and artists
of one sort or another.

The bishop continued to smile. "You have in your possession at the
moment a very unusual piece of ancient manuscript," he continued.

"It is part of an estate, and you will in due course offer it for sale, along with the rest of the books, which are insignificant in comparison. No doubt they are in good condition, but editions of them can be obtained in any decent bookshop. The scroll is unique. But then you know that already." His eyes never moved from Monty's face.

Monty was colder, as if someone had opened a door onto the night. Any idea of denying his knowledge melted away. He had to swallow a couple of times before he could speak, and even then his voice sounded a little high-pitched.

"Something as unusual as the scroll will have to wait for Mr. Williams." It sounded like an excuse, even though it was perfectly true. "I imagine you would like it verified as well. It looks old, but no expert has examined it yet, so I have no idea of price. Actually, we don't even know what it is."

The bishop's smile did not waver, but his eyes were sharp and cold. "It is an ancient and very evil document, Mr. Danforth. If it were to pass into the wrong hands and become known to others the damage it could do would be measureless. I assure you, whatever price an expert might put on it, should you take the path of demanding that price, the Church will meet it. We would hope, as a man of principle and goodwill, you would settle for its value in the market place for scrolls of its date and origin."

Monty's hands were stiff, his arms covered in goosebumps. The bishop's figure seemed to float in the air, to become darker, and then lighter, the edges to blur. This was ridiculous! He blinked and shook his head, then looked again, and everything was normal. An elderly bishop, perfectly solid and human, was standing near the door, still smiling at him, still watching him.

Monty gulped. "The price doesn't lie within my control, Your Grace, but I imagine Mr. Williams will be fair. I have never known him not to be otherwise."

"Do not put it up for auction, Mr. Danforth," the bishop said gravely, the pleasantness disappeared from his expression as completely as a cloud passing across the sun robbed the land beneath of light. "It would be a very dangerous mistake, the extent of which I think might well be beyond your imagination, fertile as that is."

"I shall pass on your message to Mr. Williams," Monty promised, but his voice lacked the firmness he wished.

"Something suggests to me, Mr. Danforth, that I am not the only person to approach you on this subject," the bishop observed. "I urge you, with all the power at my disposal, not to sell this scroll elsewhere, no matter what inducement might be offered you to do so."

Now Monty was annoyed. "You say 'inducement' Your Grace, as if I had been offered bribes. That is not so, and I do not care for your implication. That might be the case with people you usually deal with, but it is not so with this bookshop. Bribery does not work, and neither do threats." The moment the words were out of his mouth fear seized him so tightly he found himself shaking.

"Not threats, Mr. Danforth," the bishop said in barely more than a whisper. "A warning. You are dealing with powers so ancient you cannot conceive their beginning, and in your most hideous nightmare you cannot think of their end. You are not a fool. Do not, in your ignorance and hubris, behave like one." Then without adding any more, or explaining himself, he turned and went out of the door. His feet made no sound whatever on the floorboards beyond, nor did the street door click shut behind him.

Monty did not move; in fact, he could not. His imagination soared over one thing after another and he seemed at once hot and cold. Clearly in the bishop's mind the scroll had an even more immense power than Monty had already seen in his own inability to copy it by any mechanical means. Who had written it and when? Was it ancient, or a more modern hoax? Obviously it held some terrible secret, almost certainly to do with the Church. To do with greed? The Catholic Church at least had treasures beyond imagining. Or was it personal sin, or mass abuse of the type only too well known already, but involving someone of extraordinary importance?

Bribery, violence, even murder? Or some challenge to a doctrine people dared not argue or question?

The possibilities raged through his mind and every one of them was frightening.

At last he stood up, a little wobbly at first, his limbs too long cramped, went over to the telephone, and tried to get Roger Williams again. He let it ring twenty times. There was no answer. He hung up, and called instead the young man who looked after opening the shop in Roger's absence and told him that he would not be in the next day.

Monty drove to the village where Williams had his house. The countryside was silent in the morning sun, untroubled by rush hour traffic. He passed through gentle fields, mostly flat land. Much of it was agricultural; here and there sheep grazed, heads down.

He was turning over in his mind exactly how to explain to Roger the sense of evil he had felt from both the old man, and then perhaps even more from the bishop who had seemed at once benign and dangerous. Or was it Monty's own imagination that was at the heart of it, coupled with his technical incompetence in not being able to copy the scroll?

But Hank couldn't copy it either. Hank was absent-minded at times, and he had a dry and odd sense of humour, but he was never incompetent.

He glanced up at a field of crops, and saw beyond it a sight that made his heart lurch. The rich, dark earth was littered with human skulls—thousands of them, as if a great army had been slaughtered and their corpses left in the open to rot as a perpetual reminder of death.

His hands slipped on the steering wheel and the car careered over the road, slewed to one side and finished up on the verge, only a foot from the drainage ditch. Another fourteen inches and he would have broken the axle. He drew in gasps of breath. His whole body was shaking and he was drenched with sweat.

Then he steeled himself to look at the field again. He saw white sheep turnips in the mud and weeds, their skull-like surfaces mounded above the soil.

What on earth had he seen for that awful moment? A vision of Armageddon?

He put the car back into gear and backed out very slowly, then sat, still shaking, until he could compose himself and drive the last mile or so to Roger's house. He pulled in the drive and stopped. Stiffly he climbed out of the car, still a little shaky, and went to the front door. He rang the bell and there was no answer. Normally he might have waited, perhaps gone to the pub for a coffee or a beer, and returned later. But today it was too urgent. He tried the door and found it unlocked.

Inside the hall there was a harsh smell of smoke, as if Roger had burned a pan, or even a whole meal.

"Roger!" he called at the foot of the stairs.

There was no answer, and he went up, beginning to fear that perhaps Roger was more seriously ill than he had supposed. He knocked on the bedroom door and when there was still no answer, he pushed it open.

He stepped back, gasping, hand over his mouth. Now the silence was hideously plain. What was left of Roger's body lay stiff and black on the remains of the bed, charred mattress, blackened carpet beneath it. The whole room was stained with smuts and soot as if some brief but terrible fire had raged here, consuming all in its path, and then gone out.

Monty fumbled his way back down the stairs to the telephone and called the police.

They came from the nearest small town, taking only twenty minutes to get there. They asked Monty to wait.

It was nearly two hours before a grimfaced sergeant from the county town told him that they believed it had been arson, quick and lethal. They asked him a great many more questions, including some about the bookshop, Roger's personal life, and also to account very precisely for his own whereabouts all the previous day. To his great relief he was able to do so.

Then with their permission he drove back to Cambridge and went to see Roger's solicitor, both to inform him of Roger's death, and to ask for instructions regarding the bookshop, for the time being. He was stunned, grieved and too generally disconcerted even to think about his own future.

"I'm afraid it falls on you, Mr. Danforth," Mr. Ingles told him gravely. "The only family Mr. Williams had is a niece in Australia. I can try to get in touch with her, but I already know from Mr. Williams that the young woman is something of an explorer, and it could be a period of time before we can obtain any instructions from her. In the meantime you are named as Mr. Williams' successor in the running of the business. Did he not inform you of that?" He shook his head. "I'm sorry—by the look on your face, clearly he did not. I do apologize. However there is nothing I can do about it now."

Monty was appalled. The scroll! He couldn't possibly make the decision on the sale of that!

"When can you find this woman?" he said desperately. "How long? Can't the Australian police or somebody get in touch with her? Doesn't she have responsibilities? A telephone? An email address? Something!"

"I dare say we will find her within a few weeks, Mr. Danforth," the solicitor said soothingly. "Until then, I advise that you just run the business as usual."

Monty felt as if one by one the walls were falling down and leaving him exposed to the elements of violence and darkness and there was no protection left.

"You don't understand!" He could hear the hysteria rising in his voice but he could not control it. "I have an ancient scroll in the last shipment, and two people are wanting it. I have no idea what it's worth, or which one to sell it to!"

"Can't you get an expert to value it?" Inglis said, his silver eyebrows raised rather high.

"No, I can't, not if it's worth what the two bidders so far are implying. I don't know what it is . . . it's . . ."

"You're upset, Mr. Danforth," Ingles said soothingly. "Roger's death has distressed you, very naturally. I'm sure when you've had a day or two to think about it, or a good night's sleep at least, you'll know what to do. Roger had a very high opinion of you, you know."

At any other time Monty would have been delighted to hear that; right now it was only making things worse. He could see in Ingles' face that already he was thinking of Monty as incompetent and possibly wondering why on earth Roger had thought well of him.

"The Church wants it," he said aloud.

"Then sell it to them, at whatever price an impartial assessor considers to be fair," Inglis replied, rising to his feet.

How could Monty explain the power the old man had exerted, the extraordinary emotions in his face that Monty could not ignore. Put into words it sounded absurd.

"I'll get an assessment," was all he could think of to say.

Ingles smiled. "Good. I'll wait to hear from you."

Monty did not get home until late, and the following day was taken up with matters of business at the shop. There was a great deal of paperwork to be attended to, access to bank accounts, dry but very necessary details.

In the evening Monty went to his favourite pub to have supper in familiar and happy surroundings. He had called Hank to join him, but Hank had not yet returned home and was not answering his mobile, so Monty was obliged to eat alone.

He had a supper that should have been delicious: freshly cooked cold pork pie with sharp, sweet little tomatoes, then homemade pickle with Caerphilly cheese on oatcakes, and a glass of cider. He barely tasted it.

The setting sun was laying a patina of gold over the river bank and the trees were barely moving in the faint breath of wind beyond the wide glass windows. Monty was looking towards the west when he saw the man walking across the grass towards him, up from the riverside path. He seemed to have the light behind him as if he had a halo, a sort of glow to his very being.

To Monty's surprise the man came in through the door and across the room straight towards him, as if they knew each other. He stopped beside Monty's table.

"May I join you, Mr. Danforth?" he said quietly. "We have much to talk about." Without waiting for the reply, he pulled out the second chair and sat down. "I do not need anything to eat, thank you," he went on, as if Monty had offered him something.

"I have nothing to talk about with you, sir," Monty said a little irritably. "We are not acquainted. I have had a very long day. One of my close friends has just died tragically. I would prefer to finish my dinner alone, if you please." He was aware of sounding rude, but he really did not care.

"Ah, yes," the man said sadly. "The death of poor Mr. Williams. Yet another victim of the powers of darkness."

"He was burned to death," Monty said with sudden anger and a very real and biting pain at the thought. "Fire is hardly a weapon of darkness!"

The man was handsome, his face highbrowed, his eyes wide and blue, filled with intelligence. "I was speaking of the darkness of the mind, Mr. Danforth, not of the flesh. And fire has been one of its weapons since the beginning. We imagine it destroys evil, somehow cleanses. We have burned wise women and healers in the superstitious terror that they were witches. We have burned heretics because they dared to question our beliefs. We have burned books because the knowledge or the opinions in them frightened us and we did not wish them to spread. And pardon me for bringing it back to your mind, but you have seen the results of fire very recently. Did you find it cleansing?"

In spite of himself Monty's mind was filled with the stench of burning and the sight of Roger's charred and blackened body on what was left of the bed. It made him feel sick, as though the food he had just eaten were revolting.

"Who are you and what do you want?" he said harshly.

"I am a scholar," the man replied. "I am someone who could add to the world's knowledge, without judgment as to who should know what, and who should be permitted to conceal truth because they do not agree with it, or have decided that this person or that one could find it difficult or uncomfortable. I would force no one, but allow everyone."

"What do you think is in it?" Monty asked curiously.

"A unique testimony from the time of Christ," the scholar replied. "One that may verify our beliefs—or blow them all apart. It will be a new truth—or a very old one"

Monty already knew what he was going to say, but he asked anyhow.

"And why do you approach me at a time of grief and interrupt my supper?"

"Actually you have finished your supper," the man indicated Monty's empty plate with a smile on his finely sculpted face. "But I find it hard to believe that you do not already know why I have come. I wish to buy from you the scroll, at whatever price you believe to be fair. I would ask you to give it to the world, if I thought that would prevail upon you, but I know that you have some responsibility to the estate of which it is presently a part. And please do not tell me that it is not within your power. With Mr. Williams' most unfortunate death, it is more than within it, it is your obligation."

Monty felt the sweat break out on his brow in spite of the closing in of the evening, now that the sun had definitely faded.

"You are not the only person seeking to buy it," he answered.

"Of course not," the scholar agreed with amusement. "If I were, I would begin to doubt its authenticity. The Church, at the very least, will bid high for it. But surely money is not your only consideration? That would disappoint me very much, Mr. Danforth. I had thought far more highly of you than that."

"I have not yet been able to get anyone in to verify what it is," Monty prevaricated. "It is impossible to put a price on it."

"When you have verified it, it will still be impossible," the scholar responded. "But you are being disingenuous. I think you have at least an educated guess as to what you have. And I assure you it is what you believe it to be."

"I have no beliefs as to what it is," Monty insisted angrily.

The scholar's face was filled with awe, his eyes almost luminous in the waning light. "It is the lost testament of Judas Iscariot," he said so quietly his voice was barely audible. "We have known of its existence for centuries. It has been hunted by all manner of people, each with his own reasons either to hide it or to make it known."

So it was true. Monty sat on the familiar river bank in the English twilight and thought of Jerusalem two thousand years ago, of betrayal and sacrifice, of blood, pain, ordinary human feet trudging in the dust on a journey into immortality. He thought of faith, and grief, and human love.

"Is it?" he asked.

"I think you know that, Monty," the scholar answered. "It must be given to the world. Mankind has a right to know what is in it—a different story, or the one we all expect. And in simple morality, does not the accused have a right to testify?"

The thought whirled in Monty's head, and he found no words on his tongue. The enormity of it was too great. Little wonder he could not photocopy it!

The scholar leaned across the table closer to him. "You would be a benefactor to justice, Monty," he said, unable to keep the urgency out of his voice. "An honest man, a true scholar who sought the truth above all emotional or financial interest, a man of unsoiled honesty."

For a moment Monty was overwhelmed by temptation. He drew in his breath, and then he remembered the old man with his granddaughter, and the promise he had made him. Why did he want it? He was the only one who had given no reason. He remembered again the knowledge of time and pain in his eyes.

"I will consider it," he said to the scholar in front of him. "If you leave me an address I will be in touch with you. Now please leave me to have another glass of cider and a piece of cake."

Actually he did not bother with more cider, or the cake. He paid his bill and left. As soon as he was in his car he tried Hank again on his cell phone. This time Hank answered.

"I must see you immediately," Monty said before even asking how Hank was or what he was doing. "Please come to the bookshop. I'll wait for you."

"Are you alright?" Hank said anxiously. "You sound terrible. What's happened?"

"Just come to the bookshop," Monty repeated. "Ring the bell. I'll let you in."

Half an hour later Monty and Hank were sitting at the table in Monty's workroom with the scroll open in front of them.

"Who was this scholar?" Hank said gravely. "He must have given you a name."

"No, he didn't," Monty replied. "Like the old man with his grand-daughter, and the bishop, or whatever he was, they all knew about this," he glanced at the scroll. "And my name, and where to find me. But I've told no one, except you. I didn't even have a chance to tell Roger."

Hank looked at the scroll again, lifting up his glasses to peer beneath them and see it more intensely. He was silent for so long that Monty became restless. He was about to interrupt him when Hank sat back at last.

"I've been swatting up a bit on Aramaic," he said, his voice quiet and strained, lines of anxiety deeper in his face than usual, perhaps exaggerated by the artificial light. "I can only make out a few words clearly. I'm not really very good. It's a long way from mathematics, but I've always been interested in the teachings of Christ—just as a good man, perhaps morally the greatest."

"And . . .?" Monty's own voice quivered.

Hank's face lit with a gentle smile. "And I have no special illumination, Monty. I can make out a few words, but they seem ambiguous, capable of far more than one interpretation. There are several proper names and I'm almost sure one of them is 'Judas'. But there is so much I don't know that I couldn't even guess at the meaning. It isn't a matter of missing a subtlety. I could omit a negative and come with a completely opposite interpretation."

"But could he be correct . . . the scholar?" Monty insisted. "Could it be the lost testimony of Judas Iscariot?"

"It could be a testimony of anyone, or just a letter," Hank replied. "Or it could be a fake."

"No it couldn't," Monty said with absolute certainty. "Touch it. Try to photograph it. It's real. Even you can't deny that."

Hank chewed his lip, the lines in his face deepening even more. "If it is what the scholar says, that would explain why the bishop is so anxious to have it, and perhaps destroy it. Or at the very least keep it hidden."

"Why? Surely it would make religion, Christianity in particular, really hot news again."

"If it confirms what they have taught for two thousand years," Hank agreed. "But what if it doesn't?"

"Like what?" Monty asked, then immediately knew the answer. It was as if someone were slowly dimming all the lights everywhere, as far as the eye could see, as far as the imagination could stretch.

Hank said nothing.

"You mean a fake crucifixion?" Monty demanded. "No resurrection?" Then he wished he had not even said the words. "That would be awful. It would rob millions of people of the only hope they have, of all idea of heaven, of a justice to put right the griefs we can't touch here." He swallowed painfully. "Of ever seeing again those we love . . . and those who didn't have a chance here . . ."

"I know," Hank said softly. "That is a belief I would never force on others, even if I hold it myself. I would be inclined to give it to Prince of the Church, and let him burn it."

"Book burning? You, Hank?" Monty said incredulously.

"If I had to choose between truth, or what seems to be truth, and kindness . . . then I think I might choose kindness," Hank said gently. "There are too many 'shorn lambs' I wouldn't hurt."

"Temper the wind to the shorn lamb," Monty said in a whisper. "And could you do it without even knowing what the scroll said?"

"That's the rub," Hank agreed. "We don't know what's in it. It might not be that at all. Do you remember what the Bible says Christ said to Judas? 'Go and do what thou must'?"

Monty stared at him.

Hank looked at the scroll. "If there were no betrayal then there would have been no trial, therefore no crucifixion, and no resurrection. Is it possible that Judas did only what he had to, or there would have been no fulfilment of the great plan?"

Monty was speechless, his mind whirling, his thoughts out of control.

"But that would spoil the simplicity of the damnation that Christendom has always placed on Judas," Hank went on. "It would all suddenly become terribly real, and fearfully complex, much too much to be shared with the whole world, most of whom like their religion very simple. Good and evil. Black and white. No difficult decisions to be made. We don't like difficult decisions. For two thousand years we have been told what to think, and we've grown used to it. And make no mistakes, Monty, if this goes to anyone except the Prince of the Church, it will be on the Internet the day after, and everyone will know."

"The Churchman is obvious," Monty agreed. "Anyone can see why he wants it, and I can't entirely disagree. And I can see why the scholar wants it, regardless of what it destroys or who it hurts. But who is the old man? Why does he want it, and how did any of them know it exists, and that I have it?"

"What did you say his name was?" Hank asked. "He was the only one who gave you a name, wasn't he?"

"Yes. Judson Garrett."

Hank stood motionless. "Judson Garrett? Say it again, Monty, aloud. Could it possibly be . . .?" He stared at the scroll. "Lock it up, Monty. I don't know if it will do any good, but at least try to keep it safe."

Quite early the next morning Monty received a phone call from the police to tell him that it was now beyond question that Roger Williams had been murdered. They asked him if he would come down to the local station at his earliest convenience, preferably this morning. There were several issues with which he could help them.

"Of course," he replied. "I'll be there in a couple of hours."

He was met by a very pleasant policewoman, no more than in her mid-thirties. She introduced herself as Sergeant Tobias.

"Sorry about this, Mr. Danforth," she apologized straight away. "Coffee?"

"Er . . . yes, please." It seemed discourteous to refuse, and he would welcome something to do with his hands. It might make him appear less nervous. Had she seen how tense he was, how undecided as to what to tell her?

"You said Roger was murdered," he began as soon as they were sitting down in her small office. If that were so, why was a mere sergeant dealing with it, and a young woman? It did not sound as if they regarded it as important.

"Yes," she said gravely. "There is no question that the fire was deliberately set. And Mr. Williams was struck on the head before the fire started. I thought you'd like to know that because it means he almost certainly didn't suffer."

For a moment Monty found it difficult to speak. He had refused even to think of what Roger might have felt.

"Thank you," he said awkwardly. "Why? I mean . . . do you know why anyone would kill him?"

"We were hoping that you could help us with that. We have found no indication of any personal reason at all. And the fact that the house was pretty carefully searched, but many very attractive ornaments left, some of considerable value, not to mention all the cutlery, which incidentally is silver and quite old, suggests it was not robbery. All the electronic things were left too, even a couple of very expensive mobile phones and ipods, very easily portable."

Monty shook his head, as if trying to get rid of the idea. "Nobody could have hated Roger like that. Maybe it was people high on something?"

"Maybe," she agreed. "But it was very methodical and well done. The search was meticulous, and nothing was broken or tossed around."

"Then how do you know?"

She smiled a little bleakly. "Marks in the dust," she answered. "Not just here and there, as he might have pulled books out himself since anyone last dusted. They were on every shelf, all recent. What does your bookshop deal in, Mr. Danforth? What would your most expensive item be?"

Now the cold ate through him and the taste of the coffee was bitter in his mouth. There was only one possible answer to that, unless he were to lie to her. That thought was born in his mind, and died.

"Usually just a rare book, sometimes a manuscript or original folio, quite a lot of first editions, of course. They can fetch thousands, even tens of thousands. Just occasionally we get an old manuscript, possibly illuminated."

She looked at him steadily. "And at the moment?" she prompted.

He took a deep breath and let it out in a sigh. "At the moment we have an old manuscript which came in the bottom of a crate of pretty ordinary books, from an estate sale."

"Old?" she asked. "What do you call 'old'?"

What would she know about books? Probably nothing at all. World War II would be ancient history to her.

"Mr. Danforth?" she prompted.

"Possibly the time of Christ," he answered, feeling a little melodramatic.

Her interest was instant and intense. "Really? In what language? Latin? Hebrew? Aramaic?"

"I think it's Aramaic," he replied. "It seems to be important, because I have had three people asking for it already, and I haven't even had it authenticated yet."

"But you advertised it?" she said with a quick note of criticism in her voice.

"No," he answered. "No, I didn't. I don't know how anybody knew of it. And I don't know whether it is Aramaic or not. I have a friend who knows a little, just words here and there, and that's what he thinks it is. I still need an expert."

"Have you any idea at all what it is about?" she pressed. "What is it written on? Parchment, vellum? How long is it?"

He withdrew a little bit. "Why do you want to know?"

She smiled, and her expression was gentle and full of pride. "My father is Eli Tobias. He is an expert in ancient Aramaic scripts. We think Mr. Williams was killed for a rare book of some sort. That is why they put me onto the case."

He sighed. "You're right. Three different men have come to me and offered anything I want if I will sell it to them. I can't even photocopy the thing. It's as if it were . . . possessed."

"Then you need an expert to look at it," she replied. "Perhaps more than one. Did any of these men suggest what it is, or why they want it so much?"

He repeated to her what each of the men had said and she listened to him without interrupting.

"Keep it safe, Mr. Danforth," she said after he had finished and stared at her over the cold coffee. "We shall send two experts tomorrow, or the day after. I think we have found the reason poor Mr. Williams was burned to death. Please . . . please be very careful."

Monty promised to do so, and went out into the street a little shakily. He drove back to Cambridge and worked in the shop until late afternoon. He finished cataloguing the last books of the Greville estate and decided to go home for supper, and then perhaps telephone Hank and tell him the latest news. It would be comforting to speak to him. His sanity was like a breath of clean air, blowing away the stale nonsense that had collected in his mind.

He was surprised to find when he went outside that it had been raining quite heavily, and he had not noticed. The gutters were full and in places slurping over. Thank goodness it had stopped now or he would have been soaked. The sky was darkening in the east, and the red sky to the west promised a good day tomorrow, if you believe the old tales of forecasting.

He turned the corner and the sunlight struck him in the face. He shut his eyes for a moment, then opened them again. The shock took him like a physical blow. The whole tarmac surface was covered with blood. It lay in pools, shining and scarlet. It ran gurgling in the gutters.

He was paralyzed by the sheer horror of it.

A cyclist came racing around the corner, skidded, slewed across the road and hit him, knocking him over. He was bruised and his skin torn, his chest for a moment unable to move, to draw in breath. With difficulty he gasped in air at last and straightened very slowly to his knees, dizzy and aching.

An old lady was hurrying towards him, her face creased with concern.

"Are you alright?" she asked anxiously. "Stupid boys. They're going much too fast. Didn't even stop. Are you injured?" She offered her hand to help him up, but she looked too frail to take any of his weight.

He stood upright, surprised to find that apart from being thoroughly wet from the gutter, he was actually not damaged. His jacket sleeves and his shirt cuffs were sodden with rainwater, dirty grey, his trousers the same. There was a tiny red smear of blood on his palm where he had scratched it.

"Yes, I think I'm all right, thank you," he replied. "I was standing in the way, I think. Just . . . staring . . ." There was nothing left of the images of blood, just an ordinary asphalt road with puddles of rain gleaming in the last of the sunset. He wouldn't tell Hank about this. As he had always said, most supernatural phenomena were just over-excited imaginations painting very human fears onto perfectly normal situations.

Nevertheless when he saw Hank later on, having washed, changed his clothes and had a very good supper, he found him also unusually concerned.

"Can you work out why we can't photograph this scroll yet?" Monty asked as they sat with late coffee and an indulgence of After Eight mints.

"No," Hank said candidly. He gave a slightly rueful smile. "For once, logic eludes me. I can't think of any reasonable answer. I imagine there's an explanation as to how those three men knew of the scroll at all, when you didn't advertise it. I suppose since they knew you had it, it wasn't a great leap to track down poor Roger. Monty . . ."

"What?"

"We have to settle this issue straight away. I don't think I'm being alarmist, but if they'd kill Roger for it, they aren't going to accept a polite delay from you."

The increasing darkness that had been growing in Monty's mind now suddenly took a very specific shape. Heat raced through him as if he felt flames already.

"I've no idea what price to put on it," he said desperately. "I wish I'd never found the thing. Sergeant Tobias said she'd have her father come and look at it some time this week. What if they won't wait? Or won't pay what he says it's worth? I suppose I should tell the Greville Estate solicitors, shouldn't I?"

"No," Hank replied after a moment's thought. "From what you told me, Roger bought the books as a job lot at auction. They belong to his estate, not the Grevilles. But you're right, I don't think you can wait until a valuation is put on the scroll. That could take quite a while, especially if it really is what the scholar claims it is. That would actually make it almost beyond price."

"Then what the hell can I do?" Monty demanded. "Give it to the British Museum?"

Hank bit his lip. "Do you think the bishop, or Mr. Garrett will allow you to do that? Who do you think killed Roger?"

Monty shut his eyes and ran his fingers through his hair. "I don't know," he admitted. "One of them, I suppose. Hank, what can I do?"

Hank sat for a long time without answering.

Monty waited.

Finally Hank spoke, slowly and very quietly. "I don't believe we can wait, Monty. I don't know what this scroll is, but I do know it has great power. Whatever is in the scroll itself, or in what various men believe of it, that power is real, and it is very dangerous. Roger is dead already. I believe that we need to end the matter long before any experts can run their tests and verify it. For a start, I don't think the bishop, or whoever he is, is going to allow that to happen. His whole purpose in buying the scroll is to destroy it, to make sure that mankind never gets to know what is written in it—expert, scholar or ordinary man in the street, or more importantly to him, perhaps, man-in-the- pew."

"What about Mr. Garrett? What does he think it is, and what does he want it for?" Monty asked.

"I don't know who he is, but I have an absurd guess, for which I doubt my own sanity. The reason he wants it, I believe, is to reverse the verdict of history."

"What can we do?" Monty asked, searching Hank's clear blue eyes.

"Tell the men we know of who want it to meet us at Roger's house, and we will hold an auction there, privately for the three of them."

"I don't know how to contact them," Monty pointed out.

"*Times* personal column," Hank said simply. "Although they may have some way of knowing anyway. Funny they should be so wrong about where the scroll was, though."

"What? Oh . . . you mean . . . in Roger's house? Why did they think that? Why did they kill him? He didn't even know about it?"

"Was the crate with the scroll in it addressed to him?"

Monty had a sudden vivid picture of the address label in his mind's eye.

"Yes. Yes it was . . ."

"Then that may be the answer. At that time they did not realize Roger was sick and not coming in to the bookshop. They assumed he would take it home."

"How did they know about it at all?" Monty pursued.

"That is something I can't answer," Hank admitted. "I don't believe in your ghosts, all of whom have a logical explanation in either fact or hysteria. But I will admit that there are things I can't explain, and I am prepared to allow that they could have to do with a more than ordinary evil . . . albeit a highly powerful human one, with manifestations we don't yet understand."

"Generous of you," Monty said with a touch of sarcasm, the sharper because he was afraid.

Hank ignored him. "Put an advertisement in the personal column of the *Times*: 'Gentleman wishes to auction ancient scroll. Regret photocopies impossible. Auction to be held at 7:00 p.m. at home of now deceased owner of shop. Replies unnecessary.' That should reach those with an interest."

Monty's throat was dry, his tongue practically sticking to the roof of his mouth.

"Then what?" he croaked.

"Then we lock up the scroll here and go to Roger's house to wait," Hank answered, but he too was pale and there was knowledge of fear in his eyes.

At seven in the evening Hank and Monty were in Roger's sitting room, too restless to occupy the armchairs. Hank was by the window looking over the back garden and Monty paced from the center of the room to the front windows and back again. The acrid smell of smoke was still sharp in the air. The electric lights were not working since the fire, and as the room grew darker with the fading sun Hank struck a match and lit the hurricane lamp they had brought.

"They're not going to come," Monty said at quarter past seven. "We didn't give them enough time. Or else they've gone to the shop, and they'll break into the safe and steal it while we're here. We shouldn't have come."

"If they were going to steal it they'd have done so anyway," Hank pointed out. "It was there every night, wasn't it?"

"Then why didn't they?" Monty demanded.

"I don't know. Perhaps they need some legitimacy—or maybe they just aren't good at safe cracking. It's a pretty good safe, isn't it?"

"Yes . . ."

The hurricane lamp burned up, sending its glow into the corners of the room and showing the dark outline of an old man with a child beside him, a fair-haired girl of about eight, whose brilliant, ice-cool eyes gleamed almost luminously.

Monty felt the sweat break out on his skin and run down his body, cold within seconds. He turned to Hank, and instead saw in the doorway the robed and implacable figure of the bishop, his face filled with a scalding contempt.

The smell of old smoke seemed heavier, catching in the throat.

The bishop moved into the room and his place in the doorway was taken by the scholar, a smile on his handsome face, a fire of intense curiosity blazing in his eyes.

Hank looked at Monty. "Perhaps we had better begin the bidding?" he suggested.

Monty cleared his throat again. "I do not know what the scroll is, or whether it is authentic or not. Each of you has offered to purchase it, as it is. Please make a bid according to what it is worth to you."

"Where is it?" the bishop demanded.

"Hush man, it is of no importance," the scholar cut across him. "Mr. Danforth will provide it, when the time is right. We don't want to risk having it destroyed in another fire, or do we?"

The old man smiled. "How wise of you. I fear destruction is what the bishop's purpose is. He will pay any price to that end."

"May the fires of hell consume you!" the bishop shouted hoarsely.

"The fires of hell burn without consuming," the old man said wearily. "You know so little. The truth is deeper, subtler and far better than your edifice of the imagination . . ."

The bishop lunged forward and picked up the hurricane lamp. He smashed it on the floor at Monty's feet. "Betrayer!" he cried as the flames spread across the spilled oil and licked upwards, hungry and hot.

The scholar, who had been watching Hank, charged him and knocked him over, seizing the small attaché case he had been carrying. He picked it up and made for the window, leaving Hank stunned on the floor.

It was the old man who took off his coat and threw it over Monty, smothering the flames at his feet, catching his trousers already burning his legs.

But the oil had spread wider and the sofa was alight. The billows of black smoke grew more intense, choking, suffocating. The bishop was lost to sight. Hank was still on the floor and Judson Garrett was bending over him, talking to him, pulling him to his feet.

Dimly through the black swirls Monty could see the child hopping up and down, her face brilliant with glee, her eyes shining with age-old evil as she watched the fire grow and swell, now reaching the old man's clothes as he lifted Hank up. He was strong, his hair dark again, his face young. He carried Hank over to the window, smashed it and pushed him through as the fire burned behind him, swallowing him up.

Monty fought his way to the door and out into the hall, gasping for breath, the heat all but engulfing him. He flung the front door open and fell out into the cool, clean night. Behind him the flames were roaring up. There was going to be nothing left of the house. He must find Hank, get him out of the way of exploding debris.

He was as far as the corner of the house when he saw Hank staggering towards him, dizzy but definitely upright.

"Monty! Monty!" he called out. "What happened to Garrett?"

Monty caught Hank by the arm. "I don't know. We've got to get away from here. It's all going up any minute. Those dry timbers are like a bomb. Come on!"

Reluctantly Hank allowed himself to be pulled away until they were both seventy yards along the road and finally saw the plume of flame burst through the roof and soar upwards into the sky.

A cloud of crows flung high in the air like jagged pieces of shadow, thousands of them, tens of thousands, all shouting their hoarse cries into the night.

"Did anybody else get out?" Hank asked, his voice shaking.

"No," Monty answered with certainty.

"He thought the scroll was in my case," Hank said. "The bishop. I've had that case for years."

"What was in it?" Monty asked.

"Nothing," Hank replied. "He would have destroyed the scroll."

"And the scholar would have published it, no matter whose faith it broke," Monty replied. "People need their dreams, right or wrong. You have to give them a new one before you break the old."

"What about Garrett?" Hank asked, pain in his voice as if he dreaded the answer.

"He's all right," Monty said, absolutely sure that it was the truth.

Hank stared at him, then at the burning house. "He's in there!"

"No, he isn't, not now. He's all right, Hank."

"And the child?"

"Gone. I think he's free of her . . . it."

"Do you have any idea what you're talking about?" Hank asked, not with doubt but with hope.

"Oh, yes, yes, I think so. I'm talking about sacrifice and redemption, about faith, about hope being stronger than even the demons who dog you with memory and tales of hatred, and who tempt you to justify yourself, at all costs."

"And the scroll? What are you going to do with it now?"

"I think when we go and look, we'll find it's gone," Monty replied. "We aren't ready for it yet."

Hank smiled and together they turned to walk away towards the darkness ahead, no more than the soft folds of the night, with sunrise beyond.

XI

It's in the Book

Mickey Spillane & Max Allan Collins

Co-author's note: It's unclear when Mickey began this story, which I have developed from an unfinished typescript, but internal evidence suggests the 1980s, so I have made that the time period of the tale. M. A. C.

COPS ALWAYS COME in twos. One will knock on the door, but a pair will come in, a duet on hand in case you get rowdy. One uniform drives the squad car, the other answers the radio. One plain-clothes dick asks the questions, the other takes the notes. Sometimes I think the only time they go solo is to the dentist. Or to bed. Or to kill themselves.

I went out into the outer office where a client had been waiting for ten minutes for me to wrap up a phone call. I nodded to him, but the six-footer was already on his feet, brown shoes, brown suit, brown eyes, brown hair. It was a relief his name wasn't Brown.

I said, "I can see you now, Mr. Hanson."

At her reception desk to one side of my inner-office door, Velda—a raven-haired vision in a white blouse and black skirt—was giving me a faintly amused look that said she had made him, too.

Mr. Hanson nodded back. There was no nervous smile, no anxiety in his manner at all. Generally, anybody needing a private investigator is not at ease. When I walked toward him, he extended a hand for me to shake, but I moved right past, going to the door and pulling it open.

His partner was standing with his back to the wall, like a sentry, hands clasped behind his back. He was a little smaller than Hanson, wearing a different shade of brown, going wild with a tie of yellow and white stripes. Of course, he was younger, maybe thirty, where his partner was pushing forty.

"Why don't you come in and join your buddy," I said, and made an after-you gesture.

This one didn't smile either. He simply gave me a long look and, without nodding or saying a word, stepped inside and stood beside Hanson, like they were sharing the wrong end of a firing squad.

Something was tickling one corner of Velda's pretty mouth as I closed the door and marched the cops into my private office.

I got behind my desk and waved at the client's chairs, inviting them to sit down. But cops don't like invitations and they stayed on their feet.

Rocking back, I said, "You fellas aren't flashing any warrants, meaning this isn't a search party or an arrest. So have a seat."

Reluctantly, they did.

Hanson's partner, who looked like his feelings had been hurt, said, "How'd you make us?"

I don't know how to give enigmatic looks, so I said, "Come off it."

"We could be businessmen."

"Businessmen don't wear guns on their hips, or if they do, they could afford a suit tailored for it. You're too clean-cut to be hoods, but not enough to be feds. You're either NYPD or visiting badges from Jersey."

This time they looked at each other and Hanson shrugged. Why fight it? They were cops with a job to do; this was nothing personal. He casually reached in a side suit coat pocket and flicked a folded hundred-dollar bill onto the desk as if leaving a generous tip.

"Okay," I said. "You have my attention."

"We want to hire you."

The way he hated saying it made it tough for me to keep a straight face. "Who is we?"

"You said it before," Hanson said. "NYPD." *He almost choked, getting that out.*

I pointed at the bill on the desktop. "Why the money?"

"To keep this matter legal. To insure confidentiality. Under your licensing arrangement with the state of New York, you guarantee that by acceptance of payment."

"And if I reject the offer?"

For a moment I thought both of them finally would smile, but they stifled the effort, even if their eyes bore a hint of relief.

Interesting—they wanted me to pass.

So I picked up the hundred, filled out a receipt, and handed it to Hanson. He looked at it carefully, folded it, and tucked it into his wallet.

"What's this all about?" I asked them.

Hanson composed himself and folded his hands in his lap. They were big hands, but flexible. He said, "This was *not* the department's idea."

"I didn't think so."

He took a few moments to look for the words. "I'm sure you know, Hammer, that there are people in government who have more clout than police chiefs or mayors."

I nodded. He didn't have to spell it out. Hell, we both knew what he was getting at.

There was the briefest pause and his eyes went to my phone and then around the room. Before he could ask, I said, "Yes, I'm wired to record client interviews . . .no, I didn't hit the switch. You're fine."

But they glanced at each other just the same.

I said, "If you're that worried, we can take it outside . . .onto the street, where we can talk."

Hanson nodded, already getting up. "Let's do it that way then."

The three of us went into the outer office. I paused to tell Velda I wasn't sure how long this would take. The amusement was gone from her dark eyes now that she saw I was heading out with this pair of obvious coppers.

We used the back door to the semi-private staircase the janitor used for emptying the trash, and went down to the street. There you can talk. Traffic and pedestrians jam up microphones, movement keeps you away from listening ears and, stuck in the midst of all those people, you have the greatest privacy in the world.

We strolled. It was a sunny spring morning but cool.

A block and a half later, Hanson said, "A United States senator is in Manhattan to be part of a United Nations conference."

"One of those dirty jobs somebody's gotta do, I suppose."

"While he's in town, there's an item the senator would like you to recover."

Suddenly this didn't sound so big-time, senator or not.

I frowned. "What's this, a simple robbery?"

"No. There's nothing 'simple' about this situation. But there are aspects of it that make you . . .ideal."

My God, he hated to admit that.

I said, "Your people have already been on it?"

"No."

"Why not?"

"Not your concern, Hammer."

Not my concern?

We stopped at a red light at the street corner and I asked, "Where's the FBI in this, if there's investigating to do? A U.S. senator ought to be able pull those strings."

"This is a local affair. Strictly New York."

But not something the NYPD could handle.

The light changed and we started ambling across the intersection in the thick of other pedestrians. There was something strange about the term Hanson used—'recovery.' If not a robbery, was this mystery item something simply . . .lost? Or maybe I was expected to steal something. I deliberately slowed the pace and started looking in store windows.

Hanson said, "You haven't asked who the senator is."

"You said it was strictly New York. That narrows it to two."

"And you're not curious which one?"

"Nope."

Hanson frowned. "Why not?"

"Because you'll tell me when you're ready, or I'll get to meet him myself."

No exasperation showed in the cop's face, and not even in his tone. Strictly in his words: "What kind of private investigator are you, Hammer? Don't you have any other questions?"

I stopped abruptly, turning my back to a display window, and gave them each a look. Anybody going past would have thought we were just three friends discussing where to grab a bite or a quick drink. Only someone knowledgeable would have seen that the way we stood or moved was designed to keep the bulk of a gun well-concealed under suit coats and that the expressions we wore were strictly for the passerby audience.

I said, "No wonder you guys are pissed off. With all the expertise of the NYPD, the senator decides to call *me* in to find a missing geegaw for you. That's worth a horselaugh."

This time Hanson did choke a little bit. "This . . . .'*geegaw*' may be small in size, Hammer, but it's causing rumbles from way up top."

"Obviously all the way up to the senator's office."

Hanson said nothing, but that was an answer in itself.

I asked, "What's higher than that?"

And it hit me.

It was crazy, but I heard myself asking the question: "Not . . .the president?"

Hanson swallowed. Then he shrugged again. "I didn't say that, Hammer. But . . .he's top dog, isn't he?"

I grunted out a laugh. "Not *these* days he isn't."

Maybe if they had been feds, I'd have been accused of treason or sedition or stupidity. But these two—well, Hanson, at least—knew the answer already. I gave it to them anyway.

"These days," I said, "political parties and bank-rollers and lobbyists call the shots. No matter how important the pol, he's still a chess piece for money to move around. That includes the big man in the Oval Office."

Hanson's partner chimed in: "That's a cynical point of view, Hammer."

A kid on a skateboard wheeled around the corner. When he'd passed, I said, "What kind of recovery job rates this kind of pressure?"

We started walking again.

Hanson said, "It's there, so who cares. We're all just pawns, right, Hammer? Come on. Let's go."

"Where?"

"To see the senator," he said.

We might have been seated in the sumptuous living room of a Westchester mansion, judging by the burnished wood paneling, the overstuffed furnishings, the Oriental carpet. But this was merely the Presidential Suite of the Hotel St. Moritz on Central Park South.

My host, seated in an armchair fit for a king, was not the president, just a United States senator serving his third consecutive term. And Senator Hugh Boylan, a big pale fleshy man with a Leprechaun twinkle, looked as out of place here as I did. His barely pressed off-white seersucker suit and carelessly knotted blue-and-red striped tie went well with shaggy gray hair that was at least a week past due a haircut. His eyebrows were thick dark sideways exclamation points, a masculine contrast to a plumply sensuous mouth.

He had seen to it that we both had beers to drink. Bottles, not poured glasses, a nice common-man touch. Both brews rested without coasters on the low-slung marble coffee table between us, where I'd also tossed my hat. I was seated on a nearby couch with more well-upholstered curves than a high-ticket call girl.

The senator sat forward, his light blue eyes gently hooded and heavily red-streaked. He gestured with a thick-fingered hand whose softness belied a dirt-poor up-bringing. His days as a longshoreman were far behind him.

"Odd that we've never met, Mr. Hammer, over all these years." His voice was rich and thick, like Guinness pouring in a glass. "Perhaps it's because we don't share the same politics."

"I don't have any politics, Senator."

Those Groucho eyebrows climbed toward a shaggy forelock. "You were famously associated with my conservative colleague, Senator Jasper. There was that rather notorious incident in Russia when you accompanied him as a bodyguard."

"That was just a job, sir."

"Then perhaps you won't have any objection to doing a job for a public servant of . . .a *liberal* persuasion."

"As long as you don't try to persuade me, Senator."

"Fair enough," he said with a chuckle, and settled back in the chair, tenting his fingers. "I would hope as a resident of our great state that you might have observed that I fight for my constituency and try to leave partisan politics out of it. That I've often been at odds with my party for the good of the people."

"Senator, you don't have to sell me. No offense, but I haven't voted in years."

A smile twitched in one corner of his fleshy face. "I am only hoping that you don't view me as an adversary. That you might have some small regard for my efforts."

"You're honest and you're a fighter. That goes a good distance with me."

His pale cheeks flushed red. *Had I struck a nerve without intending?*

"I appreciate that," he said quietly.

Sunshine was filtering through sheer curtains, exposing dust motes—even the St. Moritz had dust. Horns honked below, but faintly, the city out there paying no heed to a venerable public servant and an erstwhile tabloid hero.

"Nicholas Giraldi died last night," he said.

What the hell?

Don Nicholas Giraldi, head of New York's so-called sixth Mafia family, had died in his sleep yesterday afternoon in his private room at St. Luke's Hospital. It had been in the evening papers and all over the media: "Old Nic," that most benign of a very un-benign breed, finally gone.

"I heard," I said.

Boylan's smile was like a priest's, blessing a recalcitrant parishioner. "You knew him. There are rumors that you even did jobs for him occasionally. That he trusted you."

I sipped my Miller Lite and shrugged. "Why deny it? That doesn't make me a wiseguy any more than taking on a job for you makes me a liberal."

He chuckled. "I didn't mean to suggest it did. It does seem . . .forgive me, Mr. Hammer . . . it does seem a trifle strange that a man who once made headlines killing mobsters would form an alliance with one."

"Alliance is too strong a word, Senator. I did a handful of jobs for him, unrelated to his . . .business. Matters he didn't want corrupted by his own associates."

"Could you be more specific?"

"No. Him dying doesn't mean client confidentiality goes out the window. That cop Hanson, in the other room, has the receipt for that C-note that I signed before coming. Spells it out in the small print, if you're interested."

The dark eyebrows flicked up and down. "Actually, that's something of a relief. What I want to ask you dances along the edges of that confidentiality, Mr. Hammer. But I hope you might answer. And that you would trust me to be discreet as well."

"You can ask."

He folded his arms, like a big Irish genie about to grant a wish. "Did you receive something from the old don, shortly before . . .or perhaps *upon* . . . his death?"

"No. What would it have been if I had?"

"A book. A ledger, possibly."

I put the beer bottle back on the coffee table. "No. Is that what you're trying to recover? A ledger?"

He nodded. Now when he spoke it was nearly a whisper: "And here your discretion is key. The don was in power a very long time . . .going back to the late forties. His ways, by modern standards, were old-fashioned, right up to the end. One particular antiquated practice peculiar to Don Giraldi was, apparently, keeping a hand-written record of every transaction, every agreement he ever made. No one knows precisely what was in that book. There were other books kept, accounting records that were largely fictional, intended for the IRS but in this particular volume he was said to record the real events, the actual dealings of his business. When asked about such matters, he would say only, 'It's in the book.'"

I shrugged. "I heard the rumors. That he kept a book under lock and key, or in a safe somewhere, and all his secrets were kept in the thing. But I never believed it."

"Why not?"

I pawed at the air dismissively. "He was too shrewd to write anything down and incriminate himself if it fell into the wrong hands? Naw. It's a myth, Senator. If that's what you want to send me out looking for, my advice is to forget it."

But the big head was shaking side to side. "No, Mr. Hammer, that book is very real. Old Nic told his most innermost associates, when his health began to fail earlier this year, that the book would be given to the person he trusted most."

I frowned, but I also shrugged. "So I'm wrong. Anyway, *I'm* not that person. He didn't send me his damn book. But how is it you know what his 'innermost associates' were told?"

"FBI wiretaps." His smile had a pixieish cast, but his eyes were so hard they might have been glass. "Do you think you could find that ledger, Mr. Hammer?"

I shrugged. "It's a big city. Puts the whole needle-in-a-haystack bit to shame. But what would you do with the thing? Does the FBI think they can make cases out of what's in those pages?"

He swallowed thickly. Suddenly he wasn't looking me in the eye. "There's no question, Mr. Hammer, that names and dates and facts and figures in a ledger would be of interest to law enforcement, both local and federal. There's also no question of its value to the old don's successors."

I was nodding. "Covering their own asses and giving them valuable intel on the other mob families and crooked cops and any number of public figures. The blackmail possibilities alone are . . ."

But I didn't finish. Because the senator's head lowered and his eyes shut briefly, and I knew.

I knew.

"You've always been a straight shooter, Senator. But you didn't come from money. You must have needed help in the early days, getting started. You took money from the don, didn't you?"

"Mr. Hammer . . ."

"Hell. And so did somebody else." I hummed a few nasty off-key bars of "Hail to the Chief."

"Mr. Hammer, your country would be very—"

"Can it. I put in my time in the Pacific. I should let you all swing. I should just sit back and laugh and laugh and let this play out like Watergate was just the cartoon before the main feature."

He looked very soft, this man who had come from such a hard place so long ago. "Is that what you intend to do?"

I sighed. Then I really did laugh, but there wasn't any humor in it. "No. I know what kind of foul waters you have to swim in, Senator. And your public record *is* good. Funny, the president having to send you. Your politics and his couldn't be much more at odds. But you're stuck in the same mire, aren't you? Like dinosaurs in a tar pit."

That made him smile sadly. "Will you walk away and just let us decay, Mr. Hammer?"

"Why shouldn't I?"

"Well, for one thing, somewhere out there, in that big city, or that bigger country beyond, are people that Old Nic trusted. People like you, who aren't tainted by the Mob. And who are now in grave danger."

He was right about that.

"And Mr. Hammer, the way we came looking for you does not compare to the way other interested parties will conduct their search—the other five families, for example. And they may well start with you."

I grunted a laugh. "So I owe you a big thank you, at least, since I would have had no idea I was in anybody's cross-hairs over this. I get that."

"Good. Good." He had his first overdue sip of beer. He licked foam off those rather sensual lips and the Leprechaun twinkle was back. "And what would you say to ten thousand dollars as a fee, Mr. Hammer?"

"Ten thousand dollars of the tax payers' money?" I got up and slapped on my hat. "Sure. Why not? It's a way for me to finally get back some of what I paid in, anyway."

"Bring me the book, Mr. Hammer." His smile was reassuring but the eyes were hard again. "Bring *us* the book."

"See what I can do."

Hoods always come in twos. The bent-nose boys accompany their boss to business meetings, often in restaurants. Sometimes they sit with their boss, other times at an adjacent table. Or one sits nearby while the other stays outside in the car, at the wheel, an eye on the entrance. Or maybe parked in the alley behind a restaurant, which is a smarter move. Mob watchdogs are always teamed up in twos. So are assassins.

This time the guy waiting in the hall outside my office in the Hackard Building was in his twenties, wearing a yellow shirt with a pointy collar and no tie under a light-blue suit that gave no hint of gun bulge. But a piece was under there, all right. He would have been handsome if his nose hadn't been broken into a misshapen thing, stuck on like clay a sculptor hadn't gotten around to shaping. His dark hair was puffy with hair spray and his sideburns were right off the cough-drop box.

Hoods these days.

"Let's go in and join your boss and your buddy," I said.

"What?" His voice was comically high-pitched and his eyes were small and stupid, all but disappearing when he frowned.

I made an educated guess. "You're with Sonny Giraldi's crew. And Sonny and your opposite number are waiting inside. I'm Hammer." I jerked a thumb toward the door. "Like on the glass?"

He was still working that out when I went in and held the door open for him.

John "Sonny" Giraldi, nephew of Don Nicholas Giraldi and assumed heir to the throne, was seated along the side wall like a patient waiting to get in to see the doctor. He was small, slender, olive-complected, with a narrow face, a hook nose, and big dark eyes that had a deceptively sleepy cast. The other bodyguard, bigger than the guy in the hall, was another pointy-collared disco dude with heavy sideburns; he had a protruding forehead and a weak chin, sitting with a chair between himself and his boss.

Sonny's wardrobe, by the way, was likely courtesy of an Italian designer, Armani maybe, a sleekly cut gray number with a black shirt and gray silk tie. No way a gun was under there anywhere. Sonny let his employees handle the artillery.

"I'd prefer, Mr. Hammer," Sonny said, his voice a radio-announcer baritone too big for his small frame, "if you'd let Flavio keep his position in the corridor. This is a . . . uh . . .transitional time. I might attract unwanted company."

"Fine. Let Flavio stand watch. Hell, I know all about unwanted company."

That got a tiny twitch of a smile from Velda, over at her desk, but prior to that she had been sitting as blankly unconcerned as a meter maid making out a ticket. The Giraldi mob's heir apparent would not have suspected that the unseen right hand of this statuesque beauty undoubtedly held a revolver right now.

I shut the door on Flavio and turned to walk toward my inner office door, saying, "Just you, Mr. Giraldi. I take it you're here for a consultation."

He rose on his Italian loafers and gave me a nod, tossing a flat-hand gesture to the seated bodyguard to stay that way. Velda's head swivelled slightly and I flashed her a look that said be ready for anything. She returned that with a barely perceptible nod.

I shut the door and gestured Sonny Giraldi toward the client's chair. I got behind the desk as Sonny removed a silver cigarette case from inside his suit coat. No chance he was going for a gun the way those threads fit. He reached his slender, well-manicured hand out to offer me a smoke from the case and I shook my head.

"I gave those up years ago," I said. "How do you think I managed to live so long?"

He smiled, a smile so delicious he seemed to taste it. "Well, a lot of us were wondering. Mr. Hammer, do you know why I'm here?"

"You want your uncle's ledger."

"Yes. Do you have it?"

"No. Next question."

He crossed his legs as he lighted up a cigarette. He was not particularly manly, though not effeminate, either. "Do you understand why I thought you might have the book?"

"Yeah. On his deathbed, your uncle said he was bequeathing the thing to somebody he trusted."

He nodded slowly, the big dark sleepy eyes in the narrow face fixed on me. "You did a few jobs for the old don, jobs that he didn't feel he could entrust to his own people."

"That's true as far as it goes."

"*Why* did he trust *you*, Mr. Hammer? And why would *you* work for *him*? You're well-known to be an enemy of La Cosa Nostra. Carl Evello. Alberto Bonetti. Two dons, representing two of the six families, and you killed them both. That massacre at the Y and S men's club—*how* many soldiers did you slaughter there, anyway? Thirty?"

"It was never proven I did that. Anyway, who's counting?"

Another tasty smile. There was an ashtray on my desk for the benefit of clients, and he used it, flicking ash with a hand heavy with bejeweled golden rings. The suit might be Armani, but down deep Sonny was still just another tacky goombah.

He was saying, "And yet Don Nicholas, Old Nic himself, not only let you live, he trusted you to do jobs for him. Why?"

"Why did he let me live? Now and then I killed his competitors. Which saved him the trouble. As for why I would do a job for Old Nic . . .let's just say he did me a favor now and then."

"What kind of favor, Mr. Hammer? Or may I call you 'Mike'? After all, you and my uncle were thick as thieves."

"Not that thick, but you can call me Mike . . .Sonny. Let's just say your uncle helped me out of the occasional jam in your world."

The hooded eyes narrowed to slits. "They say he helped you get out of town after the waterfront shoot-out with Sal Bonetti."

I said nothing.

Giraldi exhaled smoke, blowing it off to one side. Thoughtful of him.

"What is the government paying you?" he asked.

"What government? Paying me for what?"

"You were followed to the St. Moritz, Mike. Senator Boylan is staying there. The G wants the book—maybe to try to bring us down, or maybe they got entries in there themself. I don't give two shits either way, Mike. I want that book."

"You've got an army. I'm just one guy. Go find it yourself."

Again he blew smoke to one side. His manner was casual but I could tell he was wound tight.

He said, "I have a feeling you're in a position to know where it is. Call it a hunch. But I don't think that book got sent to anybody in the family business. I was close to my uncle. *He would have given it to me!*"

He slammed a small fist onto my desk and the ashtray jumped. I didn't.

Very softly he repeated, "He would have given it to me."

I rocked back. "What use would somebody outside of the family have for that book?"

"I don't know. I honestly don't know, Mike."

"Does the thing even exist? Do you really believe that your uncle wrote down every important transaction and key business dealing in some ledger?"

He sat forward and the big eyes didn't seem at all sleepy now. "I *saw* him with it. The book exists. He would sit in his study—he wasn't a big man, he was my size, never one of these big fat slobs like so many in our business—a gray little guy always impeccably dressed, bald in his later years, and like . . .like a *monk* goin' over some ancient scroll. After anything big would go down, he'd retire to his study and hunker over that goddamn book."

"What did it look like?"

"It was a ledger, but not a big one, not like an accountant uses. Smaller, more like an appointment book, but not *that* small. Maybe six by four. Beat-up looking brown cover, some kind of leather. But thick—three inches thick, anyway."

"Where did he keep it?"

"Well, it wasn't in his safe in that study, or in a locked drawer, and we've been all over his house, looking." He sat forward and did his best to seem earnest. "Mike, would it mean anything to you if I said the Giraldis are going to stay on the same path as Uncle Nic?"

"You mean prostitution, gambling, loan-sharking, that kind of thing? Am I supposed to be proud of you, Sonny?"

"You know that Uncle Nic never dealt drugs. We're the only one of the six families that stayed out of what he called an 'evil enterprise.' No kiddie or gay porn, neither, no underage hookers."

Did they give a Nobel Prize for conscientious racketeering, I wondered?

He was saying, too quickly, "And we—*I*—am gonna continue contributing to charities, through St. Pat's Old Cathedral in Little Italy. We fund orphanages and drug treatment centers and all kinds of good works, Mike. You know that. We're *alone* in that, of the six families."

"Okay. So you Giraldis are the best of the bad guys. What's that to me?"

He shrugged. "I suspect it's why you were willing to do jobs for my uncle. Not just because he bailed your ass out when crazy Sal Bonetti damn near killed you."

I trotted out my lopsided grin. "Sonny, I don't have the book."

"But you know where to look. There's one-hundred K in it for you, Mike, if you turn that book over to me. Cash."

"That's a lot of green for a ledger whose contents you aren't sure of."

"Find it, Mike. *Find* it."

Sonny got up, stubbed out his cigarette in the ashtray. Smoothed his suit coat. "Do you think I'm the only one who knows you were on the old boy's list of trusted associates? And do you think the other five families aren't going to be looking for that thing?"

Suddenly the government's ten thousand didn't seem like so much loot after all. Even Sonny's hundred K seemed short of generous.

"Of course, you can *handle* yourself, Mike. That's another reason why you're the ideal person to go looking for this particular volume. And any members of the other five families who you might happen to dispose of along the way, well, that's just a bonus for both of us."

He gave me a business card with his private numbers, an after-hours one jotted on the back. Then he went out with a nod of goodbye that I didn't bother to return.

I just sat there thinking. I heard the door close in the outer office, and then Velda was coming in. She skirted the client's chair and leaned her palms on the desk. Her dark eyes were worried.

"What's going on, Mike? First cops, now wiseguys? What next?"

"I missed lunch," I said. "How about an early supper?"

She smirked and shook her head, making the arcs of raven-wing hair swing. "Only you would think of food at a time like this."

"Give Pat a call and have him meet us at the Blue Ribbon in half an hour."

"What makes you think a captain of Homicide is going to drop everything just because you call?"

"He'll drop everything because *you* called, doll. He has a thing for you, remember. And me? I'm the guy who solves half the captain's cases."

The Blue Ribbon Restaurant on West Forty-fourth Street was in its between-lunch-and-supper lull, meaning Velda and I had the restaurant part of the bar damn near to ourselves. We sat at our regular corner table with walls of autographed celebrity photos looking over our shoulders as I put away the knockwurst and Velda had a salad. She worked harder at maintaining her figure than I did.

Pushing her half-eaten rabbit food aside, Velda leaned in and asked, "So . . .you think you can find this ledger? What leads do you have?"

"Just two."

"Such as?"

I gulped from a pilsner of Miller. "Well, one is Father Mandano in Little Italy."

"Makes sense," she said with a nod. "His parish is where Don Giraldi was the primary patron."

I laughed once. "Patron. That's a good way to put it."

"Buying his way into heaven?"

"I don't think these mob guys really believe in God—not the top guys anyway. Buying himself good will is more like it. Like Capone in Chicago opening up soup kitchens in the Depression."

"So you'll talk to the good father."

"I will."

"That's one lead, Mike. You said two."

I looked at her slyly over the rim of my glass. I was almost whispering when I said, "Remember that job we did for Old Nic about twenty years back? That relocation number?"

Velda was nodding, smiling slyly right back at me. Like me, she kept her voice low. "You're right. That's a lead if ever there was one. You want me to come along?"

"I would. She liked you. She'll talk more freely if you're around. But I'll talk to the priest on my own."

"Yeah," she said with a smirk. "Only room for two in a confessional."

Pat came in the revolving door and came straight to us—he knew where we'd be. Enjoying the spring afternoon, he was in a lightweight tan suit, chocolate tie, and no hat—though he and I were two rare New Yorkers who still wore them. He stopped at the bar to grab a beer from George and brought it along with him when he came over, sitting with me on his left and Velda on his right.

"Don't wait for me," he said, noting the meal I was half-way through. "Dig right in."

"I said thirty minutes," I said. "You took forty-five. A man has to eat."

"Yeah, I heard that rumor. You didn't say what this was about, so let *me* tell *you*—old Don Giraldi finally croaking. Everybody and his dog is out looking for that legendary missing ledger of his."

"*Is* it legendary, Pat?"

His expression was friendly but the blue-gray eyes were hard. "Legendary in the sense that it's famous in certain circles. But I think it's very real, considering the stir it's causing among the ziti set."

"The other families?"

"Just one, really—the Pierluigi bunch. They were the family that Old Nic was allied most closely with. Their territories really intertwined, you know. Talking to the OCU guys, they say Old Nic's reputation as the most beneficent of the Mafia capos is bullshit. Specifically, they say he invested in drug trafficking through Pierluigi. That and *other* nasty criminal enterprises that wouldn't have made the old don such a beloved figure around Little Italy."

"Meaning if the don really was keeping a record of his transactions," I said, "that book would be of high interest to the Pierluigi clan."

"Damn straight. But they aren't the only interested parties. There are a couple of underbosses in the Giraldi family who are looking at the old don's passing as an invitation to move up in the world."

"You mean Sonny Giraldi doesn't have the don's chair sewn up."

"He *might* . . .if he had that book. So, Mike," Pat's smile was wide but those eyes of his remained shrewd. "Do you have it?"

"Well, I may be older, but I hope I still have it. What would you say, Vel? Do I still have it?"

"I should say you do," she said.

"Can the comedy," Pat said. "It's well known you had a soft spot for Old Nic, Mike."

"That's horseshit, Pat. I had no illusions about the old boy. He was probably the best man in his world, but what a lousy world, huh?"

Pat sipped beer, then almost whispered: "Word on the street is, that book went to somebody the old don trusted. Are *you* that somebody, Mike?"

"No. Tell me about this guy Hanson."

"Hanson? *What* Hanson?"

"Hanson in the department. He didn't show me his badge but he didn't have to. He had a buddy with him whose name I didn't catch—younger guy."

"That would likely be Captain Bradley."

I grinned at him. "Captain! How about that? A young guy achieving such a rarefied rank. You must be impressed, Pat."

"Screw you, buddy. Hanson is an ass-kisser—sorry, Velda—and a political player from way back. He made inspector at thirty-five. You never ran into him before?"

"No."

"When *did* you run into him?"

I ignored the question. "So this Hanson is strictly a One Police Plaza guy? No wonder I don't know him. But is he honest?"

"Define honest."

"Is he *bent*, Pat? Not just a little, but all the way?"

Pat shook his head. "I don't think so."

"You don't sound very convinced."

"We don't travel in the same orbit, Hanson and me. Mike, I never heard a whisper of corruption in regard to him, but that doesn't make it impossible. I mean, he's a political animal."

I gave him a small, nasty smile. "Could Inspector Hanson be in that ledger?"

Pat had a sip of beer and thought about it. "If he *is* bent, of course he could. But so could any number of bad apples. Why, did he come looking for it?"

I ignored that question, too. "Seems to me there are a lot of people with guns who might like to check this book out of whoever's library it's landed in."

"Brother, you aren't kidding."

I put a hand on his shoulder. "Pat, let me treat you to a platter of this knockwurst. On me."

"What's the occasion for such generosity?"

"I just think it's a pity that average citizens like me don't take the time out, now and again, to properly thank a public servant like you for your stalwart efforts."

"Stalwart, huh? Normally I'd say 'baloney.'"

But instead he had the knockwurst.

St. Patrick's Cathedral on Fifth Avenue, built in the 1870s, was a late arrival compared to old St. Pat's on the corner of Prince and Mott. The original St. Pat's had started saving souls in Little Italy a good seventy years before that midtown upstart.

I sat with Father Mandano in his office in the Prince Street rectory—this was a Wednesday night with no mass at old St. Pat's. Velda sat outside in the reception area, reading an ancient issue of *Catholic Digest*—the desk where her nun equivalent usually sat was empty. This was early evening, after office hours.

The broad-shouldered priest, in casual black and that touch of white, sat with thick-fingered, prayerfully folded hands on the blotter of a massive contradiction of a desk, its austere lines trimmed with ornamental flourishes. The office with its rich wood paneling and arched windows had a conference table to one side and bookcases everywhere, the spacious chamber under-lit by way of a banker's lamp and a few glowing wall-mounted fixtures.

The father was as legendary in Little Italy as that ledger of Don Giraldi's—the old priest deemed tough but fair, his generosity renowned. Still, even in his seventies, he had the well-fed look and hard eyes of a line coach, his white hair cut military short, his square head home to regular features that were distorting with age.

"I have of course heard the tales about this notorious ledger, Michael," he said in a sonorous baritone schooled for the pulpit. "But the late don did not leave it with me."

"You must have had many meetings with Giraldi over the years, Father. Would you have any notion about who he might have entrusted with that book?"

He shook his head once, a solemn and final gesture. "I only met rarely with Mr. Giraldi. For many years, I dealt solely with his wife, Antoinetta, who was a wonderful, devout woman."

"How could she be devout and married to a mob boss?"

"Our Father's house has many mansions."

"Yeah, and compartments, too, I guess. And mob money can build plenty of mansions."

His smile was barely perceptible. "When were you last at mass, Michael? I assume you are of the faith, Irish lad that you are."

"I haven't been a 'lad' for a lot of years, Father, and I haven't been to mass since I got back from overseas."

"The war changed you."

"The war showed me that God either doesn't give a damn or has some sick sense of humor. If you'll forgive my frankness, Father."

The dark eyes didn't look so hard now. "I'm in the forgiveness business, Michael. You hold God responsible for the sins of man?"

"If you mean war, Father, fighting against an evil devil like Hitler isn't considered a sin, is it?"

"No. But I would caution you that holding God responsible for the actions of men is a dangerous philosophy. And I gather, from your words, that you *do* believe in God."

"I do."

There was nothing barely perceptible about his smile now. "Years ago, the headlines were filled with your colorful activities, working against evil men. You were raised in the church, so surely you know of your namesake, St. Michael."

"Yeah, the avenging archangel."

"Well, that's perhaps an over-simplification. Among other things, he leads the army of God against the minions of Satan, the powers of Hell."

"I'm semi-retired from that, Father. Let's just say you don't have time to hear *my* confession, but I bet you heard some beauts from Old Nic."

The smile disappeared and the priest's countenance turned solemn again. "Nicholas Giraldi never came to confession. Not once."

"What?"

"Oh, he will lie in consecrated ground. I gave him bedside Last Rites at St. Luke's. But he never took confession here. And I will confess to *you*, Michael, that I was surprised when, after his wife's death, he continued to fund her charities. If there was any purpose in it, other than his own self-aggrandizement, it might have been to honor her memory."

"The old don bought himself plenty of good will here in Little Italy."

"He did indeed. But I don't believe his good works had anything to do with seeking forgiveness. And, before you ask how I could accept contributions from the likes of Don Giraldi, I will tell you that even a spiritual man, a servant of God, must live in this physical world. If suffering can be alleviated by accepting such contributions, I will accept that penance, whether sincere or cynical. You might consider this in itself a cynical, even selfish practice, Michael. But we were put here in this place, this, this . . ."

"Vale of tears, Father?"

"Vale of tears, son. We were put here in this problem-solving world, this physical purgatory, to exercise our free will. And if I can turn ill-gotten gains into the work of the Lord, I will do so, unashamed."

Why shouldn't he? All he had to do was take confession from some other collar and get his sins washed away for a few Hail Marys. But I didn't say that. Hypocritical or not, Father Mandano had helped a lot of people. He was a practical man and that wasn't a sin in my book.

I got to my feet, my hat in my hands. "Thanks for seeing me at short notice, Father. Listen, if you happen to get a line on that ledger, let me know. It could spark a shooting war out on your streets. And innocent people could die."

"And that troubles you, doesn't it, Michael?"

"Don't kid yourself, Father. This is just a job to me. I have a big payday coming if I pull this off. This is one valuable book."

"In my line of work, Michael," he said, "there is only *one* book of real value."

Wilcox in Suffolk County was a prosperous-looking little beach burg with a single industry: tourism. In a month the population would swell from seven-thousand to who-the-hell-knew, and the business district would be alive and jumping till all hours. Right now, at eight-thirty p.m., it was a ghost town.

Sheila Burrows lived in a two-bedroom brick bungalow on a side street, perched on a small but nicely landscaped yard against a wooded backdrop. The place was probably built in the fifties, nothing fancy, but well-maintained. A free-standing matching brick one-car garage was just behind the house. We pulled in up front. The light was on over the front door. We were expected.

I got out of the car and came around to play gentleman for Velda but she was already climbing out. She had changed into a black pants suit with a gray silk blouse and looked very business-like, or as much as her curves, long legs and all that shoulders-brushing raven hair allowed. She carried a good-size black purse with a shoulder strap. Plenty of room for various female accouterments, including a .22 revolver.

She was looking back the way we came. "I can't shake the feeling we were followed," she said.

"Hard to tell on a damn expressway," I admitted. "But I didn't pick up on anything on that county road."

"Maybe I should stay out here and keep watch."

"No. I can use you inside. I remember you hitting it off with this broad. She was scared of me, as I recall."

Now Velda was looking at the brick house. "Well, for all she knew you were one of Don Giraldi's thugs and she was getting a one-way ride. And maybe something about your manner said that a 'broad' is what you thought she was."

"I wasn't so cultured then."

"Yeah," she said sarcastically, as we started up the walk. "You've come a long way, baby."

Twenty years ago, more or less, Velda and I had moved Sheila Burrows out to these Long Island hinterlands. That hadn't been her name then, and she'd had to leave a Park Avenue penthouse to make the move. The exact circumstances of why Don Giraldi had wanted his mistress to disappear had not been made known to us. But we had suspected.

The woman who met us at the door was barely recognizable as the former Broadway chorus girl we had helped relocate back when LBJ was still president. She had been petite and curvy and platinum blonde. Now she was stout and bulgy and mousy brunette. Her pretty Connie Stevens-ish features, lightly made up, were trapped inside a ball of a face.

"Nice to see you two again," she said as she ushered us inside. She wore a pink top, blue jeans and sandals.

There was no entryway. You were just suddenly in the living room, a formal area with lots of plastic-covered furniture. A spinet piano against the right wall was overseen by a big gilt-framed pastel portrait of our hostess back in all her busty blond glory.

She quickly moved us into a small family room area just off a smallish kitchen with wooden cabinets and up-to-date appliances; a short hallway to the bedrooms was at the rear. She sat us down at a round maple table with captain's chairs and a spring-theme centerpiece of plastic flowers.

She had coffee ready for us. As I stirred milk and sugar into mine, I glanced at the nearby wall where rough-hewn paneling was arrayed with framed pictures. They charted two things: her descent into near obesity, and the birth, adolescence and young manhood of a son. It was all there, from playpen to playground, from high school musical to basketball court, from graduation to what was obviously a recent shot of the handsome young man with an attractive girl outside a building I recognized as part of NYU.

"That's our son," she said, in a breathy second soprano that had been sexy once upon a time.

"We *thought* you were pregnant," Velda said with a tiny smile.

Her light blue eyes jumped. "Really? You knew? Why, I was only a few months gone. Barely showing."

"You just had that glow," Velda said.

Our hostess chuckled. "More like water retention. How *do* you maintain that lovely figure of yours, Miss Sterling? Or are you two *married* by now?"

"Not married," Velda said. "Not quite. Not yet."

"She eats a lot of salad," I said.

That made Sheila Burrows wince, and Velda shot me a look. I'd been rude. Hadn't meant to be, but some things come naturally.

I said, "You probably never figured to see us again."

"That's true," she said. She sipped her coffee. "But I wasn't surprised to hear from you, not exactly."

Velda asked, "Why is that?"

"With Nicholas dying, I figured there would be *some* kind of follow-up. For a long time, there was a lawyer, a nice man named Simmons, who handled the financial arrangements. He would come by every six months and see how I was doing. And ask questions about our son."

I asked, "Any direct contact with Don Giraldi since you moved out here?"

"No. And, at first, I was surprised. I thought after Nick was born . . .our son is Nicholas, too . . .that we might, in some way, resume our relationship. Nicolas Giraldi was a very charming man, Mr. Hammer. Very suave. Very courtly. He was the love of my life."

"You were only with him for, what? Five or six years?"

"Yes, but it was a wonderful time. We traveled together, even went to Europe once, and he practically lived with me during those years. I don't believe he ever had relations with his wife after the early years of their marriage."

"They had three daughters."

"Yes," she said, rather defensively, "but none after our Nick came along."

Funny that she so insistently referred to the son in that fashion— 'our Nick'—when the father had avoided any direct contact. And this once beautiful woman, so sexually desirable on and off the stage, had become a homemaker and mother—a suburban housewife. Without a husband.

Velda said, "I can see why you thought Nicholas would come back to you, after your son's birth. If he had *really* wanted you out of his life—for whatever reason—he wouldn't have kept you so close to home."

"Wilcox is a long way from Broadway," she said rather wistfully.

"But it's not the moon," I said. "I had assumed the don felt you'd gotten too close to him—that you'd seen things that could be used against him."

Her eyes jumped again. "Oh, I would never—"

"Not by you, but by others. Police. FBI. Business rivals. But it's clear he wanted his son protected. So that the boy could not be used against him."

She was nodding. "That's right. That's what he told me, before he sent me away. He said our son would be in harm's way, if anyone knew he existed. But that he would *always* look out for young Nick. That someday Nick would have a great future."

Velda said, "You said you had no direct contact with Nicholas. But would I be right in saying that you had . . .*indirect* contact?"

The pretty face in the plump setting beamed. "Oh, yes. Maybe once a year, always in a different way. You see, our Nick is a very talented boy—talented young *man* now. He took part in so many school activities, both the arts and sports. And *so* brilliant; valedictorian of his class! But then his father was a genius, wasn't he?"

I asked, "What do you mean, 'once a year, always in a different way?'"

She was looking past me at the wall of pictures. Fingers that were still slender, graceful, traced memories in the air.

"There Nicholas would be," she said, "looking so proud, in the audience at a concert, or a ball game, or a school play. I think Nick gets his artistic talent from me, if that doesn't sound too stuck up and, best of all, Nicholas came to graduation and heard his son speak."

Velda asked, "Did they ever meet?"

"No." She pointed. "Did you notice that picture? That very first one, high up, at the left?"

A solemn portrait of a kid in army green preceded the first of several baby photos.

"That's a young man who died in Vietnam," she said. "Mr. Simmons, the attorney, provided me with that and other photos, as well as documents. His name was Edwin Burrows and we never met. He was an only child with no immediate family. He won several medals, actually, including a Silver Star, and *that* was the father that Nick grew up proud of."

I asked, "No suspicions?"

"Why should he be suspicious? When he was younger, Nick was very proud of having such an heroic father."

"Only when he was younger?"

"Well . . .you know boys. They grow out of these things."

Not really, but I let it pass.

"Mrs. Burrows," I said, sitting forward, "have you received anything, perhaps in the mail, that might seem to have come from Don Giraldi?"

"No . . ."

"Specifically, a ledger. A book."

Her eyes were guileless. "No," she said. "No. After Mr. Simmons died, and his visits ended, another lawyer came around, just once. I was given a generous amount of money and told I was now on my own. And there's a trust fund for Nick that becomes his on his graduation from NYU."

"Have you talked to your son recently?"

She nodded. "We talk on the phone at least once a week. Why, I spoke to him just yesterday."

"Did he say anything about receiving a ledger from his father?"

"Mr. Hammer, no. As I thought I made clear, as far as Nick is concerned *his* father is a Vietnam war hero named Edwin Burrows."

"Right," I said. "Now listen carefully."

And I told her about the book.

She might be a suburban hausfrau now, but she had once been the mistress of a mob boss. She followed me easily, occasionally nodding, never interrupting.

"You are on the very short list," I said, "of people who Don Giraldi valued and trusted. You might *still* receive that book. And it's possible some very bad people might come looking for it."

She shook her head, mousy brown curls bouncing. "Doesn't seem possible . . .after all these years. I thought I was safe . . .I thought *Nick* was safe."

"You raise the most pertinent point. I think your son is the logical person the don may have sent that book."

She frowned in concern, but said nothing.

I went on: "I want you to do two things, Mrs. Burrows, and I don't want any argument. I want you to let us stow you away in a safe-house motel we use upstate. Until this is over. You have a car? Velda will drive you in it, and stay with you till I give the word. Just quickly pack a bag."

She swallowed and nodded. "And the other thing?"

"I want you to call your son right now," I said, "and tell him I'm coming to visit him. I'll talk to him briefly myself, so that he'll know my voice. I'll come alone. If more than one person shows up at his door, even if one of them claims to be me, he's not to let them in. If that happens, he's to get out and get away, as fast as he can. Is all of that clear?"

She wore a funny little smile. "You know, Mr. Hammer, I think my impression of you all those years ago was wrong, very wrong."

"Yeah?"

"You really are quite a nice, caring human being."

I glanced at Velda, who didn't bother stifling her grin.

"Yeah," I said. "I get that a lot."

If Wilcox at eight-thirty p.m. was a ghost town, the East Village at eleven-something was a freak show. This was a landscape of crumbling buildings, with as many people living on the streets as walking down them, where in a candy store you could buy a Snickers Bar or an eightball of smack, and when morning came, bodies with bullet holes or smaller but just as deadly ones would be on sidewalks and alleyways like so much trash set out for collection.

Tompkins Square Park was this neighborhood's central gathering place, from oldtimers who had voted for FDR and operated traditional businesses like diners and laundries to students, punkers, artists, and poets seeking life experience and cheap lodging. Every second tenement storefront seemed home to a gallery showcasing work inspired by the tragic but colorful street life around them.

NYU student Nick Burrows lived in a second-floor apartment over a gallery peddling works by an artist whose canvases of graffiti struck me as little different from the free stuff on alley walls.

His buzzer worked, which was saying something in this neighborhood, and he met me on a landing as spongy as the steps coming up had been. He wore a black CBGB T-shirt, jeans and sneakers, a kid of twenty or so with the wiry frame of his father but taller, and the pleasant features of his mother, their prettiness turned masculine by heavy eyebrows.

He offered his hand and we shook under the dim yellowish glow of a single mounted bulb. "I appreciate you helping out my mom, Mr. Hammer. You know, I think I've heard of you."

"A lot of people think they've heard of me," I said, moving past him into the apartment. "They're just not sure anymore."

His was a typical college kid's pad—thrift-shop furnishings, atomic-age stuff that had looked modern in the fifties and seemed quaint now. Plank and cement-block bookcases lined the walls, paperbacks and school books mostly, and the occasional poster advertising an East Village art show or theatrical production were taped here and there to the brick walls. The kitchenette area was off to one side and a doorless doorframe led to a bedroom with a waterbed. We sat on a thin-cushioned couch with sparkly turquoise upholstery.

He offered me a smoke and I declined. He got one going, then leaned back, an arm along the upper cushions, and studied me like the smart college kid he was. His mother had told him on the phone that I had something important to talk to him about. I had spoken to him briefly, as well, but nothing about the book.

Still, he'd been told there was danger and he seemed unruffled. There was strength in this kid.

I said, "You know who your real father was, don't you, Nick?"

He nodded.

I grinned. "I figured a smart kid like you would do some poking into that Vietnamhero malarkey. Did the don ever get in touch with you? He came to the occasional school event, I understand."

He sighed smoke. "Get in touch? No, not in the sense that he ever introduced himself. But he started seeking me out after a concert, a basketball game, just to come up and say, 'Good job tonight,' or 'Nice going out there.' Even shook my hand a couple of times."

"So you noticed him."

"Yeah, and when I got older, I recognized him. He was in the papers now and then, you know. I did some digging on my own, old newspaper files and that kind of thing. Ran across my mom's picture with him, too, back when she was a real knockout. She wasn't just a chorus girl, you know, like the press would have it. She had speaking parts, got mentioned in reviews sometimes."

"Your mother doesn't know that you know any of this."

"Why worry her?"

"Nick, I'm here because your father kept a ledger, a book said to contain all of his secrets. Word was he planned to give it to the person he trusted most in the world. Are *you* that person?"

He sighed, smiled, allowed himself a private laugh.

Then he asked, "Would you like a beer? You look like a guy who could use a beer."

"Has been a long day."

So he got us cold cans of beer and he leaned back and I did too. And he told me his story.

Two weeks ago, he'd received a phone call from Don Nicholas Giraldi—a breathy voice that had a deathbed ring to it, making a request that young Nick come to a certain hospital room at St. Luke's. No mention of old Nicholas being young Nick's father, not on the phone.

"But when I stood at his bedside," Nick said, "he told me. He said, 'I'm your father.' Very melodramatic. Ever see *Stars Wars?* 'Luke, I am your father'? Like that."

"And what did you say?"

He shrugged. "Just, 'I know. I've known for years.' That seemed to throw the old boy, but he didn't have the wind or the energy to discuss it or ask for details or anything. He just said, 'You're going to come into money when you graduate from the university.'"

"You didn't know there was a trust fund?"

"No. And I still don't know how much is in it. I'll be happy to accept whatever it is, because I think I kind of deserve it, growing up without a father. I'm hoping it'll be enough for me to start a business. Don't let the arty neighborhood fool you, Mr. Hammer. I'm a business major."

"Is that what Old Nic had in mind, you starting up something of your own?"

The young man frowned, shook his head. "I'm not sure. He may have wanted me to step into *his* role in his . . .organization. Or he may have been fine with me going my own way. Who knows? In any event, he said, 'I have something for you. Whatever you do in life, it will be valuable to you.'"

"The book?"

He nodded. "The book, Mr. Hammer. He gave it to me right there in that hospital room. The book of his secrets."

I sat forward. "Containing everything your father knew, a record of every crooked thing he'd done, and all of those he'd conspired with to break God knows how many laws."

"Something like that."

I shook my head. "Even if you go down a straight path, son, that book would be valuable."

He nodded. "It's valuable, all right. But I don't want it, Mr. Hammer. I'm not interested in it or what it represents."

"What are you going to do with the thing?"

"Give it to you." He shrugged. "Do what you will with it. I want only one thing in return."

"Yeah?"

"Ensure that my mother is safe. That she is not in any danger. And do the same for me, if you can. But Mom . . .she did so *much* for me, sacrificed everything, gave her *life* to me . . .I want her *safe*."

"I think I can handle that."

He extended his hand for me to shake, and I did.

He got up and went over to a plank-and-block bookcase under the window onto the neon-winking street. I followed him. He was selecting an ancient-looking sheepskin-covered volume from a stack of books carelessly piled on top when the door splintered open, kicked in viciously, and two men burst in with guns in hand.

First was Flavio, still wearing the light-blue suit and yellow pointy-collar shirt, but I never did get the name of his pal, the big guy with the weak chin and Neanderthal forehead. They come in twos, you know, hoods who work for guys like Sonny Giraldi.

They had big pieces in their fists, matching .357 mags. In this part of town, where gunshots were commonplace, who needed .22 autos with silencers? The big guy fell back to be framed in the doorway like another work of East Village art, and Flavio took two more steps inside, training his .357 on both of us, as young Nick and I were clustered together.

Flavio, in his comically high-pitched voice, said, "Is that the book? Give me that goddamned *book*!"

"Take it," Nick said, frowning, more disgusted than afraid, and stepped forward, holding out the small, thick volume, blocking me as he did.

I used that to whip the .45 out from under my shoulder, and I shoved the kid to the floor and rode him down, firing up.

Flavio may have had a .357, but that's a card a .45 trumps easy, particularly if you get the first shot off, and even more so if you make it a head shot that cuts off any motor action. What few brains the bastard had got splashed in a shower of bone and blood onto his startled pal's puss, and the Neanderthal reacted like he'd been hit with a gory pie, giving me the half second I needed to shatter that protruding forehead with a slug and paint an abstract picture on the brick out in that landing, worthy of any East Village gallery.

Now Nick was scared, taking in the bloody mess on his doorstep. "Jesus, man! What are you going to do?"

"Call a cop. You got a phone?"

"Yeah, yeah, call the cops!" He was pointing. "Phone's over there."

I picked the sheepskin-covered book up off the floor. "No—not the cops. *A* cop."

And I called Pat Chambers.

I didn't call Sonny Giraldi until I got back to the office around three a.m. I had wanted to get that book into my office safe.

The heir to the old don's throne pretended I'd woken him, but I knew damn well he'd been waiting up to hear from his boys. Or maybe some cop in his pocket had already called to say the apartment invasion in the East Village had failed, in which case it was unlikely Sonny would be in the midst of a soothing night's sleep when I used the private number he'd provided me.

Cheerfully I asked, "Did you know that your boy Flavio and his slopehead buddy won a free ride to the county morgue tonight?"

"What?"

"I sent them there. Just like you sent them to the Burrows kid's apartment. They'd been following me, hadn't they? I really *must* be getting old. Velda caught it, but I didn't."

The radio-announcer voice conveyed words in a tumble. "Hammer, I didn't send them. They must be working for one of my rivals or something. I played it absolutely straight with you, I swear to God."

"No, you didn't. You wanted me to lead you to the book, and whoever had it needed to die, because they knew what was in it, and I had to die, too, just to keep things tidy. Right? Who would miss an old broken-down PI like me, anyway?"

"Believe me, Hammer, I—"

"I don't believe you, Sonny. But you can believe me."

Actually, I was about to tell him a whopper, but he'd never know.

I went on: "This book will go in a safe deposit box in some distant bank and will not come out again until my death. If that death is nice and peaceful, I will leave instructions that the book be burned. If I have an unpleasant going away party, then that book will go to the feds. Understood?"

"Understood."

"And the Burrows woman and her son, they're out of this. Any harm befalls either one, that book comes out of mothballs and into federal hands. *Capeesh?*"

"*Capeesh*," he said glumly.

"Then there's the matter of my fee."

"Your *fee!* What the hell—"

"Sonny, I found the book for you. You owe me one-hundred grand."

His voice turned thin and nasty. "I heard a lot of bad things about you, Hammer. But I never heard you were a black-mailing prick."

"Well, you learn something every day, if you're paying attention. I want that hundred K donated to whatever charities that Father Mandano designates. Think of the fine reputation you'll earn, Sonny, continuing your late uncle's good works in Little Italy."

And I hung up on him.

Cops always come in twos, they say, but the next morning, when Hanson entered my private office, he left his nameless crony in the outer one, to read old magazines. Velda wasn't back at her reception desk yet, but she soon would be.

"Have a seat, Inspector," I said, getting behind my desk.

The brown sheepskin volume, its spine ancient and cracked, lay on my blotter at a casual angle, where I'd tossed it in anticipation of his visit.

"*That's* the book," he said, eyes wide.

"That's the book. And it's all yours for ten grand."

"May I?" he asked, reaching for it.

"Be my guest."

He thumbed it open. The pleasure on his face turned to confusion, then to shock.

"My God . . ." he said.

"It's valuable, all right. I'm no expert, though, so you may be overpaying. You may want to hold onto it for a while."

"I'll be damned," he said, leafing through.

"As advertised, it has in it everything the old don knew about dirty schemes and double-dealing. Stuff that applies to crooks and cops and senators and even presidents."

He was shaking his head, eyes still on the book.

"Of course, we *were* wrong about it being a ledger. It's more a how-to-book by another Italian gangster. First-edition English-language translation, though—1640, it says."

"A gangster named Machiavelli," Hanson said dryly.

"And a book," I said, "called *The Prince*."

XII

The Long Sonata of the Dead

Andrew Taylor

I HADN'T SEEN ADAM in the flesh for over twenty years. I had seen him on television, of course—it was increasingly hard to miss him—but the last time I had met him in person was when we picked up our degrees. Mary had been there too.

"Well," he'd said, punching me gently on the arm. "Thank God it's over. Let's find a drink. We need to celebrate."

"No," I'd said. "I don't want to."

Mary hadn't said anything at all.

I don't deny that it was a shock to see Adam after all this time, and it wasn't a pleasant one. It was the first of the three shocks that happened in swift succession that afternoon.

I was standing at one of the tall windows of the reading room overlooking St. James's Square. It was a Tuesday afternoon in February, just after lunch, and it was raining. I was watching the domes of umbrellas scurrying like wet beetles on the pavements and the steady clockwise flow of traffic round the square. Adam must have walked across the garden in the middle. He came out of the gate in the railings on the north side. He paused for a moment, waiting for a gap in the traffic.

That's when I recognized him. Despite the rain, he didn't have a hat or umbrella. He was wearing a Burberry raincoat but even that was unbuttoned. He had his head thrown back and his legs a little apart. He was smiling as if the weather was a friend, not an inconvenience.

He had been standing like that the very first time I saw him, which was also in the rain. That had been the first day of our first term at university. I was staring down from my room at the cobbled court below and wishing I was still at home. There was Adam, looking as if he owned the place. Thirty seconds later I discovered that he was my new roommate. He was studying English, too, so we saw each other for a large part of every day for an entire year, apart from the holidays.

The traffic parted before him like the Red Sea. He strolled across the road, swinging his bag. I realized that he was coming here, to the London Library.

Adam looked up at the windows of the reading room. He couldn't have seen me looking down at him—I was too far back from the glass. But I turned and moved away as if I had been caught doing something wrong.

❧

It will help if I explain about the London Library before I go on. It's a building, first of all, an old townhouse that was turned into a private subscription library in 1841. Its members included people like Dickens and Thackeray, Carlyle and George Eliot. Over the years it has been extended down and up, sideways and backwards, until the place has become a maze of literature.

The pillared reading room on the first floor still has the air of a well-appointed gentleman's library, with leather armchairs in front of the fireplace, racks of the latest periodicals and galleries of bookcases far above your head. In all the years I have known it, I have never heard a raised voice there.

There are over a million of books, they say, in over fifty languages, marching along over fifteen miles of shelving. Nowadays they have an electronic universe of information to back them up. But it's the real, printed books that matter. I often think of the sheer weight of all that paper, all that ink, all those words, all those meanings.

The London Library is, in its way, a republic of letters. As long as they pay the subscription and obey the few rules, its members have equal rights and privileges. Perhaps that was the main reason the place was so important to me. In the London Library I was as good as anyone else. Since my marriage had broken up three years ago, I felt more at home in the library than I did in my own flat.

Over the years the collection has grown. As the books have multiplied, so has the space required to house them. Members have free access to the stacks that recede deeper and deeper into the mountain of buildings behind the frontages of St James's Square. Here, in these sternly utilitarian halls of literature, the tall shelves march up and down.

The library is an organic thing that has developed over the decades according to a private logic of its own over many levels and floors. There are hiding places, narrow iron staircases and grubby, rarely-visited alcoves where the paint on the walls hasn't changed since the days of Virginia Woolf. Sometimes I think the library is really a great brain and we, its members who come and go over the years, are no more than its fugitive thoughts and impulses.

You never know quite what you may find in the stacks. There are many forgotten books that perhaps no one has ever looked at since their arrival at the library. Where else would I have found *The Voice of Angels*, for example, or learned about the long sonata of the dead?

Now there was a serpent in my booklined garden of Eden. Its name was Adam.

❧

I went down the paneled stairs to the issue hall on the ground floor. I arrived just as Adam came through the security barrier. He was putting away the plastic-coated membership card in his wallet. So he was a member, not just a visitor.

He turned right and went into the little side-hall where the lockers are. I was pretty sure that he wouldn't recognize me. He never really noticed people. Anyway, unlike him, I had changed a good deal since he had last seen me. I had put on weight. I had an untidy beard, streaked with grey. I was going bald.

I lingered by the window that looks down into the Lightwell Reading Room. I opened my notebook and pretended to examine one of the pages. The book fell open at the entries I had copied from the computer catalogue when I had first searched for Francis Youlgreave in the name index. Only two of his books were listed there: *The Judgement of Strangers* and *The Tongues of Angels*. They were both reprints from the 1950s.

On the edge of my range of vision I saw Adam crossing the hall to the long counter that divides the staff from the members. He laid down a couple of books for return. The nearest assistant did the little double-take that people do when they encounter the famous and smiled at him. I couldn't see Adam's face but his posture changed—he seemed to grow a little taller, a little wider; he was like a preening peacock.

He turned away and passed behind me into the room where the photocopiers and the catalogues are. The two books remained where they were for the moment. I went over to them and picked up the top one. It was a survey of fin-de-siècle British poetry; it had been written in the 1930s by a man who used to review a good deal for the *Times Literary Supplement*. I had looked at it for my Youlgreave research but there wasn't much there of value and Youlgreave himself was barely mentioned.

The assistant looked up. "I'm sorry, I haven't checked that in yet—would you like to take it out?"

"I'm not sure. But may I look at it? And at this one."

She scanned the labels and handed the books to me. I took them upstairs, back to the reading room, and settled at my table. The other book was a biography of Aubrey Beardsley. Again, I had come across the book myself—Beardsley had provided the illustrations for an 1897 collector's edition of one of Youlgreave's better-known poems, "The Four Last Things." There wasn't much about Beardsley's connection with Youlgreave—merely the usual unsupported claim that they had moved in the same rather louche cultural circle in London, together with an account of Beardsley's struggle to extract payment from Youlgreave's publisher. But the page that mentioned the episode was turned down at the top left corner, an unpleasant habit that some readers have; Adam used to do it with my books and it infuriated me.

I knew then that this must be more than coincidence. That was the second shock of the afternoon. Adam was almost certainly researching Francis Youlgreave. The bastard, I thought, hasn't he got enough already? Hasn't he taken enough from me?

I continued automatically turning the pages. A flash of yellow caught my eye. It was a yellow Post-it note that marked the reference in the sources relating to the Youlgreave commission. That too was typical of Adam—he was always leaving markers in other people's books; I once found a dessicated rasher of streaky bacon in my copy of Sterne's *Sentimental Journey*.

There was something written in pencil on the Post-it note. *You're such a complete shit. You won't get away with it.*

That was the third shock. I recognized the writing, you see, the looping descenders, the slight backward slope, the tendency to turn the dots on the "i"s into tiny but incomplete circles, drawn clockwise, from the left. It had changed significantly over time—for example, the letters were untidier in form and now ran together like a tangle of razor wire on a prison wall.

But there was no doubt about it. A working knowledge of paleography has its advantages. I knew straightaway that the handwriting was Mary's.

∾

Mary was out of my league. She was in the year below mine. I had noticed her around-going to lectures, in the faculty coffee bar and, once, in the saloon bar of the Eagle, sprawled across the lap of a post-graduate student from Harvard who drove a Porsche. As far as I knew she wasn't even aware of my existence.

This changed one night in May when I went to a party at someone's house, taken there by a friend of a friend. We had come on from the pub. Someone was vomiting in the front garden when we arrived. The music was so loud that the windows were rattling in their frames.

We pushed our way through the crowd in the hall and found the kitchen, where the drinks were. That was packed, too. Someone passed me a joint as I came in. Everyone was shouting to make themselves heard over the music. Twenty minutes later, I realized that the joint had been stronger than I'd thought. I had to get away from all the people, the heat and the noise.

The back door was open. I stumbled outside. Cool air touched my skin. There was a little garden full of weeds and rusting metal. A couple was making out on an old mattress. Light and music streamed from the house but both were softened and more bearable. I looked up at the sky, hoping to see stars. There was only the dull yellow glow of a city sky at night.

I sat down on a discarded refrigerator lying on its side against the fence. The dope was still making my thoughts spin but more slowly now, and almost enjoyably. Time passed. The couple on the mattress rustled and groaned in their private world. Then, suddenly, I was not alone.

A change in the light made me look up. Mary was standing in the kitchen doorway. She was wearing a clinging velvet dress the color of red wine. She had a mass of dark hair. Her face was in shadow. The light behind her made a sort of aura around her.

I looked away, not wanting her to think that I was staring at her. I heard her footsteps. I caught a hint of her perfume, mingled with her own smell to make something unique.

"Why do you always look so sad," she said.

Startled, I looked up. "What?"

"Why do you look so sad?"

"I don't know," I said. "I don't feel it."

"Not sad," she said. "That's the wrong word. Like you're thinking tragic, profound thoughts."

"Looks deceive," I said.

"Have you got a cigarette?"

That was an easier question to answer. I found my cigarettes and offered her one. She leant forward when I held up the lighter for her. In the light of the flame I saw the gleam of her eyes, the high cheekbones and the dark, alluring valley between her breasts.

"Move up," she said, as I was lighting my own cigarette. "There's room for two."

There was but only just. I shuffled along the refrigerator. She sat down, her thigh nudging against mine. I felt her warmth through my jeans.

"Christ, it's cold."

"Have my jacket," I suggested.

When we had settled ourselves again we smoked in silence for a moment, listening to the noises from the house and the rather different noises from the mattress.

"Anyway," she said, "you should always look sad."

"Why?"

"Because you look beautiful when you're sad. Sort of soulful."

I couldn't think of anything to say. I wondered if she was stoned. Or if I myself was much, much more stoned than I had thought, and this was some sort of hallucination.

"I've seen you around, haven't I?" she went on. "It's funny we've never actually met. Until now, I mean. What's your name?"

"Tony," I said.

"I'm Mary," she said. Then she kissed me.

❧

You're such a complete shit. You won't get away with it.

The words gave me a sweet, sharp stab of pleasure. The writing was definitely Mary's. The "you" must refer to Adam. They had been together now for nearly twenty years. They had married a couple of years after university.

Over the years I had looked up Adam in *Who's Who* and Debrett's *People of Today* on several occasions, so I knew the dates. I knew the landmarks of his career, too—the deputy literary editorship at the *New Statesman*, the years at the BBC, the handful of books and the four documentary series, linked to his later books. The documentaries were usually on BBC2, but the last one had graduated to BBC1.

Adam was my age but he looked ten or even fifteen years younger. He was one of those well-known authors who seem far too busy to have much time to write. I'd glanced through his articles in the *Sunday Times* and the *Observer*, and I'd heard him endlessly on radio and seen him on television. Two years earlier, he had chaired the judges of the Man Booker Prize. He was always judging something or another or commenting on something. Even Adam's friendships had a professional or literary flavor—he played tennis with a best-selling novelist, for example, and shared a holiday house in Umbria with the CEO of a major publisher.

I got up to put the books on the trolley for shelving. I was about to return to my seat when I saw Adam himself coming into the reading room by the north door, the one leading to the new staircase that acts as a spine connecting the disparate parts and levels of the library, old and new.

Panic gripped me. He glanced about the room. It all happened so quickly I had no chance to turn away. He was carrying three or four books. For a moment his eyes met mine. There was no sign of recognition in his face, which both relieved and irritated me. He saw an empty seat near the window end of the room and made his way towards it.

The spell that held me broke. I slipped through the glazed doors and onto the landing of the main staircase of the old building. I hurried downstairs, past the portraits of distinguished dead members, a parade of silent witnesses.

Once on the stairs, however, I could think more clearly. I saw how absurd I was being. Why was I acting as if I had done something wrong, as if Adam were for some reason hunting me down? On the other hand, what on earth was going on between him and Mary? And was he really planning something on Francis Youlgreave? I told myself that I had every reason to be curious.

Besides, Adam was unlikely to leave the reading room for a while.

I continued more slowly down the stairs and into the issue hall. I turned into the passage where the lockers are. These are on the left. On the right is a line of tall cupboards, always open, with hanging spaces for coats and shelves where you can leave your bags.

The Burberry was in the fourth cupboard down, hanging between a tweed overcoat and a torn leather jacket. Adam's bag was on the shelf beneath.

This was the moment when I crossed the line. It didn't seem like that at the time. It seemed quite a natural thing to do in terms of my Youlgreave book. One has to research the possible competition.

I looked over my shoulder. No one was paying me any attention. The bag was one of those canvas-and-leather affairs that look as if they ought to have a bloodstained pheasant or a dead trout inside. I lifted the flap and checked the main compartment and the side pockets. I found nothing but the *Guardian*, the *Spectator* and a couple of crumpled paper handkerchiefs.

Straightening up, I patted the coat. In one pocket was a packet of Polos and a shopping list on the back of an envelope. The list was in Adam's scrawled handwriting: *burgundy, flowers, milk, salad veg*. The other was empty.

I nearly missed the coat's third pocket, which was inside and fastened with a button. It contained something small and rectangular that didn't yield to the touch. I slipped my hand inside and felt the outline of a phone.

It was an iPhone. I had one myself as it happened, though mine was an older model. The ringer switch was in the off position. I pressed the control button. The screen lit up.

The phone was locked. But someone had sent a text, and this was briefly displayed on the screen.

I miss you more and more every moment we're apart. J xxxx

There was no name attached to the text, only a phone number.

So that explains the Post-it note, I thought. The complete shit is having an affair.

&

Nothing new there.

So I come back to Mary. She told me later why she kissed me in the garden at the party: as a demonstration of disdain to her newly exboyfriend, who was watching us through the kitchen window. But it developed into something else.

While the party thudded away in the house, we stayed in the garden and talked and drank and smoked another joint. I can't remember what we talked about. But I do remember that for once in my life I seemed to have leapfrogged the paralyzing shyness that usually characterized my attempts to talk to attractive girls and landed without any apparent effort into something approaching friendship.

Later I walked her home, and she kissed me again when we said goodnight. The next day we met between lectures for coffee, dispelling my lingering fear that she'd have forgotten me completely overnight. By the end of the day we had tumbled into bed together.

I felt as if I'd been turned into someone new and infinitely preferable, like the frog kissed by a princess. Mary was so beautiful, so vital. She always knew what she wanted and she was very direct about getting it. I envied her that. The mystery was why she wanted me. It was still a mystery.

We lasted nearly a term as a semi-detached couple before Adam decided he would have her for himself. He and I no longer shared a room, as we had in our first year. But we still saw a fair amount of each other. I was useful to him—I was the organized one, you see, who knew when the supervisions and lectures were, which library books we needed, how to find the material that could lift your grade from a B to an A.

In a sense, it was Francis Youlgreave who brought Mary and Adam together. I knew something about Youlgreave, even then, because my mother had grown up in Rosington. Youlgreave was a Canon of Rosington Cathedral in the early twentieth century. She had one of his collections of poems, *The Judgement of Strangers*, which had once belonged to my grandparents. I was using this as the basis for my long essay, an extended piece of work we had to do in our final year which counted as a complete module of our degree. I'd made the discovery that there were several advantages to studying obscure literary figures—fewer secondary sources, for a start, and a better than average chance of impressing the examiners with one's initiative.

Mary was waiting for me in my room when Adam turned up one evening. He said he'd wait for me and, while he waited, he investigated the papers on my desk while chatting away to Mary. He found some of the Youlgreave material and Mary told him more.

By the time I returned with an Indian takeaway for two, they were smoking a joint and chatting away like friends on the brink of being something closer. She responded to his charm like a plant to water. He had the priceless knack of seeming to be interested in a person. The takeaway stretched among the three of us. Adam and Mary got very stoned and I sulked.

Next week Mary and I officially broke up. It was one lunchtime in the pub. She did her best to do it tactfully. But all the time she was being kind to me, she was glowing with excitement about Adam like a halloween pumpkin with a candle inside.

As she was going, she said, "Don't take it personally, Tony, will you? I'm always looking for something, you see, and I never quite find it. Maybe one day I'll come round full circle. Or maybe I'll find it. Whatever it is I'm looking for."

❧

I didn't know which disturbed me more: the knowledge that Adam was having an affair and that his marriage to Mary was breaking down; or the growing suspicion that he would take Youlgreave away from me, probably without even knowing what he was doing.

I knew perfectly well that Francis Youlgreave wasn't "mine" to lose in the first place. He was just a long-dead clergyman with eccentric habits, who had written a few minor poems that sometimes turned up in anthologies. Even I accepted that most of his poetry wasn't up to much. If half the stories were true, he had taken too much brandy and opium to do anything very well.

For all that, Youlgreave was an interesting person, always striving for something out of his reach. He was also interesting in the wider context of literary history. He was not quite a Victorian, not quite a modern, but something poised uneasily between the two.

We were about to reach the hundred-and-fiftieth anniversary of his birth. Publishers love anniversaries, and I had pitched the idea of a short biography of Youlgreave with a selection of his better poems to an editor I'd worked for in the past. To my surprise she liked the proposal and eventually commissioned it. The advance was modest. Still, it was a proper book and for a decent publisher.

I knew there wasn't a great deal of material available on Youlgreave. It was rather odd, actually, how little had survived—I suspected that his family had purged his papers after his death. But when talking to the editor I made a big point of his friendships with people like Oscar Wilde and Aleister Crowley, and also his influence on the modernists who came after him. There were people who claimed to see elements of Youlgreave's work in T.S. Eliot's *The Wasteland*, which wasn't as fanciful as it might seem.

Besides, what we did know about him was intriguing. The second son of a baronet, he had published a volume called *Last Poems* while he was still at Oxford. He was ordained and spent the 1890s as a vicar in London. He was made a Canon of Rosington—some people said that his family pulled strings in order to get him away from the temptations of the capital—but had retired early owing to illhealth.

Youlgreave was only in his early forties when he died. I had seen reports of the inquest. He was living at his brother's house. He fell out of a high window. They said it was an accident. But no one really knew what had happened, and they probably never would.

I had one advantage that I made the most of with my editor. Youlgreave had been a member of the London Library for most of his adult life. After his death, his family presented a number of his books to the library.

One of them was his own copy of *The Voice of Angels*. Youlgreave's last collection of poems, published in 1903, was called *The Tongues of Angels*. *Voice* was a privatelyprinted variant of *Tongues* that included an extra poem, "The Children of Heracles." The poem, which has strong elements of cannibalism, was unpleasant even by today's standards; presumably Youlgreave's publisher refused to include it in *Tongues*.

I suspected that the cataloguer hadn't realized how rare this book was. It was not in the British Library or the Bodleian or Cambridge University Library. As far as I knew, the London Library's edition was the only known copy in a collection that was accessible to the public, though there may have been a few in private hands.

The Voice of Angels was valuable not just for its rarity and for the extra poem. This particular copy had penciled marginalia by Youlgreave himself. Some of them are illegible, but not all.

Best of all, on the endpaper at the back, Youlgreave had jotted down a number of disjointed lines and clusters of words-fragments, I believed, of a poem he hadn't lived to write. One phrase leapt out at me when I first saw it: *the long sonata of the dead.*

I recognized the phrase. This was going to be one of the main revelations of my biography. Samuel Beckett had used the identical words in his novel *Molloy*, which he published nearly half a century after Youlgreave's death. It was too unusual to be dismissed as coincidence. To clinch the matter, "The Children of Heracles" included the line: *What words and dead things know.* Beckett had used an almost identical phrase in *Molloy*.

There was only one conclusion: that Beckett had somehow seen *The Voice of Angels*, this very copy that I had found in the London Library, and he had admired it enough to plagiarise at least two of Youlgreave's lines.

Now I had to face the possibility that Adam was going to take that from me too.

∾

All this passed through my mind as I stood there with Adam's phone in my hand.

I still had one thing in my favor: *The Voice of Angels* was safe on my shelf at home. It wasn't listed in the library's computer catalogue yet, only in the older catalogue, which consists of huge bound volumes with strips of printed titles pasted inside, the margins of the pages crowded with hand-written annotations by long-dead librarians. But, if Adam were serious about Youlgreave, sooner or later he would track it down and put in a request for it. Then I would have to return it to the library.

It was possible he wouldn't notice the discrepancy in the title. It was possible, even, that he wasn't doing anything significant on Youlgreave. That was what I really needed to find out.

I thought of Mary right away. She would know—she was credited as a researcher on the documentaries and in the books. And it would give me an excuse to see her, which was what I wanted to do anyway.

But did I want to see her? The very thought terrified me. Since Adam had walked into the London Library, all the comfortable certainties that shored up my life had crumbled away. Would she even talk to me after all these years? What would happen if I showed her the message on Adam's phone and proved to her that her husband was having an affair?

I had a practical problem to solve first of all. I didn't even know where to find her. Adam hadn't included his private address in his *Who's Who* entry. The library would know it but members' addresses were confidential.

That was when I remembered the crumpled envelope I had found in the Burberry. I took it out again. It was a circular addressed to Adam. There was the address: *23 Rowan Avenue.*

I glanced over my shoulder. No one was looking at me. I slipped the phone into my trouser pocket.

The library kept a *London A-Z*. Rowan Avenue was out towards Richmond, not far from Kew Gardens.

I gave myself no time to think. I took my coat and left the library. I cut across Pall Mall and the Mall and went into St. James's Park. Hardly anyone was there because of the rain. My hair and my shoulders were soaked by the time I reached Queen Anne's Gate. A moment later I was at the Underground station. I was trembling with cold and, I think, excitement.

Proust was right about his madeleine. Once something unlocks the memories they come pouring out. I was drowning in mine just because I'd seen a man standing in the rain outside the London Library.

Adam had always been a bastard, I thought. People don't change, not really. As time passes, they just become more like themselves.

I didn't have to wait more than a couple of minutes for a Richmond train on the District Line. Kew Gardens was the last stop before Richmond. It was now late afternoon. The carriage was at the end of the train and nearly empty.

I sat down and stared at my reflection in the black glass opposite me. I saw an untidy middle-aged stranger where I half-expected to find a slim, sharp-featured student with shaggy hair.

It was still raining when I left the train and took my bearings. Kew was a nice place, just right for nice people like Adam and Mary. You couldn't imagine poor people living there. But it wasn't not for the very rich, either, for people who flaunted their money and slapped it in your face. In a perfect world I might have lived there myself.

Rowan Avenue was a gently curving road about five minutes' walk from the station. The houses were terraced or semi-detached-solid Edwardian homes, well-kept and probably unobtrusively spacious. The cars outside were Mercedes, BMWs and the better sort of people carriers designed for shipping around large quantities of nice children.

Number 23 had a little glazed porch with a tiled floor, a green front door and a small stained glass window into the hall beyond. I rang the bell. Adam and Mary had no children—I knew that from *Who's Who*—but there might be a cleaner or a secretary or something. Mary might be out. The longer I waited, the more I hoped she would be.

There were footsteps in the hall. The stained glass rippled as the colors and shapes behind it shifted. My stomach fluttered. I knew it was her.

With a rattle, the door opened a few inches and then stopped. It was on the chain. I felt unexpectedly pleased—London is a dangerous city, growing worse every year; and I was relieved that Mary was taking precautions.

"Hello," she said, giving the word a slight interrogative lift on the second syllable.

"You probably won't remember me." I cleared my throat. "It's been a long time."

I could see only part of her face. She seemed a little smaller than in memory. The hair was carefully styled and much shorter.

She was frowning. "I'm afraid I don't . . ."

"Mary, it's me—Tony." Despair nibbled at me. "Don't you remember?"

"Tony?" Her voice was the same. Slightly breathless and husky. I used to find it unbearably sexy. I still did. "Tony?" she repeated, frowning. "From university?"

"Yes," I said, more loudly than I intended. I touched the beard. "Imagine me without this."

"Tony," she said. I watched recognition creep over her face. "Tony, yes, of course. Come in."

She unhooked the chain and opened the door. She was still Mary, my Mary. She was wearing jeans and a green shirt with a jersey over it. Cashmere, I thought. She was looking at me and I was acutely aware of my own appearance, something I rarely thought about.

For the first time I saw her face properly. "What have you done?" I said. "Are you OK?"

Her upper lip was swollen on the right hand side as if a bee had stung it. Or as if someone had hit her.

"I'm fine. I walked into the bathroom door last night. So stupid."

The hall was large and long, with rugs on stripped boards. Mary took me through to a sitting room dominated by an enormous TV screen. The furniture was modern. There were hardback books lying about—new ones, recently reviewed—and a vase of flowers on the coffee table.

"This is . . . nice," I said, for want of something to say.

She switched on a couple of lamps. "Do you want some tea?"

"No, thanks."

I thought she looked disappointed.

"Do sit down. It's good to see you after all this time."

That's what she said: what she meant was: *Why are you here?*

I sat down on a sofa. There was another sofa at right-angles to mine. She chose that one.

"It's been ages, hasn't it?" she said. "How've you been?"

"Fine. I—"

"What have you been doing?"

"This and that," I said. "I review—I do odds and ends for publishers—reading for them, sub-editing, blurb-writing. I've ghosted some memoirs. That sort of thing. I'm working on the biography of a poet at present."

"Which one?" she asked.

"Francis Youlgreave."

"Really." Her eyes widened as the memory caught up with her. "You always had a thing about him. Funnily enough, Adam's thinking of doing something about him too."

"There's an anniversary coming up," I said.

She nodded. "It's part of a series for him. Another documentary."

"What's it about?"

"Literary culture in the 1890s—*The Naughty Nineties*, I think that's the working title. There's going to be a book, too."

"Of course," I said.

"It's going to be revisionist," she went on. "In the sense that they're arguing the really influential figures aren't the obvious ones like Wilde and Henry James."

"Hence Youlgreave?"

"I suppose. I don't really know. Tony—it's awfully nice to see you, of course, but is there a particular reason for you coming? Like this, I mean, out of the blue."

"This is a bit difficult," I said. I wanted so much to be honest with her. "I saw Adam today—at the London Library. I didn't even know he was a member."

"So he knows you're here?"

"No—I don't think he saw me. But I . . . I happened to see his phone—he'd left it lying around. There was a text."

She sat up sharply, her cheeks coloring with a stain of blood. "A text—what do you mean? You're telling me you've been reading Adam's texts?"

"I didn't mean to, not exactly." I knew I was coloring too. "But, Mary, I think you should see it. That's why I'm here."

I took the iPhone from my pocket and handed it to her. She stared at the screen. I couldn't see her face.

I miss you more and more every moment we're apart. J xxxx.

"He's having an affair, isn't he?" I said. "Did you know?"

She didn't look up. She shrugged.

"Did he hit you, too?"

"If you must know, yes." Mary put down the phone on the arm of the sofa. She stared at me. "We're getting a divorce. We—we can't agree about who gets what. The old story."

"I'm so sorry," I said.

Her expression softened. "I really think you are. Bless you."

"I know what it's like. I was married for a while but it didn't take. Who's 'J'? Do you know?"

"She's called Janine—she used to be his PA. About ten years younger than me." She swallowed. "Nice woman."

"Not that nice."

She stood up suddenly. "I'm going to make some tea. Will you have some now?"

"Is it OK me being here? What if Adam comes back?"

"He's meeting his agent for dinner at Wilton's at nine o'clock. That's what his diary says, anyway. He was going to work in the library until then."

I followed her into the kitchen. She put on the kettle and then stood, arms folded, looking out of the window at the back garden.

"This is going to be so bloody awful," she said. "He's got most of our assets tied up in a couple of companies. One of them is offshore, which makes it even more complicated. And he controls the companies; that's the real problem. I was so naive, you wouldn't believe. I just signed where he told me when he set them up."

I thought of the Post-it note I had found in Adam's library book. *You're such a complete shit. You won't get away with it.* But it looked as if he would get away with it.

"You've talked to a solicitor?"

"Yes. For what it's worth. If I fight Adam for my share, it'll cost a fortune. But I haven't got a fortune. I've hardly got anything. I shouldn't be telling you this—it's not your problem."

"It doesn't matter."

"Anyway, the odds are I'll lose if we go to court."

"What will you do?" I said.

"God knows."

She turned to face me. I couldn't see her face clearly; the window was behind her and the winter afternoon was fading into dusk. Neither of us spoke for a while. The kettle began to hiss quietly at first and then with steadily rising urgency. At last there was a click as it turned itself off.

"I normally have green tea in the afternoon," she said, as if this was a normal conversation on a normal day. "But there's ordinary tea if you prefer, or herbal—"

"Green tea's fine," I said.

She picked up a packet of tea and a spoon. Then she stopped moving and the conversation wasn't normal any more. "I made a mistake, Tony, didn't I?" she said. "I wish . . ."

"What do you wish?" My voice was little more a whisper.

"I wish I could put time back," Mary said. "To when it was just you and me in the garden. Do you remember? At that stupid party? It all seemed so simple then."

❧

On Tuesdays, the London Library stays open until nine p.m. When I got back it was nearly six o'clock. The Burberry was still hanging in the cupboard. I hung my own coat beside it.

I had asked Mary if I should take the phone back and leave it where I had found it. She told me not to bother. Adam often left his phone at home or mislaid it—he wouldn't be surprised if he couldn't find it in his coat. He was careless about his possessions, she said, just as he was careless about people.

The library was much emptier than it had been. I liked the place especially on a winter evening, when the only people there seemed to be a few librarians and a handful of members like me. In the stacks—and most of the place consists of the stacks—each run of shelves has its own set of lights. Members are encouraged to turn off any lights that are not in use. So, on a February evening like this, most of the library consists of pools of light marooned in the surrounding gloom. Sounds are muted. The spines of the books stretch away into an infinity of learning.

Adam wasn't in any of the reading rooms. I guessed that he was either searching for books or working at one of the little tables scattered around the stacks. It didn't matter because I didn't want to find him. I didn't want to see him ever again or hear his voice. I didn't want to think of him.

I sat down and tried to work, which was how I had always intended to spend this evening. But my mind was full of Mary and I couldn't concentrate. I had a pencil in my hand and I wrote the words *the long sonata of the dead* on the inside cover of my notebook. I looked at them for a long time and wondered whether even Francis Youlgreave or Samuel Beckett had known what they meant.

A little after eight-fifteen, I decided I'd had enough. I packed up my work and went downstairs. As I reached the issue hall I nearly bumped into Adam. He had come out of the catalogue room.

We both pulled back at the last moment before a collision became inevitable. We muttered reciprocal apologies. But his words were no more than a polite reflex. He looked through me. I didn't exist for him.

He went over to the enquiries desk. I turned aside and pretended to study a plan of the library on the wall.

"I found a book in the old printed catalogue but I can't see it on the shelves," he said to the librarian. "Can you check if it's out?"

"What is it?" the librarian asked.

"It's by Francis Youlgreave." Adam spelt the surname. "It's called *The Voice of Angels*."

A moment later the librarian said, "I'm afraid it's out. Due back on March the sixth. Would you like to reserve it?"

"Yes, please."

Afterwards Adam went upstairs, glancing at his watch. After a moment I followed him. I was wearing trainers and I made very little noise. He turned into one of the older stacks and walked steadily towards the back. I couldn't see him because the lines of bookcases were in the way. But I heard his footsteps ringing on the iron gratings of the floor. You can look down at the floor below and up at the floor above. I suppose they had to make the floors of iron in order to bear the weight of all the books.

There was a further stack beyond this one, part of the History section. Very few lights were on. I waited near the archway leading into the rear stack. I stood in the shelter of a bookcase containing books on gardening.

The levels on the older stacks are connected internally with steep, narrow iron staircases in a sort of bibliographic snakes and ladders.

Some of the staircases still have their original signs—an elegant silhouette of a hand with a pointing finger accompanied by a legend saying something like "Up History" or "Down Society." One of these was nearby, which gave me the reassuring sense that I could slip away if someone else came up behind me.

I listened to Adam's footsteps until they stopped. Then, for several minutes, I heard nothing else except the hum of the strip lighting and a faint crackling sound that might have been rain on a distant skylight or window.

He came out at last. I watched him approaching through the slit between the top of a row of books and the bottom of the shelf above. He had both arms full with a pile of four or five heavy books, a folder of notes and a slim silver laptop. He was wearing a pair of gold-rimmed reading glasses that gave him a scholarly air he didn't deserve.

He passed very close to me. He began to descend the iron stairs. He was in a hurry.

At first, all I did was touch him, rest my hand on his shoulder.

When I touched him, Adam began to turn towards me. But too quickly.

That was the thing: it happened so very quickly. His own momentum still carried him forward. He was encumbered with the weight in his arms. His awareness of the fragility of the books and the laptop perhaps made it harder for him to protect himself.

Then I pushed his shoulder. Not hard, not really—barely more than a gentle nudge, the sort of gesture you might make when you meet an old friend. If you could translate the gesture into words, it would say something like, "Hey—good to see you after all this time."

Except it wasn't good to see him. It wasn't good at all, not for me and not for him.

Adam overbalanced and fell with a terrible scraping crash. The laptop and other objects skipped and clattered down the stairs, making a sound that might have been a form of hard, atonal music.

The long sonata of the dead.

I ran down the stairs. Adam was lying on his front with his books and notes around him. He wasn't moving. He made no sound at all. His head was bleeding. I wondered if the blood would drip through the iron grating and fall to the level beneath. I hoped it wouldn't damage any books.

I listened for sounds elsewhere, for running footsteps, the sound of voices. I heard nothing but the hum and the crackling and, loudest of all, my own rapid breathing.

The laptop had skidded across the floor and come to rest against the base of a bookcase. It looked undamaged. Adam's glasses were beside his head. They were unbroken, too. I remember thinking how easy it is to miss your footing if you forget to take off your reading glasses. Especially if you are going down a flight of stairs.

There was a phone on the floor, just inches from his hand as if he had been carrying that as well.

I picked it up. It was another iPhone. The screen was shattered. Without thinking, I pressed the control button. Nothing happened. The phone was dead. But why was there a phone in the first place?

A dead phone, I thought: *What dead things know.*

∽

I left the library, walked through the rain across the park for the third time and caught a train to Kew.

At this hour, and on a night like this, the train wasn't crowded. Someone had left a copy of the evening's *Metro* on the seat next to mine and I pretended to read it as we trundled wearily westward.

There were four other passengers in the carriage. All of us avoided eye contact. One of them was a thin-faced woman sitting diagonally across the carriage from me. She was younger than I, in her early thirties perhaps, and looked like a character in a Russian novel. She ought to have been travelling by troika rather than London Underground, despite the fact that she was reading something on her Kindle.

When the train stopped at Kew, I hung back, letting the other passengers leave the station first. Three of them took the eastern exit in the direction of Mortlake Road. I left a decent interval and then followed.

It was raining harder than ever. One of the people ahead had turned off. The second one went into a house on the right. That left the thin-face woman, striding down the rainslicked pavement in her long black coat and long black boots, sheltered by an umbrella. She turned into Rowan Avenue.

I didn't want to give her the impression I was stalking her so I waited before following. I took shelter under a tree but there wasn't much point. I was already soaking wet.

A moment later, I turned the corner. Number 23 was on the other side of the road. The lights were on in the hall and behind the blinds of a ground-floor room at the front with a bay window. I had no idea what I would say to Mary. Or even if I would have the courage to ring the bell. But it didn't matter. It would be good to know she was there, in that house. It would be good to know she was alive.

The woman ahead crossed the road. I hesitated. She was approaching the gate of Mary's house. She opened it.

I darted after her and took cover beside a black SUV so absurdly large it would have concealed an elephant. I edged sideways. I could now see her standing in the little porch by the front door. She had closed her umbrella and left it on the tiled floor.

A light was on above her head and she might have been standing on a miniature stage. She glanced over her shoulder. I saw her face, all bones and shadows and glaring white skin.

The door opened. There was Mary. She had changed into a dark blue dress since this afternoon.

"Janine," she said. "Janine."

The women embraced. But it wasn't as friends embrace.

"I'm so sorry," Mary said. "He took my phone, would you believe?"

"So does he know?" Janine said.

"He must have seen the texts. Anyway, come here."

Mary drew the younger woman inside. She was smiling as if she would never stop. The door closed.

I closed my eyes. The rain fell. The raindrops tapped on the dark, shiny roof of the SUV. A car hooted on the Mortlake Road. Traffic grumbled. Tires hissed over wet tarmac. A door opened down the street and, for a moment before it closed again, I heard a piano playing the saddest tune in the world.

My eyes were closed. I listened to the long sonata of the dead.

XIII

Rides a Stranger

David Bell

M Y FATHER DIED slowly.

In his early sixties, after a lifetime of vigorous health and strength, he contracted a rare neurological disorder that killed him inch by inch. First, he couldn't walk. Soon after that, he couldn't dress himself or feed himself. Eventually he was confined to bed, wearing adult diapers. A nurse came and changed him several times a day, rolling him from one side to the other with the detached and practiced care of the medical professional.

My dad's eyes remained sharp and intelligent. He was in there. We all knew that. But his body deserted him, like an electrical device with a failing battery. He slowly wound down, losing motion and control. A slow unraveling.

The last thing to go was his ability to speak.

For several months, his voice became a raspy whisper. Every word cost him effort. To say something as simple as "yes" could take five minutes and reserves of precious energy he just didn't have.

I didn't visit as much as I should have. I lived four hours away in a small college town where I taught American Literature to the indifferent and unwashed masses of middle-class kids at a public university deep in the heart of Kentucky. It was a good job and mostly fulfilling, and I told myself it left little time for regular trips to my hometown to see my father wasting away in a hospital bed. The truth is—I didn't know what I could do for him. Even when my father was at his healthiest and in full voice, we didn't have much to say to each other. We didn't see eye-to-eye politically. His facts came from Fox News, mine from MSNBC. He spent his life working in business, selling auto parts to distributors around the Rust Belt. I spent my life in the ivory tower.

We couldn't even agree when it came to books. I wrote my dissertation on Fitzgerald, specifically *The Great Gatsby*. Dad's reading habits remained more pedestrian. He read anything that landed on the bestseller list. When I was a child, he read Alistair Maclean and Jack Higgins. Later he switched to Tom Clancy and James Patterson. Big dick books, my ex-wife—also an English professor—used to call them. Big dick books.

And Dad's favorite big dick genre of them all—the western. Oaters. Horse operas. Shoot 'em ups. He read them all. Max Brand. Will Henry. Luke Short. And his favorite of them all—Louis L'Amour. Dad read every Louis L'Amour book ever written. He read and reread them. He bought multiple copies of them. He'd wear one out from re-reading, and then he'd go out and buy the same book and wear that one out as well. It seemed like strange behavior for a man who grew up in Vermont, lived most of his life in Ohio, and never once ventured west of the Mississippi River.

So, we didn't talk about books either.

But I did hear the last words he ever spoke.

This happened about three weeks before his death. I made one of my infrequent visits. The university I teach at had a fall break, and my mother had been calling me, obliquely warning me that the old man didn't have much time left. She'd say things like, "Well, your father isn't as strong as he used to be." Or she'd say, "Well, we all just have to do what we have to do." I understood. Mom was telling me to come and say good-bye.

So I made the trip. I went into their bedroom, the bedroom in which I was conceived, and which was now filled by a large hospital bed. My dad looked small beneath the tucked in sheets, almost like a sick child. He had lost close to sixty pounds, and when I saw him that day, he looked like a sketch or an outline of himself, something without substance or heft.

I took the seat next to the bed and held his hand. I didn't like holding his hand. My dad had acquired the habit of reaching down beneath the bedclothes, trying to fiddle with or even remove the diapers he wore. I never knew if this was out of discomfort or because he rebelled against the idea of wearing a diaper at all. But his hands were often busy beneath the sheets, and while I never saw anything gross on his hands, I always wondered. Was I touching feces? Or worse? And I never failed to wash my hands when I left his bedside.

The old man looked me in the eye. His eyes were blue like mine. A little watery but bright blue. And intelligent. There could be no doubt someone—Joseph Henry Kurtwood, my father—was staring back at me. He was in there. I knew that.

"How are you, Dad?" I asked.

He didn't say anything. I reminded him that he didn't have to say anything, that I understood he might be too tired to speak and to save his strength. I didn't know—and I'm sure he didn't either—what he would be saving it for, but it was something to say, something to fill the quiet space in the house. The kind of quiet that descends on a house with a dying person inside it.

My mom hovered nearby.

"Don, honey, why don't you tell Dad about your tenure vote?" Mom said, always cheery. "Joe, Don got tenure at the university."

"I thought you wanted me to tell him?" I said.

"Don't be sassy," Mom said. "Tell him about it."

"Sure," I said. "Why not?"

I turned back to Dad. Why not, indeed? The truth is—he didn't really care. And I didn't really care. It was no great accomplishment to earn tenure at a mid-sized public institution in the south. Publish a few articles, go to a few conferences, show up for meetings on time, attend the department holiday party and get a little tipsy but not too drunk, and I was a shoo-in. The department approved me unanimously. They didn't care that Rebecca and I had divorced. Hell, Rebecca voted for me.

But it was something to talk about, the adult equivalent of bringing home a high score on a Civics exam or a report card with more Bs than Cs.

"I got tenure, Dad," I said. "I'm an associate professor of English."

He squeezed my hand.

I took this to be his way of congratulating me, so I said, "Thanks."

He squeezed again. Harder. More insistent.

"Okay," I said. "The vote was unanimous—"

This time he didn't squeeze so much as he tugged my hand, jerking me a little forward in my chair. It surprised me. I didn't know the old man had that much strength left.

"What is it, Dad?" I asked.

He didn't squeeze or tug. His face looked strained, and some of the color had drained from it. His shoulders sank down even farther into the mattress, another little bit of him disappearing.

His lips moved. They moved but no sound came out.

"What is it, Dad?"

"Is he thirsty?" Mom asked. "He always thirsty. It's those pills."

"Are you thirsty, Dad?" I asked. But I knew that wasn't it. His head moved again, almost imperceptibly. Just about a quarter inch of movement. "Do you want . . .?"

I stood up. His lips moved some more.

"Is he saying something?" Mom asked.

"I don't know. You keep talking."

"Don't sass."

"Shh."

I leaned forward, my ear almost pressing against the old man's lips. I felt his breath against my skin, hot and clammy. Dying. The last few weeks of precious breath he had left.

I stood that way for a long time, thinking the moment had passed and no words would come.

But then he said it. Two words.

I think.

He said, "Good will."

❧

The end came three weeks later.

Because it took Dad so long to die, there was a lot of time to plan. When I spoke to Mom on the phone that day, she told me that she didn't need any help.

"It's all arranged," she said. "You can come for the funeral."

Something rustled in the background. Then a ripping noise.

"Are you okay?" I asked.

"Me?" she said.

She sounded surprised that I would even ask the question. I figured a whole host of people had been asking her that question over the past few years. First, when Dad became sick, and then even more intensely in the wake of his death.

"Yes, Mom. Are you okay? How are you holding up?"

"I'm fine," she said. I heard the ripping noise again. "I'm going through your father's things. I started . . . well, you know, *before*. I took away a number of boxes. But somehow it didn't seem right. You know . . . when he was still . . . here. But now, there's a lot to go through."

My mother might sound business-like. Even cold. I don't want to give the wrong impression of her. She could be business-like, even in the most stressful situations, but she was also very loving. She read to me constantly when I was a child. She encouraged my scholarly career. She was—*is*—an excellent mother. But her and my dad? How do I put this? They really weren't in love. They were companions. Roommates. Partners in the strictest sense. They raised a son together. They rowed in the same direction. But it wasn't a love affair. I'm sure Mom saw Dad's death as a passage from one phase of her life to another. When she called to tell me Dad had died, she simply said, "It's over."

"Are you okay being there alone now?" I asked. "In the house?"

"Am I okay being alone?" she said. "Don, I've been alone in this house ever since you moved out. Your father and I were both alone here. It's no big deal." The ripping noise again. "And your father has so many books. So many."

I suddenly figured out what the ripping noise was. Tape. She was taping up boxes of Dad's books. Probably sending them to the library book sale. Mom volunteered there twice a year. It was her pet cause.

I wanted to ask her so much more. I wanted to ask her why she married Dad. I wanted to ask why they stayed married. I wanted to ask about Dad's last words. "Good will."

And I wanted to ask the biggest question of all: Did you know Dad? Did you—or anybody else—really know him?

But Mom moved things along.

"So," she said, the ripping sound of packing tape coming again. "Tuesday then? Don't be late."

In the funeral home, during the viewing, I stayed at the back of the room. The casket remained open, and even though I'd seen my dad just three weeks before his death, wasting away to a stick man, I couldn't bear the thought of being close to his dead body. Even though the funeral home had done a good job on him—according to my mother—and I imagined that he probably looked peaceful or any of the other clichés people threw around on such occasions, I knew Dad wouldn't like it. The whole event felt . . . embarrassing somehow. The old man up in a box, wearing a coat and tie he never wore when he was alive. He seemed exposed. Vulnerable.

And very, very dead.

The family members—cousins, aunts, uncles—as well as the women and men my mother knew, found me despite my lingering at the back. They shook my hand, pecked me on the cheek, hugged me, and fussed over me. I was an only child and I had lost my father. Mom remained stationed at the front, accepting condolences and occasionally smiling.

It's over.

When the man first approached me, I assumed he was another friend of Mom's, someone she knew through church or volunteering at the local school. Except he didn't look like anyone my mother would hang out with. He was short, just over five feet tall. And round, almost as wide as he was tall. His brown suit coat was frayed around the edges of the collar and the sleeves, and his once-white dress shirt looked dingy gray.

"You must be the son," he said. He shook my hand. "I'm sorry about your father."

His voice carried the trace of an accent, something from the East Coast.

"I am," I said. I did the same thing with him that I did with everyone else that night—I pretended I knew who he was. "It's good to see you."

The man smiled. "You're trying to place me," he said.

"No, I . . . well, to be honest, there are a lot of relatives here—"

"I'm no relation," he said. "And I'm really not a friend."

"Not a friend?"

He held his smile. "Not a friend of yours, yet," he said. "But hopefully soon." The man looked over both shoulders, as though he thought someone was eavesdropping. The viewing room was emptying out. Only a few stragglers remained talking to Mom up at the front. And, of course, Dad. He was still in his place.

The man reached inside his jacket and brought out a slightly wrinkled business card. He held it out to me, but I didn't take it.

"Are you a lawyer or something?" I asked. "Mom has everything taken care of—"

"Read the card." He moved his hand forward a few inches, almost forcing the card into my hands.

I took it and read. Lou Caledonia, Rare Book Dealer.

I recognized the address under the name. I knew the place. A small, cramped storefront downtown. I'd been there once, many years earlier, just looking around. But I remembered the place. It seemed to specialize in genre fiction—pulp novels, mysteries, men's adventure magazines. Not the sort of reading that appealed to me, so I never went back.

"Did you know my dad?" I asked.

"I wanted to," Lou Caledonia said. "But he didn't want to know me."

Then it slowly dawned on me. "Are you here trolling for business? Because if you are, that's pretty tasteless. This is my father's viewing. You could call next week about his books."

Lou Caledonia looked hurt. The corners of his mouth sagged and he blinked his eyes a few times.

"Please," he said. "No. I'm not that kind of man. And if I've given any offense to you or your family, I deeply apologize and will go."

He held out his hands in front of him and started backing away.

But there was something about him. Maybe it was how quickly he apologized. Maybe it was his droopy dog looks. Or maybe, just maybe, it was because I wanted to understand this man's interest in my father.

"Okay," I said. "No offense taken."

He stopped backpedaling. His smile returned.

"You're a gentleman," he said. "I can tell." He moved closer again. "You're right that I shouldn't conduct business at such a solemn occasion, but you have to understand how important this is to me. And I tried speaking to your father before . . . well, before, and I was always rebuffed."

"Why?"

"Do me a favor," he said. He pointed to the card. "Tend to your family. Tend to your mother. But when all of this awful business is done, if you can just spare a little time, come to my shop. Come by and we'll talk. Please?"

I looked at the card again. The shop was on my way out of town.

"Okay," I said. "The burial is tomorrow, and I'm leaving the day after that. I'll swing by during the day."

Lou was already shaking his head. As he shook, the loose skin around his jawline shook as well. His eyes were closed. He looked solemn as a monk.

"Tonight," he said. "Come by tonight."

"Tonight? I can't. I have my mother. And family coming over. It's already eight o'clock."

"I'll be in the shop all night," he said. He started walking away. "Just come by. Please."

"But what's this about?"

He shuffled out of the room, the worn and faded back of his corduroy pants was the last thing I saw.

"Did you see the man I was talking to?" I asked. "At the funeral home."

Mom and I ate in the kitchen. It was just after nine o'clock, and we were both hungry when we got back to my parents' house. Someone had dropped off a pan of lasagna, and Mom heated it in the oven. We both ate a lot, and only after I had the first serving down and started on the second did I ask my question.

"What man?" she asked. "There were a ton of people there. More than I would have expected, even."

"He came at the end," I said. "His name is Lou Caledonia."

"Lou Caledonia?" Mom said. She almost made the name sound like part of a song. She shook her head. "Never heard of him. And, believe me, I'd remember a name like that. How did he know your father?"

"I don't know that he did."

"What?"

"He owns a bookstore. Used books. It's downtown."

Mom stopped chewing and patted her lips with a cloth napkin. "That explains it. Books. Your father and his books. Do you know how many boxes I hauled out of here while your father was sick? I finally stopped because he saw me doing it and had a fit."

"How could he have a fit? He was bedridden."

"He knew what I was doing. He knocked his water glass off the table, then he said, 'Stop.' One word. I knew what he meant. The books. Leave them alone. And there are just as many still to go. That's one way the two of you were just alike. Obsessed with books."

"Don't compare us that way," I said.

"What way?" she asked. "Is it not true that you and your father both have an insane obsession with books? He filled this house with them, and I've seen your house down in Kentucky. You're on the way to equaling him."

"I'm an English professor," I said. "That's my life. Dad read a lot of schlocky fiction. I'm . . ."

I wanted to say I was a scholar, but was I? Just because I had the Ph.D. and wrote about books didn't mean I was a scholar. In fact, was I really contributing anything to the intellectual or cultural life of the world?

"You're what?" Mom asked.

"Nothing."

Mom pushed her plate aside. She reached out and placed her hand on my forearm. Her skin felt soft, but I could see the age spots on the back of her hand. She still wore her wedding ring.

"What's going on down there?" she asked. "In Kentucky?"

"Work goes on down there."

"Is there a special someone in your life?" she asked. "Since Rebecca?"

"No," I said.

"You know, I called there once, your apartment, on a Saturday morning. Some girl answered."

"Mom. Please."

"She sounded very young. She said you were in the shower or something."

"Mom. Enough."

"I worry. You're my only child. I don't want to think of you being alone. You're forty now. If you want to have children . . . I just worry about you living in that house full of books. Would any woman want to come into that? And how are you going to leave something behind if you're not married? Your father and I, we had you. You're our legacy."

"I have work, Mom. I have my work."

She nodded. "I know. The articles. The presentations."

"And teaching," I said. "The lives I've touched."

Mom smiled. I recognized the sly look on her face. She had something to zing me with, and she said, "I bet you were touching that girl's life, the one who answered your phone on a Saturday morning."

"Jesus. You're my mother."

She laughed. And I couldn't help but laugh a little too.

"I'm going out in a little bit," I said.

Mom turned and looked at the clock. "Are you meeting some old friends?"

"I'm going to that bookstore. To see Lou Caledonia."

"Why on earth for?" She stood up and started clearing dishes.

"He wants to see me," I said. "I think he knows something about Dad."

"Honey, the only thing to know about your dad is that he liked to sit in his chair and read more than he liked to work. And that's pretty much that. It's after nine, and you have to get up early tomorrow. We both do. Besides, maybe this guy is a crazy person? What if he's a serial killer or something?"

"A serial killer?" I said. "He looks more like a hobbit."

"A what?"

"Never mind." I brought my plate to the sink. "How much trouble could a used book dealer cause?"

It was nearly nine forty-five when I pulled up in front of Lou Caledonia's bookstore. The streets downtown were quiet and empty. No cars went past, and the streetlights all blinked monotonously yellow. The storefront looked dark. I checked his card. It gave no name for the store. Above the glass display windows the word BOOKS was spelled out in chipped gold letters. The sign looked like it came from another time.

I climbed out of the car and went to the door. I looked for a bell or an intercom, but there was nothing. I pressed my face against the glass. In the shadowy light I saw rickety wooden shelves filled with endless rows of paperback books. More books sat on the floors of the aisles, and even more were stacked at the end of aisles. Cardboard boxes on the floor overflowed with additional books. Even though I didn't think the titles interested me, I had to admit to feeling a thrill of excitement at the sight of all those books. The shop seemed crammed full of the essence of reading—the simple book. How long had it been since I'd simply taken one off the shelf and read it and enjoyed it? How long since I'd read a book without the red pen of the critic in my hand, the theorist's coldly detached eye formulating a jargony thesis as I read the words?

I didn't know what to do, so I knocked. And waited. The wind picked up a little. It was a cool fall night, the sky clear and inky black. I looked around and still didn't see anyone on the streets. No one came downtown anymore. I figured they were all home streaming movies or TV or texting. When I was a kid, we came downtown for movies, for plays, for restaurants. Most of those establishments were gone.

I knocked again. Then I tried the door. It opened.

I looked around again. I don't know what I expected. The police coming to arrest me for breaking into an unlocked and nearly forgotten bookstore on an empty street? I pushed open the door and stepped inside.

"Mr. Caledonia?" I said. "Lou?"

I considered backing up and leaving. He told me to come by anytime, but maybe it was simply too late. If I wanted, I could try again when I left town, as I had originally proposed. Or maybe I wouldn't bother at all. What could this man know about my father that I didn't know? That's when it struck me: I didn't know anything about my father.

I took a step toward the door when I heard something rustle near the back of the room. I froze in place.

"Mr. Caledonia?"

I heard the noise again. This time it was followed by a sound I definitely recognized—a stack of books falling over. Someone was in the room.

I walked down the center aisle of the store, picking my way carefully. I stepped over the many books on the floor. The musty scent, the decaying paper of the pages and the heavier stock of the covers filled my nostrils. I loved it. It comforted me. I wished my own apartment smelled that way.

"Lou? It's me. Don Kurtwood. Remember? From the funeral?"

I reached the end of the aisle. There was a door ahead of me. I assumed it led to Mr. Caledonia's office. The door sat open a few inches, and weak light from a desk lamp leaked out in a narrow sliver.

"Lou?"

I took a slow, deliberate step toward that door, my foot stretching out before me, when I figured out the source of the rustling noise I heard earlier. The fat, gray cat leaped across my path, his body brushing against my pant leg. I pulled back my foot, losing my balance. I knocked over a stack of books behind me and grabbed hold of the shelf for balance.

"Jesus," I said.

I held on longer than I needed to. I held on until my heart stopped thudding in my chest. I finally looked down. The cat stared at me, its eyes glowing yellow in the gloomy store. The cat looked edgy and agitated. Its fur stood up along the ridge of its back.

"You scared the hell out of me, cat," I said.

The cat meowed once, and then slipped through the narrow opening into the office. Was I crazy to think he wanted me to follow him?

Maybe the whole thing was crazy, but I did. I took those two slow steps to the office door and pushed it open. The light from the desk lamp illuminated the portion of the floor where Lou Caledonia lay.

He was dead. The thin trickle of blood from the gunshot wound in his temple telling me all I needed to know about that. He was most definitely dead.

I called the police from my cell phone and told them what I had found. The dispatcher sounded cool and calm. She asked me if I was safe, and I told her I thought I was. But I wasn't certain. I was still in Lou's little office, standing over his dead body. How could I feel safe?

The dispatcher also asked me if I had touched anything or moved the body. I told her I hadn't.

"That's good," she said. "Why don't you leave the premises and wait for the police outside? You shouldn't disturb the scene."

Her words made sense to me. Even though I didn't watch a lot of popular TV shows, I'd seen enough at least to know not to disturb any of the evidence. I didn't need a dispatcher to tell me that.

"The officers should be there soon," she said. "Would you like me to stay on the line with you until they arrive?"

"No," I said. "That's not necessary."

I hung up and started out of the office. I really did intend to leave. Why would I want to stand around in a cramped office with the dead body of a man I barely knew? A man who had been murdered in the last few hours?

But then another thought crossed my mind: How would I ever know what Lou Caledonia wanted from me? How would I ever know what he had to do with my father—and why he showed up at Dad's funeral?

The nearest police station was located about ten blocks away. They'd probably dispatch a detective from there, which gave me about ten minutes. And that was assuming there wasn't a patrol car in the immediate vicinity of the store. An officer could show up in a matter of seconds.

But I just wanted to take a quick glance. I moved forward, my feet getting as close as possible to Lou's body without touching it. I had to get that close in order to see what sat on the top of his desk. I could see no discernible order to the papers, pens, and books scattered there. Most of the papers were handwritten bills of sale, either for books he had sold or books he had purchased. There were a couple of flyers advertising antique sales, and in the upper right corner of the desk a thick, well-worn paperback book called *The Guide To Rare Book Collecting, 1979 edition.*

I looked around the room. The shelves above and to the side of the desk were crammed with more books and papers—again a haphazard jumble. On the floor, framing Lou's body, were more cartons of books and accordion files overflowing with papers.

I heard something from the front of the store.

"Hello? This is the police. Is anyone in here?"

"Shit," I said.

The cat jumped onto the desk and stared at me. It eyeballed me, its tail swishing back and forth across the papers on the desk. I took one more look. The cat's paw rested on a clipping torn from the local newspaper. I saw one word in bold type across the top: Kurtwood. I picked it up. Dad's obituary. Across the top someone, presumably Lou Caledonia, had written: "Stranger. Could it be?"

I stuffed the clipping into the pocket of my pants just before a young, uniformed police officer appeared behind me and said, "Sir? I'm going to have to ask you to step outside."

I thought it would take longer to deal with the police and a murder investigation. I stood in the cold with the uniformed officers for about five minutes. They took basic information from me and looked at my driver's license while I shivered, and then a detective showed up. He was a middle-aged man who wore a shirt and tie but no jacket of any kind. His hair was thick and gray, and when the wind blew it flopped around on his head. He never reached up to straighten it. His handshake felt like a vice.

"I'm Phil Hyland," he said. "Why don't you tell me what happened here?"

So I did. He didn't take notes. He listened to everything I said, a look of concentration on his face. I told him about Lou Caledonia showing up at my dad's funeral and then insisting I come down to the bookstore to talk to him as soon as possible.

"The door was open, and I found him dead back there," I said.

"You say your father just died?"

"A few days ago."

"What were the circumstances of his death?" Hyland asked.

"Natural causes," I said. "He had a neurological disorder."

"I'm sorry to hear that," Hyland said. "So you'd never met this Caledonia fellow before?"

"Never."

"And what did he want with your father?" he asked.

"I don't know," I said. "I assume was something to do with books. My father owned a lot of books. But Mr. Caledonia acted offended when I suggested that's why he was at the funeral home." I tried to remember his exact words. "He told me that he had tried to talk to my father before but had always been rebuffed. That's the word he used. 'Rebuffed.' I guess I came here to see what he knew about my dad. If anything."

"Dads can be a tricky business," Hyland said. "I never knew mine that well."

"Exactly," I said. "Do any of us really know our fathers?"

I thought I was on the brink of a connection with Hyland, but just as quickly, the moment seemed to pass.

He asked, "Did the officers take your information?"

"Yes."

"We'll be in touch if we need anything more," he said. "We're probably looking at a robbery here. The neighborhood isn't what it used to be."

He started toward the door of Lou Caledonia's shop but, before he went in, he turned back to me.

"Are you sure there isn't anything else, Mr. Kurtwood?" he asked. "Anything else you saw in there?"

I could feel the clipping in my pants' pocket. It itched and scraped against my thigh. I knew I should give it back. But . . . I didn't want to give up that scrap. I knew it made no sense, but I guess I saw it as an artifact from my dad.

"Nothing," I said.

Hyland went inside, and I went back to my parents' house.

The morning paper carried no news of Lou Caledonia's death. Either it happened too late to make the cut, or it was deemed too insignificant to mention. As we dressed in the morning, Mom didn't even ask me about my trip to the bookstore the night before. Either she was too distracted by the funeral service, or it had slipped her mind. And I wasn't going to bring it up. She had enough to worry about and I didn't want to add to her stress.

We both maintained our composure during the service. Neither of us was big on emotional displays, and the Catholic Church provided enough rigidity and structure in the service that there was little room for genuine feeling. I sat in the front pew of the church next to Mom and recited the responses and hymns by memory, even though I hadn't been inside a church in about fifteen years.

When my mind wandered, it wasn't to bad memories. I thought of my childhood and the things my dad and I did together. He took me to the library a lot. He let me wander wherever I liked and was willing to let me read whatever books I happened to find. I first read *On the Road* that way, as well as *Lord of the Flies* and *The Great Gatsby*. Dad always found something from the bestseller list, but he never commented on what I read. Except once. When I was about fourteen, I picked up a copy of *Crime and Punishment*, and he said, offhandedly, "Yeah. I read that a long time ago."

"You read this?" I asked. "For school?"

"Not for school. Because I wanted to." He looked at me over the top of his glasses. "Do you think you have the market cornered on reading the great books?"

I hadn't thought of that in a long time. But sitting there in the church, I remembered that the old man could surprise me, that I shouldn't assume I understood him—or anyone else—easily. He *was* a stranger to me in many ways, and perhaps to my mother, too. But what did that have to do with a murdered bookstore owner? I wondered if I'd ever know.

A small group travelled to the graveside service. The day started to turn cool, gray clouds building in from the west along with a stiff breeze. The priest didn't waste any time getting through his prayers and rituals. I started to think about the food spread waiting for us back in the church basement. Hot chicken salad, coffee, peach cobbler. Except for a pasty communion wafer, I hadn't eaten all day. When the service concluded and we turned toward our cars, I saw a woman standing at a distance. She wore oversized sunglasses despite the day's gloom, and a barn coat and work boots. I couldn't tell how old she was, but she seemed to move with an easy grace as she turned and climbed into the cab of a pickup truck and drove off before we reached our cars.

"Do you know who that was?" I asked Mom.

But she didn't even answer. She was talking to one of my aunts, and then the pickup was gone.

"Did you say something something, honey?" Mom asked.

"I saw someone and I was wondering if you knew who they were."

"I'm so tired," she said. "I don't even know who I am anymore. Family and friends are a great support, but they wear me out."

I hadn't slept much the night before, so I said, "I understand."

"But if you're up for it later, I'd like your help with some of Dad's things. He has old boxes in the attic I can't carry down. You don't have to sort through them, but just bring them down so I can."

"There's no hurry, Mom," I said.

"I know," she said. "But it's therapeutic. I did the same thing when my mother died, Grandma Nancy. I went through all of her clothes and pictures. It helped me cope."

"Mom?" I asked. "You know I went to that bookstore last night."

"That's right. I must have been sound asleep; I didn't hear you come in. What happened with that man? What did he want?"

"Well, it's a long story. But he had a copy of Dad's obituary on his desk." I paused. "I took it."

"Why?"

"It seemed like a keepsake of some kind," I said. "I guess it seems silly. But the bookstore owner wrote the word 'stranger' on it. Does that mean anything to you?"

"Does that mean anything to me?" she asked. "That sums your father up perfectly. Do you know we dated for two years before I even knew his middle name? Two years. At first I thought he didn't have one because he always used the initial. H. Then one day I saw his birth certificate. I saw that his middle name was Henry. Now why hadn't he ever told me that?"

"Did you ask?"

"I shouldn't have to ask," she said, sniffing. "Husbands are supposed to tell their wives these things. But not your father. Maybe he wanted to maintain some mystery in our marriage."

"Maybe."

"Let's face it," she said. "I loved the man dearly. Dearly. But I didn't know him. And now I never will."

I hauled six cardboard boxes down from the attic that afternoon. They were heavy as iron bars, and when I was finished carrying them, I slumped into a living room chair, my back screaming. Dad's prophecy about me had come true—I was too bookish and didn't spend enough time playing sports. I decided forty was too old to change and asked Mom where she kept the ibuprofen.

That evening, we ate food that a neighbor had dropped off. Chicken casserole followed by a peanut butter pie. I hated the fact that we all died, that people I loved—like my father—could be taken away so cruelly. But the food was amazing. Comfort food in the truest sense of the term.

Mom seemed distracted while we ate. I finally asked her what was on her mind.

"Are you just feeling sad about Dad?" I asked.

"Not exactly," she said. "I'm just thinking about the fact that you're going to leave and go back to your life. And I want you to do that. But the house is going to feel awfully lonely."

"I understand," I said. "But you have a lot of friends. You've always been good at keeping busy."

"Sure." She forced a smile. "Maybe I need to sell the house."

"You can think about that at some point." I gestured toward the living room. "What do you figure he has in all those boxes?"

"Knowing your dad, more books. Hell, who knows? They could be the collected love letters of some ex-girlfriend."

"Dad?"

Mom waved her hand in the air, dismissing me. "Maybe I'll self-publish them and create the next *Fifty Shades of Gray*. Except it would really be gray because of how old we are."

Like most children, I didn't like to think of my parents' sex lives. And I certainly didn't think of them as sexual creatures who had relationships before they met and married each other. But, of course, they probably did. I knew Mom and Dad married when they were in their late twenties, and Mom had me within a year of their marriage. They met through mutual friends. Mom worked as a secretary in a law office, and Dad was a casual acquaintance of the lawyer. They sometimes golfed together. So they both must have dated others during high school and college and those first few years out in the real world.

My mind flashed to the woman at the cemetery. Had she really been there to see Dad's funeral? People spent time in cemeteries for any number of reasons. Why would I assume she was there because of Dad?

"Let's open up one of the boxes and take a look," I said.

"Be my guest. It's all yours anyway. You're the heir to this great fortune."

Mom cleared the plates while I went out to the living room. I took out my key to slit the tape on the box, but before I could do anything, the doorbell rang.

"If that's Mrs. Himmel from up the street, tell her I'm lying down," Mom said.

I went to the front window and slid the curtain aside.

"It's not Mrs. Himmel," I said.

"Who is it?"

I opened the door to Detective Hyland.

"Who is it, honey?" Mom said, coming into the room. "Oh, hello."

"Mom, this is Detective Hyland from the police department. It's kind of a long story."

Mom listened while I explained the events of the previous night and the death of Lou Caledonia. Mom's face remained composed, and she didn't display much shock or dismay. She reserved her comments for the end of my story when she looked at me as only my mother could and said, "Why on earth didn't you tell me this last night?"

"I didn't want to wake you up or worry you," I said.

"Sit down, Detective," Mom said. "How can we help you with this?"

Hyland came into the room. He eyed the boxes in the middle of the floor but deftly stepped around them without comment. He wore a different shirt and tie than the night before and still no jacket. His hair looked less windblown as he sat on the couch and crossed his legs, ankle on knee.

"I'm sorry to intrude on you at such a difficult time," he said. He really didn't seem that bothered by his interruption and showed no sign that he might get up and leave. He looked settled in on the couch.

Mom and I took the hint, and we each sat in matching chairs that were arranged on either side of a small table. The boxes filled the floor space between all of us.

"Last night you told me that you didn't know Mr. Caledonia," Hyland said.

"That's right."

"And you don't know the nature of their friendship?"

"That's what I was going to the store to find out," I said. "Lou said they weren't really friends. He said something like he wanted to know Dad, but Dad didn't want to know him."

"Your father always was a bit of a loner," Mom said.

"Mr. Caledonia wrote a number of letters to your father. At least ten. They were in his office at the bookstore. All of them were returned unopened."

"My husband was bedridden for the last six months," Mom said. "He wouldn't have been able to open an envelope."

"But you would have seen the letters," Hyland said. "Or opened them?"

"I don't remember any letters like that."

Hyland's eyes narrowed. I thought he was going to press Mom further, but he didn't.

"These letters were all written over the past five years," Hyland said. "They stopped about a year ago. I'm not sure why. Maybe Caledonia got tired of being rejected."

"What were the letters about?" I asked. "What could this man possibly want with Dad that he would keep writing him for so long – without a single response?"

Hyland took his time answering. He seemed to be considering me. The clipping from Lou Caledonia's desk, the one with Dad's name and the word Stranger written on it, sat on my nightstand upstairs. My heart started to beat irrationally. If the detective decided to snoop around the house, he would find it. And he'd know I lied to him at the scene of the crime when I said there was nothing else to know.

Hell, maybe he already knew about it and was just toying with me and making me sweat.

Finally, he said, "Apparently, your father had a book Mr. Caledonia wanted."

"Which book?" I asked. "Hell, if he'd told me the title I would have brought it to him last night."

"If he'd have told me the title," Mom said, "I'd have given him *all* the books."

Hyland was shaking his head. "I don't think you understand," he said. "Caledonia didn't want one of the books your father *owned*. He wanted a copy of the book your father *wrote*."

Mom laughed. I would have laughed, but the idea of my father writing a book was so bizarre that I couldn't say anything.

"No," Mom said. "That's not true." She laughed again. "My husband never wrote a book. He couldn't write a grocery list. He once went away fishing for the weekend, and he didn't even bother to write me a note. He didn't write anything."

"My dad read a lot. But he was a salesman. He didn't write any books."

Hyland shifted around on the couch. He reached into his back pants pocket and brought out a small notebook. He flipped through it to the page he wanted.

"Well," Hyland said, "you may not think your father wrote a book, but Lou Caledonia most certainly did."

"He did?" I asked. "Is that why he came to the viewing?"

"That's a good guess," Hyland said.

"Well, what book?" I asked. "Are we talking about a novel? Or what?"

"There's no book, Donnie," Mom said.

Hyland ignored her. "We're talking about a novel," he said. "According to the information in the letters and files in Mr. Caledonia's office, he thinks your father wrote the novel, *Rides a Stranger*, under the pseudonym Herbert Henry."

"Henry," I said. "That's Dad's middle name."

Hyland said, "Believe me, Lou Caledonia was aware of that." He looked at the notebook. Apparently, he thought your father wrote this novel, which was published in 1972 by Woodworth Books as part of their Monarch Series." Hyland looked over at us. "The Monarch Series was dedicated to novels about the American west. They published twenty books in the series, and *Rides a Stranger* is number nineteen."

Rides a Stranger? The obituary I took from Caledonia's desk. Stranger.

Hyland looked at his notebook again. "But even though the books were meant to be mass produced and widely distributed to be sold in grocery stores, drug stores, airports etc., something went wrong with number nineteen. There was a printer's strike at the plant that manufactured the book. The first batch was printed by replacement workers." Hyland looked over again. "Scabs for lack of a better word."

"I see," I said.

"They printing went horribly wrong. Blurred cover. Pages cut wrong. A disaster. So they had to pulp that whole batch. Throw them out. They were worthless. The strike ended a few weeks after that, and the regular workers came back. They did a test run of about one hundred books in order to make sure the problems from the last batch—the scab batch—were corrected. And the problems were fixed. But by that point book number nineteen was so far off-schedule that they went ahead and decided to print number twenty and then go back and do number nineteen later. And guess what?"

"What?" Mom asked.

"They never did," Hyland said. "They printed number twenty, and then Woodworth Books folded their tents and went out of business. Number nineteen was never given a full print run."

"How many were printed?" I asked.

"Lou Caledonia guesses they printed about fifty. Fifty cheap paperback books were printed about forty years ago. Understandably, not very many of those fifty are still around. Some went to libraries and got worn out. Some were sold in a few places. But mostly they're gone. The book itself, your dad's book, isn't that valuable in and of itself. You see, it's the set of all twenty Monarchs that would be the real prize. Lots of people have managed to collect the nineteen mass produced titles, but to find a set with all twenty . . . well, that's a rare thing. And one of those sets is worth thousands of dollars on the collector's market."

"He didn't write the book," Mom said.

"Why is this set worth so much?" I asked. "I mean, who cares about twenty old western paperbacks? Aren't they a dime a dozen?"

Hyland flipped his notebook shut. "You would think that, wouldn't you? Except there's one catch with this Monarch Series.

Number eight in the series is a book called *The Midnight Guns*. It was written by someone named T.J. Tucker."

Hyland looked at both of us as though the name should mean something to us. It didn't.

"What's so special about a guy named T.J. Tucker?" I asked.

"T.J. Tucker isn't a guy," Hyland said. "T.J. Tucker is a woman who wrote under a pseudonym. I guess they figured men were more likely to buy a western, and they wouldn't buy a western if it was written by a woman. That was her first book, and she never published another western. Her real name is Tonya Jane Hood. You know who that is, right?"

"It sounds familiar," I said.

"Are you shitting me?" Mom said.

"I'm not," Hyland said.

I looked at Mom. "Who is this?"

"Tonya Jane Hood," Mom said. "She writes the *Glitter Blood* series. You know, the books, the movies, the TV show. *Glitter Blood*. I read all of them."

"That's right," Hyland said. "The Hood novel is very desirable, but they printed close to one hundred thousand copies of that one. And when you combine the desirability of Hood with the rarity of Henry you get a valuable series. Very valuable. Maybe even worth killing over."

"This is ridiculous," Mom said. "My husband died. We buried him today. I don't want to hear this crazy stuff about these books. It doesn't have anything to do with us."

I held out my hand, hoping to calm down Mom a little bit. But I didn't disagree with her.

"Detective," I said. "Lou Caledonia seemed like an odd guy. So he thought my dad wrote a book, a rare book. What's his evidence for this? The whole thing seems kind of far-fetched."

"You may be right," Hyland said. "Maybe Caledonia's death was just a robbery gone wrong. Maybe he was dreaming when he thought your father wrote this book. But there is the middle name. There's the fact that, according to the biography in the book *Rides a Stranger*, the author of the book lives in Cincinnati, Ohio."

I said, "Lots of people named Henry live in Cincinnati, Ohio. It's a big city."

"True," Hyland said. "Very true."

A silence settled between us. No one said anything. Hyland looked lost in thought for a moment, as though contemplating whether or not he wanted to say anything else. Finally, he just stood up. "Perhaps I'm just fishing."

Mom and I stood up as well, and Hyland nodded to us. He shook my hand.

"Do accept my sympathies," he said. "If you think of anything else that's relevant, just give me a call."

He let himself out.

When Hyland was gone, Mom started puttering around in the kitchen. She scrubbed the countertops and rattled dishes into the dishwasher. I stood in the doorway and watched for a few moments. I knew she knew I was there, but she didn't look up from her work.

"Mom?" I said.

"Yeah?"

"What do you think of all that?" I asked.

I didn't think she was going to answer me. She kept cleaning. But then she stopped what she was doing and said, "I don't put much stock in it."

"Did you ever know Dad wanted to write something?" I asked.

"Your father wanted to do a lot of things," she said. "He had a lot of dreams. He wanted to run his own business, and he wanted to retire to Florida, and he wanted us to take a trip to Europe. He did none of it. Your father was a dreamer but not a doer. There's a big difference there."

"That sounds depressing."

"Be glad you didn't get those qualities from him," she said. "You got an advanced degree. You have a good career."

"Dad had a career," I said.

"Dad had a job. That's it. He hated it, and it made him miserable."

"So maybe he really wanted to be a writer. Maybe he tried it . . ."

I stopped in mid-sentence as something occurred to me.

Mom didn't notice. She dried her hands on a red towel and turned off the light over the sink. When she turned around, she said, "What's wrong with you?"

"What year did Hyland say that book was published?" I asked. "The one Lou Caledonia thinks Dad wrote? Do you remember?"

Mom's forehead creased, but I knew she remembered.

"What's the year?" I asked.

"1972," she said.

"1972. That's the year I was born," I said. "He quit writing because I was born."

After Mom went to sleep, I tore into the boxes. I wasn't sure what I was looking for, but I hoped to find something related to all the things I had been talking about with Detective Hyland and Lou Caledonia. What did the used book dealer really want with Dad? Had the old man written a book—a novel—and a rare one at that? Could the book be so rare and valuable that someone would kill for it?

But then I had to ask myself something else: Did I really care about the book stuff at all? What was I really trying to understand? It was pretty simple, really. If I could get my hands on a copy of that book, then I assumed I would understand something about my dad. Up until that point, I really didn't understand anything about him. How did he marry my mom? What made him choose the life he chose?

And his death and the death/murder of Lou Caledonia only raised more questions. Did he really write a novel? And if he did, why did he stop? Was it just because he had a wife and a child and had to make a better, more stable living than writing could provide?

The boxes provided no answers in terms of the books. I hoped to find manuscripts and rejection letters, book contracts or correspondence with editors and agents. But there was nothing like that in the boxes. In fact, looking at the contents of those boxes, one would think my father didn't have any literary aspirations at all. I found nothing about books or writing. Nothing like that.

So what did I find? Pictures. Lots and lots of pictures. And all of these pictures were taken before I was born. Before Dad met and married Mom, I guessed. They revealed that Dad did, indeed, have a life before he was married. My father had few friends when I was growing up—and maintained little in the way of friendships even after I was an adult and he was retired from work. My mother had friends. My father had his books and sports on the television.

But the pictures in the boxes told a different story. In the pictures Dad lived in a swirl of friends, men and women. He went to parties, to bars, to nightclubs. He spent time at the beach and in the big city. He drank from beer cans and champagne bottles. He wore suits and swim trunks. He had a life, one that I never imagined. He apparently had more of a life than I ever had.

One woman showed up in more of the pictures than anyone else. She was pretty, very pretty. Slender. Her hair was blonde, her smile bright. And she stood by my father's side a lot, her head resting on his shoulder, her lips parted to laugh. Dad smiled in all of these pictures, too. He looked happy. And young.

I turned one of the photos over and found a name. "Mary Ann." On another, the same woman appeared with the nickname "Peanuts" written on the back. Mary Ann? Peanuts? My father appeared to have had a serious girlfriend before he met Mom, one he appeared to love—or at least felt an immense amount of affection for.

Who knew the old man had done so much better than me?

I must have dozed off in the chair. When the phone rang, I opened my eyes and saw my father's photographs spread out on my lap like a blanket. As I moved, the photos shifted and slid, some of them falling to the floor and others dropping into the cracks between the cushion and the bulk of the chair itself.

I checked the time on the ringing phone. 11:35. I didn't recognize the number, but it was local. I answered.

"Mr. Kurtwood?"

"Yes."

"This is Detective Hyland again. Sorry to bother you."

"It's okay. I was just . . ."

"I was hoping we could speak tomorrow, before you leave town. There are some other aspects to your father's case I was hoping to go over with you, and I'm not sure your mother would want to hear them. At least not yet."

"Is this about the book?" I asked.

"Among other things."

"I can be there at nine."

"Excellent," Hyland said. "See you then."

Before I went to sleep, I put back all the photos in their boxes and closed the lids. When I came downstairs in the morning, Mom was sitting at the kitchen table working a crossword puzzle, and the coffeemaker puffed along on the counter. She looked up expectantly and said, "So, are you all packed?"

"I was thinking I might not head back today."

"Oh."

"I only have one class tomorrow, and I don't really need to be there for it. Maybe I'll stay another day and enjoy the old homestead."

"I won't argue with you there," Mom said. "Ordinarily I have to beg you to visit. If you want to stay another day, be my guest. Did you go through any of those boxes?"

"I . . . well, I just glanced in the tops of them," I said.

"And?" She looked at me over the top of her glasses. "Any deep dark secrets contained within? Was you father a spy as well as an author? Did he cure cancer or fly to the moon?"

I hesitated. I didn't know what I was supposed to tell her. I wanted to share the truth—Dad had a girlfriend!—but she might already know that. And, if she didn't, what good did it do to dredge up anything from the past, especially just a few days after Dad's death? I wasn't even certain the thing I was thinking about was worth exploring—the book allegedly written by my father. Maybe I really just needed to go back home and get on with my life, such as it was. But Detective Hyland didn't want to let me.

"It looked like a lot of old stuff to me," I said. "Nothing too special."

"I figured as much."

"But don't throw any of it away," I said.

She perked up again. "Why? If it's junk, I can toss it."

"No," I said. "Maybe I'm just being sentimental, but I can take it all with me."

"Suit yourself," she said, returning to her puzzle.

"And," I said. "Those books you said you got rid of?"

"What books?"

"The books you took away before Dad died?"

"What about them?"

Her voice was as flat and gray as pavement.

"Where did you take those?" I asked. "The library book sale?"

"Goodwill," she said. "Nobody but Goodwill would resell them."

I nodded.

Goodwill.

I waited a long time at the police station. I assumed Detective Hyland would be eager to see me, especially since he had invited me. While I waited, I searched the Internet using my phone. I tried to find a copy of *Rides a Stranger* by Herbert Henry. A few were for sale, but none were listed for less than one thousand dollars. One thousand dollars for a pulpy western paperback published forty years earlier. On several message boards devoted to book collecting, buyers had placed the book on their most desired list, with one calling it "the white whale of vintage paperback collecting."

I wondered what Dad would have made of all of it—if he had written the book. And I wondered about those books Mom had hauled off to Goodwill. Were there copies of *Rides a Stranger* in there somewhere? Is that why Dad insisted she stop? Is that why he whispered that one word into my ear just a few weeks before he died?

Good will. Was he wishing something for me? Or Mom? Or did he mean *Goodwill?*

After keeping me waiting for an hour, Detective Hyland finally appeared. He looked to be wearing the same clothes as the night before, the tie loosened and a little askew.

"Mr. Kurtwood," he said. "I'm sorry to have kept you waiting. Something came up, something related to Lou Caledonia's case. It's had me tied up all night and most of the morning."

"I understand," I said, standing up. "Do you need me to come back another time?"

"No, no," he said. "In fact, why don't you come back? You may be interested to hear some of this."

As we walked to the cubicle where he worked, I asked if the development in the Caledonia case had something to do with what he wanted to tell me that morning.

"As a matter of fact, it does," he said. We settled into chairs at his neat and orderly desk. There were no papers cluttering the surface. Just a computer, an autographed baseball encased in glass, and a cellphone that vibrated every few minutes.

"Like I said, I didn't want to discuss this in front of your mother because I was afraid it might be a little awkward."

"Probably no more awkward than surprising her with the news that her husband was secretly an author."

"I'm not so sure," Hyland said. "You see, I contacted a book dealer online, someone who had a copy of your father's book . . . well, *Rides a Stranger*, for sale. I was looking for any information that might help us with the case."

"Of course."

"It turns out the book in question has a dedication."

I sat straighter in my chair. "Really?"

"Indeed. The book is dedicated to M.A. That's all it says. 'For M.A. with love.' Do you know what that might mean?"

"My mother's name is Elaine. My grandmother, my maternal grandmother, was named Nancy. My dad didn't have any sisters."

"It sounds like a woman, right? 'With love.' Men don't say with love to other men, even our fathers. Do we?"

I had to agree. I only told my father I loved him when he was dying. He rarely said it to me after my childhood. That didn't bother me. It really didn't. That was just how men are.

"Well, it seems like we caught a little bit of a break. We went through Mr. Caledonia's possessions in his office. His calendar, address book, computer. It wasn't an easy job. I suppose he's like most collectors of arcana—a little bit disorganized, a little bit of a pack-rat. But it turns out he's been carrying on quite a correspondence with a woman named Mary Ann Compton. Does that name ring a bell?"

"It doesn't."

"But you can see the initials, right?" Hyland asked, obviously pleased with himself.

"It seems pretty clear. M.A. Mary Ann."

"But you're not familiar with her?" Hyland asked.

"Not that I know of. Does she have something to do with my father? Or this book?"

"This is the part I didn't want to bring up in front of your mother," he said. "You see, these events having to do with Lou Caledonia, they don't really have any bearing on you. Not directly. Your father died of natural causes, of course. Mr. Caledonia's murder was only tangentially related to your father's life. If your father even wrote that book at all."

"If."

"But I think it's pretty safe to say now that he did write *Rides a Stranger*. Very safe indeed."

"Why's that?" I asked.

"Because he dedicated the book to Mary Ann Compton. Back then, when your father wrote the book, she was known as Mary Ann Gates. She was dating your father when he wrote and published the book. And she's been trying to get her hands on a copy of the book ever since then. She wanted Mr. Caledonia to grant her access to your father, which he wouldn't do. She killed Mr. Caledonia when he refused her once and for all."

"Killed him?" I said. I felt a little shaky. "Over a book?"

"Not just any book," Hyland said. "Your father's only published novel. Dedicated to her."

"How are you so certain of all of this?" I asked.

Hyland smiled. "Because we have Mary Ann Compton in custody. We brought her in last night, and she confessed to the murder of Lou Caledonia."

Detective Hyland told me at least five times how irregular it was. He muttered under his breath that if anyone found out—anyone at all— he might end up in a great deal of trouble. But as he walked me back to a small interview room, the room where I would be able to have just a few minutes alone with Mary Ann Compton, he admitted that my seeing her probably wouldn't do anybody any harm.

"She confessed," he said, his hand pulling open the door to the small room. "And, besides, I have a soft spot for this whole case. Or, more accurately, your involvement in it."

"Why's that?" I asked.

"My old man liked to read. Mickey Spillane. Donald Hamilton. Richard Prather. I sometimes wonder if I became a detective because of the books he always read."

"You never know," I said.

"I think I ought to write a book someday," Hyland said. "You know, about all the cases I've worked, all the crazy things and people I've seen. I've even tried a few times. It's not as easy as it looks, writing a book."

"No, it's not."

"She'll be here in a minute," he said, holding the door for me. "And you can only have a few. Make it quick."

"Thanks," I said.

The room held a small wooden table and a few chairs. The table looked like it had been to hell and back. The floor was dirty and stained—coffee, candy wrappers, grime. I took a seat, the chair rickety and squeaky beneath me.

I thought about the woman I was going to meet. She was my father's ex-lover. No big deal. People dated others before they got married. But this woman meant so much to my dad he dedicated a book to her, a book he published the year I was born. Wasn't he dating Mom at that time? Wouldn't they have been practically engaged by then?

I ran my thumbnail through one of the deep grooves scarred in the top of the table. Maybe Dad didn't write the book at all. Maybe the whole thing was a misunderstanding. After all, no one had completely convinced me that the old man had really written the book. An eccentric used book dealer and a jilted lover pointed their fingers at my dad. Those of us who lived with the man, who knew him better than anyone, didn't think it was possible.

Who knew best?

The door opened, and I got my first look at Mary Ann Compton. Detective Hyland led her in. She didn't wear handcuffs or a prison jumpsuit, but she looked tired. She was an attractive woman, slender and trim despite being in her sixties. Her auburn hair showed a few streaks of gray. She wore no make-up, but the lines on her face gave her character, like someone who had spent a lot of time in the outdoors, soaking up the sun and the wind.

"Five minutes," Hyland said and left us alone.

I stood up. The woman—Mary Ann—took me in from head to toe.

I held out my hand. "I'm—"

"I know who you are," she said. "You look just like him."

Her voice was warm, but not effusive. She offered me a weak smile and came into the room and sat at the table. I sat again and rested my elbows on the tabletop.

She said, "We don't have much time, so you might as well ask what you want to ask. I'm sure you have a lot of questions."

"I do."

"Then you better go for it," she said. "I doubt we'll be seeing each other again."

"But we have seen each other before, right? At the cemetery."

"Yes, I was there," she said. She looked down and picked at a piece of loose skin around one of her fingernails. "I got as close as I dared."

"So you and Dad . . . my dad . . . you were a couple."

"We were meant to be," she said. "He was the one, and we belonged together. He was the great love of my life."

The words sounded so strange. Who talked that way about my father? Not my mother, that was for certain. It was hard to imagine anyone thinking that about him, but I believed this woman when she said it. Her words carried such conviction.

I was aware of the press of time. I didn't hesitate.

"So, why weren't the two of you together?" I asked. "If you loved each other so much?"

"I suspect you know the answer to that," she said, looking up at me.

I thought about the dedication again, the publication date of the book.

"How did that happen?" I asked. "How did my mother get pregnant if you and Dad were together?"

"We weren't together at the time," she said. "We had a little bit of an on and off relationship. We were off for a while when he met your mother. He was with her when he found out two things that changed his life. One, his novel was going to be published. Two, he was going to be a father. Both things meant a lot to him, of course, but he certainly cared more about being a father than about that book. In the end, that's how he felt."

"And you know that because . . ."

"Because I got the book dedication," she said. "And you and your mom got him. I can't really blame him, of course. A child is a big deal. And he didn't want you to grow up without a father. It was the right thing all around. But . . ."

"But he could have kept writing even after I was born," I said. "Lots of writers have families and day jobs, and they still write. Why did he stop?"

It took her a moment to answer. Then she said, "We weren't together when the publishing deal went south. You know about that, right?"

I nodded.

"But we still talked from time to time. He was devastated when that happened. We didn't talk about it much, but I could tell. I think he just took it as a sign. It offered him a clean break with the past. With the time and effort he would have to put into writing . . . and with me."

"Jesus." I slumped back in my chair. "I can't imagine the disappointment he must have felt over the book. To have tried for that and then have the book just disappear, to never even hold it in his hands."

"He did hold it in his hands," Mary Ann said.

"He did?" I asked.

"Your dad received all of his author copies," she said. "He had at least one whole box, maybe twenty or thirty copies. That's what Lou Caledonia was trying to get his hands on. And that's how all of this ended up happening."

"You mean Lou Caledonia's death, right?" I asked.

She nodded. "He found out your father wrote that book. For years, no one knew who the author was. Everyone knew the book was rare, and no one knew what happened to the author. Some people assumed it was a pseudonym of a well-known author. Some people thought maybe an editor wrote the novel and used a different name."

"Who thinks these things?" I asked.

"People on rare book message boards. Book dealers and collectors."

"Are you one of those?"

"No, but I followed the discussions. I knew who wrote the book. I was curious to see if anyone else did."

"And Lou Caledonia figured it out?"

"He did. He started hinting on the message boards that he knew something about Herbert Henry, that very soon he hoped to have a big discovery about the book. He should have kept his mouth shut to be honest. But I think the guy just couldn't resist bragging. After all, they call that book—"

"The white whale of vintage paperback collecting."

"You did your homework. Anyway, Lou Caledonia had found someone who used to work for Monarch Books. He found out some things about the author of the book. Can you imagine his surprise when he found out that the author of *Rides a Stranger* lived right in the same town he did? It probably made that fat little man think he had found his destiny at long last. All I wanted was a copy of the book. Just one copy."

"You didn't have one?"

"No. Like I said, your father and I weren't seeing each other by the time the book came out. I guess I could have written to him or called him. We were right here in the same town as well. But I decided that he had moved on for all the right reasons and I needed to let that be. He had a wife and a son. I ended up getting married and moving on with my life as well. I planned to let the whole thing go. I should have, you know?"

"So why didn't you?" I asked.

She took a deep breath. When she did that, I saw the lines on her face deepen, and just for a moment, she looked her age. She let the breath out and composed herself. "I found out that your dad was dying. I ran into a mutual friend from the old days. John Colfax? Do you remember him?"

The name sounded vaguely familiar from my childhood. I couldn't attach a face to it though. "I don't know," I said.

"It doesn't matter," she said. "He heard from your dad from time to time, and he heard about the illness. He told me, and we tried to keep our conversation about it casual. We said what everyone is supposed to say in those situations. 'So young.' 'Isn't that awful.' 'I'll be thinking of him.' We said all that and parted ways. But it rocked me. I couldn't stop thinking about it. I had buried those feelings a long time ago, but that didn't mean I couldn't excavate them." She shrugged. "So I sent a card. I didn't hear anything back. So I called. The number is right there in the book. I knew the neighborhood your parents lived in. I called and spoke to your mother."

"And? What happened?"

"She pretty much hung up on me," Mary Ann said. "She said your father was too sick to come to the phone. She said it was best if I didn't call anymore and left them in peace. I got the brush-off basically."

"Mom knew who you were?" I asked. "What you once meant to Dad?"

"I'm sure she did," Mary Ann said.

"She says she never knew about the book," I said.

"I guess that's possible. I don't know if your dad talked about it with anybody once he decided he wasn't going to be a writer anymore."

"I don't understand why you killed Mr. Caledonia," I said. "You really killed him, right? That's what the detective said."

As if on cue, Hyland opened the door and stuck his head into the room. "Time's up," he said.

"Wait." I held up my hand. "Just another couple of minutes."

"Yes, please," Mary Ann said.

Hyland looked us over, and then he tapped the face of his digital watch. "Two minutes. No more." He shut the door.

Mary Ann said, "I wanted a copy of that book before your dad . . . was gone. I went to Lou Caledonia and asked him if I could have one, if he ever managed to get his hands on that box your dad had." She shook her head. "First he wanted to use me. He told me to go back to your parents' house and try again. He said if I could get inside there and get whatever copies of the book your dad had, he'd share them with me. He called it a finder's fee because he located your dad."

"But you didn't need him to locate Dad."

"I know. I guess I'm a sucker for a hard luck case. I told him he could have as many copies as he wanted, as long as I got one. That's it—I just wanted one to keep. I never got one way back then, you know."

"Did you go back to my parents' house?" I asked.

"I did. And I got the brush-off again. This time, your mom was less polite. I reported this to Lou, and then about a week later, your dad was gone. I went back to Lou to ask him if he was going to try to buy any part of the estate. He was evasive. He was giving me the brush-off as well. But I saw the obituary on his desk. I knew what he was thinking. He was going to go to the funeral and try to talk to someone, probably you. I walked out of there. I just walked out. I told myself it was all over, everything was over. Your dad was gone, that relationship was long in the past, and I really did need to just forget about it. That's what I told myself."

"But?"

"But I hated sitting home during the viewing. I wanted to see your dad one more time. I thought I should be there, but I didn't go. Instead I went to Lou's store that night. My ex-husband bought me a gun when we split up. I brought it with me. I just wanted to scare that little ogre of a man. I wanted him to know that I wanted a copy of that book. Just one." Her voice started to rise. "Is that too much to ask? Just the one copy? It's dedicated to me." She paused and gathered herself. Her voice returned to its normal volume. "He denied me again. He said he had a line on the books, and those were going to fund his retirement to Florida. I don't know what happened really. I'd been brushed off so many times . . . so many times in my life. Your mom. Lou."

"My dad?"

She nodded. "I shot the little weasel. I went to the cemetery the next day, knowing I was guilty and knowing I would turn myself in. I saw the coffin, your dad's coffin. That was as close as I could come."

"I'm sorry," I said. "I didn't know."

"It's okay," she said. "It was a crime of passion . . . committed forty years after the romance died and directed against the wrong man. That's the story of my life."

Goodwill stores smell different from bookstores. In used bookstores—like Lou Caledonia's—I could smell the pages and the dust jackets and the endpapers. It was a fresh, hopeful smell, despite the age and condition of the books. But a Goodwill store smelled like desperation. In a Goodwill store the accumulated detritus of thousands of unconnected lives merged together to create the odor of surrender, of loss. Of defeat. Goodwill provided a home for things that couldn't be discarded anywhere else. Goodwill was for everything that couldn't be sold in a consignment or an antique store. I hadn't entered one since high school.

This location sat about a mile from my parents' house in a neighborhood that had once been nicer. As I kid, I remembered driving through and seeing middle-class homes with yards that were tended and clean. Not anymore. The houses around the store looked dingier and more rundown. The yards were full of toys, the grass worn and dying. It seemed appropriate somehow.

I went into the store and walked past the musty racks of clothes and the ragged and cheap furniture. Near the back I found the books. Two tall shelves stood side by side. Near the top I saw hardcovers, mostly book club editions with missing or frayed dust jackets. I scanned down to the bottom where the paperbacks were. I ran my eyes over the spines. Lots of James Patterson, Nicholas Sparks, Mary Higgins Clark. Most of the spines were creased. I flipped through them like they were cards in a Rolodex, moving each one I touched to the left and going on to the next. I passed mysteries and romances and the occasional science fiction or fantasy title. Not many westerns. A few Louis L'Amours and one or two Max Brands. But no Herbert Henry.

I went back through the shelves again, just in case I missed something. But I hadn't. The books weren't there.

Did I think it would be easy?

I went back to the front looking for an employee. I found a longhaired, wiry guy, wearing a store smock. I explained my problem, and he went to fetch his manager. She turned out to be a middle-aged woman with hair dyed the color of honey. She also wore a store smock with a nametag that said "Patti," and her authority rested in the set of keys she wore attached to her wrist by a Day-Glo rubber cord. I thought her presence would work in my favor. I had prepared a story—which wasn't really a lie—and I assumed she'd be more susceptible to it.

"How can I help you?" she asked.

I told her about Dad dying and Mom giving the books away. I told her about the box of books that my dad had written—and I left out the part about the books being really rare and potentially valuable. I also left out any mention of Lou Caledonia's murder and Mary Ann Compton's confession. I didn't think she needed to know that.

While I spoke, Patti's face remained neutral. I felt like my words weren't getting through, that they were like darts hitting a brick wall and bouncing away, leaving behind no discernible mark or impact. But I kept talking, hoping that the more I talked the more likely she would be to understand.

When I finished, Patti remained silent for a few moments. Then she said, "I really can't let anyone back to see the donations. It takes several days for us to sort them, and lots of people would like to get back there and see what we have before it goes on the floor."

"I understand," I said, although I didn't. Were people really in such a hurry to get their hands on Goodwill stuff?

"It's not unusual for this to happen," Patti said. "Families donate things and then some other family member comes along and wants it back. It happens at least once a week."

"Of course. But . . ."

I didn't know what else to say. I had made my argument. I was at Patti's mercy, and it looked like she was going to turn me away.

"Did you say this book your dad wrote was a western?" she asked.

"Yes."

"Hmm," Patti said. "My grandpa read westerns all the time when I went to visit him. I can picture him in his chair reading Louis L'Amour or Zane Grey. Who was the other one? The one everyone used to read?"

"Max Brand?" I said.

"That's it." Patti looked lost in thought for a moment. I took that as a good sign. I wondered if she were back in her childhood somewhere, in her grandparents' house, coloring on the floor or playing with dolls while her grandmother cooked in the kitchen and the old man sat in a chair lost on a cattle drive or a gunfight or a saloon brawl.

"So what do you think?" I finally asked. "Can I take a peek?"

She snapped out of her reverie. "Sure," she said. "But don't tell anyone I let you do this."

The back room was huge. The ceilings were high, the metal beams and girders exposed. The smell I noticed at the front of the store was even more intense back there, probably because the back room held things that weren't good enough to be put out front. I didn't want to think about what those things were.

Patti led me through the racks of clothes, the shelves of toys, the clutter and refuse from who knew how many lives.

"When were these items brought in?" she asked.

"A couple of weeks, I guess."

"And you're just looking for books?"

"That's right."

"I think we keep the books over here before we sort them."

We went to the far back corner of the storeroom. There were boxes and boxes of books, and then more books that weren't in boxes. Hardcovers and paperbacks. Books for kids and books for adults.

"It's a lot," I said.

"Take your time," she said. "We're open until nine."

I found a plastic stool and pulled it over by the boxes of books. I sat down and felt my shoulders slump a little.

Did I really want to do this?

I thought back over what I knew. A couple of people—one of them a murderer—believed my dad wrote a book. And published it. And it became the rarest book in the land.

Did any of this make sense?

I had already stayed an extra day. I thought of work and my life back at the university. I was already behind and overwhelmed. Did I need to spend more time on what very well may be a wild goose chase?

But I couldn't stop. I looked at those boxes of books . . . the potential that something belonging to and created by my father . . . I couldn't turn away.

I started opening boxes and looking. I looked until my back hurt, and I had to stand up and stretch. I discovered a few things: A lot of people acquired and then disposed of Reader's Digest Condensed Books. A lot of families apparently didn't hold onto the potty training books they bought for their children. And a lot of people read mystery and romance novels. Loads and loads of them.

Patti came by once to check on me. I told her I didn't know how much longer I would keep looking, and she again told me that was just fine with her.

"I wish I could get one of our employees to help you, but we're short staffed."

"That's fine."

"Our business is up with the economy being so bad. More and more people shop here for their clothes and furniture."

"I hope they buy some books, too," I said.

"They do. Books and CDs and DVDs. We sell it all. People like to be entertained when times are bad."

"That makes sense," I said.

"Well," she said, "I'll let you keep at it."

I did. For another hour after she left my side. When I first saw the box with my mother's handwriting on the side, I almost went right past it. In a thick black marker, she had scrawled "Old Books." My mother used a distinctive "d." She always added a looping swirl to the end, her own personal version of a serif font.

I pulled that box close to me and opened it. My father's books. The big-dick books, mostly spy novels. Robert Ludlum. Ken Follett.

Frederick Forsyth. Eric Ambler. I went on to the next box with my Mom's writing on it. Same thing. Dad's books, but not Dad's *book*. I opened two more with the same results. I wanted to take them all. I wanted to tell Patti that they all belonged to me, and I was going to haul them away whether she wanted me to or not. I had no idea what I would do with them. I really didn't want to read them. I just wanted to *have* them. I wanted them in my possession instead of someone else's.

And then I found the smaller box, also with Mom's handwriting on it.

The box was sealed with several layers of packing tape. The box looked old, worn, and a little beaten, like it had been shipped and moved around more than once without being opened. I couldn't get the tape off of it. I had to use a key to dig into and slice open the thick tape. It required a lot of effort. I sliced and dug and pulled until the lid came open.

The top of the box was stuffed with bubble wrap. I pulled that off. Then there was a layer of thin cardboard. I tossed that aside.

And then I saw it. The cover showed a rugged cowboy on his horse. They stood on a ridge that overlooked a small western town. The cowboy packed a revolver on his hip, and the stock of a rifle protruded from a scabbard on his horse. The cowboy looked lean and tan and strong. He squinted into the distance, toward the town. He looked capable and alone.

Across the top in thick, Western-style lettering, it said: *Rides a Stranger* a novel by Herbert Henry. I lifted up the copies on top. There were more below. Many more. I guessed the box held about twenty of them in clean, crackling new shape despite their age. They were well preserved and perfect. If what the book collectors and Detective Hyland told me was true, I was staring at a twenty thousand dollar box of books.

I had found them.

I picked up one of them, gently, like I was handling a bird's egg. I paged to the back and looked for an author bio. There was a small one. It simply said, "Herbert Henry is an author who lives in the Midwest. This is his first novel."

I went back to the front and found the dedication, the one that had caused so much trouble. It was there, just as Hyland said. "For M.A. with love."

And that was it. No author photo. No acknowledgements. Just that little bio that could have been about anyone.

None of this told me Dad wrote the book.

I turned to the back and read the copy there:

Brick Logan rides alone. He travels the western trail accompanied only by his horse and his Colt revolver. He rides to forget his past and the tragic loss of the woman he loved.

But now he enters another western trail town, one more in a long line of stops he makes. And this time Brick finds himself drawn into the life of Chastity Haines, a beautiful widow and the mother of a young son. Brick helps save the town from the merciless influence of a ruthless cattle baron. But when the fight is done, will Brick choose the life of a family man and give up his fiddlefooting, trail-haunted days. Or will he forever remain alone . . . and a stranger.

"Jesus," I said. "Dad."

"Did you find what you wanted?"

I nearly jumped. It was Patti. She stood over me, her smile hopeful.

"I think so," I said. I gently put the copy of *Rides a Stranger* back into the box, and then I thought better of it. "I'll take all of these." I indicated the boxes that had belonged to my dad. I took my wallet out and grabbed all the cash I had. It amounted to about seventy-seven dollars. "Here. Just take this."

"We'd probably sell these for a dollar apiece. Fifty cents for the paperbacks."

"Just take it all," I said. "For your time and trouble."

"Can we help you put them in your car?" she asked.

"Yes," I said. But I picked up the box of *Rides a Stranger* to carry on my own. Before I left with it, I reached into the top of the box and took one copy out. "Here," I said. "It's a book my dad wrote."

"Really?" she said. "Wow. I'm glad you found it."

"Do me a favor," I said. "Don't put it out with the other books. Just take it. If you have the chance, look it up on the internet."

"Why?" she asked.

"Consider it a donation as well. From my family."

Patti looked puzzled. "Okay," she said. "If my grandpa were still alive, I'd give it to him. It looks like the kind of book he'd like."

I nodded. "You're probably right."

I pulled up to the door of the Goodwill store, and the same bearded guy who had directed me to Patti lifted the five boxes of books that once belonged to my dad—and now belonged to me—into the trunk of my car. I had placed the other box, the valuable one, on the passenger seat, so I could keep a close eye on it.

The Goodwill employee took being outside as an opportunity to light a cigarette. He leaned back against the side of the building while I finished situating the boxes in the trunk. I had one stop to make. I was going to go back to the police station and give a copy of the book to Mary Ann Compton. I didn't know if they'd let her have it, but I would trust Hyland to let me know. If they wouldn't take it or guarantee its safety, I intended to find her lawyer and pass the book along there. But I wanted Mary Ann to have one.

"You live around here?" he asked.

"I used to," I said. "My parents do . . . well, my mom does."

My mom's house. Mom lives around here. I had to get used to saying that.

"Neighborhood's changed a lot," he said.

"Sure." I closed the trunk.

"Houses are rundown now. People don't take care of things."

"Well, thanks for your help," I said.

"My family used to shop here all the time when I was growing up."

I looked at him. "You mean at Goodwill?"

"No," he said. "I thought you grew up around here. Don't you remember the old IGA grocery store that used to be here?"

I looked at the building. It started to come back to me. There *was* a grocery store there when I was a kid, one we went to from time-to-time. To be accurate, I should say that my dad and I shopped there. Mom didn't like it. She felt it was too small, too narrow in its selection. It was possible the store closed and became a Goodwill all those years ago because a lot of people shared my mom's feelings. But Dad liked to go there. If Mom sent him out on some errand— buy a gallon of milk, buy a loaf of bread—or if he needed something for himself—shaving cream or a newspaper or—

He always looked at the books when we went into IGA. They had a long rack of paperback books and magazines near the front of the store, and we always stopped there before we checked out. And Dad always bought a book. A spy novel, a mystery, and, yes, a western. Did he think about his own writing when he stood in front of that rack? Did he think about what might have been if he hadn't given the whole thing up for Mom and me? He never showed anything. He always seemed perfectly content, but who knew what was really going on inside of him as he looked at all of those books?

"There's a parking lot behind here as well, right?" I asked.

"That's right."

"And it looks over the lot next door? There's a fence, and you can see down into the next lot? Right?"

The guy nodded. "That's right."

"You used to come here when you were a kid. I used to come with my dad. And you know what? He used to show me the horses back there."

"Horses?"

"Yes. There was an old, abandoned house next door. Apparently, the neighborhood wasn't always great. And out back of that house, someone kept a couple of horses. They just wandered around in the yard over there, cropping grass or whatever. Do you remember that?"

The guy ground out his cigarette and shook his head. "I don't remember any horses."

"They were there," I said.

"Could be," he said and then turned and went back inside.

But I remembered. I remembered it very clearly. Dad and I used to come to the IGA, and when we came out to go the car, he would turn to me and say, "Do you want to look at the horses?"

And I always said yes. I thought it was magic that Dad knew they were there. And how did he know I would want to see them?

Did he contemplate all the western stories he could have written— *should* have written—as he looked at those horses that seemed so out of place in the middle of that neighborhood? So lonely and forgotten?

I jumped in the car and drove around back. The parking lot looked pathetic, the asphalt cracked and stained. I drove over to the edge of the lot where the rusting and rickety chain-link fence still stood. I climbed out, taking one last look at that box of books. My dad's legacy. Besides me, the most lasting mark he made on the world.

I climbed out and walked over. I put my hands against the fence, felt the ragged and flaking metal beneath my hands. I searched.

The remains of the house had sunk into the ground. Nothing remained but a pile of boards and a crumbling chimney. And no matter how long or hard I looked, the horses, of course, were long, long gone.

XIV

The Caxton Library & Book Depository

John Connolly

1

L ET US BEGIN with this:
To those looking at his life from without, it would have seemed that Mr. Berger led a dull existence. In fact, Mr. Berger himself might well have concurred with this view.

He worked for the housing department of a minor English council, with the job title of "Closed Accounts Registrar." His task, from year to year, entailed compiling a list of those who had either relinquished or abandoned the housing provided for them by the council, and in doing so had left their accounts in arrears. Whether a week's rent was owed, or a month's, or even a year's (for evictions were a difficult business and had a habit of dragging on until relations between council and tenant came to resemble those between a besieging army and a walled city), Mr. Berger would record the sum in question in a massive leather bound ledger known as the Closed Accounts Register. At year's end, he would then be required to balance the rents received against the rents that should have been received. If he had performed his job correctly, the difference between the two sums would be the total amount contained in the register.

Even Mr. Berger found his job tedious to explain. Rare was it for a cab driver, or a fellow passenger on a train or bus, to engage in a discussion of Mr. Berger's livelihood for longer than it took for him to describe it. Mr. Berger didn't mind. He had no illusions about himself or his work. He got on perfectly well with his colleagues, and

was happy to join them for a pint of ale—but no more than that—
at the end of the week. He contributed to retirement gifts, and
wedding presents, and funeral wreaths. At one time it had seemed
that he himself might become the cause of one such collection, for
he entered into a state of cautious flirtation with a young woman in
accounts. His advances appeared to be reciprocated, and the couple
performed a mutual circling for the space of a year until someone
less inhibited than Mr. Berger entered the fray, and the young
woman, presumably weary of waiting for Mr. Berger to breach some
perceived exclusion zone around her person, went off with his rival
instead. It says much about Mr. Berger than he contributed to their
wedding collection without a hint of bitterness.

His position as registrar paid neither badly nor particularly well,
but enough to keep him clothed and fed, and maintain a roof above
his head. Most of the remainder went on books. Mr. Berger led a
life of the imagination, fed by stories. His flat was lined with shelves,
and those shelves were filled with the books that he loved. There
was no particular order to them. Oh, he kept the works of individual
authors together, but he did not alphabetize, and neither did he
congregate books by subject. He knew where to lay a hand on any
title at any time, and that was enough. Order was for dull minds,
and Mr. Berger was far less dull than he appeared (to those who
are themselves unhappy, the contentment of others can sometimes
be mistaken for tedium). Mr. Berger might sometimes have been
a little lonely, but he was never bored, and never unhappy, and he
counted his days by the books that he read.

I suppose that, in telling this tale, I have made Mr. Berger sound
old. He was not. He was thirty-five and, although in no danger
of being mistaken for a matinée idol, was not unattractive. Yet
perhaps there was in his interiority something that rendered him,
if not sexless, then somewhat oblivious to the reality of relations
with the opposite sex, an impression strengthened by the collective
memory of what had occurred—or not occurred—with the girl

from accounts. So it was that Mr. Berger found himself consigned to the dusty ranks of the council's spinsters and bachelors, to the army of the closeted, the odd, and the sad, although he was none of these things. Well, perhaps just a little of the latter: although he never spoke of it, or even fully admitted it to himself, he regretted his failure to express properly his affection for the girl in accounts, and had quietly resigned himself to the possibility that a life shared with another might not be in his stars. Slowly he was becoming a kind of fixed object, and the books he read came to reflect his view of himself. He was not a great lover, and neither was he a tragic hero. Instead he resembled those narrators in fiction who observe the lives of others, existing as dowels upon which plots hang like coats until the time comes for the true actors of the book to assume them. Great and voracious reader that he was, Mr. Berger failed to realize that the life he was observing was his own.

In the autumn of 1968, on Mr. Berger's thirty-sixth birthday, the council announced that it was moving offices. Its various departments had until then been scattered like outposts throughout the city, but it now made more sense to gather them all into one purpose-built environment and sell the outlying buildings. Mr. Berger was saddened by this development. The housing department occupied a set of ramshackle offices in a redbrick edifice that had once been a private school, and there was a pleasing oddness to the manner in which it had been imperfectly adapted to its current role. The council's new headquarters, meanwhile, was a brutalist block designed by one of those acolytes of Le Corbusier whose vision consisted solely of purging the individual and eccentric and replacing it with a uniformity of steel, glass and reinforced concrete. It squatted on the site of what had once been the city's glorious Victorian railway station, itself now replaced by a squat bunker. In time, Mr. Berger knew, the rest of the city's jewels would also be turned to dust, and the ugliness of the built environment would poison the population, for how could it be otherwise?

Mr. Berger was informed that, under the new regimen, there would be no more need for a Closed Accounts Register, and he would be transferred to other duties. A new, more efficient system was to be put in place, although, as with so many other such initiatives, it would later be revealed that it was less efficient, and more costly, than the original. This news coincided with the death of Mr. Berger's elderly mother, his last surviving close relative, and the discovery of a small but significant bequest to her son: her house, some shares, and a sum of money that was not quite a fortune but would, if invested carefully, enable Mr. Berger to live in a degree of restrained comfort for the rest of his life. He had always had a hankering to write, and he now had the perfect opportunity to test his literary mettle.

So it was that Mr. Berger at last had a collection taken up in his name, and a small crowd gathered to bid him farewell and good luck, and he was forgotten almost as soon as he was gone.

2

Mr. Berger's mother had spent her declining years in a cottage on the outskirts of the small town of Glossom. It was one of those passingly pretty English settlements, best suited to those whose time on this earth was drawing slowly to a close, and who wanted to spend it in surroundings that were unlikely to unduly excite them, and thereby hasten the end. Its community was predominantly High Anglican, with a corresponding focus on parish-centered activities: rarely an evening went by without the church hall being occupied by amateur dramatists, or local historians, or quietly concerned Fabians.

It seemed, though, that Mr. Berger's mother had rather kept herself to herself, and few eyebrows were raised in Glossom when her son chose to do the same. He spent his days outlining his proposed work of fiction, a novel of frustrated love and muted social commentary set among the woolen mills of Lancashire in the nineteenth century.

It was, Mr. Berger quickly realized, the kind of book of which the Fabians might have approved, which put something of a dampener on his progress. He dallied with some short stories instead, and when they proved similarly unrewarding he fell back on poetry, the last resort of the literary scoundrel. Finally, if only to keep his hand in, he began writing letters to the newspapers on matters of national and international concern. One, on the subject of badgers, was printed in the *Telegraph*, but it was heavily cut for publication, and Mr. Berger felt that it made him sound somewhat obsessive about badgers when nothing could be further from the truth.

It began to dawn on Mr. Berger that he might not be cut out for the life of a writer, gentleman or otherwise, and perhaps there were those who should simply be content to read. Once he had reached this conclusion, it was as though a great weight had fallen from his shoulders. He packed away the expensive writer's notebooks that he had purchased from Smythson's of Mayfair, and their weight in his pocket was replaced by the latest volume of Anthony Powell's roman fleuve, *A Dance to the Music of Time*.

In the evenings, Mr. Berger was in the habit of taking a walk by the railway line. A disused path, not far from the back gate of his cottage, led through a forest and thus to the raised bank on which the railway ran. Until recently, trains had stopped four times daily at Glossom, but the Beeching cuts had led to the closure of the station. Trains still used the lines, a noisy reminder of what had been lost, but soon even the sound of them would disappear as routes were reorganized. Eventually, the lines through Glossom would become overgrown, and the station would fall into disrepair. There were those in Glossom who had suggested buying it from British Railways and turning it into a museum, although they were unclear as to what exactly might be put in such a museum, the history of Glossom being distinctly lacking in battles, royalty, or great inventors.

None of this concerned Mr. Berger. It was enough that he had a pleasant place in which to walk or, if the weather was conducive, to sit by the lines and read. There was a stile not far from the old station, and he liked to wait there for the passing of the last train south. He would watch the businessmen in their suits flash by, and experience a surge of gratitude that his working life had reached a premature but welcome end.

Now, as winter began to close in, he still took his evening strolls, but the fading of the light and the growing chill in the air meant that he did not pause to take time with his book. Nevertheless, he always carried a volume with him, for it had become his habit to read for an hour at the Spotted Frog over a glass of wine or a pint of mild.

On the evening in question, Mr. Berger had paused as usual to wait for the train. It was, he noticed, running a little late. It had begun to do so more and more of late, which led him to wonder if all of this rationalization was really leading to any kind of improvements at all. He lit his pipe and looked to the west to witness the sun setting behind the woods, the last traces of it like flames upon the denuded branches of the trees.

It was at this point that he noticed a woman passing through the overgrown bushes a little further down the line. He had noticed before a trail of sorts there, for the branches of shrubs had been broken in places, but it was a poor substitute for his own path, and he had no desire to damage his clothing or his skin on briars. The woman was dressed in a dark dress, but what caught Berger's eye was the little red bag that she carried on her arm. It seemed in such stark contrast to the rest of her attire. He tried to see her face, but the angle of her progress concealed it from him.

At that moment he heard a distant whistle, and the stile beneath him started to vibrate. The express, the last train of the evening, was approaching. He could see its lights through the trees as it came. He looked again to his right. The woman had stopped, for she too had heard the train. Mr. Berger expected her to pause and wait for it to pass, but she did not. Instead she hastened her steps. Perhaps she wishes to be across the lines before it comes, thought Mr. Berger, but that was a risky business. It was easy to misjudge distances under such circumstances, and he had heard tales of those who had caught a foot on a sleeper, or stumbled while rushing, and the train had been the end of them.

"Ho!" he called. "Wait!"

Instinctively he stepped down from the stile and walked quickly towards her. The woman turned at the sound of his voice. Even from a distance, Mr. Berger could see that she was beautiful. Her face was pale, but she did not seem distressed. There was about her an eerie, unsettling calm.

"Don't try to cross!" he shouted. "Let the train pass."

The woman emerged from the bushes. She hitched up her skirts, showing a pair of laced ankle boots and a hint of stocking, and proceeded to climb up the embankment. Now Mr. Berger was running, but he continued to call to her, even as the express grew louder behind him before passing him in a flash of noise and light and diesel. His saw the woman cast aside her red bag, draw her head between her shoulders and, with her arms outstretched, throw herself on her knees before the train.

Mr. Berger flinched. The angle of the line meant that he did not witness the moment of impact, and any sounds of distress were lost in the roar of the engine. When he opened his eyes, the woman was gone and the train was continuing on its way.

Mr. Berger ran to the spot at which he had last seen the woman. He steeled himself for the worst, expecting to see the track mired with gore and body parts, but there was nothing. He had no experience of such matters, though, and had no idea whether a train striking a person at such a speed would leave a great mess or none at all. It was possible that the force of it had sent fragments of the woman in all directions, or even that it had carried her broken frame further down the track. After searching the bushes by the point of impact he followed the line for a time, but found no blood, and no sign of a body. He could not even find the woman's discarded red bag. Still, he had seen her, of that he had no doubt. He had not imagined it.

He was now closer to the town than he was to his home. There was no police station in Glossom, but there was one in Moreham, some five miles away. Mr. Berger walked quickly to the public telephone at the old station house, and from there he called the police and told them of what he had witnessed. Then, as instructed, he sat on the bench outside the station and waited for the patrol car to arrive.

3

The police did much the same as Mr. Berger had done, only with greater numbers and at greater expense in man-hours and overtime payments. They searched the bushes and the tracks, and enquiries were made in Glossom in case any female residents had gone missing. The driver of the train was contacted, and the train was kept on the platform at Plymouth for an hour while its engine and carriages were examined for any sign of human remains.

Finally Mr. Berger, who had remained seated on his stile throughout, was interviewed for a second time by the inspector from Moreham. His name was Carswell, and his manner when he confronted Mr. Berger was colder than it had originally been. A light rain had begun to fall shortly after the search for a body had commenced, and Carswell and his men were now damp and weary. Mr. Berger was also wet, and found that he had developed a slight but constant shiver. He suspected that he might be in shock. He had never witnessed the death of another person before. It had affected him deeply.

Now Inspector Carswell stood before him, his hat jammed on his head and his hands thrust deep in the pockets of his coat. His men were packing up, and a pair of dogs that had been brought in to help with the search was being led back to the van in which they had arrived. The townspeople who had gathered to watch were also drifting away, but not without a final curious glance at the figure of Mr. Berger.

"Let's go through it again, shall we?" said Carswell, and Mr. Berger told his story one last time. The details remained the same. He was certain of what he had witnessed.

"I have to tell you," said Carswell, when Mr. Berger had finished speaking, "that the driver of the train saw nothing, and was unaware of any impact. As you can imagine, he was quite shocked to hear that a woman had been reported as throwing herself under his wheels. He aided in the examination of the train himself. It turns out that he has some unfortunate experience of such matters. Before he was promoted to driver, he was a fireman on an engine that struck a man near Coleford Junction. He told us that the driver saw the man on the rails but couldn't brake in time. The engine made a terrible mess of the poor fellow, he said. There was no mistaking what had happened. He seems to think that, if he had somehow hit a woman without knowing, we'd have no trouble finding her remains."

Carswell lit a cigarette. He offered one to Mr. Berger, who declined. He preferred his pipe, even though it had long since gone out.

"Do you live alone, sir?" asked Carswell.

"Yes, I do."

"From what I understand, you moved to Glossom fairly recently."

"That's correct. My mother died, and she left me her cottage."

"And you say that you're a writer?"

"Trying to be a writer. I've started to wonder if I'm really destined to be any good at it, to be honest."

"Solitary business, writing, or so I would imagine."

"It does tend to be, yes."

"You're not married?"

"No."

"Girlfriend?"

"No," said Mr. Berger, then added "Not at the moment."

He didn't want Inspector Carswell to think that there might be anything odd or unsavory about his bachelor existence.

"Ah."

Carswell drew deeply on his cigarette.

"Do you miss her?"

"Miss who?"

"Your mother."

Mr. Berger considered it an odd question to ask, but answered nonetheless.

"Of course," he said. "I would visit her when I could, and we spoke on the telephone once a week."

Carswell nodded, as if this explained a lot.

"Must be strange, coming to a new town, and living in the house in which your mother died. She passed away at home, didn't she?"

Mr. Berger thought that Inspector Carswell seemed to know a lot about his mother. Clearly he had not just been asking about a missing woman during his time in Glossom.

"Yes, she did," he replied. "Forgive me, Inspector, but what has this got to do with the death of this young woman?"

Carswell took the cigarette from his mouth and examined the burning tip, as though some answer might be found in the ash.

"I'm beginning to wonder if you might not have been mistaken in what you saw," he said.

"Mistaken? How can one be mistaken about a suicide?"

"There is no body, sir. There's no blood, no clothing, nothing. We haven't even been able to find the red bag that you mentioned. There's no sign that anything untoward happened on the track at all. So . . ."

Carswell took one last drag on his cigarette, then dropped it on the dirt and ground it out forcefully with the heel of his shoe.

"Let's just say that you were mistaken, and leave it at that, shall we? Perhaps you might like to find some other way to occupy your evenings, now that winter is setting in. Join the bridge club, or take up singing in the choir. You might even find a young lady to walk out with. What I'm saying is, you've had a traumatic time of it, and it would be good for you not to spend so much time alone. That way, you'll avoid making mistakes of this nature again. You do understand me, don't you sir?"

The implication was clear. Being mistaken was not a crime, but wasting police time was. Mr. Berger climbed down from the stile.

"I know what I saw, Inspector," he said, but it was all that he could do to keep the doubt from creeping into his voice, and his mind was troubled as he took the path back to his little cottage.

4

It should come as no surprise to learn that Mr. Berger slept little that night. Over and over he replayed the scene of the woman's demise, and although he had neither witnessed nor heard the impact, still he saw and heard it in the silence of the bedroom. To calm himself, he had taken a large glass of his late mother's brandy upon his arrival home, but he was not used to spirits and the alcohol sat ill with him. He grew delirious in his bed, and so often did the woman's death play out before him that he began to believe that this evening was not the first time he had been present at her passing. A peculiar sense of déjà vu overcame him, one that he was entirely unable to shrug off. Sometimes, when he was ill or feverish, a tune or song would lodge itself in his mind. So entrenched would its hooks become that it would keep him from sleep, and he would be unable to exorcise it until the sickness had passed. Now he was having the same experience with his vision of the woman's death, and its repetitive nature was leading him to believe that he had already been familiar with the scene before he was present at it.

At last, thankfully, weariness overcame him and he was able to rest, but when he woke the next morning that nagging feeling of familiarity remained. He put on his coat and returned to the scene of the previous evening's excitement. He walked the rough trail, hoping to find something that the police might have missed, a sign that he had not been the victim of an overactive imagination—a scrap of black cloth, the heel of a shoe, or the red bag—but there was nothing.

It was the red bag that bothered him most of all. The red bag was the thing. With his mind unfogged by alcohol—although, in truth, his head still swam slightly in the aftermath—he grew more and more certain that the suicide of the young woman reminded him of a scene in a book: no, not just a scene, but perhaps *the* most famous scene of locomotive-based self-immolation in literature. He gave up on his physical search, and decided to embark on a more literary one.

He had long ago unpacked his books, although he had not yet found shelves for them all, his mother's love of reading not matching his own, and thus leading to her preference for large swathes of bare wall that she had seen fit to adorn only with cheap reproductions of sea views. There was still more room for his volumes than there had been in his own lodgings, due in no small part to the fact that the cottage had more floor space than his flat, and all a true bibliophile needs for his storage purposes is a horizontal plane. He found his copy of *Anna Karenina* sandwiched in a pile on the dining room floor between *War & Peace* and *Master and Man and Other Parables and Tales*, the latter in a nice Everyman's Library edition from 1946 about which he had forgotten, and which almost led him to set aside *Anna Karenina* in favor of a hour or so in its company. Good sense quickly prevailed, although not before he had set *Master and Man* on the dining table for further examination at a more convenient time. There it joined a dozen similarly blessed volumes, all of which had been waiting for days or weeks for their hour to come at last.

He sat in an armchair and opened *Anna Karenina* (Limited Editions Club, Cambridge, 1951, signed by Barnett Freedman, unearthed at a jumble sale in Gloucester and acquired for such a low price that Mr. Berger had later made a donation to charity in order to salve his conscience). He flipped through the pages until he found Chapter XXXI, which began with the words "A bell sounded . . ." From there he read on quickly but carefully, travelling with Anna past Piotr in his livery and top-boots, past the saucy conductor and the woman deformed, past the dirty hunchback *muzhik* until finally he came to this passage:

She was going to throw herself under the first car as its center came opposite where she stood. Her little red travelling-bag caused her to lose the moment; she could not detach it from her arm. She awaited the second. A feeling like that she had experienced once, just before taking a dive in the river, came over her, and she made the sign of the cross. This familiar gesture called back to her soul a whole series of memories of her youth and childhood; and suddenly the darkness which hid every-thing from her was torn asunder. Life, with its elusive joys, glowed for an instant before her. But she did not take her eyes from the car; and when the center, between the two wheels, appeared, she threw away her red bag, drawing her head between her shoulders, and, with outstretched hands, threw herself on her knees under the car. For a second she was horror-struck at what she was doing.

"Where am I? What am I doing? Why?"

She tried to get up, to draw back; but something monstrous, inflexible, struck her head, and threw her on her back.

"Lord, forgive me all!" she murmured, feeling the struggle to be in vain.

A little muzhik *was working on the railroad, mumbling in his beard.*

And the candle by which she had read the book that was filled with fears, with deceptions, with anguish, and with evil, flared up with greater brightness than she had ever known, revealing to her all that before was in darkness, then flickered, grew faint, and went out forever.

Mr. Berger read the passage twice, then leaned back in his chair and closed his eyes. It was all there, right down to the detail of the little red bag, the bag that the woman on the tracks had cast aside before the express had hit her, just as Anna had thrown away her bag before she was struck. The woman's gestures in her final moments had also been similar to Anna's: she too had drawn her head between her shoulders and stretched out her arms, as though the death to come was to take the form of crucifixion rather than iron and wheels. Why, even Mr. Berger's own memory of the incident had been couched in similar phrases.

"My God," said Mr. Berger to the listening books, "perhaps the inspector was right and I have been spending too much time alone with only novels for company. There can be no other excuse for a man believing that he has seen the climactic scene of *Anna Karenina* reenacted on the Exeter to Plymouth railway."

He placed the volume on the arm of the chair and went to the kitchen. He was briefly tempted to reach for the brandy again, but no particular good had come of their previous shared moments, and so he opted for the routine of making a big pot of tea. When all was in place, he took a seat at the kitchen table and drank cup after cup until he had drained the pot dry. For once he did not read, nor did he distract himself with the *Times* crossword, still left untried at this late stage of the morning. He simply stared at the clouds, and listened to birdsong, and wondered if he was not, after all, going gently insane.

Mr. Berger did not read anything else that day. His two examinations of Chapter XXXI of *Anna Karenina* remained his sole contact with the world of literature. He could not recall a day when he had read less. He lived for books. They had consumed every spare moment since the revelation in childhood that he could tackle a novel alone without his mother having to read it to him. He recalled his first halting encounters with the Biggles stories of W.E. Johns, remembering how he had struggled through the longer words by breaking them up into their individual syllables, so that one difficult word became two easier ones. Ever since then, books had been his constant companions. He had, perhaps, sacrificed real friendships to these simulacra, because there were days when he had avoided his chums after school or ignored their knocking on his front door when his parents' house was otherwise empty, taking an alternative route home or staying away from the windows so that he could be sure that no football game or exploration of orchards would get in the way of finishing the story that had gripped him.

In a way, books had also been partly responsible for his fatal tentativeness with the girl from accounts. She seemed to read a little—he had seen her with a Georgette Heyer novel, and the occasional "book in brown" from the two-penny library—but he had the sense that it was not a passion with her. What if she insisted that they spend hours at the theater, or the ballet, or shopping, simply because it meant that they would be "doing things together"? That was, after all, what couples did, wasn't it? But reading was a solitary pursuit. Oh, one could read in the same room as someone else, or beside them in bed at night, but that rather presumed that an agreement had been reached about such matters, and the couple in question consisted of a pair of like-minded souls. It would be a disaster to find oneself embroiled with the sort of person who read two pages of a novel and then began humming, or tapping her fingers to attract attention, or, God help us, started fiddling with the dial on the radio. The next thing one knew, she'd be making "observations" on the text in hand, and once that happened there would be no peace for ever after.

But as he sat alone in the kitchen of his deceased mother's house, it struck Mr. Berger that he had never troubled himself to find out the views of the girl in accounts on the subject of books or, indeed, ballet. Deep inside, he had been reluctant to disturb his ordered lifestyle, a world in which he rarely had to make a more difficult decision than selecting the next book to read. He had lived his life as one removed from the world around him, and now he was paying the price in madness.

5

In the days that followed, Mr. Berger subsisted largely on newspapers and magazines of an improving nature. He had almost convinced himself that what he had seen on the tracks employed by the locomotives of the London and South Western Railway was a psychological anomaly, some form of delayed reaction to the grief he had experienced at his mother's death. He noticed that he was the object of peculiar looks, both poorly concealed and unashamedly open, as he went about his business in the town, but that was to be expected. He did hope that the town's memory of the unproductive police search might fade eventually. He had no desire to be elevated to the role of local eccentric.

But as time wore on, something odd happened. It is usually in the manner of experiences such as Mr. Berger's that, as distance grows from the event in question, so too the memory of it becomes foggier. Mr. Berger should, if the ordinary rules of behavior were being obeyed, have become ever more certain of the psychologically troubling nature of his encounter with the young woman reminiscent of Anna Karenina. But Mr. Berger found himself believing with greater and greater conviction that the opposite was true. He had seen the woman, and she was real, admittedly allowing for a certain latitude in one's definition of reality.

He began reading again, tentatively at first, but soon with his previous immersion. He also returned to walking the path that wound down to the railway line, and sitting on his stile to watch the trains go by. Each evening, with the approach of the train from Exeter to Plymouth, he would set aside his book, and watch the rougher trail to the south. It was darker now, and the trail was harder to see, but Mr. Berger's eyes were still keen, and through habit he grew practiced at picking out the difference in the density of the bushes.

But the trail remained undisturbed until February came, and the woman returned.

6

It was a cold but bracing evening. There was no damp in the air, and Mr. Berger enjoyed the sight of his breath pluming as he took his evening constitutional. There was music in the Spotted Frog that evening: some form of folk revivalism, for which Mr. Berger had a sneaking fondness. He intended to drop in for an hour or two, once he had watched the train go by. His vigil at the stile had become something of a ritual for him, and although he told himself that it was no longer connected to the business of the woman with the red bag, he secretly knew that it was. He was haunted by the image of her.

He took his seat on the stile, and lit his pipe. From somewhere to the east, he heard the sound of the approaching train. He glanced at his watch, and saw that it was just after six. The train was early. This was unheard of. If he had still been in the habit of writing letters to the *Telegraph*, he might well have popped off a missive announcing this turn-up for the books, much in the manner of those twitchers who liked to let the populace know of the appearance of the first cuckoo of spring.

He was already composing the letter in his head when he was distracted by a commotion to his right. Someone was coming down the trail, and in some hurry. Mr. Berger dropped from the stile and began walking in the direction of the sounds. The sky was clear, and the moon was already silvering the undergrowth, but even without the aid of its light Mr. Berger would have been able to pick out the woman rushing to meet the train, and the red bag that hung from her arm.

Mr. Berger dropped his pipe, but managed to retrieve it. It was, after all, a good pipe.

While it would not be untrue to say that he had become obsessed with the woman, he had no real expectation of ever seeing her again. After all, people did not make a habit of throwing themselves under trains. It was the kind of act that tended to be performed once, or not at all. In the case of the former, any possible repeat of the incident was likely to be ruled out by the action of a heavy engine or, in the unlikely event of survival, sufficient recall of the painfulness of the first attempt to render most unwelcome any further repetition of it. Yet here, without a shadow of a doubt, was the same young woman carrying the same red bag and making the same rush towards self-destruction that Mr. Berger had previously witnessed.

It must be a ghost, thought Mr. Berger. There can be no other explanation. This is the spirit of some poor woman who died some time ago—for he saw that her clothing was not of this century—and she is doomed to repeat her final moments over and over until—

Until what? Mr. Berger wasn't certain. He had read his share of M.R. James and W.W. Jacobs, of Oliver Onions and William Hope Hodgson, but had never come across anything quite like this in their stories. He had a vague notion that digging up a forgotten corpse and reburying it in a more appropriate location sometimes helped, while James tended to favor restoring ancient artifacts to their previous resting place, thereby calming the spirits associated with them, but Mr. Berger had no idea where the young woman might be interred, and he had not picked so much as a flower while on his walks, let alone some old whistle or manuscript. All of this would have to be dealt with later, he realized. There was more important business to attend to.

The early arrival of the train had obviously caught the woman, spectral or otherwise, by surprise, and the branches seemed to be conspiring to keep her from her date with mortality. They caught at her dress, and at one point she took a tumble that sent her to her knees. Despite all of these hindrances, it was obvious to Mr. Berger that she was still likely to make it to the tracks in time to receive the full impact of the train.

Mr. Berger ran, and as he did so he screamed and shouted, and waved his arms. He ran faster than he had ever run before, so that he managed to reach the base of the trail some time before the woman did. She drew up short, seemingly surprised to see him. Perhaps she had been so intent on her own demise that she had failed to hear his cries, but she was now faced with the physical reality of Mr. Berger, and he with hers. She was younger than he, and her skin was unusually pale, although that might just have been the moonlight. Her hair was the blackest that Mr. Berger had ever seen. It seemed to consume the light.

The woman tried to dart to her right, and then to her left, to avoid Mr. Berger, but the bushes were too thick. He felt the ground vibrating, and the noise of the approaching train was deafeningly loud. He was aware of its whistle sounding. The driver had probably spotted him by the tracks. Mr. Berger raised his right hand and waved to let the driver know that all was okay. The woman was not going to get past him, and Mr. Berger had no intention of throwing himself under any trains.

The woman clenched her fists in frustration as the train rushed by. Mr. Berger turned his head to watch it go, some of the passengers staring at him curiously from the window, and when he looked back the woman was gone. It was only as the rattle of the train faded that he heard the sound of bushes rustling and knew that she was making her way back up the hill. He tried to follow, but the same branches that had previously hampered her progress now delayed his. His jacket was torn, he lost his pipe, and he even twisted his left ankle slightly on a root, but he did not give up. He reached the road just in time to see the woman slip into a laneway that ran parallel to Glossom's high street. The back gardens of a row of cottages lay on one side, and on the other the rear wall of what had once been the town's brewery but was now derelict and unused, although a faint smell of old hops still hung about it.

Eventually the laneway diverged, with the path to the left eventually connecting with the main street while the path to the right twisted into darkness. Mr. Berger could see no sign of the woman to his left, for the high street was well lit. He chose instead to go right, and was soon among the relics of Glossom's industrial past: old warehouses, some still in use but most abandoned; a wall that announced the presence of a combined cooperage and chandlery, while the decay of the building behind it left no doubt that it had been some time since either barrels or candles had emerged from within; and, finally, a two-storey redbrick building with barred windows and grass growing by its doorstep. Beyond it was a dead end. As he drew nearer, Mr. Berger could have sworn that he heard a door softly closing.

Mr. Berger stood before the building and stared up at it. There were no lights burning, and the windows were so encrusted with dirt and filth both inside and out that there was no possibility of catching a glimpse of its interior. A name was carved into the brickwork above the door. Mr. Berger had to strain his eyes to read it, for the moonlight seemed to have no desire to aid him here. At last he made out the words "Caxton Private Lending Library & Book Depository."

Mr. Berger frowned. He had made enquiries in the town as to whether there was a library and had been told that there was none, the nearest, as with so much else that Glossom lacked, being in Moreham. There was a newsagent that sold books, but they were mainly detective stories and romances, and there was a limit to how many of either Mr. Berger wished to read. It was, of course, entirely likely that the Caxton Private Lending Library & Book Depository was no longer in business, but if that was the case then why was the grass growing around its doorstep trampled flat in places? Someone was still entering and leaving it on a semi-regular basis, including, if Mr. Berger was not mistaken, a woman, or something phantasmagorical that resembled a woman, with an Anna Karenina fixation.

He took out his matchbook and lit a match. There was a yellowed sign behind a small pane of glass to the right of the door. It read: "For all enquiries, please ring bell." Mr. Berger used up three matches looking in vain for a bell of any kind. There was none. Neither was there a slot or box for mail.

Mr. Berger worked his way round the corner of the building to the right, for any progress to the left was barred by the wall. Here was a smaller laneway, but it ended in another brick wall, and there were no windows on that side of the building, nor was there a door. Behind the wall was a patch of waste ground.

Mr. Berger returned to the front door. He banged on it once with his fist, more in hope than expectation of an answer. He was unsurprised when none came. He examined the single keyhole. It did not look rusted, and when he put a finger to it, the digit came back moistened with a hint of lock oil. It was all most peculiar, and not a little sinister.

There was nothing else to be done for now, Mr. Berger thought. The night was growing steadily colder, and he had not yet eaten. Although Glossom was a quiet, safe town, he did not fancy spending a long night outside a darkened lending library in the hope that a spectral woman might emerge so he could ask her what she thought she was doing, throwing herself repeatedly under trains. There were also some nasty scratches on his hands that could do with a spot of antiseptic.

So, with one final look back at the Caxton Library, and more perturbed than ever, Mr. Berger returned home, and the Spotted Frog was deprived of his custom for that night.

7

Mr. Berger returned to the Caxton Library shortly after 10.00 A.M. the next morning, on the basis that this was a reasonably civilized hour at which to appear, and if the Caxton was still in business then it was likely that someone might be about at this time. The Caxton, though, remained as silent and forbidding as it had the previous evening.

With nothing better to do, Mr. Berger began making enquiries, but to no avail. General expressions of ignorance about the nature of the Caxton Private Lending Library & Book Depository were his sole reward at the newsagent, the local grocery, and even among the early arrivals at the Spotted Frog. Oh, people seemed to be aware that the Caxton existed, but nobody was able to recall a time when it was actually in business as a lending library, nor could anyone say who owned the building, or if any books still remained inside. It was suggested that he might try the town hall in Moreham, where the records for the smaller hamlets in the vicinity were kept.

So Mr. Berger got in his car and drove to Moreham. As he drove, he considered that there seemed to be a remarkable lack of interest in the Caxton Library among the townsfolk of Glossom. It was not merely that those to whom he spoke had forgotten about its existence until Mr. Berger brought it up, at which point some faint atavistic memory of the building was uncovered before promptly being buried again; that, at least, might be understandable if the library had not been in business for many years. What was more curious was that most people seemed to be entirely unaware of its existence, and didn't care very much to investigate further once it was brought to their attention. Glossom was a close-knit community, as Mr. Berger was only too well aware, for comments about hallucinations and train delays still followed him as he asked about the library. There appeared to be only two types of business in the town: everybody's business, and business that was not yet everybody's but soon would be once the local gossips had got to work on it. The older residents of the town could provide chapter and verse on its history back to the 16th century, and every building, old or recent, had its history.

All, that is, except the Caxton Private Lending Library.

The town hall in Moreham proved to be a source of little illumination on the matter. The library building was owned by the Caxton Trust, with an address at a P.O. Box in London. The Trust paid all bills relating to the property, including rates and electricity, and that was as much as Mr. Berger could find out about it. An enquiry at the library in Moreham was met with blank looks, and although he spent hours searching back issues of the local weekly paper, the *Moreham & Glossom Advertiser*, from the turn of the century onwards, he could find no reference to the Caxton Library anywhere.

It was already dark when he returned to his cottage. He cooked himself an omelette and tried to read, but he was distracted by the fact of the library's apparent simultaneous existence and non-existence. It was there. It occupied a space in Glossom. It was a considerable building. Why, then, had its presence in a small community passed relatively unnoticed and unremarked for so long?

The next day brought no more satisfaction. Calls to booksellers and libraries, including to the grand old London Library, and the Cranston Library in Reigate, the oldest lending library in the country, confirmed only a general ignorance of the Caxton. Finally, Mr. Berger found himself talking to the British representative of the Special Libraries Association, an organization of whose existence he had previously been unaware. She promised to search their records, but admitted that she had never heard of the Caxton and would be surprised if anyone else had either, given that her own knowledge of such matters was encyclopedic, a judgment that, after an hour-long history of libraries in England, Mr. Berger was unwilling to doubt.

Mr. Berger did consider that he might be mistaken about the woman's ultimate destination. There were other buildings in that part of town in which she could have hidden herself to escape his notice, but the Caxton was still the most likely place in which she might have sought refuge. Where else, he thought, would a woman intent upon repeatedly reenacting the final moments of Anna Karenina choose to hide but an old library?

He made his decision before he went to bed that night. He would become a detective of sorts, and stake out the Caxton Private Lending Library & Book Depository for as long as it took for it to reveal its secrets to him.

8

As Mr. Berger soon discovered, it was no easy business being a detective on a stakeout. It was all very well for those chaps in books who could sit in a car or a restaurant and make observations about the world in a degree of comfort, especially if they were in Los Angeles or somewhere else with a climate noted for warmth and sunlight. It was quite another thing to hang around among dilapidated buildings in a small English town on a cold, damp February day, hoping that nobody one knew happened by or, worse, some passing busybody didn't take it upon himself to phone the police and report a loiterer. Mr. Berger could just imagine Inspector Carswell smoking another cigarette and concluding that he now most definitely had some form of lunatic on his hands.

Thankfully, Mr. Berger found a sheltered space in the old cooperage and chandlery that afforded a view of the end of the laneway through a collapsed section of wall while allowing him to remain relatively concealed. He had brought a blanket, a cushion, a flask of tea, some sandwiches and chocolate, and two books, one of them a John Dickson Carr novel entitled *The Crooked Hinge*, just to enter into the spirit of the thing, and the other *Our Mutual Friend* by Charles Dickens, the only Dickens he had yet to read. *The Crooked Hinge* turned out to be rather good, if a little fantastical. Then again,

Mr. Berger considered, a tale of witchcraft and automatons was hardly more outlandish than apparently witnessing the same woman attempt suicide twice, the first time successfully and the second time less so.

The day passed without incident. There was no activity in the laneway, the rustle of the odd rat apart. Mr. Berger finished the Dickson Carr and started the Dickens, which, being the author's last completed novel, meant that it was mature Dickens, and hence rather difficult by the standards of *Oliver Twist* or *The Pickwick Papers*, and requiring considerably more patience and attention. When the light began to fade, Mr. Berger set aside the book, unwilling to risk drawing attention by using a torch, and waited another hour in the hope that darkness might bring with it some activity at the Caxton Library. No illumination showed in the old building, and Mr. Berger eventually gave up the watch for the night, and took himself to the Spotted Frog for a hot meal and a restorative glass of wine.

His vigil recommenced early the next morning, although he chose to alternate Dickens with Wodehouse. Once again, the day passed with little excitement, the appearance of a small terrier dog apart. The dog began yapping at Mr. Berger, who shooed it ineffectually until its owner gave a shrill whistle from nearby and the dog departed. Still, the day was warmer than the one before, which was a small blessing: Mr. Berger had woken that morning with stiff limbs, and had determined to wear two overcoats if the new day proved as chilly as the last.

Darkness started to descend, and with it doubts on the part of Mr. Berger about the wisdom of his course of action. He couldn't hang around laneways indefinitely. It was unseemly. He leaned into a corner and found himself starting to doze. He dreamed of lights in the Caxton Library, and a train that rolled down the laneway, its complement of passengers consisting entirely of dark-haired ladies carrying small red bags, all of them steeling themselves for self-destruction. Finally he dreamed of footsteps on gravel and grass, but when he woke he could still hear the footsteps. Someone was coming. Tentatively he rose from his resting place and peered at the library. There was a figure on its doorstep carrying what looked like a carpet bag, and he heard the rattle of keys.

Instantly Mr. Berger was on his feet. He climbed through the gap in the wall and emerged into the laneway. An elderly man was standing before the door of the Caxton Library, his key already turning in the lock. He was shorter than average, and wore a long grey overcoat and a trilby hat with a white feather in the band. A remarkable silver handlebar mustache adorned his upper lip. He looked at Mr. Berger with some alarm and hurriedly opened the door.

"Wait!" said Mr. Berger. "I have to talk to you."

The old gent was clearly in no mood to talk. The door was wide open now, and he was already inside when he realized that he had forgotten his carpet bag, which remained on the ground. He reached for it, but Mr. Berger got there at the same time, and an unseemly tug-of-war began with each man holding on to one of the straps.

"Hand it over!" said the old man.

"No," said Mr. Berger. "I want to talk with you."

"You'll have to make an appointment. You'll need to telephone in advance."

"There's no number. You're not listed."

"Then send a letter."

"You don't have a postbox."

"Look, you must come back tomorrow and ring the bell."

"There is no bell!" shouted Mr. Berger, his frustration getting the better of him as his voice jumped an octave. He gave a final hard yank on the bag and won the struggle, leaving only a handle in the grip of the old man.

"Oh, bother!" said the old man. He looked wistfully at his bag, which Mr. Berger was clutching to his chest. "I suppose you'd better come in, then, but you can't stay long. I'm a very busy man."

He stepped back, inviting Mr. Berger to enter. Now that the opportunity had at last presented itself, that worthy gentleman experienced a twinge of concern. The interior of the Caxton Library looked very dark, and who knew what might be waiting inside? He was throwing himself at the mercy of a possible madman, armed only with a hostage carpet bag. But he had come this far in his investigation, and he required an answer of some sort if he was ever to have peace of mind again. Still holding on to the carpet bag as though it were a swaddled infant, he stepped into the library.

9

Lights came on. They were dim, and the illumination they offered had a touch of jaundice to it, but they revealed lines of shelves stretching off into the distance, and that peculiar musty smell distinctive to rooms in which books are aging like fine wines. To his left was an oak counter, and behind it cubbyholes filled with paperwork that appeared not to have been touched in many years, for a fine film of dust lay over it all. Beyond the counter was an open door, and through it Mr. Berger could see a small living area with a television, and the edge of a bed in an adjoining room.

The old gent removed his hat, and his coat and scarf, and hung them on a hook by the door. Beneath them he was wearing a dark suit of considerable vintage, a white shirt, and a very wide gray-and-white striped tie. He looked rather dapper, in a slightly decaying way. He waited patiently for Mr. Berger to begin, which Mr. Berger duly did.

"Look," said Mr. Berger, "I won't have it. I simply won't."

"Won't have what?"

"Women throwing themselves under trains, then coming back and trying to do it again. It's just not on. Am I making myself clear?"

The elderly gentleman frowned. He tugged at one end of his mustache and sighed deeply.

"May I have my bag back, please?" he asked.

Mr. Berger handed it over, and the old man stepped behind the counter and placed the bag in the living room before returning. By this time, though, Mr. Berger, in the manner of bibliophiles everywhere, had begun to examine the contents of the nearest shelf. The shelves were organized alphabetically, and by chance Mr. Berger had started on the letter 'D'. He discovered an incomplete collection of Dickens' work, seemingly limited to the best known of the writer's works. *Our Mutual Friend* was conspicuously absent, but *Oliver Twist* was present, as were *David Copperfield*, *A Tale of Two Cities*, *Pickwick Papers*, and a handful of others. All of the editions looked very old. He took *Oliver Twist* from the shelf and examined its points. It was bound in brown cloth with gilt lettering and bore the publisher's imprint at the foot of the spine. The title page attributed the work to Boz, not Charles Dickens, indicating a very early edition, a fact confirmed by the date of publisher and date of publication: Richard Bentley, London, 1838. Mr. Berger was holding the first edition, first issue, of the novel.

"Please be careful with that," said the old gent, who was hovering nervously nearby, but Mr. Berger had already replaced *Oliver Twist* and was now examining *A Tale of Two Cities*, perhaps his favorite novel by Dickens: Chapman & Hall, 1859, original red cloth. It was another first edition.

But it was the volume marked *Pickwick Papers* that contained the greatest surprise. It was oversized, and contained within it not a published copy but a manuscript. Mr. Berger knew that most of Dickens' manuscripts were held by the Victoria & Albert Museum as part of the Forster Collection, for he had seen them when they were last on display. The rest were held by the British Library, the Wisbech Museum, and the Morgan Library in New York. Fragments of *Pickwick Papers* formed part of the collection of the New York Public Library, but as far as Mr. Berger was aware, there was no complete manuscript of the book anywhere.

Except, it seemed, in the Caxton Private Lending Library & Book Depository of Glossom, England.

"Is it—?" said Mr. Berger. "I mean, can it—?"

The old gentleman gently removed the volume from Mr. Berger's hands and placed it back in its place on the shelf.

"Indeed," said the gentleman.

He was looking at Mr. Berger a little more thoughtfully than before, as though his visitor's obvious appreciation for the books had prompted a reassessment of his probable character.

"It's in rather good company as well," he said.

He gestured expansively at the rows of shelves. They stretched into the gloom, for the yellow lights had not come on in the farther reaches of the library. There were also doors leading off to the left and right. They were set into the main walls, but Mr. Berger had seen no doors when he had first examined the building. They could have been bricked up, but he had seen no evidence of that either.

"Are they all first editions?" he asked.

"First editions, or manuscript copies. First editions are fine for our purposes, though. Manuscripts are merely a bonus."

"I should like to look, if you don't mind," said Mr. Berger. "I won't touch any more of them. I'd just like to see them."

"Later, perhaps," said the gent. "You still haven't told me why you're here."

Mr. Berger swallowed hard. He had not spoken aloud of his encounters since the unfortunate conversation with Inspector Carswell on that first night.

"Well," he said, "I saw a woman commit suicide in front of a train, and then some time later I saw her try to do the same thing again, but I stopped her. I thought she might have come in here. In fact, I'm almost certain that she did."

"That is unusual," said the gent.

"That's what I thought," said Mr. Berger.

"And do you have any idea of this woman's identity?"

"Not exactly," said Mr. Berger.

"Would you care to speculate?"

"It will seem odd."

"No doubt."

"You may think me mad."

"My dear fellow, we hardly know each other. I wouldn't dare to make such a judgment until we were better acquainted."

Which seemed fair enough to Mr. Berger. He had come this far: he might as well finish the journey.

"It did strike me that she might be Anna Karenina." At the last minute, Mr. Berger hedged his bets. "Or a ghost, although she did appear remarkably solid for a spirit."

"She wasn't a ghost," said the gent.

"No, I didn't really believe so. There was the issue of her substantiality. I suppose you'll tell me now that she wasn't Anna Karenina either."

The old gent tugged at his mustache again. His face was betrayed his thoughts as he carried on an internal debate with himself.

Finally, he said "No, in all conscience I could not deny that she is Anna Karenina."

Mr. Berger leaned in closer, and lowered his voice significantly. "Is she a loony? You know . . . someone who thinks that she's Anna Karenina?"

"No. You're the one who thinks that she's Anna Karenina, but she *knows* that she's Anna Karenina."

"What?" said Mr. Berger, somewhat thrown by the reply. "So you mean she *is* Anna Karenina? But Anna Karenina is simply a character in a book by Tolstoy. She isn't real."

"But you just told me that she was."

"No, I told you that the woman I saw *seemed* real."

"And that you thought she might be Anna Karenina."

"Yes, but you see, it's all very well saying that to oneself, or even presenting it as a possibility, but one does so in the hope that a more rational explanation might present itself."

"But there isn't a more rational explanation, is there?"

"There might be," said Mr. Berger. "I just can't think of one at present."

Mr. Berger was starting to feel light-headed.

"Would you like a cup of tea?" said the old gent.

"Yes," said Mr. Berger, "I rather think I would."

10

They sat in the gentleman's living room, drinking tea from china cups and eating some fruitcake that he kept in a tin. A fire had been lit, and a lamp burned in a corner. The walls were decorated with oils and watercolors, all of them very fine and very old. The style of a number of them was familiar to Mr. Berger. He wouldn't have liked to swear upon it, but he was fairly sure that there was at least one Turner, a Constable, and two Romneys, a portrait and a landscape, among their number.

The old gentleman had introduced himself as Mr. Gedeon, and he had been the librarian at the Caxton for more than forty years. His job, he informed Mr. Berger, was "to maintain and, as required, increase the collection; to perform restorative work on the volumes where necessary; and, of course, to look after the characters."

It was this last phrase that made Mr. Berger choke slightly on his tea.

"The characters?" he said.

"The characters," confirmed Mr. Gedeon.

"What characters?"

"The characters from the novels."

"You mean: they're alive?"

Mr. Berger was beginning to wonder not only about his own sanity but that of Mr. Gedeon as well. He felt as though he had wandered into some strange bibliophilic nightmare. He kept hoping that he would wake up at home with a headache to find that he had been inhaling gum from one of his own volumes.

"You saw one of them," said Mr. Gedeon.

"Well, I saw someone," said Mr. Berger. "I mean, I've seen chaps dressed up as Napoleon at parties, but I didn't go home thinking I'd met Napoleon."

"We don't have Napoleon," said Mr. Gedeon.

"No?"

"No. Only fictional characters here. It gets a little complicated with Shakespeare, I must admit. That's caused us some problems. The rules aren't hard and fast. If they were, this whole business would run a lot more smoothly. But then, literature isn't a matter of rules, is it? Think how dull it would be if it was, eh?"

Mr. Berger peered into his teacup, as though expecting the arrangement of the leaves to reveal the truth of things. When they did not, he put the cup down, clasped his hands, and resigned himself to whatever was to come.

"All right," he said. "Tell me about the characters . . ."

It was, said Mr. Gedeon, all to do with the public. At some point, certain characters became so familiar to readers—and, indeed, to many non-readers—that they reached a state of existence independent of the page.

"Take Oliver Twist, for example," said Mr. Gedeon. "More people know of Oliver Twist than have ever read the work to which he gave his name. The same is true for Romeo and Juliet, and Robinson Crusoe, and Don Quixote. Mention their names to the even averagely educated man or woman on the street and, regardless of whether they've ever encountered a word of the texts in question, they'll be able to tell you that Romeo and Juliet were doomed lovers, that Robinson Crusoe was marooned on an island, and Don Quixote was involved in some business with windmills. Similarly, they'll tell you that Macbeth got above himself, that Ebenezer Scrooge came right in the end, and that D'Artagnan, Athos, Aramis and Porthos were the names of the musketeers.

"Admittedly, there's a limit to the number of those who achieve that kind of familiarity. They end up here as a matter of course. But you'd be surprised by how many people can tell you something of Tristram Shandy, or Tom Jones, or Jay Gatsby. I'm not sure where the point of crossover is, to be perfectly honest. All I know is that, at some point, a character becomes sufficiently famous to pop into existence and, when they do so, they materialize in or near the Caxton Private Lending Library & Book Depository. They always have, ever since the original Mr. Caxton set up the first depository shortly before his death in 1492. According to the history of the library, he did so when some of Chaucer's pilgrims turned up on his doorstep in 1477."

"Some of them?" said Mr. Berger. "Not all?"

"Nobody remembers all of them," said Mr. Gedeon. "Caxton found the Miller, the Reeve, the Knight, the Second Nun, and the Wife of Bath all arguing in his yard. Once he became convinced that they were not actors or lunatics, he realized that he had to find somewhere to keep them. He didn't want to be accused of sorcery or any other such nonsense, and he had his enemies: where there are books, there will always be haters of books alongside the lovers of them.

"So Caxton found a house in the country for them, and this also served as a library for parts of his own collection. He even established a means of continuing to fund the library after he was gone, one that continues to be used to this day. Basically, we mark up what should be marked down, and mark down what should be marked up, and the difference is deposited with the Trust."

"I'm not sure that I understand," said Mr. Berger.

"It's simple, really. It's all to do with ha'pennys, and portions of cents, or lire, or whatever the currency may be. If, say, a writer was due to be paid the sum of nine pounds, ten shillings, and sixpence ha'penny in royalties, the ha'penny would be shaved off and given to us. Similarly, if a company owes a publisher seventeen pounds, eight shillings and sevenpence ha'penny, they're charged eightpence instead. This goes on all through the industry, even down to individual books sold. Sometimes we're dealing in only fractions of a penny, but when we take them from all round the world and add them together, it's more than enough to fund the Trust, maintain the library, and house the characters here. It's now so embedded in the system of books and publishing that nobody even notices anymore."

Mr. Berger was troubled. He would have had no time for such accounting chicanery when it came to the Closed Accounts Register. It did make sense, though.

"And what is the Trust?"

"Oh, the Trust is just a name that's used for convenience. There hasn't been an actual Trust in years, or not one on which anyone sits. For all intents and purposes, this is the Trust. I am the Trust. When I pass on, the next librarian will be the Trust. There's not much work to it. I rarely even have to sign checks."

While the financial support structure for the library was all very interesting, Mr. Berger was more interested in the question of the characters.

"To get back to these characters, they live here?"

"Oh, absolutely. As I explained, they just show up outside when the time is right. Some are obviously a little confused, but it all becomes clear to them in the days that follow, and they start settling in. And when they arrive, so too does a first edition of the relevant work, wrapped in brown paper and tied with string. We put in on a shelf and keep it nice and safe. It's their life story, and it has to be preserved. Their history is fixed in those pages."

"What happens with series characters?" asked Mr. Berger. "Sherlock Holmes, for example? Er, I'm assuming he's here somewhere."

"Of course," said Mr. Gedeon. "We numbered his rooms as 221B, just to make him feel at home. Dr. Watson lives next door. In their case, I do believe that the library received an entire collection of first editions of the canonical works."

"The Conan Doyle books, you mean?"

"Yes. Nothing after Conan Doyle's death in 1930 actually counts. It's the same for all of the iconic characters here. Once the original creator passes on, then that's the end of their story as far as we, and they, are concerned. Books by other authors who take up the characters don't count. It would all be unmanageable otherwise. Needless to say, they don't show up here until after their creators have died. Until then, they're still open to change."

"I'm finding all of this extremely difficult to take in," said Mr. Berger.

"Dear fellow," said Mr. Gedeon, leaning over and patting Mr. Berger's arm reassuringly, "don't imagine for a moment that you're the first. I felt exactly the same way the first time that I came here."

"How did you come here?"

"I met Hamlet at a number 48B bus stop," said Mr. Gedeon. "He'd been there for some time, poor chap. At least eight buses had passed him by, and he hadn't taken any of them. It's to be expected, I suppose. It's in his nature."

"So what did you do?"

"I got talking to him, although he does tend to soliloquize so one has to be patient. Saying it aloud, I suppose it seems nonsensical in retrospect that I wouldn't simply have called the police and told them that a disturbed person who was under the impression he was Hamlet was marooned at the 48B bus stop. But I've always loved Shakespeare, you see, and I found the man at the bus stop quite fascinating. By the time he'd finished speaking, I was convinced. I brought him back here and restored him to the safe care of the librarian of the day. That was old Headley, my predecessor. I had a cup of tea with him, much as we're doing now, and that was the start of it. When Headley retired, I took his place. Simple as that."

It didn't strike Mr. Berger as very simple at all. It seemed complicated on a quite cosmic scale.

"Could I—?" Mr. Berger began to say, then stopped. It struck him as a most extraordinary thing to ask, and he wasn't sure that he should.

"See them?" said Mr. Gedeon. "By all means! Best bring your coat, though. I find it can get a bit chilly back there."

Mr. Berger did as he was told. He put on his coat and followed Mr. Gedeon past the shelves, his eyes taking in the titles as he went. He wanted to touch the books, to take them down and stroke them, like cats, but he controlled the urge. After all, if Mr. Gedeon was to be believed, he was about to have a far more extraordinary encounter with the world of books.

II

In the end, it proved to be slightly duller than Mr. Berger had expected. Each of the characters had a small but clean suite of rooms, personalized to suit their time periods and dispositions. Mr. Gedeon explained that they didn't organize the living areas by authors or periods of history, so there weren't entire wings devoted to Dickens or Shakespeare.

"It just didn't work when it was tried in the past," said Mr. Gedeon. "Worse, it caused terrible problems, and some awful fights. The characters tend to have a pretty good instinct for these things themselves, and my inclination has always been to let them choose their own space."

They passed Room 221B where Sherlock Holmes appeared to be in an entirely drug-induced state of stupor, while in a nearby suite Tom Jones was doing something unspeakable with Fanny Hill. There was a brooding Heathcliff, and a Fagin with rope burns around his neck, but like animals in a zoo, a lot of the characters were simply napping.

"They do that a lot," said Mr. Gedeon. "I've seen some of them sleep for years, decades even. They don't get hungry as such, although they do like to eat to break the monotony. Force of habit, I suppose. We try to keep them away from wine. That makes them rowdy."

"But do they realize that they're fictional characters?" said Mr. Berger.

"Oh, yes. Some of them take it better than others, but they all learn to accept that their lives have been written by someone else, and their memories are a product of literary invention, even if, as I said earlier, it gets a bit more complicated with historical characters."

"But you said it was only fictional characters who ended up here," Mr. Berger protested.

"That is the case, as a rule, but it's also true that some historical characters become more real to us in their fictional forms. Take Richard III: much of the public perception of him is a product of Shakespeare's play and Tudor propaganda, so in a sense that Richard III is a fictional character. Our Richard III is aware that he's not actually *the* Richard III but *a* Richard III. On the other hand, as far as the public is concerned he is *the* Richard III, and is more real in their minds than any products of later revisionism. But he's the exception rather than the rule: very few historical characters manage to make that transition. All for the best, really, otherwise this place would be packed to the rafters."

Mr. Berger had wanted to raise the issue of space with the librarian, and this seemed like the opportune moment.

"I did notice that the building seems significantly larger on the inside than on the outside," he remarked.

"It's funny, that," said Mr. Gedeon. "Doesn't seem to matter much what the building looks like on the outside: it's as though, when they all move in, they bring their own space with them. I've often wondered why that might be, and I think I've come up with an answer of sorts. It's a natural consequence of the capacity of a bookstore or library to contain entire worlds, whole universes, and all contained between the covers of books. In that sense, every library or bookstore is practically infinite. This library takes that to its logical conclusion."

They passed a pair of overly ornate and decidedly gloomy rooms, in one of which an ashen-faced man sat reading a book, his unusually long fingernails gently testing the pages. He turned to watch them pass, and his lips drew back to reveal a pair of elongated canines.

"The Count," said Mr. Gedeon, in a worried manner. "I'd move along if I were you."

"You mean Stoker's Count?" said Mr. Berger. He couldn't help but gawp. The Count's eyes were rimmed with red, and there was an undeniable magnetism to him. Mr. Berger found his feet dragging him into the room as the Count set aside his book and prepared to welcome him.

Mr. Gedeon's hand grasped his right arm and pulled him back into the corridor.

"I told you to move along," he said. "You don't want to be spending time with the Count. Very unpredictable, the Count. Says he's over all that vampiric nonsense, but I wouldn't trust him farther than I could throw him."

"He can't get out, can he?" asked Mr. Berger, who was already rethinking his passion for evening walks.

"No, he's one of the special cases. We keep those books behind bars, and that seems to do the trick for the characters as well."

"But some of the others wander," said Mr. Berger. "You met Hamlet, and I met Anna Karenina."

"Yes, but that's really most unusual. For the most part, the characters exist in a kind of stasis. I suspect a lot of them just close their eyes and relive their entire literary lives, over and over. Still, we do have quite a competitive bridge tournament going, and the pantomime at Christmas is always good fun."

"How do they get out, the ones who ramble off?"

Mr. Gedeon shrugged. "I don't know. I keep the place well locked up, and it's rare that I'm not here. I just took a few days off to visit my brother in Bootle, but I've probably never spent more than a month in total away from the library in all of my years as librarian. Why would I? I've got books to read, and characters to talk to. I've got worlds to explore, all within these walls."

At last they reached a closed door upon which Mr. Gedeon knocked tentatively.

"*Oui?*" said a female voice.

"*Madame, vous avez un visiteur,*" said Mr. Gedeon.

"*Bien. Entrez, s'il vous plaît.*"

Mr. Gedeon opened the door, and there was the woman whom Mr. Berger had watched throw herself beneath the wheels of a train, and whose life he felt that he had subsequently saved, sort of. She was wearing a simple black dress, perhaps even the very one that had so captivated Kitty in the novel, her curly hair in disarray, and a string of pearls hanging around her firm neck. She seemed startled at first to see him, and he knew that she recalled his face.

Mr. Berger's French was a little rusty, but he managed to dredge up a little from memory.

"*Madame, je m'appelle Monsieur Berger, et je suis enchanté de vous rencontrer.*"

"*Non,*" said Anna, after a short pause, "*tout le plaisir est pour moi, Monsieur Berger. Vous vous assiérez, s'il vous plaît.*"

He took a seat, and a polite conversation commenced. Mr. Berger explained, in the most delicate terms, that he had been a witness to her earlier encounter with the train, and it had haunted him. Anna appeared most distressed, and apologized profusely for any trouble that she might have caused him, but Mr. Berger waved it away as purely minor, and stressed that he was more concerned for her than for himself. Naturally, he said, when he saw her making a second attempt—if attempt was the right word for an act that had been so successful first time round—he had felt compelled to intervene.

After some initial hesitancy, their conversation grew easier. At some point Mr. Gedeon arrived with more tea, and some more cake, but they barely noticed him. Mr. Berger found much of his French returning, but Anna, having spent so long in the environs of the library, also had a good command of English. They spoke together long into the night, until at last Mr. Berger noticed the hour, and apologized for keeping Anna up so late. She replied that she had enjoyed his company, and she slept little anyway. He kissed her hand, and begged leave to return the next day, and she gave her permission willingly.

Mr. Berger found his way back to the library without too much trouble, apart from an attempt by Fagin to steal his wallet, which the old reprobate put down to habit and nothing more. When he reached Mr. Gedeon's living quarters, he discovered the librarian dozing in an armchair. He woke him gently, and Mr. Gedeon opened the front door to let him out.

"If you wouldn't mind," said Mr. Berger, as he stood on the doorstep, "I should very much like to return tomorrow to speak with you, and Ms. Karenina, if that wouldn't be too much of an imposition."

"It wouldn't be an imposition at all," said Mr. Gedeon. "Just knock on the glass. I'll be here."

With that the door was closed, and Mr. Berger, feeling both more confused and more elated than he had in all his life, returned to his cottage in the darkness, and slept a deep, dreamless sleep.

12

The next morning, once he had washed and breakfasted, Mr. Berger returned to the Caxton Library. He brought with him some fresh pastries that he had bought in the local bakery in order to replenish Mr. Gedeon's supplies, and a book of Russian poetry in translation of which he was unusually fond, but which he now desired to present to Anna. Making sure that he was not being observed, he took the laneway that led to the library and knocked on the glass. He was briefly fearful that Mr. Gedeon might have spirited away the contents of the premises—books, characters, and all—overnight, fearful that the discovery by Mr. Berger of the library's true nature might bring some trouble upon them all, but the old gentleman opened the door to Mr. Berger's knock on the glass and seemed very pleased to see him return.

"Will you take some tea?" asked Mr. Gedeon, and Mr. Berger agreed, even though he had already had tea at breakfast and was anxious to return to Anna. Still, he had questions for Mr. Gedeon, particularly pertaining to Anna.

"Why does she do it?" he asked, as he and Mr. Gedeon shared an apple scone between them.

"Do what?" said Mr. Gedeon. "Oh, you mean throw herself under trains?"

He picked a crumb from his waistcoat and put it on his plate.

"First of all, I should say that she doesn't make a habit of it," said Mr. Gedeon. "In all the years that I've been here, she's done it no more than a dozen times. Admittedly, the incidents have been growing more frequent, and I have spoken to her about them in an effort to find some way to help, but she doesn't seem to know herself why she feels compelled to relive her final moments in the book. We have other characters that return to their fates—just about all of our Thomas Hardy characters appear obsessed by them—but she's the only one who reenacts her end. I can only give you my thoughts on the matter, and I'd say this: she's the titular character, and her life is so tragic, her fate so awful, that it could be that both are imprinted upon the reader, and herself, in a particularly deep and resonant way. It's in the quality of the writing. It's in the book. Books have power. You must understand that now. It's why we keep all of these first editions so carefully. The fate of characters is set forever in those volumes. There's a link between those editions and the characters that arrived here with them."

He shifted in his chair, and pursed his lips.

"I'll share something with you, Mr. Berger, something that I've never shared with anyone before," he said. "Some years ago, we had a leak in the roof. It wasn't a big one, but they don't need to be big, do they? A little water dripping for hours and hours can do a great deal of damage, and it wasn't until I got back from the picture house in Moreham that I saw what had happened. You see, before I left I'd set aside our manuscript copies of *Alice in Wonderland* and *Moby Dick.* "

"*Moby Dick*? " said Mr. Berger. "I wasn't aware that there were any extant manuscripts of *Moby Dick.* "

"It's an unusual one, I'll admit," said Mr. Gedeon. "Somehow it's all tied up with confusion between the American and British first editions. The American edition, by Harper & Brothers, was set from the manuscript, and the British edition, by Bentley's, was in turn set from the American proofs, but there are some six hundred differences in wording between the two editions. But in 1851, while Melville was working on the British edition based on proofs that he himself had paid to be set and plated before an American publisher had signed an agreement, he was also still writing some of the later parts of the book, and in addition he took the opportunity to rewrite sections that had already been set for America. So which is the edition that the library should store: the American, based on the original manuscript, or the British, based not on the manuscript but on a subsequent rewrite? The decision made by the Trust was to acquire the British edition and, just to be on the safe side, the manuscript. When Captain Ahab arrived at the Library, both editions arrived with him."

"And the manuscript of *Alice in Wonderland*? I understood that to be in the collection of the British Museum."

"Some sleight-of-hand there, I believe," said Mr. Gedeon. "You may recall that the Reverend Dodgson gave the original ninety-page manuscript to Alice Liddell, but she was forced to sell it in order to pay death duties following her husband's death in 1928. Sotheby's sold it on her behalf, suggesting a reserve of four thousand pounds. It went, of course, for almost four times that amount, to an American bidder. At that point, the Trust stepped in, and a similar manuscript copy was substituted and sent to the United States."

"So the British Museum now holds a fake?"

"Not a fake, but a later copy, made by Dodgson's hand at the Trust's instigation. In those days, the Trust was always thinking ahead, and I've tried to keep up that tradition. I've always got an eye out for a book or character that may be taking off.

"So the Trust was very keen to have Dodgson's original *Alice*: so many iconic characters, you see, and then there were the illustrations too. It's an extremely powerful manuscript.

"But all of this is beside the point. Both of the manuscripts needed a bit of attention—just a careful clean to remove any dust or other media with a little polyester film. Well, I almost cried when I returned to the library. Some of the water from the ceiling had fallen on the manuscripts: just drops, nothing more, but enough to send some of the ink from *Moby Dick* on to a page of the *Alice* manuscript."

"And what happened?" asked Mr. Berger.

"For one day, in all extant copies of *Alice in Wonderland*, there was a whale at the Mad Hatter's tea party," said Mr. Gedeon solemnly.

"What? I don't remember that."

"Nobody does, nobody but I. I worked all day to clean the relevant section, and gradually removed all traces of Melville's ink. *Alice in Wonderland* went back to the way it was before, but for that day every copy of the book, and all critical commentaries on it, noted the presence of a white whale at the tea party."

"Good grief! So the books can be changed?"

"Only the copies contained in the library's collection, and they in turn affect all others. This is not just a library, Mr. Berger: it's the *ur*-library. It has to do with the rarity of the books in its collection and their links to the characters. That's why we're so careful with them. We have to be. No book is really a fixed object. Every reader reads a book differently, and each book works in a different way on each reader. But the books here are special. They're the books from which all later copies came. I tell you, Mr. Berger, not a day goes by in this place that doesn't bring me one surprise or another, and that's the truth."

But Mr. Berger was no longer listening. He was thinking again of Anna and the awfulness of those final moments as the train approached, of her fear and her pain, and how she seemed doomed to repeat them because of the power of the book to which she had given her name.

But the contents of the books were not fixed. They were open not just to differing interpretations, but to actual change.

Fates could be altered.

13

Mr. Berger did not act instantly. He had never considered himself a duplicitous individual, and he tried to tell himself that his actions in gaining Mr. Gedeon's confidence were as much to do with his enjoyment of that gentleman's company, and his fascination with the Caxton's contents, as with any desire he might have harbored to save Anna Karenina from further fatal encounters with locomotives.

There was more than a grain of truth to this. Mr. Berger did enjoy spending time with Mr. Gedeon, for the librarian was a vast repository of information about the library and the history of his predecessors in the role. Similarly, no bibliophile could fail to be entranced by the library's inventory, and each day among its stacks brought new treasures to light, some of which had been acquired purely for their rarity value rather than because of any particular character link: annotated manuscripts dating back to the birth of the printed word, including poetical works by Donne, Marvell, and Spenser; not one but two copies of the First Folio of Shakespeare's works, one of them belonging to Edward Knight himself, the book-holder of the King's Men and the presumed proofreader of the manuscript sources for the Folio, and containing his handwritten corrections to the errors that had crept into his particular edition, for the Folio was still being proofread during the printing of the book, and there were variances between individual copies; and what Mr. Berger suspected might well be notes, in Dickens's own hand, for the later, uncompleted chapters of *The Mystery of Edwin Drood*.

This latter artifact was discovered by Mr. Berger in an uncatalogued file that also contained an abandoned version of the final chapters of F. Scott Fitzgerald's *The Great Gatsby*, in which Gatsby, not Daisy, is behind the wheel when Myrtle is killed. Mr. Berger had glimpsed Gatsby briefly on his way to visit Anna Karenina. By one of the miracles of the library, Gatsby's quarters appeared to consist of a pool house and a swimming pool, although the pool was made marginally less welcoming by the presence in it of a deflated, bloodstained mattress.

The sight of Gatsby, who was pleasant but haunted, and the discovery of an alternate ending to the book to which Gatsby, like Anna, had given his name, caused Mr. Berger to wonder what might have happened had Fitzgerald published the version held by the Caxton instead of the book that eventually appeared, in which Daisy is driving the car on that fateful night. Would it have altered Gatsby's eventual fate? Probably not, he decided: there would still have been a bloodstained mattress in the swimming pool, but Gatsby's end would have been rendered less tragic, and less noble.

But the fact that he could even think in this way about endings that might have been confirmed in him the belief that Anna's fate might be altered, and so it was that he began to spend more and more time in the section devoted to Tolstoy's works, and familiarized himself with the history of *Anna Karenina*. His researches revealed that even this novel, described as "flawless" by both Dostoevsky and Nabokov, presented problems when it came to its earliest appearance. While it was originally published in installments in the *Russian Messenger* periodical from 1873 onwards, an editorial dispute over the final part of the story meant that it did not appear in its complete form until the first publication of the work as a book in 1878. The library held both the periodical version and the Russian first edition, but Mr. Berger's knowledge of Russian was limited, to put it mildly, and he didn't think that it would be a good idea to go messing around with it in its original language. He decided that the library's first English language edition, published by Thomas Y. Crowell & Co. of New York in 1886, would probably be sufficient for his needs.

The weeks and months went by, but still he did not act. Not only was he afraid to put in place a plan that involved tinkering with one of the greatest works of literature in any language, but Mr. Gedeon was a perpetual presence in the library. He had not yet entrusted Mr. Berger with his own key, and he still kept a careful eye on his visitor. Meanwhile, Mr. Berger noticed that Anna was becoming increasingly agitated, and in the middle of their discussions of books and music, or their occasional games of whist or poker, she would grow suddenly distant and whisper the name of her children or her lover. She was also, he thought, taking an unhealthy interest in certain railway timetables.

Finally, fate presented him with the opportunity he had been seeking. Mr. Gedeon's brother in Bootle was taken seriously ill, and his departure from this earth was said to be imminent. Mr. Gedeon was forced to leave in a hurry if he was to see his brother again before he passed away and, with only the faintest of hesitations, he entrusted the care of the Caxton Private Lending Library & Book Depository to Mr. Berger. He left Mr. Berger with the keys, and the number of Mr. Gedeon's sister-in-law in Bootle in case of emergencies, then rushed off to catch the last evening train north.

Alone for the first time in the library, Mr. Berger opened the suitcase that he had packed upon receiving the summons from Mr.

Berger. He removed from it a bottle of brandy, and his favorite fountain pen. He poured himself a large snifter of brandy—larger than was probably advisable, he would later accept—and retrieved the Crowell edition of Anna Karenina from its shelf. He laid it on Mr. Gedeon's desk and turned to the relevant section. He took a sip of brandy, then another, and another. He was, after all, about to alter one of the great works of literature, so a stiff drink seemed like a very good idea.

He looked at the glass. It was now almost empty. He refilled it, took another strengthening swig, and uncapped his pen. He offered a silent prayer of apology to the god of letters, and with three swift dashes of his pen removed a single paragraph.

It was done.

He took another drink. It had been easier than expected. He let the ink dry on the Crowell edition, and restored it to its shelf. He was, by now, more than a little tipsy. Another title caught his eye as he returned to the desk: *Tess of the d'Urbervilles* by Thomas Hardy, in the first edition by Osgood, McIlvaine and Co., London, 1891.

Mr. Berger had always hated the ending of *Tess of the d'Urbervilles*. Oh well, he thought: in for a penny, in for a pound.

He took the book from the shelf, stuck it under his arm, and was soon happily at work on Chapters LVIII and LIX. He worked all through the night, and by the time he fell asleep the bottle of brandy was empty, and he was surrounded by books.

In truth, Mr. Berger had gotten a little carried away.

14

In the history of the Caxton Private Lending Library & Book Depository, the brief period that followed Mr. Berger's "improvements" to great novels and plays is known as the "Confusion" and has come to be regarded as a lesson in why such experiments should generally be avoided.

The first clue Mr. Gedeon had that something was amiss was when he passed the Liverpool Playhouse on his way to catch the train back to Glossom, his brother having miraculously recovered to such an extent that he was threatening to sue his physicians, and discovered that the theatre was playing *The Comedy of Macbeth*. He did a quick double-take, and immediately sought out the nearest bookshop. There he found a copy of *The Comedy of Macbeth*, along with a critical commentary labeling it "one of the most troubling of Shakespeare's later plays, due to its curious mixture of violence and inappropriate humor bordering on early bedroom farce."

"Good Lord," said Mr. Gedeon aloud. "What has he done? For that matter, what *else* has he done?"

Mr. Gedeon thought hard for a time, trying to recall the novels or plays about which Mr. Berger had expressed serious reservations. He seemed to recall Mr. Berger complaining that the ending of *A Tale of Two Cities* had always made him cry. An examination of a copy of the book in question revealed that it now ended with Sydney Carton being rescued from the guillotine by an airship piloted by the Scarlet Pimpernel, with a footnote advising that this had provided the inspiration for a later series of novels by Baroness Orczy.

"Oh, God," said Mr. Gedeon.

Then there was Hardy.

Tess of the d'Urbervilles now ended with Tess's escape from prison, engineered by Angel Clare and a team of demolitions experts, while *The Mayor of Casterbridge* had Michael Henchard living in a rose-covered cottage near his newly-married stepdaughter and breeding goldfinches. At the conclusion of *Jude the Obscure*, Jude Fawley escaped the clutches of Arabella and survived his final desperate visit to Sue in the freezing weather, whereupon they both ran away and went to live happily ever after in Eastbourne.

"This is terrible," said Mr. Gedeon, although even he had to admit that he preferred Mr. Berger's endings to Thomas Hardy's.

Finally he came to *Anna Karenina*. It took him a little while to find the change, because this one was subtler than the others: a deletion instead of an actual piece of bad rewriting. It was still wrong, but Mr. Gedeon understood Mr. Berger's reason for making the change. Perhaps if Mr. Gedeon had experienced similar feelings about one of the characters in his care, he might have found the courage to intervene in a similar way. He had been a witness to the sufferings of so many of them, the consequences of decisions made by heartless authors, the miserable Hardy not least among them, but his first duty was, and always had been, to the books. This would have to be put right, however valid Mr. Berger might have believed his actions to be.

Mr. Gedeon returned the copy of *Anna Karenina* to its shelf, and made his way to the station.

15

Mr. Berger woke to the most terrible hangover. It took him a while even to recall where he was, never mind what he might have done. His mouth was dry, his head was thumping, and his neck and back were aching from having fallen asleep at Mr. Gedeon's desk. He made himself some tea and toast, most of which he managed to keep down, and stared in horror at the pile of first editions that he had violated the night before. He had a vague sense that they did not represent the entirety of his efforts, for he dimly recalled returning some to the shelves, singing merrily to himself as he went, although he was damned if he could bring to mind the titles of all the books involved. So ill and appalled was he that he could find no reason to stay awake. Instead he curled up on the couch in the hope that, when he opened his eyes again, the world of literature might somehow have self-corrected, and the intensity of his headache might have lessened. Only one alteration did he not immediately regret, and that was his work on *Anna Karenina*. The actions of his pen in that case had truly been a labour of love.

He rose to sluggish consciousness to find Mr. Gedeon standing over him, his face a mixture of anger, disappointment, and not a little pity.

"We need to have words, Mr. Berger," he said. "Under the circumstances, you might like to freshen up before we begin."

Mr. Berger took himself to the bathroom, and bathed his face and upper body with cold water. He brushed his teeth, combed his hair, and tried to make himself as presentable as possible. He felt a little like a condemned man hoping to make a good impression on the hangman. He returned to the living room and smelled strong coffee brewing. Tea, in this case, was unlikely to be sufficient for the task at hand.

He took a seat across from Mr. Gedeon, who was examining the altered first editions, his fury now entirely undiluted by any other emotions.

"This is vandalism!" he said. "Do you realize what you've done? Not only have you corrupted the world of literature, and altered the histories of the characters in our care, but you've damaged the library's collection. How could someone who considers himself a lover of books do such a thing?"

Mr. Berger couldn't meet the librarian's gaze.

"I did it for Anna," he said. "I just couldn't bear to see her suffer in that way."

"And the others?" said Mr. Gedeon. "What of Jude, and Tess, and Sydney Carton? Good grief, what of Macbeth?"

"I felt sorry for them, too," said Mr. Berger. "And if their creators knew that, at some future date, they might take on a physical form in this world, replete with the memories and experiences forced upon them, would they not have given some thought to their ultimate fate? To do otherwise would be tantamount to sadism!"

"But that isn't how literature works," said Mr. Gedeon. "It isn't even how the world works. The books are written. It's not for you or me to start altering them at this stage. These characters have power precisely because of what their creators have put them through. By changing the endings, you've put at risk their place in the literary pantheon and, by extension, their presence in the world. I wouldn't be surprised if we were to go back to the lodgings and find a dozen or more unoccupied rooms, with no trace that their occupants ever existed."

Mr. Berger hadn't thought of that. It made him feel worse than ever.

"I'm sorry," he said. "I'm so very, very sorry. Can anything be done?"

Mr. Gedeon left his desk and opened a large cupboard in the corner of the room. From it he removed his box of restorer's equipment: his adhesives and threads, his tapes and weights and rolls of buckram cloth, his needles and brushes and awls. He placed the box on his desk, added a number of small glass bottles of liquid, then rolled up his sleeves, turned on the lamps, and summoned Mr. Berger to his side.

"Muriatic acid, citric acid, oxalic acid, and Tartureous acid," he said, tapping each bottle in turn.

He carefully mixed a solution of the latter three acids in a bowl, and instructed Mr. Berger to apply it to his inked changes to *Tess of the d'Urbervilles.*

"The solution will remove ink stains, but not printer's ink," said Mr. Gedeon. "Be careful, and take your time. Apply it, leave it for a few minutes, then wipe it off and let it dry. Keep repeating until the ink is gone. Now begin, for we have many hours of work ahead of us."

They worked through the night, and into the next morning. Exhaustion forced them to sleep for a few hours, but they both returned to the task in the early afternoon. By late in the evening, the worst of the damage had been undone. Mr. Berger even remembered the titles of the books that he had returned to the shelves while drunk, although one was forgotten. Mr. Berger had set to work on making *Hamlet* a little shorter, but had got no further than Scenes IV and V, from which he had cut a couple of Hamlet's soliloquies. The consequence was that Scene IV began with Hamlet noting that the hour of twelve had struck, and the appearance of his father's ghost. However by halfway through Scene V, and after a couple of fairly swift exchanges, it was already morning. When Mr. Berger's excisions were discovered many decades later by one of his successors, it was decided to allow them to stand, as she felt that *Hamlet* was quite long enough as it was.

Together they went to the lodgings and checked on the characters. All were present and correct, although Macbeth appeared in better spirits than before, and remained thus ever after.

Only one book remained unrestored: *Anna Karenina*.

"Must we?" said Mr. Berger. "If you say 'yes', then I will accept your decision, but it seems to me that she is different from the rest. None of the others are compelled to do what she does. None of them is so despairing as to seek oblivion over and over. What I did does not fundamentally alter the climax of the novel, but adds only a little ambiguity, and it may be that a little is all that she requires."

Mr. Gedeon considered the book. Yes, he was the librarian, and the custodian of the contents of the Caxton Private Lending Library & Book Depository, but he was also the guardian of its characters. He had a duty to them and to the books. Did one supersede the other? He thought of what Mr. Berger had said: if Tolstoy had known that, by his literary gifts, he would doom his heroine to be defined by her suicide, might he not have found a way to modify his prose even slightly, and thus give her some peace?

And was it not also true that Tolstoy's ending to the novel was flawed in any case? Rather than give us some extended reflection on Anna's death, he chose instead to concentrate on Levin's return to religion, Kozyshev's support for the Serbs, and Vronsky's commitment to the cause of the Slavs. He even gave the final word on Anna's death to Vronsky's rotten mother: "Her death was the death of a bad woman, a woman without religion." Surely Anna deserved a better memorial than that?

Mr. Berger had crossed out three simple lines from the end of Chapter XXXI:

The little muzhik *ceased his mumblings, and fell to his knees by the broken body. He whispered a prayer for her soul, but if her fall had been unwitting then she was past all need of prayer, and she was with God now. If it were otherwise, then prayer could do her no good. But still he prayed.*

He read the preceding paragraph:

And the candle by which she had read the book that was filled with fears, with deceptions, with anguish, and with evil, flared up with greater brightness than she had ever known, revealing to her all that before was in darkness, then flickered, grew faint, and went out forever.

You know, thought Mr. Gedeon, Chapter XXXI could end just as easily there, and there would be peace for Anna.

He closed the book, allowing Mr. Berger's change to stand.

"Let's leave it, shall we?" he said. "Why don't you put it back on its shelf?"

Mr. Berger took the book reverently, and restored it gently, lovingly to its place in the stacks. He thought about visiting Anna one last time, but it did not seem appropriate to ask Mr. Gedeon's permission. He had done all that he could for her, and he hoped only that it was enough. He returned to Mr. Gedeon's living room and placed the key to the Caxton Library on the desk.

"Goodbye," he said. "And thank you."

Mr. Gedeon nodded but did not answer, and Mr. Berger left the library and did not look back.

16

In the weeks that followed Mr. Berger thought often of the Caxton Library, and of Mr. Gedeon, and of Anna most of all, but he did not return to the laneway, and he consciously avoided walking near that part of the town. He read his books, and resumed his evening walks to the railway track. Each evening he waited for the last train to pass, and it always did so without incident. Anna, he believed, was troubled no more.

One evening, as summer drew to its close, there came a knocking on his door. He answered it to find Mr. Gedeon standing on his doorstep, two suitcases by his side, and a taxi waiting for him by the garden gate. Mr. Berger was surprised to see him, and invited him to step inside, but Mr. Gedeon declined.

"I'm leaving," he said. "I'm tired, and I no longer have the energy that I once had. It's time for me to retire, and entrust the care of the Caxton to another. I suspected as much on that first night, when you followed Anna to the library. The library always finds its new librarian, and leads him to its door. I thought that I might have been mistaken when you altered the books, and I resigned myself to waiting until another came, but slowly I came to understand that you were the one after all. Your only fault was to love a character too much, which caused you to do the wrong thing for the right reasons, and it may be that we both learned a lesson from that incident. I know that the Caxton and its characters will be safe in your care until the next librarian comes along. I've left a letter for you containing all that you need to know, and a number at which you can call me should you have any questions, but I think you'll be just fine."

He held out to Mr. Berger a great ring of keys. After only a moment's hesitation, Mr. Berger accepted them, and he saw that Mr. Gedeon could not stop himself from shedding a tear as he entrusted the library and its characters to its new custodian.

"I shall miss them terribly, you know," said Mr. Gedeon.

"You should feel free to visit us anytime," said Mr. Berger.

"Perhaps I will," said Mr. Gedeon, but he never did.

They shook hands for the final time, and Mr. Gedeon departed, and they did not meet or speak again.

17

The Caxton Private Lending Library & Book Depository is no longer in Glossom. At the beginning of this century the town was discovered by developers, and the land beside the library was earmarked for houses, and a modern shopping mall. Questions started to be asked about the peculiar old building at the end of the laneway, and so it was that one evening a vast fleet of anonymous trucks arrived driven by anonymous men, and in the space of a single night the entire contents of the Caxton Private Lending Library & Book Depository—books, characters and all—were spirited away and resettled in a new home in a little village not far from the sea, but far indeed from cities and, indeed, trains. The librarian, now very old and not a little stooped, liked to walk on the beach in the evenings, accompanied by a small terrier dog and, if the weather was good, by a beautiful, pale woman with long, dark hair.

One night, just as summer was fading into autumn, there was a knock on the door of the Caxton Private Lending Library & Book Depository, and the librarian opened it to find a young woman standing on the doorstep. She had in her hand a copy of *Vanity Fair*.

"Excuse me," she said, "I know this may sound a little odd, but I'm absolutely convinced that I just saw a man who looked like Robinson Crusoe collecting seashells on the beach, and I think he returned with them to this—" she looked at the small brass plate to her right—"*library?*"

Mr. Berger opened the door wide to admit her.

"Please come in," he said. "It may sound equally odd, but I think I've been expecting you . . ."

XV

The Book Case

Nelson DeMille

OTIS PARKER WAS dead. Killed by a falling bookcase whose shelves were crammed with very heavy reading. Total weight about a thousand pounds which flattened Mr. Parker's slight, 160 pound body. A tragic accident. Or so it seemed.

To back up a bit, I'm Detective John Corey, working out of the First Precinct Detective Squad, which is located – if you ever need me – on Ericsson Place in Lower Manhattan, New York City.

It was a cold, blustery March morning, a Tuesday, and I was sitting in a coffee shop on Hudson Street, a few blocks from my precinct, trying to translate ham and eggs over easy into Spanish for my English-challenged waiter. "Huevos flippo. Hambo and blanco toasto. Okay?"

My cell phone rang at 8:34, and it was my boss, Lieutenant Ed Ruiz who said, "I notice you're not at your desk."

"Are you sure?"

"Where are you?"

I told him and he said, "Good. You're up. We have a body at the Dead End Bookstore on North Moore. Discovered by a clerk reporting for work."

I knew the bookstore, which specialized in crime and mystery novels, and I'd actually been a customer a few times. I love murder mysteries. I can always guess the killer – without peeking at the end. Well…hardly ever. My job should be so easy.

Ruiz continued, "The deceased is the store owner, a Mr. Otis Parker."

"Oh…hey, I know him. Met him a few times."

"Yeah? How?"

"I bought a book."

"Really? Why?"

I ignored that and inquired, "Robbery?"

"No. Who robs a bookstore? You rob places that have money or goods you can sell."

"Right. So? What?"

"Well," replied Lt. Ruiz, "it looks like a ground ball," cop talk for something easy. He explained about the falling bookcase, then added, "Appears to be an accident, but the responding officer, Rourke, says it might need another look before they clean up the mess."

"Okay. Hey, how do you say fried egg on a roll to go in Spanish?"

"You say hasta la vista and get over to the bookstore."

"Right." I hung up and went out into the cold March morning. Lower Manhattan at this hour is jammed with people and vehicles, everyone on their way to work, and all thrilled to be doing that. Me, too.

It was quicker to walk than to get my squad car at the precinct, so I began the four block trek up Hudson, bucking into a strong north wind that roared down the avenue. A flasher on the corner opened his trench coat and got lifted into a holding pattern over the Western Union building. Just kidding.

I turned into North Moore, a quiet cobblestoned street that runs west toward the river. Up ahead on the right I saw two RMPs and a bus, which if you read NYPD detective novels you'll know is two radio cars and an ambulance. One car would be the sector car that responded, and the other the patrol sergeant's car.

As I approached the Dead End Bookstore I saw there was no crime scene tape, and the police activity hadn't drawn much attention on the street; it hardly ever does in New York unless it's something interesting or culturally significant, like a mob hit. Even then, it's not worth more than a minute of your time. Also, this was not a lively street; mostly older apartment and loft buildings with lots of vacancy signs. Mr. Otis Parker had located his bookstore badly, but named it well.

I clipped my shield on my trench coat and approached a cop whose name tag said Conner. I asked him, "Is the M.E. here?"

"Yeah. Dr. Hines. I think he's waiting for you."

Hines was an okay guy. Looked like an undertaker and didn't try to play detective. I glanced at my cell phone clock. It was now 8:51 A.M. On the off chance that this was something more than an unfortunate example of Newton's law of gravity, I'd need to fill out a DD-5 and begin a homicide file. Otherwise, I was just stopping by.

I looked at the front of the bookstore which took up the whole ground floor of an old five-story brick building, sandwiched between two equally old buildings. The glass door had a Closed sign hanging on it, along with a notice of store hours – open every day except Sundays, 9 A.M. to 6 P.M. Basically, banking hours that insured the minimum number of customers. There were two display windows, one on each side of the door, and in the windows were...well, books. What this street really needed was a bar.

Anyway, in the left window were mostly classic crime novels – Chandler, Dorothy Sayers, Agatha Christie, Conan Doyle, and so forth. The window on the right featured contemporary bestselling authors like Brad Meltzer, James Patterson, David Baldacci, Nelson DeMille, and others who make more money writing about what I do than I make doing what I do.

I asked Officer Conner, "Who's the boss?"

He replied, "Sergeant Tripani." He added, "I'm his driver."

You want to get the lay of the land before you burst on the scene so I also asked, "Who else is in there?"

He replied, "The two paramedics, and the responding officers, Rourke and Simmons, and an employee named Scott who discovered the body when he came to work."

"And Otis Parker," I reminded him.

"Yeah. He's still there."

"Did you see the body?"

"Yeah."

"What do you think?"

Officer Conner replied, "My boss thinks it's an accident."

"And you think?"

"Whatever he thinks."

"Right." I advised him, "If anyone comes by and identifies themselves as a customer or a friend, show them in."

"Will do."

I entered the bookstore which looked like it did the last time I was here – no customers, no staff, cobwebs on the cash register and, unfortunately no coffee bar. Lots of books.

The store had a two-story high ceiling, and there was a wrought-iron spiral staircase toward the rear that lead up to an open loft area where I could see Sergeant Tripani, whom I knew, standing near the railing. He saw me and said, "Up here."

I walked to the staircase that had a sign saying Private and began the corkscrew climb. On the way, I tried to recall the two or three times I'd interacted with Mr. Otis Parker here in his store. He was a bearded guy in his early 60's, but could have looked younger if he'd bought a bottle of Grecian Formula. He dressed well, and I remember thinking – the way cops do – that he must have had another source of income. Maybe this store was a front for something. Or maybe I read too many crime novels.

I also recalled that Mr. Parker was a bit churlish – though I'd heard him once talking enthusiastically to a customer about collectors' editions which he sold in the back of the store. I'd sized him up as a man who liked his books more than he liked the people who bought them. In short, a typical bookstore owner.

I reached the top of the stairs and stepped up into the open loft which was a large, wood paneled office. In the office was Officer Rourke, the two paramedics, Dr. Hines – wearing the same black suit he'd worn for twenty years – and Sergeant Tripani who greeted me, "Good morning, detective."

"Good morning, sergeant."

There's always a pecking order, and Sergeant Tripani, the patrol supervisor, was the head pecker until Detective Corey from the squad showed up. Of course Mr. Parker's death was not a suspected homicide – at least not by Sergeant Tripani – but here I was to check it out, and Sergeant Tripani was happy to turn it over to me. In fact, he said, "It's all yours, John."

"Ruiz just asked me to stop by." I pointed out, "I still have my coat on."

He didn't reply.

I snagged a pair of latex gloves from a paramedic, then I surveyed the scene of the crime or the accident: It was a nice office, and there was an oriental rug on the floor, strewn with lots of leather bound books around a big mahogany writing desk. The legs of the desk had collapsed under the weight of the falling bookcase behind it, as had the legs and arms of the desk chair and side chair. The tipsy bookcase in question had been uprighted and leaned back against the wall revealing Mr. Otis Parker whose sprawled, splayed, and flattened body lay half on the collapsed desk and half on the floor. The desk items – telephone, Rolodex, pencil holder and so forth – had miraculously remained on the desk as had the blotter which was soaking up some fresh blood on and around the deceased's head and face. Fortunately, Mr. Parker's brains remained where they belonged. I don't like to see brains.

Also on the desk was a framed black and white photo. The glass was cracked but I could see a dark haired woman, maybe in her late thirties. If this was his wife, it would be an old photo. But if it wasn't old, then Mr. Parker had a young wife. Or, maybe it was his daughter. In any case, the lady was not bad looking.

Otis Parker, I noted, was wearing good shoes, and good slacks, and a nice white shirt. His snappy sports jacket hung on a coat tree nearby. I couldn't tell if he was wearing a tie because he was face down. So, obviously, he'd been sitting at his desk when the bookcase behind him had somehow tipped away from the wall and silently fallen on him, his desk and his chair. He may have seen or felt a few books landing around him, but basically he never knew what hit him. Indeed, it looked like an accident. Except, why did a thousand-pound bookcase fall forward? Well, shit happens. Ironic, too, that Otis Parker was killed by the books he loved. Okay, the bookcase killed him. But that's not what the New York Post would say. They'd say, Killed by the books he loved.

I greeted Officer Rourke and inquired as to the whereabouts of his partner, Simmons.

Rourke replied, "He's in the stockroom downstairs with Scott Bixby, the clerk who found the body." He added, "Bixby is writing a statement."

"Good." Everyone seemed to be accounted for so I greeted Dr. Hines and we shook hands. I asked him, "Do you think he's dead?"

Dr. Hines replied to my silly question, "The responding officers" – he motioned to Officer Rourke – "pulled the bookcase off the victim with the assistance of the clerk and they found no signs of life at that time." He further briefed me, "The EMTs" – he indicated the two paramedics – "arrived three minutes later and also found no signs of life." He informed me, "I have pronounced him dead."

"Assuming Mr. Parker did not object, that makes it official."

Dr. Hines doesn't appreciate the dark humor that is a necessary part of tragic situations, and he made a dismissive sound.

I asked him, "Cause of death?"

"I don't know." He elaborated, "Crushed."

"Instantaneous?"

"Probably. No sign of struggle." He speculated, "A bigger man might have survived the impact."

I looked at Otis Parker and nodded. If he'd eaten right and lifted weights...

Dr. Hines continued, "I suspect his neck or vertebrae were broken, or he died of a massive cranial trauma. Or maybe cardiac trauma." He added, "I'll do the autopsy this afternoon and let you know."

"Okay." When someone dies alone, with no witnesses, even if it's an obvious accident, the taxpayers pay for an autopsy. Why? Because the M.E. has to list a cause of death before he signs the certificate, and "crushed" is not a medical term. Also, you do the autopsy because things are not always what they seem to be. That's why I'm here.

I asked him, "Time of death?"

"Recent."

I glanced back at the body and said, "His watch stopped at seven-thirty-two. That's your time of death."

He looked surprised, then walked to the body and peered at the watch on Mr. Parker's wrist. He informed me, "The watch is still running."

"Must be shockproof."

Dr. Hines looked at his own watch and announced, "I have another call." He said to me, "If you discover anything that doesn't look like an accident, let me know before I begin the autopsy."

"I always do, doc." I added, "Hold off on the meat wagon until you hear from me."

"I always do, detective." He added, "But let's not take too long. I want the body in the cooler."

"Right." The drill is this: the ambulance can't take a dead body away, so we needed the morgue van, affectionately known as the meat wagon. But, if I, Detective John Corey, suspected foul play, then we actually needed the Crime Scene Unit who would take charge of the stiff and the premises.

But maybe we didn't need the CSU people at all. I needed to make a determination here and I needed to do it in a relatively short amount of time. I mean, if you cry wolf and there is no wolf, you look like an idiot. Or worse, you look like a guy who has no regard for the budget. But if you say "accident," and it turns out later that it was something else, then you got some explaining to do. I could hear Ruiz now. "Do you know what the word detective means? It means detecting things, detective." And so on.

Dr. Hines had left during my mental exercises and so had the two paramedics. Remaining now in the loft office with me was Sergeant Tripani and the responding officer, Rourke. And Mr. Parker, who, if he could talk might say, "How the hell do I know what happened? I'm just sitting here minding my own business and the next thing I know I'm pressed meat."

I already knew what Sergeant Tripani thought, but in case he'd changed his mind, I asked him, "What do you think, Lou?"

He shrugged, looked at the body and said, "I think it is what it looks like." He explained more fully, "An accident waiting to happen."

I nodded, but it wasn't a real positive nod. I looked at the bookcase that had been leaned at a steep angle against the paneled wall to ensure that it didn't repeat its strange forward motion away from the wall. "Objects in motion," I said, quoting Sir Isaac Newton, "tend to stay in motion. Objects at rest tend to stay at rest."

Sergeant Tripani had no comment on that and asked me, "Do you need me here while you're deciding what this is?"

"No. But I need to speak to Officers Rourke and Simmons and the clerk who found the body."

"Okay."

I asked him, "Do we know next of kin? Any notifications made?"

He replied, "Wife. The clerk called her after he found the body and after he called us. He left a message on her cell phone and home phone saying there's been an accident. Then when Rourke and Simmons arrived, Rourke did the same thing, and he asked Mrs. Parker to call his cell and/or to come immediately to the store."

"Where does she live?"

"The clerk said East Twenty-third."

I asked, "Did you send a car around to her home?"

"We did. No reply to the buzzer and no doorman."

"Does she have a place of business?"

"She works at home, according to the clerk."

"Doing what?"

"I didn't ask."

I wondered why Mrs. Parker had not answered her home phone or even her cell phone and why she hadn't returned those obviously urgent calls or answered her door. Sleeping? Long shower? Doesn't pick up her messages? I'm not married, though I do date, and my experience with ladies and phone messages is mixed. I will say no more on that subject.

Sergeant Tripani started toward the spiral staircase, then turned and said to me, "If you find anything that doesn't look like an accident –"

"Then you buy me breakfast."

"You're on."

"Can your driver get me a ham and egg on a roll?"

"Sure. You want a Lipitor with that?"

"Coffee black. Get a receipt."

Lou Tripani made his way down the spiral staircase and I asked Officer Rourke, "What do you think?"

He replied, "With all due respect for other opinions, I'm just not buying that this bookcase tipped over by itself." He added, "Or that it tipped over at the exact time when this guy was at his desk – when the store was empty with no witnesses to see it and no one around who could've helped him."

I informed him, "Shit happens." I did concede, "Could be more than bad luck."

"Yeah."

"Did you interview the clerk?"

"Sure." He informed me, "He seemed not quite right."

"Meaning?"

"Something off there. Like he seemed more nervous than shocked."

I don't like to be prejudiced before I do an interview, but the clerk's reaction, close to the time he discovered the body, was important and interesting. By now Scott had calmed down and I might see another emotion. I said to Rourke, "Stick around. Put the Open sign on the door and if by some miracle there's a customer, let them in and give me a holler."

"Right."

"And if and when Mrs. Parker shows up, let me handle the notification."

He nodded.

"And let me know when my breakfast arrives."

Officer Rourke went down the staircase. Not every uniformed cop wants to be a detective, but most of them have good instincts and experience, and a lot of cases have been solved or advanced because of the cop who first came on the scene. Rourke seemed smart and he had a suspicious nature. I wouldn't want to be Mrs. Rourke.

I looked at the bookcase again. It looked like an antique, like most of the expensive junk in this office. It was one of those...let's say, ponderous Victorian pieces that decorators hate, but men like.

I looked back at the deceased and mentally pictured the bookcase falling on top of him while he worked at his desk. The force of the object would be increased by its falling speed, like that apple that hit Sir Isaac on the head. But if this was murder, it was a risky way to do it. I mean, there was no guarantee that the bookcase would kill him. Score one against homicide.

But if it was murder, how was it done? It would take two people – or maybe one strong guy – to topple this bookcase. And obviously, it would be someone he knew who was in his office at this hour. And the person or persons would say to him, "You just sit there Otis while we stand behind you and admire your books." Then, "Okay, one, two, three – timber!"

Maybe. But without the one, two, three.

I noticed that the ten-foot high bookcase was taller than it was wide, and the depth of the bookcase at the bottom was the same at the top, making it inherently unstable. Score another point against the bookcase being a murder weapon; it was, as Tripani said, an accident waiting to happen.

I looked at the splatter pattern of the books, the way you look at blood splatter, and I noticed that most of the books were laying near the front of the desk, with only a few toward the rear, indicating to me that the shelves had held more books toward the top, adding to the instability. Mr. Parker, who seemed smart to me, was not too smart about the danger of top-heavy objects.

I looked at the wall behind the bookcase and at the solid back of the piece to see if there were any screws or bolts that had pulled loose from the wood paneling. But there was nothing securing this massive piece of furniture to the wall – though I did see some old holes in the bookcase, indicating that previous owners had screwed this monster to something solid.

Most accidents, I'm convinced, are God's way of getting rid of stupid people. Or if you believe in Darwinism, you wonder why there are any stupid people left in the world. Well, I guess they can reproduce before they remove themselves from the gene pool.

I also noticed that the oak floor had a slope to it, not uncommon in these creaky old buildings. The floor pitched a bit toward the desk and toward the edge of the loft. I've been in a thousand buildings like this, built in the last century, and the wooden rafters that hold up the floors are uneven, bowed, or warped, giving the floors some interesting tilts.

But what was it that caused this stationary object to suddenly topple away from the wall? Objects at rest, and all that. Well, if not human hands, then a few other things could have done it, the most obvious being the building settling. This can happen even after a hundred years. That's how these places collapse now and then. Also, you get some heavy truck rumbling on the street, and that can cause a vibration that would topple an unstable object. Same with construction equipment and guys working underground. Vibrations are also caused by heating and air conditioning units starting up. Even badly vented plumbing or steam pipes could cause a bang in the pipes which could possibly topple something that was on the verge of toppling. That's exactly what happened in my old East Side tenement building to my mother's prized Waterford crystal vase that her rich aunt gave her. Actually, I broke it. But that's another story.

I was about to rule this a dumbicide, but then something caught my eye. I noticed on the oak floor that there was a faint outline where the bookcase had sat for some years, caused obviously by the fact that no one had washed or waxed the floor under the bookcase since it had been there. And I also noticed that there were outlines of two small objects that had sat on the floor and protruded from the front of the bookcase. You don't have to be a detective to determine that these two outlines were made by furniture chocks or wedges – wood or rubber – that tipped the tall, heavy piece back against the wall for safety. So, Mr. Parker was not so stupid – though I would have also shot some big bolts into the wall.

Point was, the bookcase was probably not on the verge of toppling forward by itself if those wedges were there. And they were there. But where were they now? Not on the floor. I looked around the room, but I couldn't find them.

I went to the rail and saw Officer Rourke sitting behind the counter reading a borrowed book. I called down to him, "Hey, did you see any furniture wedges on the floor when you got up here?"

"Any...? What?"

I explained and he replied, "No. Simmons and I ran up the stairs with the clerk and we lifted the bookcase and leaned it back against the wall where you see it. I didn't notice any furniture wedges on the floor." He let me know, "Other than feeling for a pulse and heartbeat, we didn't touch anything." He added, "EMS arrived about three minutes later."

"Okay." So, this has become the Case of the Missing Furniture Wedges. Let's assume that no one who responded to the 911 call stole two furniture wedges. Let's assume instead that the killer took them. Right. This was no accident. Otis Parker was murdered.

I said to Rourke, "Mum's the word on furniture wedges."

I turned away from the rail and stared at Otis Parker and the bookcase. Someone was in this room with him, someone he probably knew, and that person – or persons – had previously removed the two wedges from under the bookcase. Right. Two people. One to tip the heavy bookcase back a bit and the other to slide the wedges out and pocket them. Now the bookcase is unstable, and maybe made more so if someone transferred some of the books from the lower shelves to the higher ones. Maybe this was done yesterday, or a few days ago. And unfortunately for Otis Parker he hadn't noticed this slight lean of his bookcase away from the wall or that the wedges were missing.

So, early this morning, Otis Parker arrives and sits at his desk. Someone accompanied him, or met him here, probably by appointment. That person – or persons – goes to his bookcase to admire his leather bound collection, or maybe get a book. And while they're at it, he, she, or they cause – in a manner not yet known – the bookcase to topple away from the wall, and the expected trajectory of the falling bookcase intersects with the seated victim. Splat! No contest.

I looked around the room. Now that I suspected murder, everything looked different. And everything and anything could be a clue. Stuff in the waste basket, the victim's date book, his cell phone, the contents of his pockets and the contents of his stomach, and on and on. Hundreds of things that needed to be looked at, bagged, tagged, and parceled out to the forensic labs, the evidence storage room, and so forth, while Otis Parker himself was sliced and diced by Dr. Hines. What a difference a few minutes can make.

I surveyed the office, noting its masculine, old clubby feel. There was a large leather couch to the right of the bookcase, a few book-themed prints on the walls, and a rolling bar near the spiral staircase. I pictured Mr. Parker in here, entertaining an author, or even a lady friend, after hours.

On the far side of the room was a long table stacked with books and I realized that all the books were the same. Beneath the table were five open boxes that had obviously held the books. I walked to the table and saw that the book title was *Death Knocks Once*, and the author was Jay K. Lawrence, an author whom I'd read once or twice. I also noticed a box of Sharpies on the table, and I deduced that Jay K. Lawrence was going to be here today or in the very near future to sign his new book for the store. Or, he'd already done so.

I snapped on my latex gloves and opened one of the books, but there was no autograph on the title page. Too bad. I would have liked to buy a signed copy. But maybe Jay Lawrence would be arriving shortly, and in anticipation of this I opened to the back flap where there was a bio and photo of Jay K. Lawrence. Most male crime writers look like they used their mug shot for the book jacket, but Mr. Lawrence was a bit of a pretty boy with well-coiffed hair, maybe a touch of makeup, and a little air brushing. Jay Lawrence's main character, I recalled, was a tough Los Angeles homicide detective named Rick Strong and I wondered where in Mr. Lawrence's pretty head this tough guy lived.

I read the short bio under the photo and learned that Jay Lawrence lived in L.A. There was no mention of a wife and family, so he probably lived with his mommy and ten cats, and he loved to cook.

The next thing I had to do was call Lieutenant Ruiz. But if I did that, this place would get real crowded. I needed to talk to Scott the clerk and to Mrs. Parker before this was announced as a homicide investigation, because when you say "homicide" the whole game changes and people get weird or they get a lawyer. So, for the record, I didn't see anything suspicious, and this is still an accident investigation.

I heard the door open below, and I looked down to see if it was Mrs. Parker, or maybe Jay Lawrence. But it was Officer Conner with my egg sandwich which made me just as happy. I asked Conner to leave the bag on the counter.

My tummy was growling, but I needed to get as much done here as I could before Ruiz called me to ask what the story was. I called down to Rourke, "There may be an author coming in to sign books. Jay Lawrence. Just say there's been an accident. I want to talk to him."

He nodded and I turned back to the office.

I'm not supposed to touch or move too many things, but I did eyeball everything while my mind was in overdrive.

There was a door to the left of the bookcase, and I opened it and walked into a small room filled with file cabinets. To the right was an open bathroom door and I stepped inside. The lights were on, and the toilet seat was down, indicating that a lady had used it last, or that Otis Parker had a bowel movement. I also noticed that the sink was wet, and there was a damp paper towel in the trash can, and that paper towel would have lots of someone's DNA on it. It's amazing how much evidence is left behind in a bathroom. I'd have the CSU people start here.

I also noticed a toilet plunger standing on the floor in the corner. In the back of my mind I'd been looking for something…I didn't know what it was, but I was sure I'd know it when I saw it. And this could be it.

Somebody – a Greek guy – once said, "Give me a lever long enough, and a place to stand, and I can move the world." Or a bookcase.

Still wearing my latex gloves, I picked up the plunger, and examined the wooden handle. One side of the rounded tip was slightly discolored and there was a small dent or crease about halfway up the handle, on the opposite side of the discoloration.

I carried the plunger into the office and stood on the left side of the bookcase. I now noticed two things – a small dimple in the wood paneling and a small crease in the back edge of the bookcase, both about chest high. These marks were barely noticeable in the hard, dark wood, but they would match perfectly with the marks on the lighter and softer wood of the plunger handle. So, it was obvious to me, as it would be obvious to the CSU team, the D.A., and hopefully a jury, that the killer, after excusing him or herself to use the bathroom, returned quietly to the office and quickly slipped the plunger handle between the bookcase and the wood paneled wall. Then that person pulled on the handle, using it as a lever to tilt the unbalanced bookcase an inch or so forward until gravity took over. For every action, said Sir Isaac Newton, there is an equal and opposite reaction.

I returned Part B of the murder weapon to the bathroom.

Now I knew two things: Otis Parker was murdered, and I also knew how he was murdered.

The only thing left to discover was who murdered him. And why. If you get the why, you usually get the who. As I've discovered in this business, when motive and opportunity coalesce, you get a crime. And when the crime is made to look like an accident, you look for someone close to the victim.

I needed a lot more time in this office, but the office wasn't going anywhere and someone close to the victim – Scott the clerk – was cooling his heels in the stockroom and he needed to be interviewed.

I removed my gloves and went down the stairs. I asked Rourke, "Where's the stockroom?"

He indicated a closed door in the rear of the long bookstore. My ham and egg on a roll was calling my name, but it's not professional to interview a witness with your mouth full, so I just grabbed the coffee and went through the door into the stockroom.

It was a fluorescent-lit space lined with metal shelving that held hundreds of books. The deep shelves looked stable enough, but after seeing what happened to poor Mr. Parker, the place made me nervous.

There was a long table in the center of the room, also stacked with books and paperwork, and at the table sat a uniformed officer – Simmons – and a young gent who must be Scott. I thought I may have seen him once or twice in the store.

There was a metal security door that lead out to the back, and I opened the door and looked out into a paved yard surrounded by a brick wall about ten feet high. There were no gates leading to the adjoining backyards, but the walls could be scaled if you had something to stand on – or if you had a cop hot on your tail. Been there, done that – on both sides of the law. There was also a fire escape leading up to the top floor.

I closed the door and turned to Scott. I identified myself, pointing to my shield – the way the lady cop did in Fargo. Funny scene.

Officer Simmons, who'd been babysitting the witness as per procedure, asked, "Do you need me?"

"No. But stick around."

He nodded, got up and left.

I smiled at Scott who did not return my smile. He still looked nervous and unhappy, maybe concerned about his future at the Dead End Bookstore.

My coffee was tepid, but I spotted a microwave sitting on a small table wedged between two bookcases, and I put my paper cup in the microwave. Twenty seconds? Maybe thirty.

There was a bulletin board above the table with a work schedule, and I saw that Scott was scheduled to come in at 8:30 A.M. today, and someone named Jennifer had a few afternoon hours scheduled this week. Not much of a staff, which meant not many people to interview. There was also a post-it note saying, "J. Lawrence – 10 A.M. Tuesday." Today.

I retrieved my coffee from the microwave and sat across from

Scott. He was a soft-looking guy in his mid-twenties, short black hair, black T-shirt and pants, and a diamond stud in his left earlobe which I think means he's a Republican. Maybe I got that wrong. Anyway, I did remember him now – more for his almost surly attitude than his helpfulness.

I flipped through the dozen or so pages of Scott's handwritten statement and saw he hadn't yet finished with his account of who, what, where, and when. In this business, short statements are made by people with nothing to hide; long statements are a little suspicious and this was a long statement.

As I perused his tight, neat handwriting, I said to him, "This seems to be a very helpful account of what happened here."

"Thank you."

I asked him, "Do you think the police arrived promptly?"

He nodded.

"Good. And the EMS?"

"Yeah..."

"Good." And are you now thinking I'm here to evaluate the response to your 911 call? I'm not. I dropped his written statement on the table and asked him, "How you doin'?"

He seemed unsure about how he was doing, but then replied, "Not too good."

"Must have been a shock."

"Yeah."

"How long have you worked here?"

"Three years this June."

"Right after college?"

"Yeah."

"Good job?"

"It's okay." He volunteered, "Pays the bills while I'm writing my novel."

"Good luck." Every store clerk and waiter in this town wants you to know they're really a writer, an actor, a musician or an artist.

Just in case you thought they were a clerk or a waiter. I asked Scott, "What time did you get here this morning?"

He replied, "As I told the other policeman, I got here about seven-thirty."

"Right. Why so early?"

"Early?"

"You're scheduled for eight-thirty."

"Yeah...Mr. Parker asked me to get here early."

"Why?"

"To stock shelves."

"The shelves look stocked. When's the last time you sold a book?"

"I had some paperwork to do."

"Yeah? Okay, take me through it, Scott. You got here, opened the door – front door?"

"Yeah." He reminded me, "It's all in my statement."

"Good. And what time was that?"

"I opened the door a little before seven-thirty."

"And it was locked?"

"Yeah."

"Did you know that Mr. Parker was here?"

"No. Well, not at first. I noticed the lights were on in his office up in the loft, so I called up to him."

"I assume he didn't answer."

"No...he...so, I thought maybe he was in here – in the stockroom – so I came in here to get to work."

"And when you saw he wasn't here, what did you think?"

"I...thought maybe he was in his bathroom upstairs."

"Or maybe he ducked out for a ham and egg on a roll."

"Uh...he...if he went out, he'd turn off the lights." Scott informed me, "He's strict about saving energy. Was."

"Right." Now he wasn't using any energy. I said, "Please continue."

"Well...as I said in my statement, after about twenty minutes I carried some books to the counter up front, and I called up to him again. He didn't answer, but then I noticed something…I couldn't see the top of his bookshelf."

In fact, I'd noticed that bookshelf myself on my two or three visits here. You could see the top two or three shelves from the front of the store. But not this morning.

Scott continued, "I didn't know what to make of that at first… and I kept staring up at the office…then I went half way up the stairs and called out again, then I went all the way up and…"

Rourke said Scott looked nervous, but now Scott looked appropriately distraught as he relived that moment of horror when he found his boss flattened by a half ton of mahogany and books.

I didn't say anything as he spoke, but I nodded sympathetically.

Scott continued, "I shouted his name, but… there was no answer and no movement…"

"How'd you know he was under there?"

"I could see…I wasn't all the way up the stairs, so I could see under the bookcase…"

"Right. I thought you said you went all the way up the stairs."

"I…I guess I didn't. But then I did. I tried to move the bookcase, but I couldn't. So I called 911 on my cell phone."

"Good thinking." I glanced at his statement and said, "Then you called Mrs. Parker."

"Yeah."

"How well do you know her?" He thought about that, then replied, "I've known her about three years. Since they started dating."

"So they're newlyweds."

"Yeah." He volunteered, "Married last June."

"Previous marriage for him?"

"Yeah. Before my time."

"How about her?"

"I think so."

Recalling the photo on the deceased's desk, I asked Scott, "How old is she?"

"I...guess about forty."

Booksellers always get the young chicks.

I asked Scott, "Was she a nice lady?"

"I...guess. I didn't see her much. She hardly ever comes to the store."

By now Scott was wondering about my line of questioning, so I volunteered, "I like to get a feeling for the victim's next of kin before I break the news to them."

He seemed to buy that and nodded.

I asked Scott directly, "Did the Parkers have a happy marriage?"

He shrugged, then replied, "I don't know. I guess." He then asked me, "Why do you ask?"

"I just told you, Scott."

Recalling that Scott told Tripani that Mrs. Parker worked at home, I asked him, "What does she do for a living?"

"She's a decorator. Interior designer. Works at home."

"Do you have any idea where she is this morning?"

"No. Maybe on a job."

"Could she be out of town?"

"Could be." He informed me, "She's from L.A. She has clients there."

"Yeah?" L.A. Who else do I know from L.A.? Ah! Jay Lawrence. Small world. I asked him, "Did she decorate this place?"

He hesitated, then replied, "No. I mean, not the store."

"His office?"

"I don't know. Yeah. I guess."

"That's three different answers to the same question. Did she decorate his office? Yes or no?"

"Yes."

"How long ago was that?"

"Uh...I think about two years ago."

"When they were dating?"

"Yeah."

"So she put the bookcase up there?"

He didn't reply immediately, then said, "I guess."

Scott was a crappy witness. Typical of his generation, if I may be judgmental here. A little fuzzy in his thinking, his brain probably half baked on controlled substances, educated far beyond his ambitions, marking time while he wrote the Great American Novel. But he did get to work early. So, he had some ambition.

As for Mrs. Parker, I was concerned that she'd take it very badly if she was the person who bought that bookcase and failed to secure it to the wall. I mean, that would be hard to live with. Especially if she took those furniture wedges for another job…well, too early to speculate on that.

I asked Scott, "Was her business successful?"

"I don't know."

"Is this bookstore successful?"

"I don't know. I'm just a clerk."

"Answer the question."

"I…I think he makes ends meet." He let me know, "I get paid."

"Does the rent get paid?"

"He owns the building."

"Yeah? Who's on the top three floors?"

"Nothing. Nobody. Loft space. Unrented."

"Why unrented?"

"Needs heat, a new fire escape, and the freight elevator doesn't work."

And there's no money to do the work. I was wondering what Mr. Parker was thinking when he bought this building, but then Scott, reading my mind, volunteered, "He inherited the building."

I nodded. And he should have sold it to a developer. But he wanted to own a bookstore. Otis Parker, bibliophile, was living his dream, which was actually a nightmare. And Mrs. Parker's decorating career could be a hobby job – or she did okay and had to support her husband's book habit.

Motive is tricky, and you can't ascribe a motive and then try to make it fit the crime. I mean, even if Otis Parker was worth more dead than alive – this building, or at least the property, was worth a couple mil, even in this neighborhood – that didn't mean that his young wife wanted him dead. She might just want him to sell the building and stop sinking time and money into this black hole – this Dead End Bookstore – and go get a real job. Or at least turn the place into a bar.

Maybe I was getting ahead of myself. For all I knew the Parkers were deeply in love and his death – caused by her bookcase – would cause the grief-stricken widow to enter a nunnery.

Meanwhile, I made a mental note to check for a mortgage on the building, plus Mr. Parker's life insurance policies, and if there was a prenup agreement. Money is motive. In fact, statistically, it is the main motive in most crimes.

I returned to the subject at hand and said, "So, after you called 911, you called her."

He nodded.

"From upstairs or downstairs?"

"Downstairs. I ran down to unlock the door."

"And you used your cell phone."

"Yeah."

"Her home number is in your cell phone?"

"Yeah...I have their home number to call if there's a problem here."

"Right. And you have her cell phone number in your cell phone in case...what?"

"In case I can't get Mr. Parker on his cell phone."

"Right." And when I look at everyone's phone records, I might see some interesting calls made and received.

The thing is, if a murder actually does appear to be an accident, there's not much digging beyond the cause and manner of death. But when a cop thinks it looks fishy, then the digging gets deeper, and sometimes something gets dug up that doesn't jibe with peoples' statements.

It had taken me less than fifteen minutes to determine that I was most probably investigating a homicide, so I was already into the digging stage while everyone else – except maybe Officer Rourke – thought we were talking about a bizarre and tragic accident.

Scott – baked brains aside – was getting the drift of some of my questions. In fact, he was looking a bit nervous again, so I asked him bluntly, "Do you think this was something more than an accident?"

He replied quickly and firmly, "No. But that other officer did."

I suggested, "He reads too many detective novels. Do you?"

"No. I don't read this stuff."

He seemed to have a low opinion of detective novels and that annoyed me. On that subject, I asked him, "Is Jay Lawrence scheduled to come in today?"

He nodded. "Yeah. To sign his new book. He's on a book tour. He's supposed to come in sometime around ten A.M."

I looked at my watch and said, "He's late."

"Yeah. Authors are usually late."

"Where's he staying in New York?"

"I don't know."

"Do you have his cell number?"

"Yeah…someplace."

"Have you met him?"

"Yeah. A few times."

"How well does he – did he – know Mr. Parker?"

"I guess they knew each other well. They see each other at publishing events."

"And Mrs. Parker?"

"Yeah…I guess he knew her, too."

"From L.A.?"

"Yeah…I think so."

Out of curiosity, or maybe for some other reason, I asked Scott,

"Is Jay Lawrence a big bestseller?"

Scott replied with some professional authority, "He was. Not anymore." He added, "We can hardly give his books away."

"Yeah? But you bought five boxes of them for him to sign."

Scott sort of sneered and replied, "That's a courtesy. Like, a favor. Because they know each other and because he was coming to the store."

"Right." It could be awkward if there were only two books here for Jay Lawrence to sign.

Well, you learn something new every day on this job. Jay Lawrence, who I thought was a bestselling author, was not. Goes to show you. Maybe I make more money doing what I do than he makes writing about what I do.

I had more questions to ask Scott, but there was a knock on the door and Officer Simmons opened it and said, "There's a guy here – a writer named Jay Lawrence, to see the deceased." He added, "Rourke notified him that there had been an accident in the store, but not a fatality."

I looked at my watch. It was 10:26, for the record, and I said to Simmons, "Keep Scott company." I said to Scott, "Keep writing. You may have the beginning of a bestseller."

I went out into the bookstore where Mr. Jay K. Lawrence was sitting in a wingback chair, wearing a black cashmere topcoat, his legs crossed, looking impatient. He should be looking concerned – cops, accident and all that – and maybe he was, but he hid it with feigned impatience. On the other hand, authors are all ego, and if they're detained or inconvenienced by, say, an earthquake or a terrorist attack, they take it personally and get annoyed.

I identified myself to Mr. Lawrence and again pointed to my shield. I have to get that stupid movie scene out of my head or people will think I'm an idiot. Actually, it's not a bad thing for a suspect to think that. Not that Jay Lawrence was a suspect. But he had some potential.

Before he could stand – if he intended to – I sat in the chair beside him.

He looked like his photo – coiffed and airbrushed – and I could see that under his open topcoat he wore a green suede sports jacket, a yellow silk shirt and a gold-colored tie. His tan trousers were pressed and creased and his brown loafers had tassels. I don't like tassels.

Anyway, I got to the point and informed him, "I'm sorry to have to say this, but Otis Parker is dead."

He seemed overly shocked – as though the police presence here gave him no clue that something bad had happened.

He composed himself, then asked me, "How did it happen?"

"How did what happen?"

"How did he die?"

"An accident. A bookcase fell on him."

Mr. Lawrence glanced up at the loft, then said softly, "Oh, my God."

"Right. The bookcase in his office. Not the stockroom."

Mr. Lawrence didn't reply, so I continued, "Scott found the body."

He nodded, then asked me, "Who's Scott?"

"The clerk." I said to him, "We left a message on Mrs. Parker's cell phone and home phone, but we haven't heard from her." I asked, "Would you know where she is?"

"No…I don't."

"Were you close to the Parkers?"

"Yes…"

"Then it might be good if you stayed here until she arrives."

"Oh…yes. That might be a good idea." He added, "I can't believe this…"

I had to keep in mind that this guy wrote about what I do, so I needed to be careful with my questions. I mean, I wouldn't want him to get the idea that I suspected foul play. On that subject, there was no crime scene tape outside, and no CSU team present, so he had no reason to believe that he'd walked into a homicide investigation. If he had nothing to do with that, it was a moot point. If he did have something to do with it, he was breathing easier than he'd been on his way here for his scheduled book signing. Also, I'd left my trench coat on, giving him, and anyone else, the impression that I wasn't staying long.

To make him feel a little better, I said to him, "I read two of your books."

He seemed to brighten a bit and asked, "Which ones?"

"The one about the writer who plotted to murder his literary agent."

He informed me, "That was a labor of love."

"Yeah? I guess that's what all writers dream about."

"Most. Some want to murder their editors."

I smiled, then continued, "And I read *Dead Marriage* about the young woman who kills her older husband. Great book."

He stayed silent a second, then said, "I didn't write a book with that theme."

"No? Oh...sorry. Sometimes I get the books confused."

He didn't reply, and in what may have been a Freudian slip, he asked me, "Does Mia know?"

"Who?"

"Mrs. Parker."

"Oh, right. Mia. No. We never say that in a phone message." I added, "We'll wait another fifteen minutes or so, then we have to get the body to the morgue." I suggested, "Why don't you call her?"

He hesitated, then said, "That's not a call I want to make."

"Right. I'll call. Do you have her number?"

"Not with me."

"Not in your cell phone?"

"Uh...I'm not sure." He asked, "Don't you have her number?"

"Not with me." I suggested, "Take a look in your directory. I really want to get her here. That's better than her having to go to the morgue."

"All right..." He retrieved his cell phone, scrolled through his directory and said, "Here's their home phone...Otis' cell phone... and yes, here's Mia's cell phone."

"Good." I put my hand out and he reluctantly gave me his cell phone. If I was brazen, I'd have checked his call log, but I could do that later, if necessary. I speed-dialed Mia Parker's cell phone and she answered, "Jay, where are you?"

Sitting next to a detective at the Dead End Bookstore. She had a nice voice. I said to her, "This is Detective Corey, Mrs. Parker."

"Who...?"

"Detective Corey. NYPD. I'm using Mr. Lawrence's cell phone." Silence.

I continued, "I'm at the Dead End Bookstore, ma'am. I'm afraid there's been an accident."

"Accident?"

"Did you get the messages that were left on your cell phone?"

"No...what message?"

"About the accident."

"Where's Jay?"

Who's on first? I replied, "He's here with me."

"Why do you have his cell phone? Let me speak to him."

She didn't seem that interested in the accident, or who had the accident, so I handed the phone to Jay.

He said to her, "It's me."

Me, Mia. Mama mia, Mia. Otis is rigor mortis.

He informed her, again, "There's been an accident at the bookstore. Otis is..." He looked at me and I shook my head. He said, "Badly hurt."

She said something, then he asked her, "Where are you? Can you get here quickly?" He listened, nodded to me, then said to her, "I'll be here."

He hung up and said to me, "She's in her apartment. She'll be here in about ten or fifteen minutes."

Thinking out loud, I said, "I wonder why we couldn't reach her earlier?"

He explained, "She said she was writing a proposal. She has an office in the apartment, and she blots out the world when she's working on a project."

"Yeah? Do you do that?"

"I do."

"I need a room like that." Actually, I drink Scotch whiskey to blot out the world and any room will do. I said to him, "She took your call."

"She just finished."

"I see." Again, thinking out loud, I said, "Most accident victims who are badly hurt wind up in the hospital. Not the bookstore."

He didn't reply.

"And yet, Mrs. Parker saw nothing odd about coming to the bookstore."

We made eye contact, and he said to me, "I think she knows it's more than an accident, detective. I think, like most people who get a call like that, she's very distraught and partly in denial." He asked me, "You follow?"

"I do. Thank you."

Two things here. First, I didn't like Jay Lawrence and he didn't like me. Loathing at first sight. And to think he glamorized the police in his novels. Rick Strong, LAPD. This was really a disappointment. But maybe he did like cops. It was *me* he didn't like. I have that effect on pompous asses.

Which brought me to my second point. He was a smooth customer and he had a quick reply to my somewhat leading questions. I've seen lots of guys like this – and they're mostly guys – egotistical, self-absorbed, usually charming, and great liars, i.e., sociopaths. Not to mention narcissistic. Also, as a fiction writer, he bullshitted for a living.

But maybe I was judging Mr. Jay K. Lawrence too quickly and too harshly. And it didn't matter what I thought of him. I'd never see him again – unless I locked him up for murder.

For sure, I wouldn't read any more of his books. Well, maybe I'd take them out of the library to screw him out of the royalty.

I said to Jay Lawrence, "I noticed a pile of your books in Mr. Parker's office." I asked him, "Would you like to sign them while you're waiting?"

He didn't reply, perhaps actually considering this. I mean, a signed book is a sold book. And he needed the sales. Right? I assured him, "You don't have to go upstairs. Unless you want to. I can have Scott bring the books down here."

He replied, a bit coolly, "I don't think it would be appropriate for me to sign books at this time, detective."

"Maybe you're right. But…I hate to ask, but could you personalize one for me?" And leave your DNA and fingerprints on the book?

"Maybe later."

"Okay." I remained seated beside him and asked, "Where are you staying?"

"The Carlyle."

"Nice hotel."

"My publisher pays for it."

"When did you get to New York?"

"Last night."

"How long are you staying?"

"I leave tonight for Atlanta."

"Do you think you can make it back for the funeral?"

He thought about that, then said, "I'll have to check with my publicist." He explained, "These tours are scheduled months in advance. I know it sounds callous, but…"

"I understand. A busy life is scheduled – a sudden death is not." I offered, "You can use that line in your next book."

He ignored my offer and said, "If you'll excuse me, I have some phone calls to make." He explained, "I need to let my publicist know I can't make my other bookstore appointments today, or my media interviews."

"Right." I stood and said, "When Mrs. Parker arrives, I'll let you break the news to her."

He didn't reply.

Well, Mr. Lawrence was sitting in the bookstore with Officer Rourke keeping him company, Scott was in the stockroom with Officer Simmons, writing his bestseller, and Otis Parker was alone in his office, reaching room temperature by now. Time for breakfast.

I retrieved the brown paper bag from the counter and went outside. It was still cold and windy and there weren't many people on North Moore Street. I noticed now that in the store window was a copy of *Death Knocks Once* by Jay K. Lawrence, and a small sign under the book announced, Autographed. Well, not yet.

I got in the passenger seat of Rourke's patrol car, unwrapped my ham and egg sandwich and took a bite. Room temperature.

I called Lieutenant Ruiz before he could call me. He answered, and I said, "I'm still at the Dead End Bookstore."

"What's the story?"

"Well…" I'm about to lie to you. No. Not a good idea. Ruiz, like me, is more interested in results and arrests than silly technicalities, so I said to him, "I have some reason to believe this was a homicide."

"Yeah?"

"But I don't want to announce that at this time."

No reply.

I took another bite and said, "I think the bookcase was tipped over by a person or persons unknown."

"Are you eating?"

"No. I'm chewing on my tie."

He ignored that and asked, "You need assistance?"

"No. I need about thirty or forty minutes."

"Where's the body?"

"Where it was found."

"Suspects?"

"Looks like an inside job."

"I heard from Sergeant Tripani. He says it looks like an accident."

"No. It looks like he owes me breakfast."

Rule number one between cops who are making shit up is Get Your Stories Straight, and Lieutenant Ruiz said to me, "So you're saying you believe it was an accident."

I replied, "At this time, I believe it was an accident."

"Call me in half an hour."

I hung up and got out of the car. I went back into the store and saw that Mr. Lawrence was on his cell phone at the back of the store, out of earshot of Rourke. I didn't know who he was calling, but I'd know when I subpoenaed his phone records.

I stood near the door and looked into the street as a taxi pulled up and discharged a lady who, based on the photo I saw, looked like Mrs. Parker.

She glanced at the police car and strode quickly toward the door. The expression on her face showed some concern, but not exactly sick with worry over her husband's accident. I mean, I've seen it all by now, and Mrs. Parker looked to me like someone who needed to get through some slightly unpleasant business.

She opened the door, glanced at me, then at Officer Rourke, then spotted Jay Lawrence in the rear of the store as he spotted her. They hurried toward one another and met at the Bargain Book table.

It was an awkward moment as they vacillated between embracing, grasping each other's hands, or high-fiving.

He took both her hands in his, and I heard him say, "Mia, I am so sorry...Otis is..."

Dead. Come on, Jay. I've got thirty minutes before I have to announce a suspected homicide.

She got the drift and they embraced. He looked over her shoulder at me and caught me looking at my watch while I took another bite of my sandwich. I really felt like a turd.

I mean, what if neither of them had anything to do with Otis Parker's murder? I knew it had to be an inside job, but it could have been Scott or Otis' ex-wife, or Jennifer the part-time clerk, or other persons not yet known who had off-hour access to the store and to Otis Parker. Right?

On the subject of motive, there are, generally speaking, six major motives for murder. Ready? They are: profit, revenge, jealousy, concealment of a crime, avoidance of humiliation or disgrace, and homicidal mania. There are variations, of course, and combinations, but if you focus on those, and try to match them to a suspect – even to an unlikely suspect – then you can conduct an intelligent investigation.

Sometimes, of course, you don't need to go that route. Sometimes you have lots of forensic evidence – like someone's fingerprints on the murder weapon. But that's not my job. I'm a detective and I deal with the human condition first, then the clues I can see with my own eyes, and the statements people make, or don't make. If I'm smart and lucky, I can wrap it up before the CSU people and the Medical Examiner are done.

While I was thinking about all this, I was observing Mr. Lawrence and Mrs. Parker. They were sitting side by side in the reading chairs now, he with his hand on her shoulder, she dabbing her eyes with his handkerchief.

For the record, she was easy to look at. A little younger than Scott thought – maybe late thirties, long raven black hair, Morticia makeup, and I'm sure a good figure under her black lambskin coat, which was open now revealing a dark gray knit dress that looked expensive. She also wore long, black boots, a cashmere scarf, and gloves which she'd taken off. A well-dressed lady, complete with a gold watch, wedding band, and a nice rock.

I tried to picture her plodding away at her paperwork in her apartment in this outfit. Well, maybe she had an appointment later.

I had let a respectable amount of time elapse, so I ditched my sandwich on the counter, then I walked over to the grieving widow and her friend. I introduced myself to her without pointing to my shield.

She looked up at me but did not respond.

I said, "I'm very sorry about your husband."

She nodded.

I spoke to her, in a soft and gentle voice, "Sometimes the bereaved wants to see the body. Sometimes it helps bring closure. Sometimes it's too painful." And sometimes the bereaved totally loses it and confesses on the spot. I assured her, "It's your choice."

She didn't think too long before replying, "I don't want to…see him."

"I understand." I said to her, "I'd like you like to stay here until the body is removed." I explained, "You may have to sign paperwork."

She replied in a weak voice, "I want to go home."

"All right. I'll call for a police car to take you home." Later.

Jay Lawrence, without consulting the bereaved widow, said, "I will accompany her."

I really wanted to question Mia Parker, but I couldn't keep her here. I also wanted to question Jay Lawrence, but he was latched onto the grieving widow, and you want to question suspects separately, so that you can pick up inconsistencies in their stories. Also, the courts have ruled that a cop is allowed to lie to a suspect in order to draw out some information. Like, "Okay, Mr. Lawrence, you say A, but Mrs. Parker and Scott told me B. Who's lying, Mr. Lawrence?" Actually, it would be me who was lying. But you can't play one against the other if both suspects are sitting together. I did, however, have some info from Scott, though not a lot.

Also, of course, this was not a homicide investigation and therefore there were no suspects, and therefore I couldn't pull these two off separately for questioning.

I mean, I knew beyond a doubt that Otis Parker had been

murdered, and I was fairly sure there were two people involved, and it was an inside job, and it was premeditated. And the two people sitting in front of me filled the bill as potential suspects. But I had to tread lightly and treat them as a bereaved widow and a very upset friend, who was also a crime writer with some savvy. Basically, I was at a dead end at the Dead End Bookstore, and the clock was ticking.

So maybe I should just say it. "Sorry to inform you, but I believe Otis Parker was murdered, and I'd like you both to come to the precinct with me to see if you can help the police with this investigation."

I was about to do that, but I had some time to kill before I had to call Ruiz, so I pulled up a chair, put on my sympathetic face and asked Mrs. Parker, "Can I get you some water? Coffee?"

"No, thank you."

I offered, "I can see if there's something stronger in Mr. Parker's office."

She shook her head.

I said, conversationally, "I understand you decorated his office. It's very nice."

Our eyes met, and she hesitated, then said to me, "I *told* him...I told him to have it fastened to the wall...and he said he'd done that."

"You mean the bookcase?"

She nodded.

"Well, unfortunately he didn't."

"Oh..." She sobbed, "Oh, if only he'd listened to me."

Right. If men listened to their wives, they'd live longer and better lives. But, married men, I think, have a death wish. That's why they die before their wives. They want to. Okay, I'm getting off the subject.

I said to her, "Please don't blame yourself." Let me do that.

She put her hands over her face, sobbed again, and said, "I should have checked when I was in his office...but I always believed what Otis said to me."

Making you the first wife in the history of the world to do that. Sorry, I digress again.

Actually, I could imagine that she did like her husband. Maybe he was a father figure. Despite her Morticia look, she seemed pleasant and she had a sweet voice. Maybe I was on the wrong track. But... my instincts said otherwise.

Under the category of asking questions that you already know the answer to, I asked her, "Do you and Mr. Lawrence know each other from L.A.?"

It was Mr. Lawrence who replied, "Yes, we do. But I don't see what difference that makes."

Of course you do, Jay. This is the stuff you write about. Anyway, I winged a response and said, "I need to say in my accident report what your relationship is to the widow."

He didn't say, "Bullshit!" but his face did. Good. Sweat, you pompous ass.

Mia Parker, who seemed clueless from Los Angeles, said to me, "Jay and I have been friends for years. We saw each other socially with our former spouses."

I nodded, then said to her, "Scott tells me you were married last June."

At the mention of her June wedding, her eyes welled with tears, she nodded and covered her face again.

I let a few seconds pass, then I said, "I've spoken to Scott and I think I have enough details for my accident report, but if not I'll speak to him again, and bother you as little as possible."

She nodded and blew here nose into her friend's handkerchief.

Her friend understood that I had a statement from the clerk and that I was, perhaps, a tiny bit suspicious.

There wasn't much more I could do or say to these two at this time, but I had at least hinted to Jay Lawrence that he probably wasn't getting on that flight to Atlanta. I could see he was a bit concerned. I mean, if he'd plotted this – like one of his novels – he had fully expected it to be ruled an accident, and he'd hoped that the body would be gone when he got here half an hour late, and the sign on the door would say Closed. Or, if the cops were still here, they'd say, "Sorry, there's been an accident. The store is closed."

Right. But Mr. Jay K. Lawrence did not imagine a Detective John Corey, called on the scene because a patrolman was suspicious. The ironic thing was that Jay Lawrence's cop character, Rick Strong, was smarter than his creator. But neither Jay Lawrence nor Rick Strong were as smart as John Corey. I was, however, out of bright ideas.

I stood and said to Mrs. Parker, "To let you know, the city requires an autopsy in cases...like this. So, it may be two days before the body is released." I added, "You should make plans accordingly." I also added, "In the unlikely event that the Medical Examiner feels that he needs to...well, do further tests, then someone will notify you."

Mr. Lawrence stood and asked, "What do you mean by that?"

I looked him in the eye and replied, "You understand what I mean."

He didn't reply, but clearly he was getting a bit jumpy.

I was now going to call Ruiz and advise him that I was officially making this a homicide investigation. I had two suspects, but no evidence to hold them. In fact, not enough evidence to even advise them that they were persons of interest – though I'd ask them to meet me later at the station house, to help in the investigation.

But just when you think you've played your last card, you remember the card up your sleeve. The Joker.

I said, "The Medical Examiner should be arriving shortly. Please remain here until then." I assured them, "I'll call for a police car to take you home after the M.E. arrives."

Mr. Lawrence reminded me, "You said we could leave now. And we can find our own transportation."

"I changed my mind. Remain on the premises until the M.E. arrives."

"Why?" asked Mr. Lawrence.

I replied a bit curtly, "Because, Mr. Lawrence, the Medical Examiner may want a positive identification. Or he may need some information as to date of birth, place of residence, and so forth." I said to him, "Actually, *you* may leave. Mrs. Parker cannot."

He didn't reply, but sat again and took her hand. A real gentleman. Or maybe he didn't want her alone with me.

I went to Officer Rourke who was still sitting behind the counter, apparently engrossed in his book, but undoubtedly listening to every word. I made eye contact with him and said, "Let me know when the M.E. arrives and send him up." Wink.

He nodded, and I could see his brain in high gear wondering what the brilliant detective was up to.

I climbed the spiral staircase into Otis Parker's office and looked at his body. Right. He could have survived. Then he could have told me what happened.

But I already knew what happened. I needed Otis Parker to tell me who did it.

Cops, as I said, are allowed to lie. Half the confessions you get are a result of lying to a suspect.

I let a few more seconds pass, then I shouted, "Get an ambulance!" I ran to the rail and shouted to Rourke, "He's alive! He's moving! Get an ambulance!"

Rourke, thank God, didn't shout back, "He's dead as a doornail!" Instead, he got on his hand radio and pretended – I hope – to call for an ambulance.

I glanced at Mia Parker and Jay Lawrence. They didn't seem overjoyed at this news. I shouted to them, "We'll have an ambulance here in three or four minutes!" Great news. Right? Try to contain your feelings of hope and joy. I resisted shouting, "It's a miracle!" I did say, "Mrs. Parker can ride in the ambulance."

They looked…well, stunned. And that wasn't play acting. Also, I didn't see Mrs. Parker running up the stairs to smother her awakening husband with kisses. If she did come upstairs, it might be to smack him in the head with a book. Well…that's just me being cynical and suspicious again.

I disappeared from the rail and let a minute pass, then I walked slowly and deliberately down the spiral staircase and headed toward two worried-looking people. The expression on my face told them they were in deep doo-doo. Actually, if this didn't work, I *was* in deep, deep doo-doo.

I stopped in front of them and said, "He's speaking."

No response.

I looked them both in the eye and said, "He spoke to me."

Very smart people would have shouted in unison, "Bullshit!" But they were so unstrung – actually shaking – that all they could do was stare at me. Also, I'm a good liar. Ask the last guy I tricked into a confession.

I let a few seconds pass, then said, "I saw that someone had removed the furniture wedges from under the bookcase. I also saw that someone had used the toilet plunger to lever the bookcase away from the wall." I paused for dramatic effect, then said, "And now I know who that was." Actually, I didn't. But they did.

I would have bet money that it would be Mia Parker who cracked – but it was Jay Lawrence. He said, "Then you know I had nothing to do with it. I was in my hotel all morning and I can prove it."

When someone says that, you assume they're telling the truth, i.e. they've established their alibi for the time of death. Or they think they have. Meanwhile, Mia Parker was staring at her friend, who continued, "I had room service at six-thirty, then I had it cleared at seven-thirty."

"All that proves is that you had breakfast." And I didn't.

I looked at Mia Parker and said to her, "Mrs. Parker, based on the statement your husband just made, I am charging you with attempted murder."

I was about to go into my Right-to-Remain-Silent spiel, but she fainted. Just like that. Crumbled to the floor. Ideally, a suspect should be awake when you read them Miranda, so I turned my attention to Jay Lawrence.

He was just standing there, looking not too well himself. Hello? Jay? Your friend just fainted.

I would have come to Mrs. Parker's assistance, but Rourke was already coming toward us.

I looked at Jay Lawrence and I said, "I have reason to believe that you were an accomplice. That it was you who assisted Mrs. Parker in removing the two furniture wedges from under the bookcase. Probably last night after you arrived from L.A." I informed him, "So your alibi for this morning, even if it proves to be true, does not exclude you as an accessory to attempted murder." He didn't faint, but he did go pale.

Rourke had run out to his squad car and returned with a first aid kit. He was now reviving Mrs. Parker with an ammonium nitrate capsule. This was good because now I only had to give the Miranda warning once. A small point, I know, but...anyway, I asked Jay Lawrence, "Do you have anything to say?"

He did. He said, "You're out of your mind." He added, "I had nothing to do with this."

"That's for a jury to decide."

Rourke had gotten Mrs. Parker into the wingback chair and she looked awake enough, so I began, "You both have the right to remain silent –"

Jay Lawrence chose not to remain silent and interrupted, "I can prove conclusively that I came directly to the hotel from the airport and that I was in the Carlyle all evening, and until ten this morning."

That wasn't what I wanted to hear, but I needed to hear more, so I asked, "How can you prove that?"

He hesitated, then said, "I was with a woman. All night."

Apparently he did better than I did last night. I watched *Bonanza*.

He continued, "I will give you her name and cell phone number and you can speak to her, and she will confirm that."

Okay…so we have the nearly airtight in-bed-with-a-lady alibi. But sometimes this is not so airtight. Still, this was a problem.

I was about to ask him for the lady's name and number, but Mrs. Parker, fully awake now, shouted, "You were *where*?" She stood and shouted again, "You said you had interviews to do. You bastard!"

I've been here, and so has Rourke apparently, because we both stepped between Mrs. Parker and Mr. Lawrence to head off a physical assault.

Mrs. Parker was releasing a string of obscenities and expletives which Jay Lawrence took well, knowing he deserved them. And knowing, too, that his lover's wrath was a lot better than being charged with accessory to attempted murder – which was actually a successful attempt. But that was my secret.

Mia Parker was still screaming and I had the thought that I should have left her on the floor. But my main concern was that I'd gotten this wrong. About Jay Lawrence, I mean. But not about Mia Parker, who confirmed my charge of attempted murder by shouting, "I did this for *you*, you cheating bastard! So we could be together! You *knew* what I was going to –"

Jay Lawrence jumped right in there and shouted back, "I did *not* know what you –"

"You did!"

"Did not!"

And so forth. Rourke was nodding, letting me know he was a witness to this while at the same time he kept repositioning himself so that the wronged lady could not get at her two-timing lover. I kind of hoped that she got around Rourke and dug her nails into Jay's pretty face. I certainly wasn't going to get between them. Hell hath no fury and all that.

Well, I was sure that the Dead End Bookstore hadn't seen so much excitement since the upstairs toilet backed up.

Meanwhile, neither of the now ex-lovers seemed to notice that over five minutes had passed and there was no ambulance pulling up to rush Otis Parker to the hospital.

By now, I should have had Rourke slap the cuffs on Mia Parker, but, well...I was enjoying this. She was really pissed and she shouted to her fellow Angelino, "We could have bought that house in Malibu...we could have been together again..."

Where's Malibu? California? Why did she want to go back there? No one wants to leave New York. This annoyed me.

She broke down again, sobbing and wailing, then collapsed in the chair. She was babbling now. "I hate it here...I hate this store...I hate him...I hate the cold...I want to go home..."

Well, sorry, lady, but you're going to be a guest of the State of New York for awhile.

As much as I wanted to cuff Jay Lawrence, I wasn't certain what his role, if any, was in this murder. Well, he *knew* about it, according to Mia Parker. But did he actually *conspire* in the murder? And assuming she had help, who helped her? Not Jay who was in the sack with his alibi witness.

I motioned for him to follow me and he did so without protest. I led him to the rear of the store, away from his pissed off girlfriend, and I said to him, "You get one chance to assist in this investigation. After that, you get charged with conspiracy to commit murder, and/or as an accessory. Understand?"

He didn't respond verbally, and I didn't even get a nod. Instead, he just stood there, with a blank expression on his face.

I glanced at my watch to indicate the clock was ticking. Then, I said, "Okay, you're under arrest as an accessory –"

"Wait! I...okay, I knew she wanted him...out of the way...and she asked me...like, how would you do this in a novel...but I didn't think she was serious. So, I just made a joke of it."

I informed him, "I think Otis Parker will live, and he can tell us what happened up there and who was in the room at that time."

"Good. Then you'll know that I'm telling the truth."

And he probably was. Mia Parker committed the actual murder herself. But, with all due respect to her apparent intelligence, she didn't think of that bookcase and that plunger and those furniture wedges by herself. That was Jay Lawrence. And that's what she'd say, and he would deny it. She said, he said. Not good in court.

I said to him, "She seemed to think she was going to be with you in…" Where was that place? "Malibu."

He replied, "She's…let's say, mistaken. Actually, delusional. I made no such promise." He made sure I understood, "It was just an affair. A long distance affair."

He was desperately trying to save his ass, and not doing a bad job of it. He was clever, but I am John Corey. Arrogant? No. Just a fact.

I said to him in a tone suggesting he was my cooperating witness, "That bookcase has been sitting there for over two years. Do you think she put it there – right behind his desk – knowing what she was going to do with it?"

He hesitated, then replied, "I don't know. How would I know that?"

He was smart, and he didn't want to admit to any pre-knowledge of premeditated murder – not even as speculation. But he *was* willing to throw his girlfriend under the bus if it kept him out of jail. He was walking the old tightrope without a balancing bar.

By now, Jay Lawrence was thinking about exercising his right to remain silent and his right to an attorney. So I had to be careful I didn't push him too far. On the other hand, time was ticking by and I needed to go in for the kill. I said, "Look, Jay – can I call you Jay? Look, *someone* removed those wedges from under the bookcase, and it wasn't little Mia all by herself. Hell, I don't think I could do that without help. Are you telling me there was someone *else* involved?"

He seemed to think about that, then said, "I haven't been to New York in several months. And I can account for every minute of my time since my plane landed at five-thirty-six last night." He informed me, "I have a taxi receipt, a check-in time at the Carlyle, dinner in the hotel…with my lady friend, the hotel bar –"

"All right, I get it." I didn't want to hear about the adult movie he'd rented from his room. Basically, Jay Lawrence had covered his ass and he had the receipts to prove it. And he'd done this because he knew, in advance, what was going to happen early this morning. But maybe he didn't know about an accomplice.

I asked him for the name and phone number of his lady friend which he gave me. It was, in fact, his publicist in New York; the lady who booked his publicity tour and who could also provide an alibi for his free evening. *Bang publicist*: 7 P.M.-10 A.M. Dinner and breakfast in hotel.

Jay Lawrence was, as Mia Parker said, a two-timing bastard. And also a conniving coward who let his lover do the dirty work while he was establishing an alibi for the crime. He totally bullshited her. And if it had gone right, he was onboard for the payoff, which I guess was his share of all the worldly possessions of the deceased Otis Parker – including his wife. The wife, I'm sure, thought it was all about love and being together. In Malibu. Wherever that was. And none of this would have happened, I'm sure, if Jay Lawrence had sold more books.

Meanwhile, there was still the question of the furniture wedges. Who helped her with that? Jay didn't seem to know, or he wasn't saying. But Mia knew.

I said to him, "Stay right here."

I walked to where Mia Parker was sitting in the wingback chair, looking a bit more composed, and without any preamble I asked her, "Who helped you remove the furniture wedges?"

She replied, "Jay."

I was fairly certain that was not true and not possible.

"When?"

"Last…early this morning."

"Are you telling me the truth?"

"Why would I lie?"

Well, because Jay was screwing a babe all night, and you are very pissed off.

Mrs. Parker needed less sympathy and understanding and more shock treatment, so I said to Rourke, "Cuff her." But softie that I am, I instructed front cuffs instead of back – so she could dab her eyes and blow her nose.

Rourke told her to stand, gave her a quick but thorough pat down, then cuffed her wrists in the front.

I said to Rourke, "Call for a car." I added, "I'll be riding with her to the precinct."

Mia Parker, now cuffed, under arrest, and about to be taken to the station house for booking, was undergoing a transformation. Early this morning, she was a married lady with a boyfriend and an inconvenient husband. Now she had no boyfriend and no husband. And no future. I've seen this too many times, and if I said it didn't get to me, I'd be lying.

The person who I felt most sorry for, of course, was Otis Parker. He ran a crappy bookstore and he didn't give service with a smile, but he didn't deserve to die.

I asked Mrs. Parker, "If he dies, is all this yours?"

She looked around, then replied, "I hate this store."

"Right. Answer the question."

She nodded, then informed me, "We had a prenup...I didn't get much in a divorce...but..."

"You got a lot under his will." I asked, "Life insurance?"

She nodded again, then, continued, "I also got the building and the...business." She laughed and said, "The stupid business...he owes the publishers a fortune. The business is worth nothing."

"Don't forget the fixtures and the good will."

She laughed again. "Good will? His customers *hate* him. *I* hate him."

"Right."

She continued, "This store was draining us dry...he was going to mortgage the building…I had to do something…"

"Of course." I've heard every justification possible for spousal murder, and most of them are amazingly trivial. Like, "My wife thought cooking and fucking were two cities in China." Or, "My husband watched sports all weekend, drank beer and farted." Sometimes I think being a cop is less dangerous than being married.

Anyway, Mrs. Parker forgot to mention that she'd planned this long before the marriage, or that she had a boyfriend. But I never nitpick a confession.

I inquired, "Do you have a buyer for the building?"

She nodded.

I guessed, "Two million?"

"Two and a half."

Not bad. Good motive.

She also let me know, "His stupid collector books are worth about fifty thousand." She added, "He buys them, but can't seem to sell them."

"Has he tried the internet?"

"That's where he *buys* them." She confided to me, "He's an idiot."

"Put that in your statement," I suggested.

She seemed to notice that she was cuffed, and I guess it hit her all at once that the morning had not gone well, and she knew why. She let me know, "All men are idiots. And liars."

"What's your point?"

She also let me know, "Those books in his office are worth about ten thousand."

"Really?" Poetic justice?

As I said, I'm not married, but I have considered it, so to learn something about that I asked her, "Why'd you marry him?"

She didn't think the question was out of line, or too personal, and she replied, "I was divorced…lonely…"

"Broke?"

She nodded and said, "I met him at a party in LA…he said he

was well off...he painted a rosy picture of life in New York..." She thought a moment, then said, "Men are deceitful."

"Right. And when did you think about whacking him?"

She totally ignored my question and went off into space awhile. Then she looked at Jay in the back of the store and asked me, "Why isn't *he* under arrest?"

I don't normally answer questions like that, but I replied, "He has an alibi." I reminded her, "The lady he spent the night with." I shared with her, "His publicist, Samantha –"

"That whore!"

The plot thickens. But that might be irrelevant. More to the point, Mrs. Parker was getting worked up again and I said to her, "If you can convince me – with facts – that he conspired with you in this attempt on your husband's life, then I'll arrest him."

She replied, "We planned this together for over two years. And I can prove it." She added, "It was *his* idea." She let me know, "He's nearly broke."

"Right." I confessed, "I didn't like his last book." I already knew the answer to my next question, but I asked for the record, "Why'd you wait so long?"

"Because," she replied with some impatience, "it took Otis two years to marry me."

"Right." Guys just can't commit. Meanwhile, that bookcase is just waiting patiently to fall over. This was the most premeditation I'd ever seen. Cold, calculating and creepy. I mean, when Otis Parker said, "I do," his blushing bride was saying, "You're done."

The good news is that property values have gone up in the last two or three years. I don't know about collectible books, though.

I tried to reconstruct the crime, to make sure I was getting it right. D-Day for Otis Parker was the day after Jay Lawrence came to town to promote his new book. Today. Jay was supposed to help Mia last night to set up the bookcase for a tumble, then maybe a drink and a little boom-boom at the Carlyle, and some pillow talk about being together, and psyching each other up for the actual murder. And this morning, Jay would be here to comfort the widow.

But Jay, at some point, as the big day approached, got cold feet. All his Rick Strong books ended with the bad guy in jail, and Jay didn't want that ending for himself. So he made a date with his publicist and ditched Mia, leaving Mia to do it all by herself. She had the balls. He had the shakes.

One of the things that bothered me was that Otis Parker was in his office early on the morning that he was going to be whacked. That wasn't coincidence. Not if this was all planned in advance.

I went back to my original thought that Otis Parker had an appointment. And who was that appointment with? And why didn't Scott know about it?

Maybe he did.

I said to Rourke, "I'll be in the stockroom. Keep an eye on these two. Let me know when the car gets here."

That made Mia think of something and she asked me, "Where's the ambulance?"

"I don't know. Stuck in traffic."

She stared at me and shouted, "You bastard! You lied to me!"

"You lied to me first."

"You...you..."

I was glad she was cuffed. Rourke put his hands on her shoulders and pushed her into the chair.

Meanwhile, Jay heard some of this, or figured it out and he walked quickly toward me and asked, "Why isn't the ambulance here?"

I confessed, "Otis Parker doesn't need an ambulance."

Jay looked as stunned as when I had pronounced Otis alive.

People don't like to be tricked, and Mia let loose again. Sweet voice aside, she swore like a New Yorker. Good girl.

Jay Lawrence recovered from his shock and informed me, "You... that was not...that's not admissible..."

"Hey, he looked like he was trying to stand. I'm not a doctor."

"You...you said he spoke to you..."

"Right. Then he died. Look, Jay, here's a tip for your next book. I am allowed to lie. You are allowed to remain silent."

"I'm calling my attorney."

"That's your right. Meanwhile, you're under arrest for conspiracy to commit murder." I gave Rourke my cuffs and said, "Cuff him."

I walked to the back of the store and into the stockroom.

Officer Simmons was talking on his cell phone and Scott was still at the table, reading a book – *How to Get Published for Dummies*.

I sat opposite Scott and asked him, "Why was Mr. Parker here so early?"

He put down his book and said, "I don't know. I guess to do paperwork."

"Did he tell you he was coming in early?"

"No...I didn't know he was going to be here."

"But he asked you to come in early."

"Yeah..."

"But never mentioned that he would be coming in early."

"Uh...maybe he did."

"That's not what you said to me, or what you wrote in your statement."

Officer Simmons was off the phone, and he took up a position behind Scott. This was getting interesting.

Scott, meanwhile, was unraveling fast, and he swallowed, then said in a weak voice, "I...guess I forgot."

"Even after you saw the lights in his office?"

"Yeah...I mean...I remembered that he said he might be in."

"Who put those five boxes of books in his office?"

"I did."

"When?"

"Last night."

"Why last night?"

"So…Jay Lawrence could sign them…Mr. Parker likes the authors to sign in his office."

"Jay Lawrence wasn't coming in until ten A.M."

"Yeah…but…I don't know. I do what I'm told."

"What time did Mr. Parker think that Jay Lawrence would be in?"

"Ten –"

"No. Otis Parker thought that Jay Lawrence was coming in very early. About seven-thirty or eight in the morning. That's why he asked you to bring the books up last night, and that's why he was here this morning."

Scott didn't reply and I asked him, "Who wrote that note on the bulletin board that said 10 A.M.?"

"Me. That's when he was supposed to come in."

My turn to lie. I said, "Mrs. Parker just told me that her husband said he had to get to the store early to meet Jay Lawrence."

"Uh…I didn't know that."

"Mr. Parker never told you that when you carried the books upstairs last night?"

"Uh…I don't –"

"Cut the bullshit, Scott." I informed him, "Two people are going down for murder. The third person involved is the government witness." I asked him, "Which one do you want to be?"

He started to hyperventilate or something, and I said to Simmons, "Get him some water."

Simmons grabbed a bottled water off the counter and put it on the table in front of Scott. I said to him, "Drink."

He screwed the cap off with a trembling hand and drank, then took a deep breath.

I took a shot and said to him, "Mrs. Parker told me you met her here last night, after Mr. Parker left for the day."

He took another deep breath and replied, "I…she asked me to stay and meet her here."

"And she asked you to help her with some furniture in her husband's office"

He nodded.

"And you did that."

He nodded again.

"Did you know *why* you were doing that?"

"No."

"Try again. I need a truthful witness for the prosecution."

He drank more water, then said, "I told her…it wasn't safe to –"

"One more time."

"I…didn't know…she said don't ask questions…"

"What did she offer you?"

He closed his eyes, then replied, "Ten thousand. But I said no."

"Yeah? Did you want more?"

He didn't reply.

I thought a moment and asked, "Did you both have a drink in his office?"

He nodded.

"On the couch?"

"Yeah…"

What a deal. He gets ten thousand bucks, drinks the boss' liquor, and fucks the boss' wife on the boss' couch. And all he has to do in return is push the bookcase back a bit while Mia Parker slides the wedges out. How could you say no to that? Well, Jay Lawrence said no, but he was older and wiser, and he already fucked Mia Parker. Also, he got scared.

I made eye contact with Simmons, who was shaking his head in disbelief.

As I said, I've seen it all, but it's new and shocking every time.

Scott was staring blankly into space, maybe thinking about Mia Parker on the couch. Maybe thinking it seemed like a good idea at the time.

Well, aside from money, you have what I call dick crimes. Dicks get you in trouble.

I had another thought and asked Scott, "Did she say she'd get Jay Lawrence to help you get your book published?"

He seemed surprised that I knew this. I didn't, but it all fit.

Scott was fidgeting with the empty bottle now, then he said, "I didn't know what she was going to do...I *swear* I didn't."

"Right. So, this morning you let her in at about seven-thirty."

He nodded.

"Mr. Parker was already here."

He nodded again.

"He told you his wife was coming by to say hello to Jay Lawrence, her friend from L.A."

"Yeah..."

"She went up to his office and they waited for Jay Lawrence."

He nodded.

"And you went...where?"

"Out back."

"Could you hear the crash?"

He closed his eyes again and said, "No..."

"What time did you come back to the stockroom?"

"About...seven forty-five..."

"Then you carried some books to the counter, just like you said in your statement, and you called up to him."

He nodded.

"And there was no answer, so you knew she was already gone. And where did you think he was? In the bathroom? Or under the bookcase?"

No reply.

"Did you actually go up the stairs?"

"Yeah...I didn't know...I swear I didn't know what she –"

"Right. She needed the furniture wedges for another job. And she paid you ten thousand bucks and had sex with you for your help. And she gave you a script for this morning."

He didn't reply.

I looked at my watch. 11:29. Almost lunch time. I stood and said to Scott, "I'm placing you under arrest as an accomplice to murder."

I nodded to Officer Simmons, who already had his cuffs out, and he said to Scott, "Stand up." Scott stood unsteadily and Simmons cuffed his hands behind his back.

I said to Simmons, "Read him his rights."

I walked toward the door, then turned and looked at Scott. I almost felt sorry for him. Young guy, bad job, lousy boss, maybe short on cash, and wishing he was back in college, or wishing he could be the guy autographing his books. Meanwhile, other peoples' unhappiness and money problems – Mia's and Jay's – were about to intersect with his life. Of course, he could have just said "no" to Mia and called the police. Instead, he made a bad choice, and one person was dead, two were going to jail for a long time, and Scott, if he was lucky and cooperative, would be out before his thirtieth birthday, a little older and wiser. I wanted to give him an enduring piece of advice, some wisdom that would guide him in the future. I thought of several things, then finally said to him, "Never have sex with a woman who has more problems than you do."

I walked back into the store as my cell phone rang. It was Lieutenant Ruiz who said to me, "I'm waiting for your call, John."

"Sorry, boss."

"What's happening?"

"Three arrests. Wife for premeditated murder, her boyfriend for conspiracy to commit, the clerk who found the body as an accomplice."

"No shit?"

"Would I lie?"

"Confessions or suspicion?"

"Confessions."

"Good work."

"Thank you."

"You coming to work today?"

"After lunch."

We hung up, and I looked at Mia Parker and Jay Lawrence, both sitting now side by side in the wingback chairs, cuffed and quiet. They were together, finally, but they didn't seem to have much to say to each other. I had the thought that the marriage wouldn't have worked anyway.

I also thought about telling Jay that his girlfriend banged the clerk to get the kid to do what Jay wouldn't do. But that would make him feel bad – and he felt bad enough – though it might shut her up about Jay banging his publicist. I resisted the temptation to stir the shit a little, and I let it go. They'd find all this out in the pre-trial anyway.

Later, while we were waiting for the three squad cars to take the perps away, I asked Jay Lawrence to sign a book for me. He graciously agreed, and I took his book out of the display window.

He was able to hold a Sharpie with his cuffed hands, and I held the book open for him. "To John," I requested, "The greatest detective since Sherlock Holmes."

He scrawled something, and I said, "Thanks. No hard feelings."

I put thirty bucks in the cash register.

When all the perps were in the cars, I opened the book and read the inscription:

To John, Fuck You, Jay.

Well…maybe it will be worth something someday.